Pr

'A fascinating and absor

'Beguiling and entertaining … Simpson's novel has a poetry to it and a feel for the natural environment. Simpson is a bower bird whose ability to derive existential truths from the game is aided by an ability to decorate the novel's nest with gems from recent history'
PETER LALOR, ***Weekend Australian***

'Joyous storytelling at its best. I was enthralled'
SARAH WINMAN, author of ***Still Life***

'A fabulous novel. Inga Simpson brings all her craft and sensitivity to a story that has never been told, and now that she has done it, it feels like this was a story that was needing to be told. With her art, Inga joins the likes of Meg Lanning, Ellyse Perry and Alyssa Healy in the vanguard of cricket's exciting new revolution. Long may it last'
MALCOLM KNOX

'Heartfelt … Uplifting … Simpson explores family, priorities, the pain of making difficult choices and the knowledge that it's never too late to start over. This is an uplifting book that will satisfy both cricket lovers and readers who enjoy loving stories about beginning again'
Books+Publishing

'*Willowman* may well be the perfect Australian novel' **Readings**

'Told authentically and with consummate affection' ***Good Reading***

'Moving, gripping, authentic, so tenderly told; at once a page-turner and a life-giving meditation – *Willowman* is just magic'
BROOKE DAVIS

'What a wonderful book. What a read. A love story to cricket, to families, to craft and to music. Beautifully written'
MICHAEL BRISSENDEN

Also by Inga Simpson

Mr Wigg
Nest
Where the Trees Were
Understory
The Last Woman in the World

For children
The Book of Australian Trees (with Alicia Rogerson)

Inga Simpson

Willowman

hachette
AUSTRALIA

Australian Government
Australia Council for the Arts
This project has been assisted by the Australian Government through the Australia Council, its arts funding and advisory body.

State Library of Queensland
Queensland Government

This project has been assisted by the Queensland Writers Fellowships. The Queensland Writers Fellowships are presented by the State Library of Queensland and Arts Queensland in partnership with the Queensland Writers Centre.

hachette
AUSTRALIA

First published in Australia and New Zealand in 2022
by Hachette Australia
(an imprint of Hachette Australia Pty Limited)
Gadigal Country, Level 17, 207 Kent Street, Sydney, NSW 2000
www.hachette.com.au

This edition published in 2023

Hachette Australia acknowledges and pays our respects to the past, present and future Traditional Owners and Custodians of Country throughout Australia and recognises the continuation of cultural, spiritual and educational practices of Aboriginal and Torres Strait Islander peoples. Our head office is located on the lands of the Gadigal people of the Eora Nation.

NATIONAL LIBRARY OF AUSTRALIA

A catalogue record for this book is available from the National Library of Australia

ISBN: 978 0 7336 4959 2 (paperback)

Cover design by Debra Billson
Cover images courtesy of Alamy, Getty Images and iStock
Author photograph courtesy of Red Berry Photography
Image on Part title pages courtesy of iStock
Typeset in Horley Old Style by Kirby Jones
Printed and bound in Great Britain by Clays Ltd, Elcograf S.p.A.

FSC www.fsc.org MIX Paper from responsible sources FSC® C001695

The paper this book is printed on is certified against the Forest Stewardship Council® Standards. McPherson's Printing Group holds FSC® chain of custody certification SA-COC-005379. FSC® promotes environmentally responsible, socially beneficial and economically viable management of the world's forests.

For my grandfather,
J.A.F. Simpson

author's note

Willowman is a novel, a work of fiction. It is set around the time that T20 cricket emerged at the international level: 2006–2009. To serve the story, however, I have taken many liberties with recent cricket history, including the timing of the Sheffield Shield, international series, and the make-up of contemporary teams. Longer cricket history, and the spirit of the game, remain intact.

The elements are cricket's presiding geniuses.

~ Neville Cardus

For all its apparent artificiality,
cricket is a sport in nature.

~ Joseph O'Neill, *Netherland*

THE TOSS

Who ever hoped like a cricketer?

~ R.C. Robertson-Glasgow

white willow

Cricket has a willow heart. Batmakers around the world have crafted bats from birch, maple, ash, bamboo, even poplars – but nothing else measures up. I've tried Australian timbers, too: huon pine, red cedar, bunya. You can shape a bat, sure, and it will hit the ball, but it doesn't have the right sound, the right qualities. Despite what administrators, sponsors, broadcasters, even the players would have us believe, without the tree, there'd be no game. After two hundred years, cricket batmaking is still beholden to a single species: *Salix alba caerulea* or white willow.

Willow grown in Kashmir – that long-contested high ground – is the best alternative, but the bats are heavy and yellow, good enough for some. Those who don't believe in magic.

It's no coincidence that white willow and cricket come from the same place: the south-east of England. While ever white willow has water, it grows *fast*. For the best cricket bat willow, you need plenty of rain. A consistent water supply means consistent growth, which produces an even grain. And even grain is more likely to produce a good cricket bat.

Now, with the twenty-first century underway, I'm growing white willow here. It began as a bit of an experiment, after my year working with the willowmen in Essex. Thanks to a government grant, back when I was still young, when people thought I was someone, going somewhere.

Australian farmers and environmentalists call willows the rabbits of the rivers, clogging up our waterways – just another feral colonial fuck-up. But white willows do not weep. Their trunks are tall and straight, their leaves upward-facing. They prefer fertile river flats to stream banks. Their roots run deep, travelling far and wide to feed the network of tubes pumping water up to the tree's crown.

Australia might beat England more often than not these days, but the Poms still have the wood on us. Every high-grade bat in the world is made from white willow, grown in England. The top players want English willow for their bats, and for good reason. It's the best. All that rain has to be good for something.

It's frustrating, to say the least, having to import willow from the old enemy. They're still making us pay for that first Ashes win in 1882, and every win since. Two big companies have the market stitched up. The best clefts go to local English makers and, these days, to big buyers in India. With its exponentially expanding population and cashed-up passion for the game – especially this new twenty-over version – India will soon be the superpower of cricket. I'm lucky enough to have a contact, from my summer with the willowmen. If it wasn't for him, I wouldn't be able to get my hands on English willow, not in such small quantities.

That's why I started growing my own little willow republic. My grandfather, one of the last traditional batmakers back in the old country – as hallowed as Lord's and the Ashes themselves – said it couldn't be done. Plenty of others have said it, too. But here I am all the same, growing white willow and making bats. England may have given cricket to the world, but it's a world game now.

The collective noun for willows is a prayer. And reverence is warranted. Walking these rows, surrounded by uniform trunks, morning sun filtering through the canopy, the leaves shimmering silvery-blue, it's as picturesque as any landscape.

Frank and I surrounded our little Gippsland grove with blue gums. You won't see that back in England. They're good companions, protecting the willows from the wind and shading them while they grow. But the willows have already caught up. White willows – like many of us who have been transported or transplanted – grow quicker in the Antipodes, as if anxious to get somewhere, prove something, or make up for a dubious start.

Most people wouldn't recognise white willows from the road. If they notice them at all, they probably assume they're poplars. That's just as well, given what the timber is worth. Some mornings I wake up in a sweat from a dream that someone has come in overnight and cut them all down, carted them away. So far, it hasn't happened. Touch willow.

Every single one of my trees is female, not a rooster among them. Cricket bat willow only comes from female trees. And, at sixteen years, these are just reaching maturity. That's why I've come, hat in hand, to bring one down – to see if the timber is any good for making bats.

As with any farming, growing willow is subject to the vagaries of weather and chance. It's a fool's game, like cricket itself. But cricket is more than just a game. It's a lot like life, and it all begins here.

blue note

Frank's battered hat appears from behind the hill, followed by a raised arm, as if to distinguish his lanky frame from the tree trunks. In my own plantation, we fell willows in February, when there's still enough heat to get the moisture out of the timber. But this is Frank's first. He's anxious to see what we've grown, and today is the only day we managed to align our schedules ahead of summer.

'Morning, Allan.' His cheeks are the colour of the cool-climate shiraz he's so fond of drinking.

'Frank.'

'This is the one, then?'

I manage a nod. My guts are churning worse than on Katie's first day at school. I've taken my time picking out the tree but we'll have to see inside first. She'll be a good indicator for the grove. There's no use cutting a heap down if they can't make top-quality bats.

I put on the earmuffs and fire up the chainsaw. Frank stands back, gauging the height, second-guessing whether there's room to bring the tree down inside his fence, rather than on it. Farmers always seem to think that owning land means they're the only ones who can operate machines or manage anything practical outdoors.

In the old days, they felled willows with big cross-cut saws, two men on each end. There was none of this cutting a notch first; that would waste precious timber. They just drove a wedge in behind the saw. Even back in Essex they use chainsaws now, felling twenty-five or thirty trees a day and trucking them back to the yard. The scale of production would have Grandfather turning in his grave.

I offer my thanks, for what I'm taking. It's not quite a prayer, but I ask that the timber will allow me to create good cricket bats and, maybe, even one or two that are really special.

Those remarkable bits of willow are what I live for, making the work not work, more like delivering something into the world, peeling away the layers to reveal what's already there inside, waiting. On those days, I think it's what I was put on this good earth to do.

It was calm earlier, a nip in the air. But there's a breeze now, which I'll need to allow for. I make the cut low to the base, so as not to lose any more timber than necessary. Having already calculated exactly how many bats are in the tree – forty-four in this case – any less would be a failing. I cut the usual narrow wedge, to control the direction of the fall. The extra-long saw blade allows me to work my away around without switching sides. I just keep on going right through. Even after all these years, it's nerve-racking. There's an element of chance: how she'll fall, the whim of the wind. And, no matter how I school myself, I'm bringing down a living thing. It costs me something, and so it should.

She starts to give, and the weight of her crown pulls at the last line of fibres holding her trunk together. And then she's cracking, tipping, and gravity, momentum, pull her down, *whoomphing* into the soft ground, sending up a golden cloud of wood dust.

Once cut, the bark separates from the timber, coming away in a fashion human skin isn't inclined to – thank goodness. I tap Frank's arm, and point. When the smooth willow is first exposed, it has a blueish tinge. It fades as we watch, oxidising and turning brown, as if the spirit of the tree is slipping away, into the soil. Or burrowing deep into the fibres of the timber.

Examining the stump, the growth rings, is always a revelatory moment, the tree's story laid out, the first insights into her character. This one isn't as symmetrical as she first appeared, slight ridges and furrows are exaggerated in the timber, appearing to flow in, like waves, from the edge. That's the way the human eye works, the brain, but of course the tree's movement is from the centre out, the way she grew.

Frank lets his cattle in among the willows to control the grass. Maybe they gave this tree a little nudge, early on. They've damaged one or two over the years, even ripping off the bark one hot day, chewing it to cool themselves down. There's a compound in the cambium, salicin, the basis of aspirin. In medieval times, people used willow bark to relieve headache and toothache. How cattle know to chew the bark is another marvel, evidence that other creatures are a whole lot smarter than we give them credit for.

'What do you think?' Frank says. He peers at the grain through his frameless glasses.

'Pretty good.' Good but not great, is what I'm thinking, but best to reserve judgement.

The tree's growth rings are relatively even, considering the drought years, but there are a couple of compacted bands, ridges and variations. There's a lot of sapwood on a willow, more than a third on this one, though not quite centred. Heartwood has more colour, and is more brittle, so the less of it, the better for bats.

Willow grown back in England is creamy white, like the Royals. Australian-grown willow is more of a pinky-brown, as if darkened by the sun even beneath the bark. I used to bleach it but gave that away. There are enough chemicals in the workshop to worry about, and colour doesn't make a spot of difference to performance.

We measure out twenty-eight inches, the maximum length for the blade of a bat, and start cutting the trunk into sections. Chainsawing is a whole lot easier once the trunk is horizontal. I used to allow more margin for error, but these days I don't make many mistakes – and there's less and less room for margins.

Pale sawdust streams out, over my jeans and boots, raw and sappy, as if from the earth itself. I tell myself I'm not really killing the tree. Not quite. When I work the willow, back at the bench, it's still living tissue; I'm just changing her form.

'Give me a hand?' I say.

We manoeuvre the first round onto the ground and level it. I cleave it along the grain with the block splitter, into eight three-sided *billets* or wedges. If the timber splits easily, and feels light, as if it wants to come apart, it's good. If it's hard to split, and heavy – then not so good. The first round is somewhere in between.

The next few rounds go a little easier, but perhaps it's just that I'm warmed up, getting my swing right. The last two, approaching the top of the tree, are smaller, enough to split into only six billets.

The upper trunk and crown are a lichen forest. One variety is flat and vivid green, a bit like young willow leaves, with orangey spots, its flowers perhaps. The other is grey-green and shaggy, with all sorts of branchlets and leaves.

'Quite the ecosystem, isn't it,' says Frank.

'Every tree is a whole world, my grandfather used to say.'

We stack the blocks onto the back of the ute. Not as rough as I would firewood, but not as delicately as I handled willow when I first went off to Essex, either. They're heavy to lift, still rough and full of moisture, still blocks of wood.

While Frank has his back turned, I lean on the side of the ute to catch my breath. The work knocks me up more than it used to. I should have gone easy on the red wine last night – and the nights before that.

Frank tests the weight of a good-looking piece with his long fingers, nails clean and neatly clipped. 'Decent grain on this one.'

I nod. The lines aren't too far apart, and aligning nicely with what will be the hitting surface of the bat, but grain isn't everything. Sometimes it's the imperfections that a batter will fall in love with.

Frank is a dentist, in the city. He grew up on a big property, but this one – at five hundred acres – is just a hobby farm: Belted Galloways, or Belties, as he calls them. Cricket is another one of his passions. He only plays socially, but watches every game on television and reads every book going. He's built up quite the library, and not just on his shelves. He has volumes of cricket trivia stored away in his archive of a mind. He's always the first asked to quiz nights. Frank collects information the same way he collects books, ephemera, furniture, and weird antique dentistry contraptions. Instruments for torture I call them, not having been blessed with the best teeth.

When the last of the lengths are on board the ute, I raise and latch the sides of the tray, sucking in big breaths as quiet as I can.

'Did you know that Bradman numbered his bats?' Frank says.

'You think he knew they'd be worth something?'

'He was a smart fellow.' Frank is hovering. He's a man used to being in control and I'm not giving him what he wants. 'What's next?'

'I'll stack it away back at the workshop. And then we wait.'

Frank nods. 'You travelling all right, Allan?'

'I'm doing okay.'

'I'm glad.' He shakes my hand. 'I'll call in to the workshop sometime.'

'Look forward to it.'

I turn up the radio in the ute. They're playing Mendelssohn's overture, *The Hebrides,* featuring not one but two oboes. The tones, and cascading notes, are somehow sympathetic with the sugar gums and dry-stone walls criss-crossing the paddocks. It was Scots immigrants who built them, hauling the greystone by hand and using their stonemason traditions to reshape the landscape. People carry their music with them.

It's drier than it should be; summer has come early. There's a lot of traffic on the highway for a Thursday, too. More and more folks commuting. More and more tourists heading down to Mornington and the Otways, the Great Ocean Road. Council is widening another stretch of road, great tracts of bare earth and a mountain of trees turned to mulch. I shake my head. In Europe they grow white willows on the verges, as a buffer along highways and factory zones to scrub the air clean. Even in those murky settings, the timber remains pale, unscarred by the poisons of human industry. Only the red leather of a cricket ball leaves a mark.

Willow is, though – like many of us hailing genetically from the north – prone to sunburn. And, like all trees, white willow has its share of pests to contend with: sally sawfly, borers, giant willow aphids and, these days, a warming world. Anyone can see nature's balances are out of whack. It would only take one disease, one tiny predator. Like those bark beetles in the northern hemisphere turning spruce and pine forests to rust.

It's well past lunch by the time I back the ute down the lane, and my stomach is telling me about it. When I get out to open the gates, the tray is low over the axles, weighed down with willow. The ground in front of the shed, between the workshop and the house, is soft and the tyres leave two deep trenches. Marlene would have something to say about that if she was still here.

I ferry the billets, three at a time, to the drying shed. As I lift each one, my feeling is that they're too heavy. There are maybe a couple, all sapwood, that have a bit of potential. My arms are blocks of wood, too, tired from all the sawing, lifting, carrying.

I make a cup of tea and put together a sandwich from what's left in the fridge, which isn't much, but it's fuel, and head back out. I pull an old brush from the jar and paint the ends of each block with resin to prevent them splitting while they dry. Batmakers used to dip each end in wax, like a maturing cheese. The resin is easier to work with. As a one-man show, I've had to adapt, to minimise labour and costs, energy expenditure. So far, the willow keeps on giving.

The drying process will take between three and twelve months, depending on the whims of weather and willow. Last winter it was so cold I brought the best of them inside, to be near the fire. They weren't bad company, actually, didn't complain or criticise, just went about their quiet transformation. These billets will become *clefts*, the raw blades I shape into bats. As the blocks release moisture, they shrink and lighten, taking on a fibrous quality. That's when the alchemy begins.

field of dreams

Mid-morning, I down tools and wander across the paddock and over the hill to the local ground. It's a walk I find myself taking more often than I can really afford during summer. It costs nothing to sit in the tiny stand or on the grass up the back, in the shade of the sugar gums, but I should be shaping, pressing, sanding – not watching the game. There are customers waiting, and the season is short enough as it is.

I could sit there for hours, days. And I have. It would add up to years of my life. *Her* life was how Marlene liked to put it, as if it had been misspent. I never played seriously or had aspirations, just turned up for club games. Until I was married. It's something about the close-cropped green turf, the pitch out in the middle rolled flat, the neatly chalked white lines, the peeling corrugated iron roof of the clubhouse, the black and white letters of the old scoreboard, and the Maribyrnong snaking away behind. It's the orchestra of leather meeting willow, the whoop and huddle of players when a wicket falls, and the generous applause each time a player hits a boundary, takes a wicket or reaches a milestone, no matter which side they're on. With the backing hum of cicadas, the weight of eucalyptus in the warming air, it all adds up to a kind of meditation.

There's something about the start of the season, too: the lengthening days, the mounting expectation. The echoes of summers past, games won and lost, greats come and gone. The hope twitching in the still-growing bones of the young players that *this* will be their breakthrough season. Or, among the more hardened, who have long let go of that dream, the gratitude at being back with their mates, hoping they can contribute, that this will be the year their club holds up the trophy, and that they will be there on the podium, spraying beer over their mates and belting out the team song in the sheds afterwards.

In many ways, I prefer grade games to the Sheffield Shield. I enjoy picking the batters on the rise, those who will go on to play for their state and, perhaps, represent their country. I like to think I've developed an eye for it, seeing in them what they cannot yet see themselves: that particular combination of natural talent and technical skills. There's a purity to their game before pride, entitlement and anxiety set in – before they become conscious of the selectors on the boundary fence. They're raw product, all possibility; how their story will play out is yet to be told.

It's not unlike the process for crafting a bat. Picking out the best pieces of willow from their sound and feel, bringing all my knowledge and experience to bear. And still, the best bats just have something about them that I can't predict or explain. It's the same in great batters: a lightness of touch, the unquenchable desire to score runs, a fierceness of spirit – something inside that needs to be expressed. Technique is important but batting is an *art*.

My brother had the gift. He was a talented all-rounder, needing to be constantly involved in the game. For a time, we both worked the willow, our inheritance, just from different sides of the fence. Natey had a taste of playing for the national team – only four Tests, one season. His performances were solid but unremarkable. 'Never thought I'd choke,' he said. After he was dropped, and then did his Achilles, he never was able to fight his way back. It's a particular pain, to know the game at that level; to play, train and travel with legends, only to feel it slip away – destined never to be one yourself. The game made him – and broke him. Sometimes I think it would've been kinder not to have played those Tests at all.

Club and grade cricket are where I sell most of my bats. Only a few are good enough for the top-level players, and these days they're all sponsored by the big companies anyway. But I'm not at the ground for sales. Melbourne is hosting the Under-19s National Championships – a one-day competition – with a few of the games to be held at Footscray Oval. It's a rare chance for a close look at the nation's emerging talent pool – the next generation of Test players. There's a crowd of a couple of hundred compared to the usual couple of dozen, so I'm not the only one. Everyone has been talking about a young batter from Queensland and I want to see him for myself.

I'm still waiting at the bar when that particular *crack* makes me turn – as pure a sound as I've heard for years. The boy, fresh off the plane from Brisbane, found the bat's sweet spot first ball. The next shot is a front-foot drive through the covers, so beautifully executed, holding his shape even as he watches the ball run down to the fence for FOUR, that it brings tears to my eyes. *Oh.* Just when I'd been feeling jaded, with cricket, with life, along comes this gift.

I wander down to the fence, thinking I'll stay for half an hour. He's small for a Queenslander, and far from imposing as an opener. But he backs himself and isn't afraid to play the hook and pull shot, which you don't see so much these days. When Harrow drops to one knee, slashing the ball through the covers, the crowd groans with pleasure. The power and ease in the young man's body is a kind of grace. The grace everyone wishes they had.

After he reaches fifty, he begins to pull and cut anything short and wide, his horizontal bat shots finding the fence either side of the wicket. And the *way* he cuts. His wrists seem to swivel on the finest mechanism, caressing the ball. He sees the ball early and plays it late, never seems caught in two minds. He and fellow opener, Reid, are grinding Victoria's young pacemen into the turf.

When Harrow is just two boundaries short of a century, the crowd spills from the bar and out of their cars down to the fence. He drops his knees and runs the ball down to third man for two. A simple, low-scoring shot, but there's something about the way he plays the ball, as if he had all the time in the world. A sign of a mature head on such young shoulders. When I look around, men, women and children are applauding, smiling, shaking their heads, murmuring to each other. The sparkle in their eyes is a question: *Is this the one?*

My gut, my heart, tell me he is. That once-in-a-generation player. After losing the Ashes over there, in England, Australian cricket could do with the boost, a promising young batter on the rise, a name on everyone's lips. Someone to carry the country's hopes, to lift the team back to greatness. Someone who can live up to their promise, fulfil their potential. The potential we all like to believe we have inside us. To deliver us our dreams.

Harrow's bat is a decent piece of willow. With timing like that, he doesn't need to strike the ball hard. But the bat I would make him would have a larger centre, less weight and more air. With a little help, he could work magic with those hands, play for his country, be the best in the world. Maybe there's something of Natey about him, with his curls and open, smiling face. I want so much for him to succeed.

As if sensing the possibility, Harrow dances down the pitch and strikes the ball back over the Victorian spinner's head and beyond the white picket fence for SIX.

It's the perfect way to bring up a hundred. When he raises his bat, the crowd, almost all Victorians, are on their feet to applaud him. Harrow grins, with the pride, joy and embarrassment of a young man whose whole life is ahead of him, the future his for the taking.

Under-19s championships

Harrow hadn't even been sure he'd play, with four openers in the squad so, given the opportunity, he was never going to waste it. His hundred, in front of an appreciative Footscray crowd, was the backbone of a good total, but they'd have to bowl well, too. Victoria was one of the fittest teams, training with the AFL players in the off-season, and a tight unit. But Queensland had William Walker. He'd moved down from a big property up north to play cricket, living in a caravan out the back of his aunt's place at Eumundi. He practically had to fold himself in half to fit inside. The boys warmed to him from the start. He was funny, and your typical gentle giant. Off the field, anyway. Once he had the ball in his hand, you didn't want to get in his way. Talk about white line fever.

They called him Skywalker, because his head was so high up, in the clouds. He also had a tendency to drift off while fielding down on the boundary. The boys had to yell and point to the ball heading his way. But far out, could he bowl. It was like he mesmerised the batters with the *idea* of speed, coming down from such a great height.

Harrow watched from second slip as Skywalker ran in to bowl, all limbs in motion, a blur at the point of delivery. It was quick, hurrying the Victorian batter, who fended at the ball. The nick came hard and fast. Harrow didn't so much see the trajectory of the ball as sense it. His body, his weight, moving in line, watching the ball all the way into his hands, scooping it up and closing his fingers around it. OUT.

Skywalker roared, arms raised. The whole team ran in and mobbed him, like boys clamouring over a giant.

From there, the Victorian boys caved. Sky ended up taking six for thirty-nine to bring home the first Queensland win. The perfect way to start the competition.

'The Force is with us,' Harrow said. And it became their motto, pulling them together as a group.

Sky's parents and three brothers were all there in the stands, rugged up, the tallest family by far. It was one of those moments when Harrow felt the world shifting, propelling him forward. And he found himself missing Mum, Dad and even Liv, wishing they were there, too. With the gum trees all around and the river flowing by, Footscray Oval reminded him a lot of his home ground, back at Landsborough, where it all began.

When Mum pulled into Bill Morris Field that Saturday morning, the freshly mown green grass shimmering before them, something settled in Harrow's blood. With its white picket fence and rainforest backdrop, it was the most beautiful ground on the Sunshine Coast. The fence was hand-painted every winter by club volunteers to keep it perfectly white in a sub-tropical climate. The pickets only actually made it two-thirds of the way around the ground. Beyond that, south-east Queensland burst through any pastoral dreams. Rose gums dwarfed fences, stumps and bats. Remnant rainforest crowded along the creek line, as if trying to retake the ground.

There was even a tree *in* the ground. A big old fig near the main gates. The gentlemen who built those four pillars and wrought-iron gates, like the entrance to some grand county ground back home, just didn't understand how *big* that tree would grow with a hundred inches of rain a year and the ground warm through all four seasons. Its buttressed roots had spread and risen, almost blocking the entrance. Vehicles could no longer pass in or out, and spectators had to enter and exit single file.

If he hit the trunk on the full, it was SIX. But if the ball went up into the crown, bouncing down through the branches and leaves, it was still in play. And, if a fielder was fast enough to get there, anticipate its fall, and take the catch, it was OUT. It brought a random element to the game, and always made for a good story afterwards. Somewhere along the way, a kurrajong and feijoa had got into the act, on the other side of the gates, and no one had discouraged them. Now they were established trees, too.

If he hit the ball into the creek, it was SIX. No one even tried looking in that tangle of trunks, vines, lantana and brush-turkey nests anymore. Not since Bob Giscock cut his shin to the bone on a piece of rusted corrugated iron, staining his whites red. The club went through a shitload of extra balls, a hundred and fifty a season, but it saved a lot of time.

Hitting the Landsborough Loggers president's car, a blue-and-white striped limited-edition Ford Falcon Cobra, was a two-week suspension, effective immediately. A whole generation of cricketers was scared of slogging it to cow corner, where he parked. He liked to say it was thanks to him that young Landsborough players learned to work the ball right around the field, developing a full range of shots.

The stand wasn't much, just a green shed with room for the members and a dozen volunteers (the old boys) but a crowd would gather on three sides of the ground. Covered benches went first, bagsed by devoted dads and mums hours before the toss. Families parked their cars on the fence line, or backed up the ute, wagon, van or truck, staging their own picnics in the back. Kids clambered all over the playground and, when things got started, found a spot on top of the swings or the slide, even in the branches of the old rose gums. Plenty just wandered up and leaned on the fence for an hour or two; it was the right height for that.

The pitch itself was the low point: cement with synthetic grass laid over the top. It was a long way from Lord's or the Sydney Cricket Ground. The upside was that bounce and spin were consistent; those variables hadn't yet come into his game. It was a batter's paradise.

Ever since he'd started in the Under-12s, Harrow had wanted to smash the ball into the tennis courts. It was on the short side of the ground, but often into the afternoon sea breeze; there was an element of risk. But the satisfaction, of his game dropping in on theirs, would be worth it. For one month the tennis and cricket seasons overlapped, and there were four matches going on every Saturday morning. Parking spots were in short supply and, for some parents, a tough choice to be made about which child to watch.

Harrow was already playing for the Under-15s but, at thirteen, was yet to put on any muscle. He'd been earmarked as a prodigy, whatever that meant, but was still learning how to bring his skills together on game day. Coach had moved him up the order to open the batting, thinking that, lacking the power of the bigger boys, he could use the pace of the new ball to score.

The Loggers hadn't had the greatest start to the season; they needed to win the game to have any chance of making the finals. And Sally Newman, who'd asked him out after school the day before, would be there for her tennis match. He spat out his gum, swallowed a couple of mouthfuls of water, and walked out behind Breddo, swinging his arms like Ricky Ponting. He didn't have words for it yet, but he was learning to carve out a little space around himself to play within, a kind of bubble.

Woombye, the team everyone loved to hate, had one really good fast bowler, Gazza Keen. The rest were ordinary. Breddo didn't get off strike until the fourth ball of the opening over, with a single down to fine leg. Keen had two balls left; Harrow only had to see them out. Breddo walked down from the other end. 'Watch out for the fuller one. His arm comes over higher.'

Harrow nodded and walked back to take strike. The ball was on a fifth stump line, trying to tempt him into a shot. He let it go through to the keeper. Gazza gave him a bit of an eyeful, trying to intimidate with height and age. Harrow just smiled, and went for a walk towards square leg, staring into the forest, where the cicadas were working up to full throttle.

The next one was a beauty, and nearly snuck through him, but he managed to get his bat down in time. Breddo was right, you could see the extra extension of Gazza's arm.

Breddo made easy work of Woombye's medium pacer, Abbey, flicking one off his pads. They ran three, putting Harrow back on strike. Abbey dug one in, trying to bounce him, but it was wide, giving Harrow room to top edge it into the old metal scoreboard, just above his name. Streaky, but the clang of it got the crowd up and his blood pumping.

Abbey's next ball was overpitched. Harrow spanked it back past the bowler on the up, into the fence of the tennis courts. SIX. The *crack* of bat on ball, hitting it right out of the middle, and seeing it land just where he wanted, had him grinning.

Abbey was not smiling. 'Let's see if your head goes the same distance, kid.'

The bowler ran in hard but put the next ball in exactly the same spot. This time, Harrow stepped into it, cleared his hip to get a bit more elevation, and dropped the ball right in the middle of the court where Sally was playing. There were squeals, and then cheers, and a car horn sounding. That would be Liv, his little sister, watching from the ute.

Breddo started to come down for a chat, but Harrow took his three-step walk out towards the forest, sucking in big breaths through his nose. He was keeping them busy at the scoreboard, changing the big white numbers.

The crowd was really watching now, watching him in the middle. The whole district would know his name. Those that followed cricket anyway. He gave the last ball of Abbey's over the same treatment, timing it perfectly to land on the other side of the net. No one was hit, but the girls ran from the court covering their heads. All tennis matches were halted, and Sally joined her friends on the boundary line to watch. For that Saturday, cricket trumped tennis. Seeing the ball so well, finally executing the shot he'd been practising with his family and friends (plus his girlfriend) watching, his team cheering him on, had to be the best feeling in the world.

Breddo punched Harrow's new gloves with his worn old mitts. 'Let's take it deep, eh?'

Harrow brought up his fifty with a pull shot, timing it so well he could scarcely believe it, watching the ball fly away to the fence. He grinned and raised his bat to applause and honking car horns.

The innings, the game, the ground – it was the whole universe, with him at its centre.

Eventually Breddo mis-hit one, sending the ball high in the sky. Gazza ran around to get under it and held the catch. That brought Landsborough's captain, Russ, to the crease. His father owned the local IGA, the Loggers' main sponsor, making everyone even more eager to please him. He and Harrow got through to lunch and then set about building a big total, finding the gaps in the field, running hard between wickets. Their season wasn't done yet.

The train came through every hour, the alarms on the level crossing flashing orange. Weekend traffic churned up and down the Blackall Range, cars slowing as they passed. The sun dropped lower, allowing the heat and humidity to ease.

Wickets fell at the other end, but Harrow batted on. And on. Just before tea, he hit another SIX, into the fig tree this time, to bring up his hundred. Mum and Dad were standing on the back of the ute, arms raised, fists clenched. Liv honked the horn in a three-note tune, which began a procession of honks all around the ground.

Russ called them in, clapping Harrow on the back as he ran past. 'Well played, kid,' he said.

He finished on a hundred and four not out. It was 'raining cricket balls', the *Range News* would report. It was his best innings ever, and his first century. But it was more than that. It was the feeling of finally hitting the ball out of the ground, of tapping into something larger when the team needed it. He'd turned a corner and found what was there all along. He would play cricket. And one day, he would play cricket for Australia.

cleft

I walk the rows with Harrow in mind, between the willow clefts stacked high on timber pallets, their rough-cut ends with two walls, a floor and a roof. Each one is unique, its qualities dependent on the original character of tree, soil, weather, the rate of growth, the culmination of seasons. I do a quick grading as I cut them from the billets, looking for those that are light and furry off the saw. First, second, third and fourth grade.

The English clefts I buy in are all firsts or seconds. All the finest prospects are up the back, in row X, including a few of mine that just have something about them. Like my wine cellar, I need to make the good stuff harder to reach, to save them for that special occasion. There is no W or Y. X is for X-factor, all those things that can't be fully explained.

I used to dry the clefts in the kiln at the old sawmill, but the mill is long gone now. In theory, all clefts are dried to about fifteen per cent of their original weight. But two initially identical clefts can end up varying in weight by a pound or more. In a bat weighing five pounds, that's a lot. It isn't really about moisture, but the density of wood that remains. A good bat is light and dry, a bit like balsa wood. All those fine water tubes running through the willow are the secret, filling the timber with air.

It's the widest grain I'm after, the sign of younger, more resilient timber. I scan for the fuzziest clefts, as if they have kept on growing after being cut, like human nails and hair after death, taking one last gasp of life – or undergoing a transformation.

I tap each one with two fingers, listening for the low note, an indication that the timber will give the rebound I need. Back and forth, playing a willow tune, until I'm sure. Each blade needs to be expressed in the right shape, matched to the right player. Even then, it's one-part mystery. But get the right combination, the perfect bat for a great player, and something mythic can happen. That's the possibility that keeps me going. I see it in timber, and it's there in music, art, literature and sport – those rare moments of transcendence. It's the story everyone wants to be part of.

For the clefts, it's all about how they'll respond to a cricket ball. In a player, talent is easy to spot. How they'll respond to coaching, opportunity, pressure and setbacks is harder to predict.

It's a kind of gambling, not that I ever put any money down. Perhaps I should, I certainly invest enough time following particular players. Living their career, their life, with them. *Through* them, Marlene used to say.

Sometimes I wonder if willow has a will. If some trees are just more aware than others, more determined to shine. It's as if some clefts *want* to be made, need a particular player to carry them out onto a cricket field. As if they have a way of finding their perfect match. Even people who really live and love the game – cricket nuffies – don't realise that it's white willow that has enchanted them.

Of the tens of thousands playing, only a few have what it takes to make it at the top level. Add to that the element of luck: selection, injury, conditions, team composition, the umpiring decisions that can make the difference between scoring zero and a hundred, finding form and losing it. 'It's a bloody casino,' Nate used to say. Only the crazy and the brave would embark on a journey so unlikely to succeed.

Better to play for the love of the game than ambition, because disappointment is guaranteed in cricket, as it is in life. Or for the team, to be part of something larger. I wipe my cheeks. Nothing gets me emotional quite like our great game.

The sun drops below the tree line, the tangle of old casuarinas at the end of the lane casting a pinkish glow over the rough-cut ends. One in particular lights up, its furred surface swollen with warmth. From the first harvest from my original plantation, out at Shepherds Flat. When I lift it from the rack to feel its weight, the hair on my forearms prickles. For a moment, the timber appears blue again, and butterflies start up in my belly. This is the one.

Marlene didn't start out hating cricket. She came to a few games early on and used to watch the big ones with me on television. The Boxing Day Test, any series decider and, later, every one-dayer Michael Bevan played in. Fair enough, too; he was a good-looking bloke who won plenty of matches for Australia. He should probably have played more Tests.

It was my devotion to the game she came to resent. All that time I spent down at the ground, watching the up-and-coming instead of watching my own daughter growing up. The time I put into shaping bats was time I should have spent shaping our own family. I threw balls to Katie in the nets in the afternoons and we had the occasional family backyard game. But once she hit her teens, she lost interest in cricket.

I don't know what she did. Studied, I guess. Her last few years of school she was always in her room or at the library, or out with friends. We just ran out of things to talk about.

Katie never got into any trouble, did well at school, finished intact. She's an accountant now. Good and safe, already independent and living with a fella. A sensible girl – woman; I should be thankful, I know.

Somehow, by the time Katie left home, Marlene had stopped watching the game or asking about the Test in progress. She even stopped coming down to the workshop. In the early days she baked a cake every week, and brought me a slice with a mug of steaming tea every morning. Chocolate or lemon and poppyseed, a Bundt cake for special occasions. When I was away, or down at a game, she would pack me sandwiches and a thermos, and leave little piles of willow shavings on the bench, in the shape of a tree or animal, sometimes a heart.

To be fair, I didn't try hard enough to support her passion: painting. Not that I didn't recognise her talent. But even when we were in the same room, at the breakfast table or in bed, I wasn't always listening properly. My mind was on the game.

Marlene was a promising visual artist, big landscapes – experimenting with pastels. When we met, making signs for a student protest, she was just finishing art school. Her first exhibition was a sell-out and got a little write-up in *The Age*. I was at the Conservatorium up the road: oboe, of all the instruments. Our courtship unfolded in concert halls and gallery openings. Second-hand suits and dresses, too many glasses of champagne. What a pair of dreamers!

Once we got pregnant, we had to face facts: we probably weren't quite good enough to make it at the elite level. And there wasn't much money in it even if we did. How would we manage the travel with a baby? It would be hard. Too hard. That's what we told ourselves. Looking back, that was my father talking. And when had I ever listened to him? It was an excuse not to try, not to risk failure.

In those lean years, when Marlene's art teaching kept us afloat, I did thank her. But I was more than a little ashamed, not being able to provide for my family. A *real* husband would have supported her art, was always the subtext. She actually said it out loud once, in an argument, forgetting that batmaking was not my first choice, either. It was all wrong from the start, letting marriage limit our dreams rather than enable them.

doubling up

Queensland Under-19s flogged Northern Territory in the second round and then edged out Tasmania in a thriller. Harrow contributed eighty and sixty, plus a couple of catches. He sent all the results home, in detail. Liv said his scores, and Queensland's progress through the competition, were updated on his school noticeboard when she and Mum drove past every morning. That was pretty funny, seeing as they weren't even going to let him come.

His Year 12 patron, Miss Meadow, had turned him down initially, saying he needed to spend the time studying. 'Your English essay is overdue. And final exams are only a few weeks away.'

He was passing all his subjects, but everyone knew playing on the University of Queensland oval was as close as he was going to get to a higher education.

'With respect, exams and essays aren't much use to me. I'm going to play cricket for Australia.'

'That's a nice dream, Todd. But I think you need a backup plan.'

He flopped back in his chair and raised his hands, palms open. 'Have you seen me bat, Miss?'

In the end, Mum rang the principal for 'a conversation'. And he was going after all.

Queensland Under-19s' next game was against New South Wales, where he'd be facing his nemesis, Robert Hilton. It was only the moment he'd been imagining every night since he'd read the team lists. And just about every night since he'd first come up against Hilton, when they were still boys, at the regional schools comp at Port Macquarie. He'd been the stand-out fast bowler for the locals, Hastings Valley, and probably the tournament. There was already talk back then of him playing for New South Wales.

Oxley Oval's picket fence was yellow instead of white, and right next to the sea. Lorikeets and cockatoos screeched from the Norfolk Island pines. The human crowd, such as it was, sat on the stone wall cut into the grassed hill or the benches beneath the pines. The only thing that reminded Harrow of home was the proximity of the tennis courts. He set his sights on a SIX or two, something to stir up the crowd.

Hilton was a tree of a boy, and a handful. His first ball rose steeply and struck Harrow flush on the chest, knocking all the air out of him. He wasn't sure his heart was still beating. He walked away, head up, refusing to rub it, channelling Justin Langer (perhaps not the best opener ever, but the toughest). When the pain crept in, he just grinned back at Hilton. He wasn't going to be hit twice.

He took position again, shutting everything out: the birds, the sea, the breeze in the pines, the home crowd clapping the bowler in. Everything but the ball. It was a narrowing of focus, but an expansion of consciousness, awareness. He sighted the ball out of Hilton's hand, off the pitch, coming for his head, but this time he was ready, and hooked it over deep square for FOUR.

Wittling gave him a nod from the other end, raised his gloved hand in a fist. Respect, and a measure of the work they had to do. Together they took the shine off the ball, and then started smashing Hilton around the ground. Hilton was muttering under his breath, shaking his head. Eventually Wittling lost his off stump. Others came and went. Harrow carried his bat right through the innings. Even the locals applauded when he launched a half-volley into the tennis courts to reach his hundred.

When he called home that night, it was Liv who answered. 'A century already,' she said. 'What are you going to pull out for the final?'

'Shut up,' he said.

His mother was more worried about whether his helmet was up to the older boys' fast bowling. 'This Robert Hilton, they say he can already bowl a hundred and forty kilometres an hour!'

'He's not that quick, Mum.'

A narrow win over Northern Rivers saw Sunshine Coast into the semis, where Harrow took a wicket and scored fifty, part of their best team performance yet, to edge out Central Coast. Vickers, their bowling all-rounder and captain, hit fifteen off the last over, including a SIX off the final ball, earning him the moniker Iceman. The local paper labelled Sunshine Coast 'the new Invincibles'. Meanwhile, Hastings Valley had beaten Coffs Coast in a thriller of their own. Harrow would face off with Hilton again in the final.

At dinner that night, the teams started mingling. Harrow chatted to Reid, the stocky Gold Coast batter who was about to move to Brisbane for a contract with the Queensland Bulls. They were both openers, competing with each other, in theory, for higher honours, but it didn't feel like that. Not yet. He caught Hilton looking over from the rear of the wood-panelled bowling club function room. He gathered from the honour board that Hiltons were town royalty: football, golf and cricket achievements in gold letters going back three generations. No one from Sunshine Coast had that sort of pedigree. And the name Harrow didn't exactly strike fear into any bowler's heart. But one day it would.

He'd psyched himself up for the final down at Main Beach with his headphones in, listening to Powderfinger and watching the gromms carving it up on one side, the skaters on the other. All the off-field movement gave him room to rest, clear his mind. They had it pretty good in Port; no wonder not many played cricket. The nasty bruise flowering on his chest was a badge of honour, seeing him go without a shirt at any opportunity.

On game day, Sunshine Coast won the toss and batted. He got off the mark first ball, playing positively and turning over the strike. When Hilton came on to bowl, Harrow prepared himself for the bouncer. He had to take him on early, show him who was boss. Instead, the ball came for his stumps. And *fast*. He just managed to get his bat down but overbalanced, nearly falling flat on his face. When he took guard again, his breathing was all over the place. He barely saw the next ball, played at it anyway, and missed. He shrugged and replayed the shot, suggesting it had moved off the pitch, but it had beaten him for pace. Hilton knew it, too. His smirk said everything.

For the next three balls, he was stuck on the crease. Wittling kept backing up aggressively, trying to sneak through for a single and get him off strike, but Harrow couldn't hit the ball off the square. The following over, Wittling smashed a loose ball back past their seamer's head for FOUR, which kept the scoreboard ticking but meant Harrow would face Hilton again next over.

Two more dot balls, tight in at his pads, and he was feeling the pressure. He needed to get in the game, score. And sure enough, when a wider one came through, he slashed at it. The ball found the outside edge of his bat and was easily pouched by first slip. OUT. He'd fallen right into Hilton's trap.

The game went down to the final overs. And it looked like Hilton was going to bring Hastings Valley home with the bat. He didn't have many shots, but with levers like that he only had to connect with the ball. He hit a massive SIX into the car park, setting off all the alarms.

Blaxland and Redman, their big quicks from Caloundra, practically had steam coming out their ears. But Blax got him in the end, with a cross-seam ball, and Red came running in to take the catch off the top-edge off Hilton's bat. It all came down to a very simple equation: one wicket to win, seven runs to lose. Six balls remaining.

It was all on Red in that last over, sweat pouring out of him. Hastings' number eleven was a real bunny, coming out with a shoelace trailing, so they rated their chances, especially after a big swing and miss first ball he faced. But then he got off strike with a bunt ball. Six runs; one wicket; four balls. The win was within their reach. And they wanted it. They all wanted it so *very* much. And Red knew it. He stood at the top of his mark, wiped his forehead with his wristband, and glanced around the field. They were attuned to each other's every move, pushing in as the ball was bowled, trying to force an error. The boys clapped two dot balls like they were wickets.

Hastings' tubby spinner swatted one that could just as easily have been caught but landed safe between two fielders and bounced off the running track into the boundary. FOUR. The crowd was on their feet, yelling and screaming for the home win. One ball; one wicket; two runs.

Red ran in, and the boys were all with him, behind him, willing him to bowl the ball of the tournament, to get a nick, hit the player's pads, knock over his stumps, break his jaw. They didn't care *how*. And Red really bent his back. It was his fastest ball of the day for sure: straight and full, cannoning into the batter's pads, right in front of the stumps. Red turned and appealed, running backwards, both arms raised in glorious certainty. They were all leaping, hands to the sky. It was *plumb*. Even the local umpire couldn't deny it.

But he did. He refused to raise that finger. Just stood there, shaking his thick head. Meanwhile, the batters had scampered through for a single. Scores were tied. The boys stood around with their mouths open, hands on heads. No one had thought to field the ball.

Red was getting stuck into the umpire. 'Were your fucking eyes even open?'

Ice and Harrow had to hold Red back. And then Coach ran on to the field clapping his hands. 'C'mon boys, you played out of your skins. This is a great result. A tied final!'

As they trudged off, muttering about the injustice, Harrow couldn't help thinking of his own dismissal, the difference a few runs could have made.

In the sheds it didn't seem so bad, after hot showers and food and drink on tap. The boys gathered around Red, trying to comfort him. No one could help it if the umpire was biased. A tied game was a result so rare it would be legend. Like the two tied Tests. Maybe they didn't quite play with the grace of the West Indians, or scrap like Allan Border's Australians, but they believed that one day they could.

They cleaned themselves up for the presentations, finding fresh shirts and pants. Ice spent twenty minutes polishing his shoes and Coach turned up in a jacket and tie, which was a first. With the most runs and highest strike rate, Harrow was awarded best batter, Hilton best bowler. They'd matched themselves up, out of some sort of primal instinct. But sitting at those long tables, the hollow feeling he was nursing, of not delivering when it mattered, was in the way of fully enjoying the occasion. It was a lesson he wouldn't forget.

Hilton came over to shake his hand afterwards. 'That's some pull shot you've got there.'

Harrow grinned. 'It was that or let you take my head off.'

Under-19s finals

Hilton was a man now, four inches taller and all bulked up. Harrow was watching him train, in the Footscray nets, now sporting a sharp haircut and an armful of tatts. Not that he needed any help looking mean; he'd picked up a few yards of pace, too. Harrow had been standing there for half an hour, cap down over his eyes, as Hilton peppered the New South Wales batters with bouncers, before the quick even acknowledged him. Harrow nodded. There weren't words for what he was feeling; a little fear, sure, but that was part of the challenge.

Queensland won the toss and batted first. Harrow ran out ahead of Reid, swinging his arms, bouncing on his toes, to take his mark. He knew Hilton would be expecting his pull and hook shots, so he put those away for now. He didn't play the bouncer at all, just swayed out the way and smiled. He wasn't going to be drawn into any big shots early or lose his head. Not this time. He got off strike with a flick off his pads and called Reid through for a single.

The other opening bowler was fast but wayward. Harrow tucked one down to fine leg for FOUR and pushed an easy single through mid-wicket. Reid hit a straight drive down the ground and they ran four on a misfield and poor throw. Harrow should've been out next over, caught at first slip. But the fielder put it down. Harrow shook his head and took strike again. It was the lucky break he needed.

New South Wales were getting frustrated. The pitch was an absolute road, the ball didn't seem to be swinging or seaming. The third delivery of Hilton's next over gave Harrow room to cut, running the ball away for another boundary.

They put on forty-nine before Reid lost his middle stump. Hilton gave him a big send off and Reid had plenty to say in return, forcing the umpire to step in. Harrow turned his back, determined not to get caught up in the emotion. Instead, he watched the low clouds scudding in over the ground. Melbourne's weather never did seem to be able to make up its mind.

Once he posted his century, Harrow accelerated, taking Queensland past three hundred, and his own score within four runs of a double century. Hilton came on to bowl the last over. Of course. Harrow got the first ball away and ran three, which was looking like a mistake, with one of the Gold Coast twins Harry Dean swinging and missing, nearly turning himself full circle.

Next ball was wide, beating Dean and the keeper, running away for four byes. Harrow was starting to wonder if he would ever get back on strike, but just grinned and shrugged. More pressure wasn't going to help Dean. At least Hilton had to bowl the ball again. This time Dean clubbed it out to mid-wicket, and they jogged through for a single.

Final ball of the innings, Harrow had his eye on the short boundary at deep square leg. There were two fielders out there but if he got any width at all, he reckoned he could send it over their heads. The ball was overpitched; it was Hilton feeling the pressure now. Harrow stepped into the shot and lofted the ball down the ground, over long on. It landed on the roof of the clubhouse, lodging in a gutter.

He leapt high in the air and pumped his gloved fist. He'd joined the double hundred club, which only nine batters had managed in the competition before him. And most of them had gone on to play for their country. Even Hilton came over to shake his hand as they ran from the field.

Then Sky found something in the pitch that had eluded the New South Wales bowlers, reducing them to five for forty-two. They never recovered, all out in the thirty-fifth over. It was a massive win for Queensland. They'd surprised everyone, even themselves.

When Liv rang, he already knew what she was going to say.

'A double, Toddy!! Hope you've left something in the tank.'

Western Australia was going to be tough to beat, armed with the usual battalion of fast bowlers. Coach took a gamble and played two spinners, thinking the Footscray pitch, well-worn now, might turn, and Western Australia wouldn't play them as well as the pacers.

McCain, their number three and captain, from Toowoomba, lost the toss, but Western Australia sent them in when they would have batted anyway. Harrow raced to fifty, and then pulled himself back, determined to be there at the end. He was on seventy-nine when he chopped an inside edge onto his stumps. The most disappointing sound in cricket.

He trudged from the field and stood under the showers until the hot water ran out. When he joined the others, to watch the rest of the boys do the work, Coach said, 'Bad luck, mate.'

He nodded. But it wasn't luck. He'd gotten ahead of himself and checked his shot, rather than just playing his natural game. The rest of the batters chipped in, Reid top-scoring with ninety-one. And then Sky was an absolute legend, taking three wickets and fluking a diving catch in the outfield. It was like watching a skyscraper fall, but in the end, he held up the ball. OUT.

The spinners cleaned up the rest, with Harrow chiming in to take his first wicket (a skied ball off a half-tracker), and Western Australia was all out in the forty-eighth over, well short of the required total. Their gamble had worked. Or, as Liv put it, Queensland was on a roll.

Meanwhile, Victoria had lost the other semi. Queensland would play New South Wales in the final. They'd only won the championship four times to New South Wales' fifteen, but it was a challenge the boys were ready for.

They spent their rest day at St Kilda, chilling out with a game of touch footy in the park, amid picnickers and buskers, and a swim afterwards. The water was so cold their lips turned blue, and McCain reckoned his balls had shrunk permanently. After that they took to calling Victoria the Arctic instead of Mexico, as in south of the border, and McCain Captain Frozz, as in frozen peas.

Harrow had never seen so many cake shops in his life, let alone on one street. He couldn't decide between a poppyseed roll and the layered chocolate torte, so ordered both, and a cappuccino so big even he couldn't finish it. When he sent Liv a picture of the cake shop window, she warned him not to pig out. But it was too late.

Whether it was all the caffeine and sugar or visualising how he was going to bat the following day, he didn't really sleep that night. He couldn't wait to get back out to the middle and score more runs.

The big game was at Punt Road, in the shadow of the mighty Melbourne Cricket Ground. Frozz lost the toss again; they would field first, which meant waiting – and chasing. But at least they'd know exactly what they had to score to win.

The bowlers didn't start well; their lengths were off, bowling too short or too full. New South Wales got away early and they couldn't peg them back. Their openers both passed fifty and were starting to smash the ball around when Sky finally got the breakthrough: an edge that Harrow had to dive for and take with his left hand.

Sky plonked one of his great mitts on the back of Harrow's head and pulled him towards his chest in a half-embrace. 'Nice, Hars.'

It was a big moment in the game. Sky took two wickets in his next over, and they were back in the battle. Some big-hitting from the tailenders in the final overs took New South Wales to two hundred and ninety-nine. Queensland had a lot to do, under pressure. Pressure not helped by the media showing up with their long lenses and two old blokes in sunglasses, leaning on the fence, who could only be selectors.

Harrow and Reid ran from the field ahead of the others to go through their respective routines amid the chaos of gear, clothes, towels and half-dressed men and boys: fresh shirt, socks, thigh guard, box, rib protector, forearm guard, pads, inners and gloves laid out, bat leaning against the locker. Deep breaths all the while. Reid went right side to left, Harrow left to right. Reid was always ready first but waited, without impatience, by the door, eyes closed, visualising what he wanted to do out in the middle. Harrow, on the other hand, could not be still for a moment. Not until he was facing that first ball.

Frozz called everyone together in a huddle, arms around one another. 'Boys, we're *here*, in the final. No one expects us to win. But we *can*! Let's show them how we play cricket in Queensland.'

Reid went early, losing his leg stump to a Hilton yorker, but Harrow and Frozz dug in. Harrow was feeling good, hitting them clean, building his innings to pass fifty. He raised his bat, but he wasn't done. There was the next ball, and the one after that. Frozz got a beauty that squared him up, hitting him flush on the pads. Harrow was pretty sure it was going down leg, but he knew the umpire was going to give it out. Frozz had left himself wide open. Sure enough, the umpire raised his finger. Harrow went on the attack, building another partnership with Harry Dean. But he fell, and then his brother, Gill. They were still in touch with the required run rate but kept losing wickets.

There was too much left to do in the final over: sixteen from six balls. And Hilton to bowl it. But Harrow was still there, and on strike. He walked down to bump fists with Sky. 'I've got this,' Harrow said, squinting up at him.

'And I've got your back.'

He swung hard at the first ball, only managing a top-edge but it flew over slip and away to the boundary for FOUR. Hilton shook his head and walked back to his mark. The next one was meant to be a yorker but ended up a waist-high full toss, which Harrow pulled for SIX.

'Shot, Hars,' Sky said.

New South Wales pushed a fielder out. The next one would be at his head, for sure. He was ready, but again, didn't get hold of it. There was a single there, but Harrow called NO. He managed to flick the next ball off his pads, and they scampered through for two, Sky only just grounding his bat as the keeper removed the bails.

Four runs, two balls.

The next ball was too good, spearing in at his toes. Harrow could only defend. He took a breath and walked out towards square leg, focusing on the breeze in the treetops, the crowd gone quiet. Hilton and his captain were still strategising, placing their field.

It was Dad's voice he heard in his head, quiet and steady. *Back yourself.*

He took his mark, tapped his bat three times, looked up at Hilton running in hard, jaw set. He read it on length – and swung. The ball flew above the leaping fielder's hands, bounced once, and ran over the boundary rope for FOUR. Right in front of the selectors. Queensland WIN!

Sky was down the pitch in two strides, lifting Harrow high in the air. Harrow was unable to speak, only grin. National Champions!

He was the tournament's leading run scorer and Sky leading wicket-taker, edging out Hilton by two wickets. All three were named in the team of the championship. Looking back through past lists, there were plenty of names he recognised. It was the seeding ground for national players. Now his name was there, too.

They celebrated with a few VBs in the change rooms, not a XXXX to be found. Frozz and Reid were the only ones over eighteen but that didn't slow the party. There was the usual half-dressed carry-on in front of the lockers, and more than one beer poured over Harrow's head. Sky's skinny white legs took up half the narrow space, as the boys gathered in to hear him call the final over, beer bottle as microphone, as seen from the non-striker's end. He really hammed it up, how stressful it was just standing there, and the miracle of the final four. The boys fell around laughing, a loose-limbed contentment settling in.

They gathered in a stumbling circle, arms around each other's shoulders, the floor awash. Reid sang the team song, off-key but full of heart. The boys' eyes were glassy, and not just from the beers. Harrow had to work hard not to let a tear escape. It all meant so much.

Once he was cleaned up, and buttoning his shirt for the final dinner and presentations, Coach clapped his hand on Harrow's shoulder. 'Selectors came asking about you.'

'What did you tell them?'

'That you're the real deal,' he said. 'That you'll play a hundred Tests for Australia.'

press and splice

My days in the workshop all begin the same way: turn on the lights, open the windows, switch on the radio. The Classic FM breakfast presenter not only knows her music but has a sense of humour – and a voice like a cello. She's good company, as is the selection she plays. Today she's included 'Shepherd's Song' from Beethoven's *Pastoral Symphony* – an old favourite. It's impossible not to feel happy among those notes. Hopefully it gives Shepherd a lift, opening for the Vics today. He really faded at the end of the last Shield season.

Pastoral was Beethoven's hymn to nature. As the presenter puts it, he loved trees more than humans. The more I look at the face of Harrow's cleft, the more excited I am about this particular bit of tree. The grain is fine, straight and blemish free, except for one little butterfly knot, like a magic kiss. I can already see the bat in my mind; it's a matter of releasing what's inside without injuring it too much.

I fire up the bandsaw and take off the rough lacquered ends, then trim a thin strip from each side, bringing the face down to four-and-a-quarter inches, the standard size since 1774. You can have less but never more. Once I've planed the face, brought it back to a smooth surface, I switch over to the cricket.

During summer, I structure my schedule around the sessions of play. Today it's the first Shield game: those old arch-rivals, New South Wales and Victoria, playing at the Sydney Cricket Ground. New South Wales has more than a home ground advantage; they field more national players than any other team. It may be the most populous state, for now, but there are plenty who suggest it has more to do with the volume of New South Wales selectors stacking the committee. It backfires in the second half of the season though, when most of the team disappears to play for Australia, leaving New South Wales to field a second-tier side. Meanwhile, Victoria has won the Shield final more than any other state. There were plenty of Victorian players who could, and should, have worn Australian colours, or worn them more often.

But it's the Queensland team I'm interested in. After Harrow's performance in the Under-19s Championship, he has to be in their sights. The commentators are talking him up, too. When Harrow gets his opportunity, I want to make sure he seizes it. It's a big step up, playing against seasoned adults, facing some of the best bowlers in the country. He'll need all the help he can get.

The bat is impatient in my hands, as if it, too, can't wait to get out into the middle.

It was probably ordained that I work the willow. My grandfather, and three generations before him, were batmakers. My great-uncle was a quilt winder, one of the secretive guild entrusted with the mysteries of making cricket balls from cork and thread. I still have his old black stool in the workshop, under the skylight. Sometimes, when I'm sitting there doing repairs or sanding, I think of him stitching leather by hand. He seemed such a calm, quiet man; you'd need patience for that work. But Grandfather said he had a filthy temper. He'd tear strips from anyone who wasn't absolutely dedicated to their work.

My father was the throwback. He emigrated after the war, turning his back on Europe, on tradition, to work the assembly line for Ford, out at Campbellfield. No one spoke of dreams and ambitions, they couldn't afford to. He followed the game and played with Nate and me. We listened to the first tied Test against the West Indies in Brisbane on the radio that summer, which would make anyone fall in love with the game. He took us to a few matches, too, when we were young. When you could still sit on the grass at the Melbourne Cricket Ground and take in an esky full of beers. Dad couldn't have done any more for Nate, driving him to and from training and games, going without to keep him in gear. We had hopes, even then, of him playing for Australia.

Dad and Nate were close, and got closer still when Mum was sick. Nate stayed at home to help, while I was sent off to England, spending the English summer with Grandfather, in St John's Wood, near Lord's. He taught me his craft, let me make my first harrow bat – a smaller bat for young or shorter players – from scratch. He still wore the white apron over his dress shirt, baggy sleeves rolled up, vest and suit pants, though by then he'd given the tie away.

It was up the back of Grandfather's workshop, swirling willow dust caught in the light shafting through the saw-tooth roofline, while he explained that every piece of willow is unique, varying in weight, density and responsiveness, that I first saw all those willow clefts as living things. And I understood, in some vague and unconscious way, though I could never have verbalised it at the time, that the heart of the game was in the hands of those craftsmen.

He'd worked in the bat factory, like his father before him, grown up with the family company as a way of life. There were men there with twenty, thirty and forty years' experience and loyalty to the firm, which made cricket balls, too, in those days. When the factory was bombed during World War II, destroying all their stock, it was Grandfather's mother, my great-grandmother, who rebuilt, with all the men away or killed in action.

During the 1950s there were twenty batmaking factories in London, a hundred and sixty thousand handmade bats a year. Grandfather's alone made twelve dozen bats a week. When they lost the factory in a fire, they rebuilt again. They just kept making bats.

But by then things were changing. There were fewer firms, and a handful of those dominated production. The big retailers had started commissioning bats to their own specifications. A couple of companies were headed by former players; personalities were coming into it, selling an aspiration.

Grandfather used to say 'batmaking belongs to England'. He knew we grew willow here but just shook his head. 'The timber is the wrong colour. The trees can't be happy, so far from home.' Perhaps it was how he imagined us, too, living down under. Mum was in the middle of her cancer treatment by then, chemo, and Dad was doing it tough, trying to hold everything together. I should have been more worried, but everyone kept telling me that Mum would get through it.

The secret of batmaking, the real transformation of the willow, is in the pressing. They used to do it by hand, with bone, a horse's femur. But in the early twentieth century, as with most other aspects of our lives, machines started to take over. The first were still part-manual, you had to adjust the weights by hand, increasing them after each press. Now it's all automated; the weights adjust themselves, responding to the willow. Every maker has their own version, made or adapted themselves, which they like to keep secret. My machine was Grandfather's. I had it shipped over, with most of his other gear, after he died. It was partly nostalgia, but they're all high-quality tools, which I still use every day.

The noise of the machines means missing moments of play, an occupational hazard. I envy the old makers, working away quietly in teams under a master batmaker, everything done by hand. It was more in tune with the game itself. Cricket may seem slow, but it can all change in a moment. The build-up to those moments, and the subtle shifts in momentum as a result, are what the game is all about.

I linger near the radio for the start of play. Victoria has won the toss and will bat first. It means a stressful start for Victorian fans, with Shepherd slow to get going, and King still new to the role. It might be better to miss the first few overs; all that can happen is someone getting out.

I dust off the press and fire it up. Once bright green, it has dulled with oil, age and good use. I set the bat in face up, make some adjustments. The cleft passes under the three metal rollers, stops and reverses. Each roller presses down on the face more and more heavily, squashing all the air from those tiny tubes within the willow, compacting the surface layers. The cleft goes in as softwood and comes out as hardwood.

It's the pressing that makes the face of the bat tough enough to hit the ball repeatedly but still light enough to wield. Much like the grass and soil of the cricket pitch is compacted under a heavy roller to make it durable enough to last five days. If you think about it, the game is played between those two hardened surfaces.

I pause, alerted by the rising tone of the commentators. King has fallen, given out leg before wicket. They're not convinced the ball was going on to hit the stumps, but he played across the line, and missed, leaving his pads exposed. He has to go. Not a good start. A batter's mind needs hardening, too, to focus under pressure and for long periods. Not every player can manage it, and few manage it all the time.

I find the stub of my blue carpenter's pencil to mark out the V for the handle at the top of the blade, and return to the bandsaw to cut away the wedge. Already it's more like a bat and less like a block of wood.

I buy the handles these days. It's cheaper than my time and they're better than I can make. Four rods of the best Sarawak cane – from Borneo or Vietnam – spliced together to make a slip, and four slips glued together to make a handle, interspliced with three layers of the best Indian rubber. The layers of flex absorb the shock of ball hitting bat.

Harrow uses a short handle, but not super short. I choose the best looking of those from the stack above my bench and mark out a complementary wedge to splice into the V of the bat. It's the trickiest part of the process; nothing keeps the handle in place but accurate measurement and glue. If I cut it too small, it will not hold. Too large and it will split the bat right down the face.

The commentator calls the fall of the second wicket, dismay dripping from his voice. The ball is nipping around in overcast conditions, but it was a poor shot from the number three and captain, Scott. It's a good excuse to start up the bandsaw again. I slip on a face mask first. Cane dust is carcinogenic. They found that out the hard way in the factories.

The handle is the other batmaker's secret. There's a natural 'spring' in the cane and a well-made splice. The first bats were solid timber, stinging the player's hands whenever they hit the ball. Coming towards you at up to a hundred and fifty kilometres an hour, the red missile of leather, twine and cork carries enough force to fracture a forearm – or a skull. The handle was always the first part of the bat to break, absorbing the initial shock of impact.

The history of the cricket bat handle is another colonial story. When the English went to South-East Asia in the 1830s, they discovered cane and rubber. For a time, makers trialled steel springs wrapped in rubber, running through the splice, from the handle down into the bat. The bats all split, splintered and broke, of course. As Grandfather put it, 'metal and willow never was a natural pairing.'

Someone had the bright idea to use a cane handle to repair a broken bat. And, by 1893, *every* bat had a cane handle. Then makers started experimenting with rubber to further reduce the jarring on the batter's hands. We makers shape the game, just as the game shapes us.

I set up the bat in the vice – lined with wood to protect the willow – and test the fit of the handle into the blade, making fine adjustments to the V with a chisel. The secret is to keep it tight at the top and loose at the bottom. Then I hammer in the cane, tilted slightly forward. I use high-quality animal glue, made from goatskin. It stinks, but marine glue sets too quickly unless the temperature is just right. Which, in Melbourne, is a fleeting rarity. I loosen the vice, wipe off the excess glue with a rag, and clamp the bat in tight. It will take twenty-four hours to fully set.

I tidy up as I go: tools away, glue back on the shelf, sweep down the bench. Not just in case someone wants to look around, to see how their bat is coming along, but for the work to keep flowing, and the bats to come out right, without mistakes or accidents.

The house is a different story. When I go in for lunch, I make a half-hearted attempt to clear clutter from surfaces. It's been building for weeks, reaching some sort of tipping point while I've been focused on Harrow. There would probably be room to eat at the table, among all the old newspapers and unopened mail. But there's a particular A4 envelope, still lying where I threw it after signing for it, registered post, that I'm avoiding.

It's been over a year now, since Marlene left, so I expect it's the divorce papers. I'll sign them; there's no point fighting it. I'm just not ready. And I won't have one ounce of negativity coming anywhere near that precious piece of willow, lest it spoil its magic.

It wasn't all work that summer with Grandfather. We watched plenty of cricket, too. Mostly county games at some of his favourite grounds. Lord's of course, just over the road and home of Middlesex, with its famously sloping ground and the weathervane featuring Father Time removing the bails from the stumps, as if batting is life itself. The Ashes urn is there, in the museum, from the first time Australia beat England. The English thought their throats cut at the time, the game over for good, but it was just the beginning.

Grandfather didn't attend church on Sundays; he went to the cricket. His eyes took on a particular shine watching a game, his face akin to rapture. If Lord's was the field of heaven, the picturesque rural grounds were gardens of Eden.

My favourite was New Road, in Worcester, with the Severn flowing along one side and Worcester Cathedral – a hotchpotch of English architectural styles from Norman to Gothic – on the other. He bought me my first pint up in the Members' – although, strictly speaking, I was not yet of age – on a perfect summer's day, while we watched a scene that could have been two hundred years old but for the neon sign on the ice-cream van. A full crowd turned up, ready to appreciate a day's play.

The view of the Cathedral from the ground is so grand it was on the twenty-quid note, along with Edward Elgar, who was born only a few miles away, at Broadheath. When the game against Hampshire was washed out, we spent the afternoon at The Firs, Elgar's childhood home turned museum, among musical instruments rather than cricket equipment. It was the items in Elgar's study, and the empty music stand, that allowed me to imagine his process, the creative mind that composed a masterpiece like the *Enigma Variations* without any formal training.

Afterwards, over a pie and a pint, I told Grandfather about the moment when I first saw and heard the oboe, at a visiting school concert. How I'd sat up, skin and scalp tingling, as if electrified. I knew immediately that I wanted to play that instrument, and to live a life surrounded by music. When I looked up, Grandfather was watching me intently. 'Then you must do it. Take it all the way. To follow your calling, to create something, is to truly live.'

The conversation that followed, about my playing, the musical qualities of timber and the concerts his own grandfather had taken him to at Royal Albert Hall, was a turning point in my life.

The year after I was at New Road, the Severn overflowed its banks and flooded the ground completely, which helped explain the timber rowing boat I saw hanging in the groundsmen's sheds. There was no play at the ground for the rest of the season.

Grandfather's factory had closed down in the 1970s, but he was still making high-end bats on commission for the company who bought him out. Sometimes he'd have to make up the time we spent talking or at games, toiling away in the workshop until late at night. But he never complained. He didn't seem to have much, if you measured wealth by possessions, but it was a rich life, and he was generous with what he had.

Despite his patience, I felt the weight of Grandfather's disappointment that neither my father nor my uncle, Rory, had kept up the family craft. On the last night, after a few pints, and a whiskey, he admitted he felt it his duty to keep the tradition alive. 'We're the standard bearers, Allan.' His voice quavered, and I saw the years on his face then. He must have been in his early-seventies, though being such a slim and fit man, he seemed much younger. He saw what was coming: the mass production, slipping standards. 'The game depends on us,' he said. I was flattered to be included, but also afraid. Of the responsibility, I suppose. They say things always skip a generation. Back then, it looked like it was going to skip two, and maybe the light would sputter out. But there are unseen currents at work in our lives.

While I was at the Con, I started making reeds for the oboe. I already had the skills, confidence with my hands, and had worked with cane. Grandfather gave me that. Reeds are somewhat smaller than a bat, but the same principles apply; it's all about expression and responsiveness. I scraped them for myself at first, from the proper French cane – *Arundo donax*. It was much cheaper than buying them and, with a fine gouger and knife, I could shape them just the way I wanted. My preference was for the German style, giving my playing a heavier, darker tone. Then I started making reeds for the other oboists. Before I knew it, I had a little cottage industry going on.

That led to getting a job repairing bats in the old Taylor cricket bat factory, to support myself through my honours year. They hired me, work unseen, on the basis of the Reader surname, I think. I was back among the willow shavings, thinking batmaking would be the hobby. But, like a game of cricket, you can prepare well, make all the plans you like, and still nothing turns out as you expect.

Harrow ground

Harrow sat on the back step to tie the laces of his runners. The heat had gone out of the day and Liv and his parents wouldn't be home for another hour. Time to sneak in a run, to clear his head and keep on top of his fitness. Studying for exams was harder than any cricket training. Sitting still for so long, for a start. He'd be thankful when it was all over.

It was just English to go, his weakest subject. He'd hoped *Ender's Game* was a book about cricket, but it was set in the future. Still, Ender was a child prodigy who had to overcome bigger and bigger challenges, which Harrow could identify with. Not that anybody expected him to save the planet.

He set off around the oval, easy at first, to warm up. All the great batters always talked about growing up playing in the backyard. How it was having to avoid the rose garden, the neighbour's birdhouse or whatnot that shaped their game. But he and Liv had had a whole field.

Dad always said it was reading about the great W.G. Grace, who grew up playing matches at home with all his brothers, that convinced him to turn the grassy patch between the house and the milking sheds into a cricket oval. He kept the water up to it in winter and mowed it every week with the ride-on. Over the years, the grass grew tight together, closing out any weeds. He cut the pitch super close and nourished it with fertiliser. When the bowling club was upgraded, he bought the old roller, to compact the Harrow pitch before games.

He even built an industrial-strength sprinkler system that watered the entire ground at once. Not that they often needed it.

The greater challenge was keeping it dry. Mum sewed covers for the pitch, a giant tarpaulin lined with old sheets. The outfield, though, was often wet and slow through summer. One of the challenges of playing cricket in Queensland. Summer was the wet season, hot and humid. Really, cricket should have been a winter sport, but that would put them at odds with the rest of the country. 'Not that that stopped the Queensland government opting out of daylight saving,' Mum said.

They used the oval most through autumn and winter, when there wasn't any other cricket going on. The days were clear and cool, and the ground dry. They began as family matches, just a bit of a backyard game on Sundays: him and Mum against Liv and Dad. Mum bowled a clever underarm with a couple of variations, which were hard to score off. They trained the dog, Catch, to fetch the ball.

Every year they played one proper Test, Australia versus England: the full five days. They'd rope in friends and neighbours. The Flanagans had four boys, so they were good for stacking a team. The Langs from over the road were like the Brady Bunch, with an extended step-family of eight during the holidays. Every October long weekend, if it was fine, would see two uneven teams of eleven battle it out. The trophy was one of his father's old Gray-Nicolls bats, spray-painted gold. The losing team had to host dinner, including drinks. As the years went by, the stakes got higher, with so many growing bodies consuming truckloads of food, and their parents putting away more and more wine.

Dad was always threatening to print a business card: dairy farmer, cricket coach, greenkeeper, spin bowler, parent, taxi driver, househusband. He and Liv rolled their eyes, though it was true. Between them, Mum and Dad spent half the week in the car, driving to and from school, to and from training, to and from weekend games. One of them, at least, hung around for every match, to watch him play, and provide feedback afterwards, whether it was asked for or not. 'I have a degree in cricket,' Mum said. 'Not that it qualifies me for anything.'

Sometimes she admitted it was 'better than smelling of manure', which would be the case if she was working in the paddocks or milking sheds. She started scoring the games, watching every ball, filling in all the columns and lines in 2B pencil. 'It's like doing a crossword,' she said. 'Keeps me awake.' Then she started filling in as umpire, too. Since she knew all the rules. 'I'm just standing around anyway. May as well do something with all this useless information.'

It was being left in the car while Mum was out on the field that got Liv playing. Phil Lavers hadn't shown up (again) and their twelfth man was interstate for a funeral, leaving them one short. Liv, yet to turn eleven, just put on one of Harrow's spare shirts, wiped a stripe of zinc on her nose, found someone's floppy hat, and ran out onto the field.

It was pretty embarrassing, but within the first five minutes she'd hung on to a difficult high catch. Liv had a cool head, even then. They batted her at eleven but she second top scored, with twenty-nine, and they won the game.

Liv's love of cricket started exactly when his did, when Dad took them to see their first international game: Australia versus South Africa at the Gabba. Walking around that great labyrinth to find their bay, and taking the steps down to the fence to see the ground, impossibly green, rise up before them, as if levitating, was a fairytale come true. The curve was for drainage, Dad said, to clear heavy rain, which they got plenty of. While most of the local grounds would close after storms, at the Gabba, the show had to go on.

They saw Damien Martyn score a century that day. From that first back-foot cover drive, the shape of his body, the fluidity of his stroke play, the clean sound of the ball off his bat, Martyn was perfect. And the South Africans were suddenly at odds with that perfection; their bowlers lost their rhythm, their fielders chased futilely as ball after ball went to the boundary, and the momentum shifted back towards Australia.

Martyn manipulated the field, thwarted their plans, won all those little battles that go on in a session, to wrest the game away from them. For those hours, it was as if he was playing a different game, a hero or god, and the rest mere mortals. Nothing could compete with the beauty of his innings. Harrow sensed that most people would never know that feeling, on or off the field, but he *wanted* it – more than anything.

Liv was quiet for the first time in her life, watching every ball with a great intensity, until the moment she stood on her seat, screaming, with the rest of the crowd, to celebrate Martyn's century. When they sat down again, her eyes were bright, and Dad was wiping his face.

Liv was a little trouper from the start. Harrow cut down one of his old bats for her, so he could practise his bowling. He was without mercy, bowling flat out from when she wasn't much higher than the stumps. More than a few sessions ended in tears, and one with a visit to the local hospital, with what turned out to be a broken collarbone. She toughened up pretty quick, learning how to use the pace of the ball to score behind and square of the wicket.

And later, when he needed to focus on his batting, she learned to bowl loopy off-breaks that made him slow down and watch the ball. There were plenty of times he lofted them over the shed, but by the time she was twelve or thirteen, she'd switched to medium pace, coming off a longer run, ponytail swinging, and started knocking over his stumps. She didn't crow about it, either, just smiled. It meant it was her turn to bat.

Sally had started coming over for Sunday lunch and, that winter, she played in their Test match. She was on his team, which he worried was going to be embarrassing, but playing tennis and softball, her hand-eye coordination was excellent. When she connected with the ball, it really went. She could run faster between the wickets than any of them and had a killer throwing arm. Even Dad was impressed.

After Harrow ran Liv out for only three runs with a lucky throw, things got a bit intense, with Sally caught in the middle. He and Sally opened the batting for their team, and at first Liv was just tossing them up, but after Sally thumped one into the wall of the milking shed, Liv surprised everyone with a perfectly placed bouncer, forcing Sally to duck out of the way, losing her balance and falling to her knees.

'Easy now, Liv,' Dad said. He was coaching them both, which was becoming a conflict of interest.

At the other end, Harrow copped them to the body: forearm, thigh, ribs. He hadn't worn proper padding for the home game, having never needed it. Mum covered her mouth with her hand. Whether she was laughing or concerned, Harrow couldn't tell. Before he'd reached twenty, he hit one straight back to Liv, who dived to catch it in her outstretched left hand. She leapt to her feet and ran around in circles, celebrating like she'd won the Ashes all on her own. The game had changed.

From then on, he had to pay Liv (in red frogs) to bowl to him in the nets at school. A dollar's worth for every half-hour. It was no longer just batting practice, either. They were competing. She seemed to take more and more pleasure in getting him out. She wasn't as quick as the boys, not yet, but somewhere along the line she'd learned how to land the ball on the seam, which created some natural variation. Luckily there were no slips catchers in the nets, but she hit his stumps far too often for his liking.

She'd also started running, setting off on a long route around the farm boundary in her white shorts and singlet, and back along their steep, winding driveway. He went with her once, and managed to keep up, despite suffering a stitch and cramp. When they sprinted for home as if it were a time trial, it was only pride that kept him going. He was sore for two days, and whenever he tried to stretch out, found his calves cramping up again. The following week, he'd started his own training regimen.

He got a new bat that Christmas. Well, new for him: a Gray-Nicolls Scoop. Retro. With the extra weight, he was working on stepping back in his crease and cutting the ball. It was the only way he was going to survive playing against men.

'Bowl me another one, pipsqueak,' he'd say. 'Fourth stump line.' And Liv would fire up and run in with everything she had.

When he smashed the kitchen window with an accidental ramp shot, the ball flying off the face of his bat, up and over his shoulder, Liv said it was her, knowing Mum wouldn't get as mad. And the pace on the ball had been all hers.

drawing out the bat

The bat is waiting when I open up the shop. It's been on my mind since I woke and I'm pretty sure I dreamed about it. Harrow, too. I put on my once-white apron and roll up my sleeves. It's old school but good practice when working with machines, reducing the likelihood of a button or cuff, a flap of shirt, getting caught in any moving parts. My father was forever coming home with stories of this or that horrific injury at the factory. Blokes now missing fingers, thumbs, hands, and even an arm. He worked metal, machining identical precision car parts. When he taught me to use a lathe, it was strict and joyless, step by step, but I understood that it was based in his experience, and from a place of care.

I release the bat from the vice and give it a few swings through the air. Still way too heavy but growing into its personality. The handle needs to come down a little. I fire up the old lathe and fit the bat into the chocks, tighten them, and again. Even a wooden bat spinning at speed is a weapon if it comes off. I press down on the accelerator, a bit like an old car, and the bat disappears into a blur. I've got the mask on, plastic goggles, too, for the cane chips that shower out as I take it down, working on the taper, first with a gauge and then with a broad chisel. The blade against timber still has something about it, a mix of precision and feel, timber and steel.

I switch off the lathe and release the bat, testing the handle in my own hands, somewhat bigger than Harrow's. Not perfect yet, but good for now.

Once I graduated from finishing to shaping at the Taylor bat factory, I experimented at home, for myself mainly. I still played on the weekends then. Like a surfboard shaper, I had a whole rack of bats. Then it was for the neighbourhood kids. No one made proper bats in smaller sizes. Word got around. Before I knew it, I had another backyard business, making bats for the girls and boys of the blokes I played with. For some of the blokes, too.

The garden shed out the back of our rented duplex was less than ideal – cramped, cold and damp. As were the rooms inside. We needed more space. Space of our own. Especially once we knew Katie was coming.

I'd had my eye on the property since the tyre shop moved out. The little cottage had been empty for too long and the workshop, out the back, was worse for wear. But the adjoining shopfront was north-facing, the morning light streaming in through the old glass louvres. The rear rooms had high ceilings, brick floors and a saw-tooth roofline, like Grandfather's old workshop. And they opened onto the lane at the back, allowing for a second entrance.

When the place came up for auction, we went along, 'just to see'. It was passed in and, with a little help from Marlene's parents, we made a ridiculous offer a few days later. Which the seller accepted! We worked nights and weekends to make the cottage liveable, sealing up the gaps and repairing the doors and windows, learning how as we went. We'd collapse into bed at the end of each day, exhausted and entangled, finding cuts, scrapes and splodges of paint on each other's skin.

Taylor's had closed down by then, the factory demolished to make way for another ring road. It made a lot of sense to continue on my own. Old Steve Taylor gave me his contact list, and any leftover gear – boxes of grips and handles. I had my own stickers printed, which Marlene designed, and just like that, I was a batmaker.

She did the sign over the front of the shop, too. And the mural on the wall in the lane. It's just the right mix of old-school tradition and funky street art of its day: a young batter – in Victorian colours, of course – bursting out, Reader bat at the centre, like a superhero. The name would not die out after all but have a new life down under.

The workshop brought people, and helped create an atmosphere, build a community even. Kids played backyard cricket in the shaded lane of an afternoon, with a wheelie bin and tennis ball. The suburb grew and changed around us, couples and families moved into the worker's cottages, businesses into empty shops. And, for a time, we grew along with it.

Having grown up in a small town – Metung, in East Gippsland – Marlene soon knew everybody's name, finding time somehow to learn all their stories. She'd share the best of them over a glass of wine on the back deck, her feet touching mine, the sun going down on another perfect day.

It's been a mental exercise I've practised as long as I remember, watching a promising new batter, designing them a perfect bat in my head. It keeps my skills sharp and it's not exactly something I can turn off. I make bats every day, or every time someone walks into the workshop wanting one. That's the job. But they're mostly second, third and fourth-tier players. To craft a bat for a top batter, to have a hand in their destiny, is every maker's dream. But I've never done it for real before.

There's just something about this Harrow. And if not now, then when? I can't remember the last time I risked anything.

I have Harrow's height, weight, arm span, grip, stance, statistics, and scoring patterns, to get the measure of the man and his batting, but those are only technical parameters. Creating a bat takes imagination. It comes from watching Harrow play: his grip, his stance, the range of shots he plays, the way he cuts and pulls, his strengths and weaknesses. His personality, too.

Day two of the Shield is underway. The Vics have regrouped, thanks to a hundred from Shepherd, effectively batting against the Test attack, with one current and two former Test bowlers in the New South Wales team, as well the young gun, Hilton.

I set up the bat in the vice again: face down, toe to my belly, which is bigger than it used to be, making it harder to reach the top of a full-sized bat. It should be incentive enough to hold off on that third glass of cabernet of a night but isn't. I pull down the biggest drawknife from the wall, the double-handled blade for removing the bulk of the willow. Drawing off the back or 'podshaving' is the most laborious part of the job but has to be done. The face and edges don't change, all the variation is in the back, taking the weight out.

My draw knife is German-made and a pleasure to use, its oak handles worn smooth. Another inheritance from Grandfather, who inherited it from his father. A simple tool, but it took a few years to feel confident wielding it. It's been shaping cricket bats for a century and it's still the most efficient and accurate way to remove the excess willow.

A podshaver is what I am, the proper name for a batmaker. And batmaking hasn't really changed much since the 1700s. I skim off the *curf*, the rough surface left on the willow after the timber was sawn, then work at taking down each shoulder, the first step in defining the bat's shape. When I draw the knife along the length of the cleft, towards my body, I'm aiming for fluid, even movements, keeping my mind on the shape wanting to express itself inside, which I sometimes catch myself thinking of as an animal, a little fox or mink.

Drawing out a bat reminds me a lot of rowing. It was only for two seasons, when I was first at the Con. I soon tired of the early starts once I met Marlene, but gliding over the Yarra in the mist before the city awoke was one of those in-between worlds that settled in me. There were willows, too, growing all along the banks in those days, softening the edges.

When we had that 'swing' – all four of us rowing in time, the boat moving fast and light over the water, to its full potential – it was as if we flew above the water. A rare moment of synchronicity between men, in the fine fabric of the universe. That kind of flow happens in batmaking, too. When I have a good bit of willow to work with, I can lose myself in the process. Like playing in the orchestra and coming to, almost, with the audience's applause. You see it in great cricketers sometimes, as if they are swept up in something larger, all of the parts moving perfectly. Every now and then you see it in great teams.

Victoria is not one of those teams at the moment. Shepherd has come out trying to smack them around this morning, as if carrying on from the evening before, rather than starting again. He's already swung and missed and mis-hit another that was lucky to avoid a fielder's waiting hands. He's going *against* the flow, thinking too much about national selection, proving himself, and not enough about working with his partner to build a big lead for his team.

I make more swift, sweeping cuts along the back of the bat, aiming for perfect balance and pick up. Once I scoop out the toe, I stop to consider it. I have my ideas, about the shape, weight, proportions, but you can't hang on to them too tight. The willow has a say, too.

Chips and flakes pile up on the bench and tumble over the floor, the subtle smell of fresh-cut willow filling the workshop. I pause at the rise in the commentator's voice. Shepherd is out, caught behind, to a shot he didn't need to play. That brings in former Test keeper, Matterson, a bloke with a good head on his shoulders but too often left with too much to do.

I hang up the draw knife and pull down the spokeshave – my favourite tool, for its precision. Fine curls of willow cascade onto the brick floor, cuddling together under the bench. I use a smaller spokeshave to chamfer the toe of the bat, refining the curve. Some players like a square-toed bat, just for that little bit extra surface area, to feel more willow on the ground, but a rounded toe is more elegant.

I shave any rough spots from the face and smooth the sides. Then I test the weight and balance, play a few air shots. My efforts are rewarded, on-field, with a boundary from Matterson. The Vics are fighting. Batting and batmaking are all about skill of eye and hand. Weight, balance, pick up, the spring in the handle – it all has to come together.

The commentators are not bothering to hide their disbelief: the Vics have lost another wicket, Matterson run out in a 'total brain fade' from his partner. It's a shame for Matterson, trying to demonstrate his batting ability to win back his Test spot. He was one of the casualties of us losing the Ashes. Hard done by, if you ask me.

The run-out, as often happens, sparks a collapse, with the home team all out, missing the opportunity for a big total. By the time I finish, my arms are aching, and my lower back. I bounce an old cricket ball against the face of the bat, testing the 'sweet spot', where the ball flies best from. Every bat has one, but I can control where it is, and how big, with the weight and shape of the back.

Last, I flick the bat with my fingers. When it makes the right noise, I know I'm done. Grandfather used to say the best bats sounded like a screaming cat. I've never heard it that way. It's more like music, striking the perfect note.

competition

It was still dark when he got up, slipping into his socks, work jeans and shirt, already laid out on the chair. Game day did not excuse him from helping Dad bring in the cows for milking. He could hear his parents talking, in low voices, already making breakfast in the kitchen.

'Morning,' he said.

'Morning,' Mum said. She handed him a piece of peanut-butter toast. 'We leave at seven.'

'Got it.' The game was down at Sandgate. A fifty-minute drive if the traffic ran smoothly.

Dad was drinking his coffee at the bench, watching the first light hit the ridgeline, a touch of mist from the showers overnight. 'See you out there.'

Harrow slipped on his gumboots at the back step and shoved the last of the toast in his mouth. A whipbird called from the edge of the garden and was answered. Liv's light came on, a bright square on the lawn. Things kept changing, every year, but there was a rhythm and routine to their lives, with cricket at the centre.

After only one year in the Under-15s, he'd moved up to the Landsborough open team, playing with the men. He'd turned fourteen during the winter, and was starting to fill out, but he was never going to be tall. Already they'd taken to calling him Runt, which rhymed with another word in frequent use on the field. And that was just his own team. The 'batting prodigy' label had its downsides. Everyone (all the players who weren't prodigies) seemed to feel the need to bring him down a peg or two.

Opposition bowlers' eyes lit up seeing him at the crease. 'Small target,' Palmwoods' quick, Beasley, liked to say. 'Lucky his head's so big.' Just before he fired another bouncer at Harrow's helmet. Or, everyone's old favourite, 'That's my rabbit.'

It was like starting all over again. But that was true of every innings, Dad said. 'No matter how well you've done, the next time you go out to bat, you begin on zero.' Harrow made three of those in a row: caught behind trying to hook a bouncer; caught at first slip, edging one that moved away; and leg before wicket, to a yorker that crushed his big toe. They started calling him Ducky, quacking every time he turned up for training.

When he dropped an easy catch in their first game, they called him a lot of things. Coach had said he was ready, that he couldn't keep 'coasting with the boys', but now he was out of his depth. It was tough love, he figured, like pushing him off the high diving board. But not what you'd necessarily expect from your own father. In some ways it was a relief not having him as coach anymore. It was a role that had no bounds: before the game, during the game, after the game, on the way home in the car, at the dinner table, in the hallway, in the bathroom while he was brushing his teeth.

The open team's coach, Waymouth, was a former state player. He'd been a particularly good player of spin bowling. His match-saving sixty, the last time Queensland had won the Shield, was one of Harrow's top-ten innings of all time, and a measure of the sort of batter he wanted to be when he played for Australia.

Playing at home was fun again now that Dad had loosened his hands on the wheel. He was still coaching Liv, but handing Harrow over had freed him up to focus on his great love, the art of leg-spin bowling. He still trundled in for the veterans' games, cleaning up the tail mainly, but he'd taken a few five-wicket hauls back in the day at district level. Bowling to Harrow was part of his own training regimen. And, although Harrow's heart was set on being a batter, it was Dad's theory that he had to be able to contribute something else to make it at top level. 'It could be the difference between being picked and missing out at a selection meeting.'

Harrow didn't mind. He liked the feeling of his fingers on the seam, flicking the ball from one hand to the other, and the motion of rolling his arm over, feeling the force moving through his body.

Landsborough was having an average season: winning one game, losing the next and he had yet to make any real contribution. He scored a quick thirty-five in their win over Beerwah. Then, the next weekend, he was out for nine, caught in the covers, sparking a collapse that saw them lose to Woombye.

In the game up at Yandina, he was given another stint at second slip, courtesy of the vice-captain's fractured thumb. It was a chance to be closer to the game, build some energy, rather than dozing off in the outfield. He could also listen to Captain's chatter, at first slip. And maybe even get on his ear about having a bowl. They needed the win or their season was as good as over.

Yandina's number three, an old bloke who liked to hit boundaries to save him doing any running, had been pinned down for a couple of overs, and Landsborough's quick, Stinger, hit him flush on the forearm. They could see the egg rising from slips. It had to hurt. A big shot was coming.

Harrow spat on his palms, rubbed them dry, and squatted down, watching the ball leave the bowler's hand, hit the pitch, and set its trajectory for just outside off stump. He saw the movement off the seam, the batter's swing, the click as the ball kissed the outside edge of his bat. He was already diving, arm outstretched, hand soft. The ball hit his palm, bobbled, but he closed his fingers around it and hung on. The boys were yelling, dragging him up off the ground and roughing his hair. 'Nice work, Harrow.'

Sting, all smiles now, said, 'So, the runt *can* catch.'

It was the break he needed. When he walked out, they still had ninety runs to get. He batted with the tailenders, taking the bulk of the strike, working it around for ones and twos, and cutting any loose balls to the boundary. It was a tight finish, coming down to the second last ball, before he hit the winning runs – a lofted drive down the ground.

After the game, Dad came into the sheds for the first time. He didn't say anything, just smiled and sat beside him on the bench, as if they were teammates. When Sting offered Harrow a beer, he took it, though he didn't really like the stuff. It was as if he'd passed some sort of test, become one of them.

Halfway through Harrow's last summer with the Loggers open team, he'd thrown his kitbag in the boot and opened the passenger door on game day, only to find Liv already sitting in the back, in her brand-new whites.

'What're you doing?'

'Playing, obviously.'

It was so embarrassing, having his little sister on the team, though there were two other girls in the competition. The boys were not keen. There were a lot of hands on heads and muttered complaints. But Waymouth gave her a bat, late in the innings, and she scored nineteen, including a lovely cover drive, which everyone applauded. She bowled a couple of overs, too. Didn't land them quite how she would have liked, but she got Maroochy's wicketkeeper, who could be a handful if he got a start, with a sharp caught and bowled. With the boys, they'd slap the bowler on the butt, but they hadn't figured out what to do with Liv. In the end they high-fived her and patted her on the shoulder.

Liv grinned all the way home in the car, nose burned pink, and even more hyper than usual, still talking about the game right through dinner. As she reminded Harrow more than once, her debut was way better than his duck and a couple of very expensive overs. Mum and Dad shook their heads over the chicken casserole. Cricket had taken over their lives.

For the rest of that summer, he and Liv had trained one evening a week with the Loggers, and every other night in the school nets. As annoying as she was, no one else loved cricket as much as he did or understood how much work it took to be the best.

On weekends they played each other on the home pitch. Liv was England, Harrow Australia, with witches' hats for fielders and the new puppy, Sixer, fetching the ball.

When he hit Liv flush on the helmet, he ran straight to her. But she just held up a gloved hand.

'Another one,' she said.

Maybe he'd been too tough on her; there was no way she wasn't shaken up. He put the next ball in the same place, though not quite as quick, and she watched it closely, swaying out of the way. Liv nodded to herself, as if she'd learned something. It was okay to let the ball go.

They threw each other impossible close catches, hit high balls into the outfield for each other to run and dive for, practised throwing down the wickets from all angles. They did their chores as a team, hosing out the milking bays, washing the buckets, and bringing the cows in together, so there was more time for cricket.

Afterwards, they stood side by side in the shed, each hitting a cricket ball in one of Mum's old stockings for hours. *Tok, tok, tok, tok* until they were called in for dinner.

If it was raining, they played Test Match at the kitchen table or classic catches on their knees in the lounge. Until a vase was smashed or a disputed decision descended into a wrestling match and Mum appeared in the doorway, hands on hips.

Even when they were doing their homework, Mum and Dad safely installed in front of the television, one of them would invariably produce a ball from a pocket and roll it across the table or toss it up. Catching whatever the other threw was how they related.

When Sally came over on Sundays, they toned it down, adapting their game to include her. Not that she was any less of an athlete. Sally was playing regional softball and needed to practise her pitching, so he and Liv hit her full tosses, trying to hook them into the outfield. Sally was meant to be *his* girlfriend, but after lunch, Sally and Liv teamed up, as bowler and keeper, trying to get him out. Somehow Sal kept it from getting too serious, making him laugh at himself, and some of the more obscure rules of the game. It was fun being around her, whatever they were doing.

By the end of her second summer with the open team, Liv was leading wicket-taker, highest run scorer, and voted best and fairest. It was easier for everyone by then; he was off building a career in premier cricket. They were each free to play their own game.

finishing

I arrived home from Grandfather's in time to attend my mother's funeral. When I left London, she'd just gone into hospital, and the doctors said it was a matter of weeks. But by the time I landed, she was gone. Nate and my father were hollowed out, barely functioning. Dad apologised, on the way home from the airport, for reading the situation wrong, not giving me the chance to say goodbye. But Nate said, later, that perhaps it was better I didn't see her like that.

I had spoken to her, a few weeks earlier. And, looking back, she must have known. She told me she loved me, which we just didn't do in our family. And said, 'Look after Nate. He's not as tough as he likes to make out.'

It was Nate who comforted me, at the funeral, all trussed up in our suits. His teammates were there, and wore black armbands when they next took the field. Father returned to work the next day. While Nate worked double shifts at the Ford factory around his playing schedule, I went back to finish high school, three months behind and just going through the motions. Except for cricket and music.

The music teacher, Mrs Troy, with her plaid skirts and thick glasses, was kind and encouraging. When I broke down one afternoon, at practice, she put her hands on my shoulder while I cried – back in the day when you could still touch students.

'Allan, you play like dream. Pour it all into your music.'

I flip the sign on the door and carry the board out into the lane. I open the shopfront Thursday to Saturday. The rest of the time it's by appointment only. I'd never get any bats made otherwise.

The morning sun streams over the old bricks on the floor. There's a warmth to them I'm fond of, not just the earthy terracotta but their irregularity, in shape and shade. Handmade, like everything else in those days. People pass by on their way to the bus, the train, the corner café, or walking their dogs. A few look in and smile, show some curiosity and friendliness, but most have their heads down, eyes front, plodding through their lives.

I use the rasp on the bat handle to make it slightly oval-shaped, so it's more comfortable and won't spin in Harrow's hands. Then I use the machine for the coarse sand, pushing the willow to the spinning glasspaper, finishing the surfaces, the last shaping of the toe. Willow dust hangs in the air, coating every surface, clogging my hair and skin. I love it all the same.

I'm keeping an eye on my phone. Katie often rings on a Saturday but she's missed the last few. Perhaps they're busy or doing something to the flat. A holiday even, they must be due. Though she didn't mention it. Neither of us are big phone talkers – but I do like to hear her voice. I can't help thinking she could do a lot better than accounting – better than David, too. He just doesn't have that spark I like to see in a person. Her mother would probably say I'm being judgemental, but I want my daughter to have a rich, full life.

I always do the final, ultrafine sand by hand. The more love and tradition, the more time my hands spend caressing the willow, the more chance there is for magic to happen. And this is a *fine* piece of willow. It has a kind of glow about it. So many miracles of tree, soil and weather, to end up in my workshop.

It's the same with a player. It's not just their DNA, but the home environment: family, backyard, local landscape, the club cricket they played, their coaches, captains, mentors and teammates. The combination of those, how they pull it together, and conceive of themselves in the world.

I shut the door through to the shopfront, and settle into Great-uncle's stool, positioned, as it always was in his own workshop, to catch the best of the light, for all that fine stitching. Sanding is a form of meditation. Doing something semi-mechanical with your hands allows the mind to wander. Watching cricket does that for me, too, engaging the brain with all the possibilities, but soothing, as well, with all the pleasing familiarities. Ideally, I have both going on at the same time – working on a good piece of willow while listening to a good game of cricket.

The Victorian bowlers have pegged back New South Wales, knocking over their top five for under a hundred. They just need to finish the job.

I stop sanding. In news around the grounds, Queensland's veteran opener, Frazer, has torn a calf muscle while stealing a quick single in the game against South Australia and Harrow is the name on everyone's lips to replace him. Queensland are to make an announcement in the morning. I'd better get a move on.

opening partnerships

Harrow found out while he was in the nets at training. Coach Carter took a call and then gestured to him.

'Take a break there, Harrow.'

'What's up?'

'We're going to have to replace you at the top, next game, I'm afraid.'

Harrow blinked. 'Why?' He'd had a breakout season, averaging a hundred and fifty, and Sunshine Coast was at the top of the table.

Coach's face split into a grin. 'Because you'll be playing for Queensland, son.'

Harrow laughed but it was more of cough, just from the relief of it.

'Really?'

'Really. They want you down there today,' he said. 'Better get going.'

He stripped off his gloves, pads, thigh guard and protector, threw them in his kitbag after his bat, hoisted his bag on his shoulder and ran to the car. His heart was pounding, and not from the exertion. Playing for his state! It was another big step. But he'd done it before.

Everyone had said premier cricket was the biggest step up. They were seriously good players, and serious about their cricket. Their bodies were older, hardened to the game. Some of the Test players still made occasional appearances and there were blokes who might have played for Queensland if they'd peaked at a different time, played in a different era, or been given an opportunity. It wasn't just the skill levels but the intensity of the competition. Harrow didn't dare open his mouth for the first few weeks, just did what he was told and tried to take everything in, to learn as much as he could before someone tapped him on the shoulder and told him the dream was over.

But somehow he had to do more than survive; he had to figure out how to thrive, how to be better than them. As tough as those old blokes were, they'd settled, given up on the dream of playing for their country. He wasn't ever going to give up. He just had to work harder.

The drive down to Mooloolaba for training, and then to Redlands or Toombul or Kedron or wherever they were playing, soon filled Harrow's week. His mother's, too. She was teaching him to drive on the backroads. 'The minute you get your P-plates, you can deliver yourself,' she said.

He couldn't help thinking that she'd miss the games. The parents carpooled, cooked cakes and quiches. It had become almost as competitive as the games themselves, and Mum was the loudest on the sidelines by far. But things were shifting on the farm. Supermarket milk was sending the small dairy farmers broke. Mum and Dad had decided not to join the others in the cooperative but to go old-school and bespoke, making their own cheese and yoghurt. Mum had been making yoghurt and cheese for their own table for years; it was just a matter of refining the process and figuring out the packaging and labelling, she said. Positioned on the tourist trail between Maleny and Montville, they built a shopfront and tasting room. It was a big risk. Everyone had to pitch in, Dad said, like any good team. His sacrifice was to officially retire from cricket. He joked that two players in the family were quite enough, but his face was sad.

Harrow and Liv stocked the fridges and took a shift behind the counter on weekends and during holidays (when they weren't playing cricket). During winter Sally did every second Saturday shift with him. It was the only way they saw each other, apart from school. There was no longer time for long Sunday lunches or home Test matches.

But there were upsides. To save on driving, Dad had kept aside a little concrete from all the building to lay a practice pitch by the milking shed and strung up a net around it. He and Liv could put in their training sessions at home, where it was only a two-minute walk to dinner.

And Sally sometimes stayed over, the Saturdays she worked, and Mum okayed her sleeping in his room.

'Better than you sneaking off in a car somewhere,' she said.

He blushed at that. It was exactly how most of his friends had fumbled through their first time. He was grateful for the space to make things a little less awkward, to show Sally that he cared about her. He spent all day cleaning his room, washed the sheets and made the bed properly. He'd left it too late to get flowers but found a candle in the hall cupboard and set it up on the bedside table. And wrote her a card, telling her he loved her.

It was a beautiful night in the end. They were able to laugh their way through the awkward moments. And Sally said afterwards that it was special to be able to hold each other until morning. He tried not to grin too much over breakfast, thankful his parents were already out working.

Liv made sure to hang around the kitchen longer than she needed, rolling her eyes whenever he and Sally kissed or held hands. Those were the still moments, when he could imagine being a normal teenager, someone who didn't play cricket.

With three other openers, he batted the first few games for Sunshine Coast at six. Back to square one. He didn't want anyone to get out, but waiting wasn't really his thing. Plus the shine was well and truly off the ball by the time he got out there, which meant it didn't come onto the bat as well. And he didn't often get a chance to play a long innings. It did mean he got to play a lot more against spin, improving that aspect of his game. He'd also been working hard on his bowling. The pitches they played on spun more than back home, which was good motivation.

Finally, in the game against University of Queensland, Captain asked him to bat up top.

'Mo isn't feeling so great today,' he said. Mo *had* copped a nasty one on the fingers in the nets. From Skywalker, who'd joined the squad. A friendly face at least.

Harrow was pretty sure that Mo's real problem was a hangover, given his best mate's bucks night had only finished at dawn. He was probably still drunk. That was one mistake he wouldn't make, the drinking that was part of the game.

Before he knew it, he was out there facing the first ball from University's frontline bowler. He wasn't big but whippy. It was on him quicker than he expected and, though he felt the bat make contact, he had no idea where it had gone. Kev called him through for a single, and he was away. They hadn't batted together much before, but they just seemed to click. Kev was fast between the wickets, with a good eye, and good judgement. Harrow would come to trust him implicitly. And Kev seemed to appreciate a youngster to nurture. He'd grown up practically next door, at Mooloolah. They played their shots, kept the scoreboard ticking over, with the sun shining and Citycats passing by on the wide brown river. At the end of the day, he was covered in bruises, but his wicket was intact.

He wasn't sure what was said, but next game it was Mo batting at six and him batting with Kev. It was his first real opening partnership. Not just for one innings but the season. Their opening stands got the team off to a great start, setting them up for a win more often than not, and taking them all the way to the semi-finals. Kev's steadiness at the other end gave Harrow the space to play his own game, and accelerate the scoring once he was set. There was ten years between them, but Kev was more like a big brother. His casual words of advice on the art of being an opener, like getting through those first ten balls, were delivered with the implied expectation that Harrow would go on to open for his state. Despite Harrow's eagerness to get there, some of Kev's patience rubbed off on him.

As if to balance out his on-field success for Sunshine Coast (five centuries, three fifties, and a fluky five-wicket haul down at Manly), Sally broke things off with him at the end of the school year. They hadn't been able to spend much time together, and he was never around for the things she wanted to do, the things the rest of his mates were doing: hanging out, going to parties, bands, drinking, staying up late. He was in bed by nine most nights or still on his way back from a game. He had his chores at home and was trying to keep up with his schoolwork in the gaps.

It hadn't been a complete surprise; she'd stopped coming to games, even stopped playing tennis and softball, and he'd heard a rumour something was going on with Bruce Pedder. He probably could've made more of an effort. The truth was, spending so much time with adults, he found most people at school a bit immature, without any real plans or dreams.

But when she told him, by the school oval during lunch on Thursday, it hurt more than he expected. There was an actual pain in his chest, like when he'd been struck. He'd had the feeling they weren't exactly setting the world on fire, but she was his first girlfriend, and practically part of the family. Mum and Liv would take it hard, too.

Sally said she didn't want her life to revolve around cricket and she knew there was no point asking him to give it up. He nodded and looked at his shoes. She was right, but he still loved her and said so. They'd grown up together. She'd been the only island outside of cricket that he was moored to. Sally cried and he found his own face was wet. They hugged each other, and said they would 'stay friends', that hollow consolation prize.

completion

I rub the dust from the surface with my hands, a final caress, and wipe it over with a soft cloth. Then one more time back in the lathe, to string the handle. It's another layer between the batter's hands and the timber, to absorb the shock of the ball. I attach the end of the white twine at the base of the handle and hold it taut while the bat spins, running it back and forth until the cane is well-covered. Then I stop the machine, cut the end of the string and tuck it under.

At last the bat is free. I hold it between my knees, and roll the grip down over the handle. It sounds like a simple thing, but actually takes some technique to get right, the tight rubber grabbing in all the wrong places.

I place one of my stickers on the back of the bat and another, smaller, at the top of the face, careful to line them up straight.

The bat goes back in the vice, for a going over with the shin bone soaked in linseed oil. I used to buy bullock or horse bones, but this one is a kangaroo bone I picked up in Frank's paddock and does just as well. That's what gives the bat the sound everyone loves to hear. I polish the leading edges hard as glass, so the ball will really fly, making it more difficult to catch. It might give Harrow a life when he most needs it.

I release the bat from the vice for the final time. 'Time to sally forth.' The verb *to sally*, as in go forth boldly on an adventure, comes from the same stem as *Salix*, the Latin for willow.

At the close of the day's play, the Vics are back in, with a thirty-run lead and no wickets down. I can rest easy for the night. I switch off the radio and carry the bat inside, to admire it for a while before I package it up. It's hard to take my eyes off it, actually. I've found myself talking to it more than once. But it was never meant for me.

The sound quality in the house is of a much higher standard than the workshop. My stereo is an old Yamaha from back in the day when things were made properly, with quality components. The turntable is a genuine Michell GyroDec I bought with my first real pay cheque from Taylors. And the Tannoy speakers, big enough to blow the roof off any concert hall, were a gift from my old mate, Garry, from the Con, before he went into the AIDS hospice. They wouldn't let him take them with him. It wouldn't be appropriate, they said. They wouldn't let his partner, Colin, visit either. Garry didn't last long after that. Who would, without affection or music. There was a man with real talent, a composer and fine violinist, one time concertmaster. It's hard when anyone dies young, but he was just hitting his peak as a musician.

The speakers came with a condition, that I get back into my playing. My practice, as we call it. I'll never forget the look on his face when he said it, holding me by the shoulders. There was a man desperate for life, not just another drone going through the motions. The speakers stand here every day, like his long shadow, reminding me that my oboe remains in its case, unplayed.

By way of apology, I put on one of his favourite records. Liszt's 'La Campanella', one of the most difficult piano pieces, based on the final movement of Paganini's second violin concerto. Its intricacy somehow acknowledges the process I've just completed. And the neighbours are away; I can really crank the volume. Up in Queensland they said, the Sunny Coast: Harrow country. If I'd known, they could have delivered his bat in person and saved me the courier fee.

I pick out a Coonawarra cabernet, a gift from a customer. It had a few years on it then, and a few more now. It's not like I can smash it over the bow, but I do want to send the bat off in style. In the last of the light, it's a warm presence in the room, almost speaking back to me. The true test will be when Harrow wields it, but I'm pretty sure it's my best work yet.

starting on zero

Harrow stood on the edge of the group, listening, while the Queensland Bulls coach, Albert, gave them the rundown on the training session, and the batting order for their game against Western Australia. Allan Border Field was out near Albion Park Raceway, and the ground still had a country feel. Except the airport wasn't far away, planes leaving and landing, road traffic churning by.

The boys nodded or raised a hand when Albs introduced him. He'd played with or against a lot of them before, in premier cricket, but they were a tight-knit group and obviously fond of Frazer. The overall feeling he got was that he was temporary. He understood; it was up to him to prove his worth.

When they broke into groups, Copes, the Bulls captain, shook his hand. 'Welcome, Todd. Looking forward to seeing you bat.'

It was their all-rounder, Klimt, who offered to team up with him for sprint training. Harrow tried not to overdo it with his speed. Klimt was underdone and carrying a little weight. When Klimt pulled up, heaving for breath, he shook his head.

'Don't you go easy on me, little fella,' he said. 'I need the work-out.'

Klimt certainly didn't go easy on him in the nets, bowling him three times, and striking him on the glove. His fingers were still numb when he packed up his gear, the other boys all laughing and joking around, heading back to the change rooms in groups.

Harrow followed them in, watching the gulls wheeling overhead, looking forward to a cool shower.

Klimt, arm over their keeper's shoulder ahead of him, turned to look back. 'See you tomorrow, rookie.'

Cricket. It was the great leveller, they said.

The Bulls were putting him up in a hotel until he found his own place, but he had to go home, first, to pick up his things. Mum had made lasagne, his favourite, and opened a nice bottle of red. 'For the sauce,' she said. But they were already having a glass and, at the table, offered him and Liv a taste, to toast his success.

'It's just until Frazer gets back,' he said.

'But they're keeping you in the squad for the summer?'

'Yep.' He cut through the stringy cheese and loaded another forkful. He'd been starving since mid-afternoon. Lately he just couldn't get enough food into his body.

'That's my new mozzarella,' Mum said. 'What do you think?'

'So good,' he said, mouth still half full.

It took Liv kicking him under the table to register their matching Harrow Dairy shirts. *Real Cream, Real Taste.* 'How did the food fair go?'

'Lots of interest,' Mum said. 'People seem to like the double brie the most.'

Dad closed his eyes. 'This. Is. Delicious,' he said. 'This meal, this moment. This family. I'm so proud of you, son. Playing for Queensland! Hard work is always rewarded, eventually.'

Liv made a noise in her throat. She'd been quiet through dinner, her plate a reverse salad-to-lasagne ratio to his. She was still playing for Landsborough opens, a better all-round package than blokes he played with and against in premier cricket. Unlike him, Liv was a brainiac at her private school. He'd been held back a year, because of cricket, whereas she'd started a year early. Everyone assumed she'd go to university, and she'd already decided on law, but she loved cricket as much as he did.

'I'll clean up,' Liv said.

He shook his head. 'We can do it together.'

Their parents headed into the lounge room to watch the latest episode of *Prime Suspect* with the last of the wine.

He walked through the kitchen door, a pile of plates in one hand, his glass in the other, only to find an orange flying for his head. He managed to catch it in his glass and fling it straight back at Liv, just out of her reach, so that she had to lunge to save the glass-fronted cabinet, taking the ball in her fingertips.

'Okay, Livs?'

She hopped to her feet, dropped the orange back in the bowl. 'Yep. Happy for you.' But her jaw was tight. She rolled the band from her wrist and tied her hair back, all in one movement, before filling the sink with water.

He wiped down the stovetop and splashback, sneaking glances at her. 'Has the board made a decision?'

Liv shook her head. 'They'll cave, to all the old boys. I told them Margaret Peden played cricket at school in *nineteen eighteen*. And she went on to become Australian captain. They didn't even know who she was!'

There'd been objections from the school board to Liv playing on the representative team with the boys. A girl wearing their precious private school colours in the inter-school competition was 'unpalatable'. Even a five-wicket haul and a century, practically winning them the cup singlehanded last season, hadn't persuaded everyone. Mum and Dad were furious, having paid a small fortune for her to attend the school, and driving an extra half-hour each morning.

Mum had scheduled a meeting with the principal and prepared a list of dot points for 'discussion'.

'Don't they want to win?'

Liv gave an exaggerated shrug. 'Get me something for the leftovers?'

He chose a round Tupperware container from the cupboard above his head and handed it to her. 'Change schools?'

Liv sighed, as if he didn't understand anything. 'It's not like there's a pathway for me anyway.'

'Are you saying I've had it easy?'

'No,' she said. 'It's just harder. I have to bank on my brains. My marks.'

'At least you have that option.'

She snorted. 'True.'

delivery

I slip the bat into a soft felt cover and then its waterproof case, and spread bubble wrap out over the shopfront counter. Three layers folded into an envelope and secured with packing tape, then I slide the bat into the cylinder and seal it. The traffic is building outside, a line of people across the road waiting for the bus into the city. I'm still addressing the labels when the courier pulls into the laneway. The van door opens, the bell on my shop door rings. I place both hands on the package and take a breath.

'Morning, Bruce.'

'Allan.' He glances down at his clipboard. 'This one's off to Queensland?'

Bruce doesn't recognise Harrow's name yet, but he will. If he's to open the batting for his state this weekend, the bat should arrive just in time.

'Sign here.'

I make my squiggle and flourish.

'The Vics came back well from that bad start.'

'A team effort, too. I like that about the Victorian boys. Prima donna players don't play, no matter how good they are.'

'I really think this is their season,' Bruce says.

I wait until Bruce's van has rejoined the flow of vehicles rushing by. Focusing on one special project required pushing everything else aside. Life, meanwhile, tends to go on. I stand at the top of the steps, looking down over the workshop. It's a bit empty with the bat gone, like when your child leaves home. Will Harrow use it? Will they be a match? Will he be the once-in-a-generation player I think he is?

My stomach is full of butterflies. I'm invested in Harrow now, my happiness tied to his career, his success. It's almost as terrifying as falling in love. But that's life, caring about anything; it makes us vulnerable.

My bats are beautiful, but they're not forever. Every bat is dying, from the day it's made. The process of pressing the fibres begins their separation – and disintegration. Most bats only last between a few hundred and a thousand runs before a crack, a split, a break, and they're retired. Sixteen, twenty years of growth, a living thing of great majesty, felled, dried, shaped, pressed and finished – all for a couple of seasons on a cricket field. But I wouldn't do anything else. Not for love or money.

We're all dying, of course. That's what it is to be human. For a player, their cricketing life is shorter still. Like white willow, it's an accelerated growth, and the higher the zenith, the harder the fall. No sooner do players reach their peak than their reflexes start slowing, their eyesight dulling, hand-eye co-ordination softening, muscles weakening, joints wearing, niggles turning chronic. Even passion for the game fades. It's subtle but relentless. Until, all too soon, it's over. All that training, all that hard work, sacrifice, for a decade at the top of the game – at best.

And afterwards, with those repeated actions so deeply ingrained in muscle memory, they play on, through their memories and in their dreams. To peak so young, to burn so bright, is the gift – and the burden – elite cricketers carry for the rest of their lives.

There's a new game in town that might prolong cricketers' careers. An even shorter version – just twenty overs per side – all bash and bling. T20 is the end of cricket as we know it, some people are saying. That's what diehards have said every generation, every iteration, every change. When the first international one-day game was played at the MCG in 1971, after the third Ashes Test was washed out, people said it would never take off. But then World Series Cricket came along, with its corporate sponsorship, coloured clothes and colourful characters, and changed the game forever. A lot of it was for the better, too. Players weren't even paid properly before that.

The changes now are being made to bring an attention-deficit generation back to the game. Or, more cynically, so cricket corporations can make more money. It was the marketing manager of the English Cricket Board who proposed bringing in a twenty-over county competition to remedy dwindling crowds and declining sponsorships. The idea is to deliver fast-paced, exciting cricket to younger fans, who are apparently put off by the longer versions of the game. Grandfather would be turning in his grave.

It was the English and New Zealand women's teams who played the first T20 international. New Zealand won by nine runs – another satisfying moment in cricket history, with the colony beating the mother country at their own game all over again. Now, T20s are bringing the women's game back into the public eye. Even if it is a warm-up game before the men's match, it's in front of an audience at least, rather than empty stadiums.

At the first men's international T20, Australia versus New Zealand, in Auckland a year later, players turned up in retro eighties kit and moustaches, and one of our bowlers replayed the infamous Trevor Chappell underarm ball from the 1981 one-day game between the sides. Umpire Billy Bowden held up a mock red card in response. It was a funny moment, but I found it hard to take the game seriously.

When we played South Africa at the Gabba for the first T20 game in Australia last year, the informality continued, with players' nicknames – rather than their surnames – printed on the back of their uniforms. I was sceptical, to say the least, but nearly forty thousand people turned up to watch. And even I was thankful for the opportunity to see the glorious Damien Martyn, in one last bonus outing, fall just short of a century to bring home the Australian win.

But it's in India that T20 is really taking off, with the launch of the Premier League, a city-based competition with unprecedented prize money. The founder says he's aiming to entice 'a new generation of sports fans', including women and children. Players from all over the world will go up for auction, to the highest-bidding clubs. Auctioning people has never turned out well in the past, but I'll reserve judgement. It's the exciting players who'll go first, the big hitters, the all-rounders, the hundred and fifty kilometre an hour bowlers. It's all about entertainment. Next, we'll be playing Tests at night so that people can watch over dinner.

I could get all depressed about it, but cricket has always been changing. It's a continual process of adjustment between batter and bowler. Bodyline was a response to the dominance of Bradman, and a reflection of the violence and ferocity of a war-torn age. Fast bowling sent more than one player to hospital during World Series Cricket, and then in came the protective gear, to level the playing field again.

The regulations are sometimes a little slow to come into line, but they do keep the game in order. When Daddy White faced up with a bat as wide as the wicket in 1771, the game replied by bringing in the 'shall not exceed four-and-a-quarter inches' rule. After Dennis Lillee carried out an aluminium bat in 1979 and – not before an A-grade fast-bowler tantrum – was sent back to fetch a real bat, came the 'bat shall be made solely of wood' rule. To this day, they are the only two commandments of batmaking.

That still leaves makers a little latitude. T20 players want bigger bats, so they can hit bigger shots. Lighter bats with thicker edges for boundary hitting – even a nick flies for SIX. They don't last long, but there are plenty more; commercial companies are churning them out by the thousand.

As a result, handmade bats have fallen out of fashion, like conventional stroke play, floppy white hats, and Test cricket. But I'll just keep on doing what I do best. The regulations will eventually address the imbalance. Cricket is a game that always falls back on tradition.

I eat my lunch at the kitchen bench, leaning over the sport pages, my back to the kitchen table. England have started well in the series against India. Their captain, Ashton, is a run machine, best batter in the world at the moment, but he's yet to prove himself away from home. Our bowlers will want to find a way to keep him quiet.

When I've read every word of every article, examined the scorecards, and even read the tennis news, I flick on the kettle. The sun comes out for a moment, lighting the piece above the dining table, one of Marlene's first big landscapes – river red gums leaning over the upper reaches of the Maribyrnong, late afternoon. The river's surface is mesmerising, always moving. It's my favourite of all her work, because she didn't keep tinkering with it. It's a little raw compared with her others but all the better for that, in my opinion. It was a gift, so she couldn't take it with her when she moved out.

While the tea is steeping, bergamot steam filling the kitchen, I select a first pressing of Mahler's 'Death in Venice' – suitably dramatic – and lower the needle. It was written as a love story, though most now associate it with death, probably because the slow fourth movement, the Adagietto, featured in Visconti's film *Death in Venice*. To my ear, his Fifth Symphony is all about longing.

With the pot of tea for fortification, I sit at the table, among the piles of unopened mail and unpaid bills. Father and Grandfather both drank Earl Grey. Although it comes in plastic-wrapped boxes and silk sachets now, there's still something medieval about the blend that seems appropriate for batmakers. Something that will endure well beyond whatever I am about to read.

I sip, swallow, set the cup in its saucer, and slice the thick envelope with my letter opener. The firm is a name I recognise, from just down the road. They could have dropped it around in person, saved the cost of delivery. The legalese takes some deciphering, but it's not as simple as signing papers. First, we have to divide our assets and debts, place a 'net worth' on our relationship.

Marlene's proposal, which takes all the breath from my body, is that I sell the house and workshop to pay her out. There are figures and calculations going back three decades but the details blur. I've been paying everything on my own since she left, working longer hours, scraping along in every sense. I knew it would be tough, that we'd have to work something out, but I never even considered she'd make me leave.

with both hands

The parcel was waiting for him when he turned up for training. A delivery woman had been allowed into the rooms, and the Bulls stood around giving him shit as he ripped away the bubble wrap. He'd just arrived and already he had mail. He was pretty sure it was a bat, but other blokes' bats came from their sponsor, in packs of six, with a whole lot of other kit. This one was handmade, a one-off, just for him.

He assumed it was something the Bulls had organised, like the piles of maroon playing and training gear with *Harrow* printed on it, but Coach said it wasn't his doing. Harrow looked through the packaging for a note but there was only a business card: *Allan Reader, batmaker.*

Harrow knew before he even picked it up that it was special: sleek lines, a gentle curve from handle to base, a slight scallop in the back. There was something about the timber that drew his attention. And the tiny flaw in the face already made him fond of it, like it was alive. But the feel, the balance in his hands, was something else. He tapped it on the carpet, as if he was already facing up, and played a few air drives. It was light as, just an extension of his arm, but it had him feeling powerful, as if he were wielding a sword.

He carried it everywhere, leaning it against the kitchen bench while he had breakfast, sitting it next to him on the passenger seat on the way to and from training, resting it across his legs while he watched television, even sleeping with it beside him on his bed, something he hadn't done since he was a little boy. He couldn't take his eyes of it. The bat was so beautiful, but it was more than that.

It was the validation, that someone believed in him, in his ability. Like being chosen to represent his state.

In the nets at practice, the *crack* of the first shot he played was as pure and true as his love for the game. The young net bowler stopped, mid follow through, to stare after the ball.

'What the fuck?'

Harrow grinned. It was a magic bat. His secret weapon.

When he worked up the courage to call the mobile number on the card, he was more nervous than made any sense. 'Mr Reader. It's Todd Harrow.'

'You got the bat all right, then?'

'It's a beauty. Thank you. It was very generous of you.'

'Pleasure. I hope it's a fit.'

'It's perfect. I'll be opening with it tomorrow.'

'And I'll be watching. Go well, son.'

When Liv called, she was emotional, he could tell. 'Make sure you take this opportunity with both hands, Toddy,' she said.

He'd always imagined debuting for Queensland at the Gabba but, if he was honest, he was more comfortable at Allan Border Field. With the white picket fence, the fig trees and eucalypts leaning in as if to watch, it was like a second home. The crowd scattered across the hill and stands, plenty of maroon on display. There was a fresh wave of hope for the Bulls' Shield chances off the back of the buzz from a debut player.

Border himself presented Harrow's maroon cap before the game. 'You're coming into an experienced team,' he said. 'Great players learn from the greats, soak everything up. But don't forget to enjoy yourself out there. This is your day.'

When Harrow introduced AB to Liv afterwards, she was all serious, nodding and shaking hands. But when AB said, 'I've heard you're quite the cricketer yourself. All-rounder?' the corners of her mouth twitched and her face lit up.

'Yeah, I play,' she said.

Queensland won the toss and chose to bat. Thank goodness! He couldn't have stood a whole day waiting in the field, separated from the bat, burning nervous energy. He got the feeling the bat couldn't have waited either. Liv, Mum and Dad were up in the stand, beneath the scalloped orange awning. He could see the blue and white checks of their blanket. Mum would have packed a good picnic, based around their cheeses. She was probably handing samples around right now, to anyone who'd take them. The whole team would be wearing Harrow Dairy shirts out in the middle if she had her way. Liv and Dad were sitting still, as nervous as he was. He'd rather be playing than watching, that's for sure.

Sky was there, on the hill, with his brothers. They were all the same height now, but Aaron was playing AFL. What a waste! Sky had an infection in his big toe nail. Surgery, he reckoned. Or he'd be playing, too. Some of the old boys from Landsborough and Sunshine Coast said they'd be at the ground. Probably talking up their role in Harrow's success.

He was almost out first ball of the match, going at it too hard. The dream might have ended right there. But the edge flew past the outstretched fingertips of the West Australian slipper. It was the scare, and the lucky break, he needed. He just had to watch the ball and trust his skills, like starting any other innings. *Trust the bat.*

Copes came down the pitch. All-rounder, journeyman, and long-term captain, he was the kind of guy everyone wanted on their team. He never stopped giving. Last season Albs, who'd been a decent all-rounder himself, had convinced him to move up the order to open, as their most reliable batter. It had paid off, solidifying their top order.

'Don't forget to breathe, Hars.' The way he said it was more like *breeve* but breathing was good.

He tapped the bat on the pitch, three times. The last ball of the over was a half-volley, giving him room to free his arms. He swung, lifting the ball over the mid-on fence. He didn't even bother running. It was FOUR from the moment it left the bat. The bowler followed the trajectory of the ball, mouth open, and spun his head back to glare at Harrow.

They thought he'd be easy pickings: green and nervous. But the bat had gifted him additional powers, taking his game to the next level. He cut, he hooked, he pulled, he drove, and he smashed one straight back over their seven-foot fast bowler's head. That earned him some sledging, something about 'imp' or 'gimp', maybe both, but he hardly heard it. Everything he hit found the middle and just ran away to the boundary. He scored seventeen in one over off their spinner, forcing Western Australia to take him out of the attack.

He played shots right around the ground, just to see what the bat could do. The bowlers were swearing under their breath, trying to intimidate him, but the day was so bright, his body in such perfect motion, he couldn't stop grinning.

First ball after lunch, he paddled one out towards mid-wicket and ran a quick two, taking him into the nineties. Copes did his best to give Harrow the strike. Too much waiting wasn't good. Western Australia's big fast bowler (with an even bigger moustache) was trying to bounce him out, but Harrow rocked onto the back foot and hooked, sending the ball flying over square leg to the boundary. FOUR. The bowler stood, hands on hips, and gave him a serve. Harrow just smiled.

They moved a man out, and Harrow knew the next one would be another bouncer; the bloke couldn't help himself. This time he was ready, but took no risks, just swaying back and watching the ball fly past. He threaded the last ball of the over between covers fielders for a single to keep the strike.

It wasn't until the third ball of the next over that he got bat on ball again, driving down the ground, and for a moment he thought he was there, but their tallest bowler, fielding at long off, ran, dived and threw out his hand, flicking the ball back from the boundary. Harrow and Copes ran three, leaving Harrow on ninety-nine. Something was happening to his hearing and vision. He was conscious of all the fluttering flags, the crowd on the grassed area clapping and whistling. The houses looking down from between trees on the hill behind them. He thought he could hear Liv's voice, yelling his name from high up in the orange stand.

Copes pushed the ball into a gap and called him through for a single. Harrow just ran, trusted. The throw came as he was grounding his bat, missing the stumps by millimetres. The Sand Gropers brought in all their fielders to stop the single. So much effort, just to stop a kid getting a hundred in his first innings for his state. It was a desperate attempt to build pressure, make something happen.

The bat was alive in his hands, humming like a tuning fork, connecting him to the pitch, the ground. It was as if the willow was doing it all for him. He didn't intend stopping at a hundred, so why get so caught up in one run? He checked the field placings again and, as the bowler ran in, focused on his breathing, watching the ball intently. It was a slower one, held deeper in his hand, but Harrow picked it. He set himself and moved into a front-foot drive. *Crack.*

There wasn't a huge crowd, but more than there'd been at the start of play. They were on their feet, for him. Harrow raised the bat, displaying its beautiful face and Reader's sticker. Once he removed his helmet, he was sure it was Liv screaming *'Toddy!'* And her wolf-whistle. She had the loudest whistle of anyone he knew – male or female.

Copes slapped his back, hard enough to knock the wind out of him. 'Well done, Youngster. Well done.'

He grinned at the boys, who'd come down to the gate, applauding him. Up in the stand, Mum, Dad and Liv were standing on their chairs, fists in the air. Mum would be crying, for sure. He saluted them with the bat, held his gloved hand over his chest; it was their day as much as it was his. Whatever happened, no one could ever take the moment away.

batch

I down tools to turn up the radio. Harrow is into the nineties again. The kid is just so hungry for runs, especially in lots of one hundred. Frazer, although recovered from injury, is going to struggle to force his way back. Queensland are playing Victoria – my boys – and look like winning, too, but there's no conflict in wanting a good player to do well. And I have a vested interest; the bat and Harrow appear to be a match.

Harrow's pull shot is on full display at the Gabba. Even through the radio I can tell when the ball is headed for the boundary. The sound is so pure I could pick it out of a line-up. Thank goodness for stump mikes. In the old days, they'd clap two coconut halves together. All bats sounded equal over the radio. Technology has a role to play in the game, bringing it closer to the fans. Nothing beats the real thing in real time, of course. Maybe I'll get to the Shield final, if it's in Melbourne. And definitely the Boxing Day Test.

Another *crack*, an on-drive this time, echoing around the empty ground, and Harrow has his hundred. '*Oh*, that's classical,' the commentator says. I shake my head. Cricket has a long history, but not so long that it can be considered classical. Classi*cal* music, classic cricket shot.

'Harrow's holding his bat aloft for the fourth time this summer. I'm guessing Reader bats, down in Melbourne, is fielding a few calls at the moment.'

I smile at that; it's not often a batmaker gets a mention. Not many watch the Shield these days, so not so many calls, but a few extra walk-ins, wanting a bat just the same as Harrow's. As if there's a line of them waiting on the shelf.

The commentators are already weighing up Harrow's chances for higher honours. He's the opener Queensland needs to take them all the way to the final, Border says. And maybe the opener Australia needs. 'He definitely has the skills, and that attacking style of play.'

'And again. Harrow's down on one knee, guiding that ball to the boundary rope. You won't see a better shot. It's just a different sound when Harrow hits the ball.'

'You got that right,' I say. If they don't choose him for the upcoming Australia A tour to Sri Lanka, I'll write to the selectors myself.

Just as well for the extra orders. I'm paying the solicitors more per day than I make in a week. It's beyond me how can anyone justify charging six hundred dollars for a phone call, no matter how nice their suit. Talking used to be free. I can't help but think of all the musicians I've known, the thousands of hours of practice they put in before an international concert, while barely earning enough to make rent. What we value reveals a lot about us.

I did try to talk to Marlene myself. Once I'd recovered from the shock of finding the house stripped of her things – many of which I considered *our* things – and the station wagon missing, I called and left messages for days. I emailed. I wrote a long letter to the address Katie gave me in Sydney. All asking her to come home, which was a further demonstration of my inability to understand her position. I should've just asked to speak face to face. When she did reply, months later, it was only to explain that she wasn't coming back, and that it would be best if we let our solicitors handle it. Talk about cold!

I've reread that letter a hundred times, hanging onto one line. Saying that she would always love me, and value our time together, but she needed to live her own life. I understand, I think. But I just can't forgive her for leaving without so much as a conversation. As if all those years counted for nothing.

I open the windows and lean against the bench, watching a butterfly lit by the sun, touching one leaf of the lemon tree, before moving on to another. I'll have to go over the leaves by hand later, looking for the caterpillars they've left behind, but it's worth it, for the moment of beauty.

I move back to the vice, where I'm finishing off a bat with the spokeshave. It's a satisfying tool, so snug in my hand, so particular. The current batch is for the local women's side. Off-the-shelf bats are too heavy for a lot of the girls. There's no sexism in saying that, only pointing out the big manufacturers' failure to cater for players with a smaller frame. I chose half-a-dozen clefts from the same tree, knowing there'll be subtle differences between them, just as there are among the players. Hopefully the bats will find their way into the right hands. With white willow coming from female trees, there's a certain synchronicity about making bats for women.

Not that it's anything new. Batmakers produced women's bats from the very beginning. A Hampshire women's team played a Surrey women's eleven way back in 1811. Things went into a bit of a decline under Queen Victoria, who believed cricket was unladylike – one of many things she got wrong – but with her out of the way, women returned to the game in the 1890s. They wore calf-length dresses, sashes, sailor's collars and cricket caps. Striking, but altogether impractical. The Red and Blue Elevens, as they were known, played exhibition matches all over England, accompanied by a 'chaperone'. A tour of Australia was proposed, but their parents vetoed it, afraid of what might happen in the wilds of down under. Yet another example of one poor decision thwarting a generation of players and the development of the game.

My great-uncle trialled a blue ball for the women's game, referencing the Red and Blue Elevens, or blue stockings, perhaps. Grandfather took me to see the one on display in the Lord's pavilion. Some experiments don't stick, but you have to give it a go, and learn from your mistakes.

I hear the postie stop and my gut clenches. I head out, to save him the trouble of trying to reach the slot from the bike. Or in case it's the package I'm dreading: the next instalment of the legal drama that has become my life.

It's a woman postie today, dreadlocks hanging out the back of her helmet.

'Morning.'

She nods, hands me the heavy envelope.

'Thanks,' I say, though I do not feel thankful. Only nauseous.

She continues down the lane on the old Honda 90, stopping every few houses, like the butterfly, to leave a little something behind.

After stumps, and the post-game analysis, I switch off the radio, shut the windows and lock the workshop. There's the usual satisfaction as I close the timber doors and look up the lane into the dropping sun. Kids playing and adults making their way home from work in golden light. Harrow was not out on a hundred and sixty when the Bulls declared. And the Vics, after an early wobble, are still fighting. There aren't any stand-out players this season, but someone always seems to put their hand up when needed. That's the measure of a good team, and the way the Vics play the game.

Around the grounds, there aren't too many other big scores. Not even from the current Test players. Harrow is already in my Ashes squad. Sometimes you've just got to give talent a clear run. It's still ten months away but he needs to have a chance to bond with the team, learn what's expected at that level.

That's how I get to sleep at night, picking my squad, then the final eleven for that First Test in Brisbane, then the batting order. The selectors will be doing the same. We shouldn't have lost last time, over there. Let alone disgraced ourselves the way we did. A lot of that was down to selection, all the chopping and changing. Though it was the players who had to wear the public ire. And the captain, as always, who fell on his sword.

I put on Sibelius' 'Finlandia' and sit on the deck looking out over the garden with the solicitors' envelope, brandishing my letter opener like a conductor. The composition's middle section is a bit turbulent for my taste but it's worth it for the calm at the end. It's another tone poem, a bit like a landscape painting. Sibelius was a nature lover and Romantic – a nationalist, too – trying to portray Finland's lakes, forests and birds in his music. But after composing his eighth symphony, he burned it, along with all his manuscripts. It's one of music's great mysteries, why he chose to live the last thirty years of his life in silence. As I cut open the envelope, and plough through the words on the printed pages before me, it's not so hard to imagine.

set, tod and match

I throw an empty tube of glue at the bin and miss, splattering the wall with goop. 'Bah.' Through a bizarre confluence of outcomes that only cricket can throw up – a drawn game, a wash-out, and Tasmania upsetting South Australia in Adelaide – Queensland are out of the running for the Shield. The final will, once again, feature those old adversaries, New South Wales and Victoria. It's a rivalry that runs blood-deep. I still haven't really forgiven Keith Miller for defecting to New South Wales in 1947. And I'm not the only one. He was the first ever superstar of the game, good-looking, irreverent and ours.

Harrow finished his first Shield season with an eighty-plus average. He fell away a bit at the end as bowlers started to figure him out. But it's been a convincing start. Of the openers, he's the leading run scorer, with the highest run rate, despite missing the first few games. But Shepherd, playing in the final, still has the opportunity to finish first.

The sun may be shining in Melbourne for the moment but at the Sydney Cricket Ground, the commentators are describing a pitch that is uncharacteristically green, the air damp after overnight rain, and the morning overcast. Victoria have won the toss and, for reasons not entirely clear, have chosen to bat. The ball is swinging – sideways movement through the air – and the New South Wales quicks are charging in. Both Shepherd and King have played and missed, a nick fell short of the slips and a difficult chance was put down at mid-on. The tension is unbearable. Sanding is too slow; I can't sit still. And I don't dare fire up a machine. I don't want to miss a moment.

I lock the shop door, flip the sign to closed and start cleaning the windows with the radio turned up loud. It was one of the many jobs Marlene did without being asked and I took for granted. The little panes are a pain, but I get better, averaging one an over, about the same as the Vics. Shepherd, as ever, is steadfast but ordinary. I'd never say so outside my own head, not in this state anyway, but for all his experience, all the runs on the board, I'd choose Harrow over him any day.

By the time I see the boys through to lunch, the shop and workshop windows are gleaming. Shepherd is gone but King is supporting his captain, Scott, turning over the strike and running hard between the wickets, showing a lot of grit.

I take my tea and sandwich down to the glasshouse. It's homemade, patched together with second-hand windows and doors. My folly, as Marlene liked to call it. But it keeps the frost from my tomatoes, houses my willow cuttings, and it's a warm place to sit through the long grey months.

In summer I open both ends and let the breeze run through. Sitting among the green, with a matching cup, saucer and plate, reminds me of Essex on a good day. My time with John May and his willowmen down on the Moorlands was as rich as the soil. John has a way of bringing good people together and bringing out the best in them. He was firm but fair and, once I'd proven myself, warm and funny. His jokes were always delivered out the side of his mouth, to keep his rollie in place.

I brought a stash of seedlings back with me. John didn't let me take the best genetic material, he's not that silly, but those first trees are a forest now, west of the city. A proper plantation. I work with my local nurseryman, Roger, to propagate them. It's not so much growing or seeding as such – but cloning. Each willow sapling starts out in the nursery as a *set*, a cutting from a *tod*, a pollarded mother tree cultivated from pedigree stock.

It's a passion project. Roger sells a few in the nursery but we mainly plant them out ourselves. Mates of ours, and farmers up for a windbreak or a little extra income. That's how I met Frank.

Thanks to us, there are now little willow groves all around Gippsland, Daylesford and Healesville.

It's an investment that's starting to pay off. With timber – as with cricket – you have to keep investing in the future. Roger keeps most of the seedlings out the back of the nursery. But I like to raise some myself. It gives me pleasure to see them grow, and to have them on site. Every now and then someone asks about the tree – and I can show them how it all begins.

It's also a sensible security measure, like the royal family travelling on separate flights. During the last bushfires, when the power went out, Roger's watering system failed, and we lost all his seedlings. If it hadn't been for me watering my lot by hand from the tank, we'd have been back to square one. They're replaceable, but it means losing a year or two of growth.

I fill the old metal watering can and make rain over the young willow sets, plucking a stray weed from one tube, noting the root tip protruding from another. I should get back to the game, and to work, but sit with the willows while I finish my tea, just to hear them growing.

A few too many things are cluttering my headspace. Marlene didn't respond well to my counter-offer. 'A flat no', my solicitor said. She didn't specify whether it was B flat or D flat, major or minor. I guess she's not musical. Katie still hasn't called. It's months now. Living in Sydney, and closer to her mother, maybe she doesn't feel she can. It must be hard for her, stuck in the middle.

People describe their memories as a series of images recurring. I get that, too. But for me more often it's like a soundtrack. Sometimes it was music actually playing during the scene, or music I was hearing in my head in the moment. Other times it gets laid down later. There couldn't really have been music playing down at St Kilda that hot summer's evening, when weekend temperatures hit forty-five. It was an awful day but we were happy, as a family, throwing Katie back and forth between us in the water, as if she weighed nothing at all. Her pink salty face and gleeful giggles were more than enough. Business was picking up, Marlene had sold a big painting, and Australia had just won the Ashes. A breeze finally came up, lapping little waves to shore. There were hundreds of people in the water, smiling with relief. When I remember that day now, it's always accompanied by the opening of the second movement of Dvořák's *New World Symphony*, a joyous harmonic progression.

the call

The call came while he was driving. On his way back up the coast for the weekend, to help out on the farm. Not that he needed an excuse. His room in the Albion share house was small, the street noisy and the fridge mostly empty. And he rarely crossed paths with his flatmates. Matt was studying at Griffith Uni and working at the bottle shop around the corner. Liam was at QUT, the Kelvin Grove campus, and working at some fancy bar in the city. Neither of them liked cricket.

The Sydney number on the phone's screen raised the possibility, never far from the front of his mind, of national selection. He pulled over in front of the New Farm bottle shop to answer.

'Todd speaking.'

'Steven Inverell here. I'm calling to let you know that you've been selected for the Australia A squad, to tour Sri Lanka.'

Harrow grinned at himself in the rear-view mirror. 'That's excellent.'

'You've had a wonderful season. We really need an opener like you, who can take the game on. We think you have loads of potential. Congratulations, son.'

'Thank you.'

'We'll send you an email with all of the details, but the squad will meet up in Brisbane next month.'

'Okay.'

He saved Slogger's number. He wouldn't ever want to miss a call from him. The world outside looked just the same, people heading into the bottle shop in ones and twos, emerging with a bottle of wine, a case of beer, or something stronger in a brown paper bag.

The sun was a low red ball, flaring on his chipped windscreen. He'd *hoped*, of course. But now it was actually happening.

He opened the car door and placed his feet on the ground, the warmth from the bitumen still rising. He nodded at the bottle shop attendant as he entered and headed to the fridge. Not for beer and wine, as he'd planned, but champagne. The one with the orange label that Mum liked was on special, so he splashed out. And why not. Perhaps the bubbles would help make it all feel real.

When he called home, it was Dad who answered. 'You on your way?'

'Leaving the city now,' he said. 'But I have news. Is everyone there?'

'Your mother's just picking up Liv. What is it?'

'Guess.'

'Australia A.'

'Yep.'

'Yes! That. Is. Fantastic,' he said. 'Todd. I can't tell you how proud–'

'Don't tell them until I get there,' he said.

'Hurry up then,' he said. 'But don't speed!'

He sat the bottle on the seat, strapped himself in, and rejoined the flow of cars. Traffic was thinning, as people pulled into their driveways, sat down to dinner with their families, in the city he had yet to really warm to. He'd worked hard, he'd wanted this for as long as he could remember. But the moment, now that it had finally come, wasn't as simple and joyous as he'd imagined. There was relief; it would've hurt to miss out. He was in the squad, that was one thing, but would he make the team? And Sri Lanka. He'd never played on spin-friendly pitches. Would his defence hold up? There was so much to get his head around. He didn't even have a passport!

At least he'd handle the humidity all right, unlike the southerners who usually made up the bulk of the team. Sky would be there, for sure, now that he was back fit, and Hilton. Probably Reid. Definitely Shepherd. Maybe they'd open together. Now that would be something. It was as it had always been; they were just getting closer to the top.

He glanced at his kitbag, on the back seat, the bat on top. He could picture carrying it out to the middle on grounds he'd only seen on television, holding it up for the crowd. Together, they'd find a way.

He should wait until the team was announced, but he wanted to tell Reader about his selection. That he was repaying his faith. At the lights, he reached for his phone and sent a message: *It's not public yet but I'm going to Sri Lanka! Todd.*

The light switched to green, the traffic back in motion. Things were shifting all around: the cooling air, the leaves on the trees, and the river, coursing along beside him. He'd just taken a call from the Chair of Selectors, who'd spoken to him like an adult, with respect. All the training, playing and travelling, moving out of home, had been worthwhile. He was only one step away from playing for Australia.

MORNING SESSION

What do they know of cricket who only cricket know?

~ C.L.R. James, *Beyond a Boundary*

see ball, hit ball

The night before they flew out, the Australia A squad went out for a few quiet beers at a bar near the hotel. Harrow found a table outside in the breeze and Mads went in to order the first round. As captain and keeper, with experience at the national level (including two Ashes series), he was taking charge, shaping their experience. He made training fun, always positive, looking to build their confidence. And after training there was always some surprise team activity, like barefoot bowls by the river or a mountain-bike ride on Mount Cooth-Tha. The boys were gelling as a unit, which would make the tour a good one, on and off the field.

AB had popped in a few times; they trained at his ground, after all. He watched them go through their batting drills and had a chat with each player. Harrow couldn't help but feel that he favoured the Queenslanders, though, spending a little more time with him. He was chuffed when AB sat next to him at drinks and was determined to ask him all the questions he'd been dying to, like what was it like to captain Australia, and his tips for batting in the subcontinent.

But when it was Harrow's turn to go in, he couldn't help but notice the blonde across the room, under the palm trees the bar had been built around.

'What'll it be, mate?' The barman was tapping a ringed thumb on the counter.

'Three schooners of XXXX, two bourbon and cokes, and a rum and coke, please.'

She was beautiful, the absolute stand-out in the room. But when he saw her laugh, throwing her head back, he knew he had to talk to her. He paid for the drinks, ferried them back to the table, not hearing a word the boys said. He walked across the room without taking his eyes from hers, without thinking of all the reasons why it was a ridiculous thing to do. She held his gaze and her smile didn't falter. It was the sort of smile that would light up the room for the rest of your life – if he didn't stuff it up. When he reached their table, he realised he hadn't planned what to say. Or counted on her two grinning friends as an audience.

'Evening, ladies,' he said. He held out his hand. 'I'm Todd.'

She stood to shake his hand. 'Megan.'

'Can I buy you a drink?'

She gestured to an empty chair, 'We just ordered another bottle. Why don't you have a glass of champagne with us?'

'What are we celebrating?'

'Nina here has just landed a job in London,' Megan said. 'And Jill and I are pretending to be happy for her, even though she is abandoning us. And clearly insane, trading sunny Queensland for fog, rain and pasty Poms.'

The fresh bottle arrived, and the waiter had his eye on the ball, bringing an extra glass. Megan didn't know about cricket, none of them did. They hadn't noticed the huddle of current, former and future Australian players. Not even AB, who still looked much like he had when he was captain.

'Well, cheers then, Nina. Congratulations.' He raised his glass to theirs and sipped, bubbles fizzing on his tongue. He couldn't see the label but he figured it was good stuff. Megan was dressed smart. She *was* smart, he could see that. Way too good for him. But when they made eye contact over the clinking glasses, his skin tingled all over, and he hoped maybe she'd see something worthwhile in him. The world was full of possibilities, if you just believed.

Something about the way they spoke reminded him of his sister, always on about injustice. 'Lawyers?'

'Yes. Solicitors,' Megan said. 'How did you know?'

He shrugged. 'Just a guess.'

'What do you do, Todd?' Nina said.

He grinned. 'I play cricket.'

Jill's head turned. 'Like for Queensland?'

'Like for Australia.' It would take too long to explain that the A team was actually a B team or development squad. He was representing his country, that was a fact. He tried to ignore the boys, who hadn't missed what was going on, waving and goofing around. 'We fly out to Sri Lanka tomorrow.'

keeping your shape

He waited four days to message Megan. Four whole days and nights. He didn't want to seem too keen and he wasn't so great at writing. What to say? But he couldn't stop thinking about her. They'd talked right into the early hours. He'd never been able to talk to anybody like that. She seemed to really *listen*, not just switch the conversation back to herself. She asked questions about things he'd never really thought about but found that he wanted to. If he was ever afraid. What it felt like to know what he wanted to do so young. And having a sister that played cricket, too. And when he asked about her work, for a big firm, he gathered, she didn't let him feel stupid.

Between the boys hanging around and Nina hovering, there hadn't been any chance of stealing a kiss. But she'd let him know she was single, ending a long relationship earlier in the year. With another solicitor, she said.

When he asked for her number, she gave it, and said that she'd like to hear from him while he was away. It felt a little cruel, meeting her just as he was going on tour, but it was only three weeks. Dad said that if you really liked a woman, you had to treat her like you would a good friend, until she let you know otherwise. 'If she's worth it, you'll wait.'

Mum had made Dad wait a whole year, until she returned from backpacking around Asia. He still had her postcards in a box, one from every country, getting closer and closer to home. Until he couldn't stand it anymore and drove all the way up to Darwin to meet her in his beat-up old Datsun.

It had taken Harrow a few days to get over the flight anyway.

He hadn't slept on the first leg, into Singapore. There was so much to take in and think about, the boys being rowdy, ordering drinks and snacks from the smiling stewards, working out their nerves with jokes and tall tales. Only Mads and Sangha (their left-arm spinner) had toured before. And their coach, Freddie, of course. He went to South Africa, back in the day, as a spare bowler, and played a handful of Tests at home. Harrow swore to himself that if he got the chance to play for Australia, he'd go the whole way, not just dabble.

Sky was always clowning around, giving the boys shit – but deadly serious at cards. It wasn't just his poker face; he was so into it. He and Hilton got on like a house on fire. If they bowled that well together it would be a good start. Mads seemed happy, but was quiet, spending a lot of time with his headphones on. He had more responsibilities, and more at stake, relegated to the rookies to try to work his way back into the Australian team.

The second leg was only four hours but felt longer, as if they had a headwind, flying the wrong way around the world. Harrow put his seat back, headphones in and eye mask on but only managed to doze off for an hour or so. By the time they arrived at Colombo, he was fuzzy around the edges, struggling to pull his bags off the belt, distracted by the armed security guards. And that was before they walked out of the terminal to load their gear on the waiting tour bus. With the dust, heat and noise, it was as if he'd landed on another planet.

He wasn't the only one who hadn't flown overseas before, but the boys gave him plenty for pulling up so rough. They looked after him, too, making sure he slotted into the new time zone and got out for a training session and a meal, rather than just sleeping it off in his room. The hotels had a lot more character than the ones they stayed in at home. Even if things were sometimes a bit haphazard, like the patterned rugs thrown out at breakfast, curries instead of cereal, and the coffee not necessarily arriving when or where it was meant to, the staff were always smiling and he could look out over the smog-hazed city from his window, trying to get his head around it all.

The humidity was a shock, even for him. In Shield cricket they didn't play right by the ocean, except in Hobart, and that was always freezing. By the end of their first net session, all his gear was soaked through. Half their on-the-ground time went into keeping their fluids up. The first game wasn't until the weekend, which was a relief because he wasn't timing the ball that well. They'd tried to prepare them at the Brisbane training camp, bringing in a young Indian spinner to bowl on pitches meant to replicate subcontinent conditions, but actually being out there was like batting on the surface of Mars. The practice pitches were not much more than dirt and the ball reacted so differently once it landed. The humidity meant it behaved differently through the air, too.

But the biggest problem was that somehow, during the flight, with his bat down in the baggage hold, they'd lost their synchronicity. It didn't feel right in his hands.

He'd grown used to Brisbane, being in a city, but it was an orderly country town compared with Colombo. The crowds, the noise, the colours and smells, markets and stalls; it was a mass of constant seething movement. The traffic, for a start, was completely crazy. Not just cars, but bikes, mopeds, and the three-wheeled tuktuks careering in all directions – things he didn't even have words for. Palm trees and neat white colonial buildings seemed at odds with the crowding figs, mangos and banyan trees, Buddha statues. The constant haze meant he couldn't quite bring anything into focus.

On their excursion to donate cricket equipment to a local high school, just a broken-down building at the end of a maze of laneways, the kids hung all over them, wanting any old bit of gear, clothing or paper signed. He couldn't help smiling back. Although he didn't really know Megan at all, not yet, he was sure she would've known what to say as he handed out bats and gloves.

Harrow started thinking of himself as an astronaut; he just needed time to acclimatise to the lack of gravity. Once he gave himself permission for a period of adjustment, his body relaxed. He started connecting with the ball in the nets at least.

Freddie spent hours chucking the odd-shaped training ball (googly) that could go all ways. The googly wasn't that easy to play at home but here the ball was slower off the pitch, and the spin so exaggerated it practically turned corners.

He'd been working extra-hard on his slips catching and close fielding, figuring that as a newbie, and the shortest member of the team, he'd find himself under the helmet in front of the batter at some stage. He had his mind set on being the best short leg fielder in the game, taking a blinder to turn a match around. In the hotel room, he spent hours rolling an orange off the bench and diving to catch it before it hit the ground, the way he and Liv used to at home.

His hard work seemed to be paying off. His balance was good, forward on his feet, and his confidence was on the up. But it was just as well he'd been imagining himself as an astronaut. When they inspected the ground they'd be playing on, the outfield was green but the pitch was a moonscape, all dirt and craters. Holding his nerve, when he got out there, was going to be the first challenge.

He lay sprawled out beneath the fan in his boxers. He could get used to big beds and clean white sheets. There was barely room for his old double mattress in his rented room back in Brisbane, and the only view was of the back of another block of flats. The hotel was a welcome respite from the dust, heat and crowds outside at the end of the day. He was watching *Field of Dreams* again. A Harrow family favourite, if only because there weren't many films about cricket.

Costner's character building a baseball field in the middle of a cornfield brought on a bout of home sickness, reminding him of Dad, Mum, and training with Liv on their ground at home. How lucky had they been, to have that? The pitch was still there, but

Dad had built the new cheese room over part of the outfield. It made sense, with him and Liv gone.

Megan said her favourite film was *The English Patient*. Epic, like a Test Match. Romantic, too. He'd been thinking about ways he could show her he was serious. Like the soldier in the film who lit the trail of candles to lead the nurse through the ruins, while he waited patiently in the dark. A trail of text messages was all he'd left so far, asking questions and letting her know he was thinking of her.

Shoeless Joe and the crew had just turned up to play a game of baseball, and Harrow settled back, hands behind his head, to watch the final scenes. But someone was banging on his door. One of the boys no doubt. When he opened up, Mads, Sky, Shep and Hilt were standing in the hallway, wearing collared shirts and aftershave.

'We're going out for something to eat. Coming?'

'Well–'

'C'mon, Youngster. Best street food you've ever tasted. Trust me.'

No didn't appear to be an option.

He pulled on a pair of jeans and a crumpled short-sleeved shirt. In the heat he hadn't been able to stand anything but thongs and shorts outside of training but the breeze was cool, and there was a buzz about the evening.

When Mads said they were off to Galle Face Green, he assumed it was a cricket ground. And cricket must have been played on that wide green lawn, but it was more like Brisbane's Southbank, a ribbon of parkland running next to the city, though with the Indian Ocean on the other side. On shore it was a sea of street stalls, music, lights and people, like some kind of festival.

They pointed at things they wanted. Mads ordered and paid. 'It's next to nothing,' he said, waving away their cash.

They were the best samosas he'd eaten in his life, and the fish curry served in a kind of pancake (hoppers, Mads called them) nearly blew his head off. Mads put away a soft-shell crab and half-a-dozen of the little green cakes with a deep-fried prawn on top.

Shep loaded up his curry with sambal and chutney, and Hilton came back with a round of Lion Beers. The food was like the city, full-on, engaging all of their senses. Only the sea was calm and pale in the moonlight.

Mads stopped shovelling food into his mouth for a moment to sip his beer. 'How good is this?' he said. 'This is the secret to playing cricket on the continent right here, boys. Just embrace the experience. You'll all get a game. Let's just enjoy ourselves, eh?'

Harrow nodded, eyes still watering from the chilli. It sounded so simple, when he put it like that.

Freddie announced the team and batting order the next morning at training. Harrow was to open, with Shep. Harrow was shouting *yes!* inside but kept his face blank; it wasn't cool to gloat. Reid and the other blokes left out made a brave effort to hide their disappointment. They still had a role to play, supporting the group. Any win or loss would be shared among the whole squad, Mads said. Their opportunity would come, next game, or down the track.

He messaged Megan as soon as he got back to his room. It wasn't like she could watch it on television, or would even want to, but he was making progress and he wanted her to know. When he asked for her home address, to send her a postcard, she gave it to him. He figured that was a good sign. She said that work was dull without Nina, and that she'd been trying to learn a bit about cricket. Someone in her office followed the game, and she was picking her brains, to decipher all the *jargon*, she said. Pretty funny from a solicitor, all *subpoenas* and *depositions*. Surely it meant she liked him, to bother with cricket.

The idea of it had him grinning, dancing around the hotel room, hitting a cricket ball against the wall for hours. *Thunk, thunk, thunk*. He played a whole century innings that way. Until Peters, their big all-rounder in the room next door, called time on that, saying it was driving him fucking nuts.

So Harrow shadow batted instead, visualising the bowler running in, the ball they'd bowl, where he'd hit it. The bat felt right again, balanced. As if it had adjusted to the new climate, too. It wasn't like he'd been out of form but now he and the bat were back in synch, moving as one. He leaned it against the bedside table, and touched it every time he passed, talking to it like a friend. Outside, with the boys, he had to tone it down, but he was walking on air. Which would come in handy against the Sri Lankan spinners, because his footwork was going to have to be good.

Harrow was putting in extra time in the nets, finally taking his father's advice and getting into his bowling. He stayed back after training to spend some time with their leg spinner, Cowp, working on a wrong 'un, the one that spun the other way. There was more turn than he was used to, though less bounce. Cowp suggested developing another stock ball that went straight on. 'So you can put together a few overs, build pressure.'

The sun was setting red. He knew it was the smog that gave it so much colour, but it was beautiful, with all the palms and strange, noisy birds. The sounds and shapes were of another world, but cricket made it home.

He watched a group of children playing a game on a neighbouring patch of dirt. Harrow didn't understand what they were saying, but the joy on their faces was unmistakeable. One of the girls hit the taped-up tennis ball for miles, again and again, reminding him of Liv. She'd been messaging every day, asking for updates. Better than boring textbooks, she said. And he knew his little sister; she'd be following his tour on a map of Sri Lanka, monitoring the scores, and wishing she was in his shoes.

In their final net session before the practice game, the bat took on that eager feeling in his hands, and he started really connecting with a few. Their bowlers needed to step things up, too, so he smashed back anything loose. Hilton gave him a bit of a stare, out of habit, though they were on the same side now. Sure enough, the next one reared up, forcing Harrow to sway out of the way.

Against the spinners, he focused on his footwork, using all of the crease, playing forward and back. Afterwards, Freddie made time for some throwdowns, feeding him ball after ball from different angles in close, until he was in the flow, a batting machine.

'You don't need to overhit the ball out there tomorrow, Hars,' he said. 'Most of their players are no bigger than you; it isn't about power. Just focus on soft hands, keeping your shape, your follow-through. If you can be patient early, the runs will come.'

Harrow nodded, took a deep breath and let it out. He was ready for the next step up, or as ready as he going to be.

building an innings

When game day dawned, he'd had hardly slept. A combination of nerves and a touch of the stomach bug a few of the boys had. He'd got up in the middle of the night to ring Megan, when she should've been home from work, but she hadn't answered. He knew she was for real, but in the dark, he started to imagine all sorts of stupid things – all the well-dressed brainy men she could be out with.

Mads lost the toss and they were sent out to field in the heat. The Sri Lankan openers, Pradeep and Mathews, got off to a steady start. Heading into lunch they were none down for seventy-nine and didn't look like getting out. Hilt and Sky were working hard but getting nothing from the pitch.

Harrow took a moment between overs to soak up the atmosphere. Most of the crowd were on the grassed banks, a few in the low-slung pavilions or white sponsors' tents, unfamiliar branding on the signboards. The numbers on the Singer scoreboard were still changed by hand and moved slowly. The young men charged with the task spent as much time leaning out from the viewing slot, watching the game.

Australia A's fast bowlers had finished their spells without making much impact, and the shine was well and truly off the ball. Cowp had dried up the scoring, and the boys sensed an opportunity coming. But when the ball found the edge of Mathews' bat, it fell just short of Shep at first slip.

'C'mon, boys, we're close here.' Mads clapped his gloves together, dancing around, trying to keep his energy up. The boys echoed his calls around the ground, keeping everyone focused.

Last ball of the over, Pradeep went for the big sweep and missed. The ball rapped into his front pad. Cowp was down on one knee, both arms in the air. 'How was that?'

The umpire's hand twitched but he did not raise his arm. 'Not out,' he said. 'Over.'

Cowp covered his mouth with his hands, as if to stop the expletives pouring out, and glared at the batter.

Sangha was quality, a left-handed wrist-spinner, but he wasn't having any luck. Australia so rarely played more than one spinner that the number two spinner in the country could spend most of his life playing Shield cricket. Then, when he got an opportunity, there was a lot of pressure to perform.

Harrow started warming up, stretching his bowling arm, wrists and shoulders, to let Mads know he was ready, if needed.

Mads waited until the second last over before lunch to bring him on, desperate to break the partnership. Harrow's first ball was a bit of a half-tracker that disappeared over his head for FOUR. He didn't bother looking around to see where it went. He fired the next one in flatter and quicker, and hit Pradeep on the pad. They all went up, even though there'd been two sounds, a bit of bat probably. The umpire shook his head. The third ball spun a mile, beating batter and keeper, running away for four byes. Pradeep would play for lunch now, not take any chances. With eight runs from the over already, he didn't need to.

Harrow steadied himself, and threw the next one up, put as many revs as he could on the ball, hoping for some dip and turn. It floated up, right in the batter's eyeline, tempting him. Pradeep came out of his crease, swished – and missed. Mads pouched the ball and broke the stumps all in one movement. Pradeep tried to get his foot back over the line, but his weight was forward, his recovery too slow.

Harrow turned, his whole body asking the question. Mads was screaming; he knew they had him. After what seemed like an age, the umpire at square leg raised his finger. OUT.

The boys were all around, messing up his hair, slapping Mads on the back. It was a great stumping. Mads wasn't flashy, but the bowlers all knew they could rely on him absolutely.

The umpire removed the bails. LUNCH. Harrow couldn't stop grinning as they walked off. He'd contributed, shifted the game. And he'd have two balls to the new batter to start the next session. The pressure was right back on the Sri Lankans.

It wasn't until after tea the following day that they bowled Sri Lanka out and Harrow finally had a chance to bat. They were chasing a massive total, but he put that out of his head. He'd seen from the Sri Lankan innings that once you got in, got used to the pitch, you could score runs. But it was slow going, no pace on the ball, no pace off the wicket, and a *lot* of spin.

He and Shep focused on rotating the strike, keeping each other's energy up. Harrow survived a couple of close calls, scooping one to mid-on, just short of the fielder, and a leg-before shout. Their twelfth man ran out wet towels and iced drinks to keep them cool. It was a battle out there, but they were holding their ground. At close of play, they walked back to the dressing rooms side by side, bats tucked beneath arms, relieved to be none down for forty-one.

'Nice job, partner.'

Harrow smiled. 'We did good.'

He showered, rehydrated, ate, sent an update to Megan, and was in bed before nine, bat beside him. He passed out before he could finish replaying his innings so far.

They started fresh the next morning. Shep went in the fourth over, the ball bobbling up off his glove, into the waiting hands of short leg. Harrow started again, building a new partnership with Hall, the left-hander from Canberra. It was *all* about building, slow and steady, including the humidity. It was forty degrees but felt way hotter.

When they went in for lunch, still only one down, Harrow headed straight for the showers. His socks and jocks were so soaked with sweat, he threw them in the bin. He could only force himself to eat a few mouthfuls, bat between his knees, but tried to replace his fluids and electrolytes.

They'd scrabbled their way to a hundred and seventy when he top-edged one to the waiting leg slip, falling right into a trap he'd seen the Sri Lankans set. A momentary lapse in concentration was all it took, and he was walking back to the sheds for eighty-seven, shaking his head. Just thirteen short of a hundred. It was amazing how often something happened on that cursed number, even when you put it out of your mind.

He stood under the tepid water, head against the tiles, physically and mentally tired after only three days. Playing cricket on the subcontinent was like running a marathon.

In the dressing room, clean and cool again, Freddie clapped him on the back and handed him a bottle of cold water. 'Good work, Hars. It was tough out there. But you were tougher.'

'Thanks, Coach.' But he'd thrown his innings away after all that hard work and let the team down.

The second time around, Sri Lanka finished with a flurry before declaring, leaving Australia two hundred and sixty-four runs to get on the final day. With oven-like conditions and the pitch turning square, it would take a miracle.

Shep got out early but Harrow put on another good partnership with Hall, getting to fifty-three with only one down. Then Hall was run out, thanks to a late call from Harrow and an unbelievable throw from the young Sri Lankan fielder roaming the covers. They'd only just settled, and started rebuilding, when Harrow pushed too hard at one. The ball hit the splice of the handle and flew straight up, easily gloved by their keeper.

He threw his head back, closed his eyes. He'd been too busy brooding about the run-out. *Rookie mistake.* As the player who was 'in', and used to the conditions, he should have put that out of his mind and batted through till the end. It was a waste of another start. He trudged off, sick to the stomach.

The boys fought hard, getting within sixty runs of the required total. With Mads hitting boundaries straight down the ground, they thought they were a chance. Until he got a dodgy leg before wicket decision. Mads stood staring at the umpire, and for a moment Harrow thought he was going to explode, but he turned and walked. Hilt was out first ball, leaving Sky and their number eleven with too big a mountain to climb. They lost by forty-one runs. The way Harrow saw it, they were the runs he'd left out there. Or the ones he'd stopped Hall scoring.

They were glum in the sheds, but Freddie praised them for fighting hard in what were, for most of them, foreign conditions. 'You've learned a lot about yourselves, and each other. We'll take all that down to Galle.'

trimming

I hear the bell on the shop door, which triggers another in the workshop, and the red ribbon jags, so as to alert me if I have machinery running. Sometimes I still don't hear or notice, and the person has to stick their head in and sing out. Some people like seeing me among the shavings, for others it's too real, or perhaps they just don't want to intrude.

For a moment I think it's Katie, pale hair poking out from under her beanie. But this woman is younger and more muscular. Still, she looks familiar.

'Morning,' she says.

'How can I help?'

She places a bat on the counter, its toe smashed and splintered. 'Can you fix this?'

I take a closer look. The face is still good, the handle sturdy. A decent bit of willow from one of the better companies. Her forearms are well-developed, strong wrists, hands.

'Yours?'

She nods.

'I can fix the bat.' The real problem is that she goes too hard at the ball, with too much bottom hand, hitting the ground too often and the bat is paying the price. She's tallish but the bat is a little long, and too heavy.

'How much?'

'Forty bucks.'

Her face softens, and her smile, when it comes, is spectacular. 'Cool.'

'Local?'

'Just here for a few days.'

'I can have it ready tomorrow? About ten?'

'Perfect.'

'Can I just grab a name and contact number?'

'Olivia,' she says and writes down her mobile number.

She's reluctant to let go of the bat, which tells me a lot. 'Thanks, Olivia.' I watch her walk out the door and up the street. To the train station probably. It's turned out to be a sunny day after all.

I find myself whistling a tune of my grandfather's and pick up a cricket ball from the counter to practise my bowling action against the back wall of the workshop. The release still feels good, though it brings a twinge in my shoulder. It was actually women players who invented overarm bowling. Until then, batters had dominated play. The change allowed fast bowlers to dictate terms on rough, unplayable wickets. It took the great W.G. Grace to turn that around. Bradman may have piled up the centuries, but Grace was the original genius of the game. Crowds flocked to see him play. In 1873 he made a thousand runs and took a hundred wickets in a season, the first man to do so. And, three years later, he scored the first ever triple century in first-class cricket.

Before Grace, batters played either a forward game or a back-foot game and only specialised in a couple of strokes. Grace switched effortlessly between forward and back, playing a full range of shots. He was a giant of a man and, striding out from the pavilion with his great beard and red and yellow striped Marylebone cap, must have struck fear into the hearts of the opposition.

I never saw him play, of course, just a few bits of scratchy footage, and the countless books Frank has loaned me. Grace somehow embodied the everyday lives of English people, carrying a nostalgia for the bespoke crafts of pre-industrial England into the Victorian Age. Cricket became a moral discipline, compulsory for school children. For a time, competence in cricket was valued more highly than intellectual achievements.

As C.L.R. James argues, Grace was as influential as any general, politician or writer. Yet he's only discussed in cricket books, separated out from the rest of history, as if the game can be separated from life.

I trim back the toe of Olivia's bat, first on the bandsaw and then with my niftiest spokeshave, as if I'm shaping musical instruments rather than repairing the toe of a club. She can afford to lose some length, so I have plenty to work with. It needs a little weight taken out of the back, too. Maybe it's the mad Mendelssohn piece playing on the radio, all that dramatic violin, or the rain now dashing against the windowpanes, but my hands are itching to shave the bat down. My eye can't help but see what should be in her hands.

I'm watching the clock. Even eloquent Elgar can't distract me. Now there's a man who specialised in D minor, the saddest key. Olivia is due and I'm regretting tampering with her bat like a crazy conductor. I just couldn't help myself. Marlene liked to say I was controlling, always wanting to set the course of our lives. And here I am changing a woman's bat without her permission.

I've been thinking a lot about my daughter. Worrying really. The longest she's ever gone without calling before was a month, and that was when she was travelling.

The sun has broken through the clouds for the first time in days when the bell rings, the ribbon jags. Time to face the music.

'Morning,' Olivia says. She's puffed up in one of those black jackets everyone seems to be wearing, although the sun is out.

I place the bat on the counter, face up.

'Oh, great.' She runs her hand over the toe and smiles.

'I have a confession to make,' I say. 'I've taken a little weight out of the back.'

'Right.'

Her face is still. For a moment, I'm terrified. Katie would have had something to say by now, and it would probably be cross.

Olivia grips the bat, plays a cover drive through the air, towards the gaggle of uniformed school kids on the street. The corners of her mouth turn up. 'That feels good, actually.'

'If you don't play better, I'll replace it.'

She grins. 'Deal.'

'Here for a game?'

She shakes her head. 'School excursion. Checking out the universities.'

'Well, Melbourne Uni is one of the best. And, you know, this is the sporting capital of the world.'

'So I've heard.'

I take her cash and write out a receipt. 'Judging by the state of the toe when you brought it in, maybe watch that bottom hand.'

'I know, I know. Our coach says the same thing.'

I spend lunchtime in the glasshouse. It's warming up but there are still no leaves on the willows – the perfect time to take some cuttings or sets. I cut a thin branch, newer growth – about eighteen months – but firm, with little buds emerging. With the secateurs, I snip it into lengths, about six inches, cutting just below a node at each end.

When I have a handful, like a bunch of green pencils or woody asparagus without the tips, I drop them into a jar, making sure all the buds are pointing upwards, pour in a couple of inches of water, and place them in the sun. It's that easy. Willow contains a natural rooting hormone; water and sun are all you need. In a week or so, tiny shoots will appear from the buds and a new generation of willows will be born.

the cauldron

He was starting to enjoy the jostling crowds and noise. Galle, the fort town by the sea at the bottom of the island, had a holiday feel. They sure loved their cricket, playing on the street, in the parks, the beach, anywhere they could mark out some sort of pitch, with a beat-up old garbage bin, fence paling, or just half a cardboard box for a wicket.

When they turned up for game day, spectators were crowding onto the grassy slope around the ground, in the open stands, and spilling over the stone fortress walls. Sri Lankan flags flew high on the ramparts, like some ancient battle site. He knew from their tour in the team bus the day before how good the view was from up there, not just of the ground but the harbour and the Indian Ocean stretching away on either side.

They were still rebuilding, after the tsunami. From the pictures, it must have been scary: surging brown water, cars floating through the city. More than thirty thousand people died, their guide said. The cricket ground had been thirty feet under water, outbuildings washed away, the pitch destroyed. Only the fort had remained. It had been touch and go whether it could be restored, and the Australia A boys were the first 'internationals' to play there since.

Most grounds were cordoned off, ticketed and regimented. At Galle, anything seemed to go. Hands reaching over fences, legs dangling off roofs, flags draped over the walls, cobblestones and trip-hazards, buses parked wherever. It wouldn't take much for someone to plummet over the edge celebrating a wicket a little too enthusiastically.

The crowd was already banging out music as the teams went through their warm-ups out on the ground. Drums, cymbals, trumpets, anything that made a noise. In a strange way all the chaos helped settle his nerves. It was what it was to be an international cricketer, travelling the world. He and the bat stayed the same, wherever they went, whatever happened, a team within the team.

He and Shep were starting to build a bit of a bond, too. Time out in the middle helped. Time together off the field, too. On the long bus ride down to Galle, Harrow had found that they had more in common than he thought, even though Shep was a city boy, from inner Melbourne. They both loved Coldplay and it turned out that his parents ran a gourmet foods store, which stocked his mother's brie. The Reader bat workshop was just down the road, Shep said, as if it was something ordinary and every day.

When Shep reached out to touch Harrow's bat, set across his knees as usual, Harrow pulled it away without thinking.

Shep laughed. 'Not superstitious, are you?'

He'd be getting plenty of shit once the boys heard about that, for sure.

When Mads won the toss and elected to bat, Harrow and Shep did a bit of a subdued high five; it was way better to just get out there than stand around in the sun getting nervous. The pitch was so dry and cracked, he'd be happy if he survived a session.

'Let's do this,' Shep said. 'Let's be better than anyone expects.'

They headed off to their respective dressing room corners to kit up. Harrow's area was neat, compared with some of the boys, and he'd developed a particular order he needed to go about things. Thigh guard and box, then chest guard, pads on: left then right, double-check his laces: double knots and tucked away under the pads. Inners and gloves: left then right. Helmet on. Only now did he touch his bat, though he'd been conscious of it the whole time. He ran his hands over the face, clearing any stray grit or fibre.

The crowd noise had already built to a roar, and Harrow could see through the arch to the movements of the dusty city outside, that other world. He was in Galle! Opening against what was effectively the Sri Lankan national team, warming up for their tour of India. He only had to participate in the wonder of it all.

He and Shep nodded at each other and walked out onto the field, looking up at the sky to adjust to the light. They took their respective positions at either end. Shep would face the first ball. That was his preference, whereas Harrow liked a little extra time to calm his breathing, take in the ground and its atmosphere. To remember where he was in the world, how lucky. It meant he was officially number two in the batting line-up, rather than number one, but that suited him fine.

While Shep was taking guard, scratching out his mark on the crease, between centre and leg stump, Harrow focused on the big old tree below the fort, people crowded in beneath its shade. Already hot and humid; it would be a long day in the sun for the fans too.

He recognised many of the Sri Lankan players by their faces and body language: their captain, Ranwala, the keeper, Hopman, their strike bowler Aziz, who was coming back from injury and in need of a good run, and their second spinner, de Silva, a little tubby now. In person, you could see the greats all had something about them, an ease with themselves and their bodies. The rest were young guns, like them, not quite grown into their hands and feet.

One of the Sri Lankan youngsters, the tallest of their team, was to open the bowling. His face was tense, the adrenaline pumping. The noise as he ran in was like being in the middle of a music festival. The first few balls were too full and wide, and Shep put the third one away for FOUR.

When Harrow took strike, the fielders seemed to have come in closer, the boundaries to have moved back. He barely saw the first ball, a red blur going by while he was still trying to control his breathing. At least he didn't dangle his bat out at it. His body moved well, giving the impression of a batter.

The next one bounced a little more off the pitch, and hit him on the glove, jamming his fingers against the bat handle. He gave the bowler nothing, just walked away and back. It stung, and he let himself feel a little anger.

Shep came down, said something. Harrow nodded though he barely heard him above the din. He looked at his bat, the beautiful bit of willow, patiently waiting for him to wield it like he owned it, and tapped it hard on the ground, three times. *Trust the bat.*

He could no longer hear the crowd when the bowler ran in; he was in the tunnel. Seeing that red ball out of the bowler's hand, its trajectory through the air, off the pitch. Moving in line to play the ball, glancing it away to leg. Hearing the right sound, leather on willow, feeling bat on ball, breathing, Shep calling him through for a single. He sprinted, grounded his bat at the other end, and pulled up. His vision and hearing returned to normal. He was off the mark.

Shep raced to thirty, while Harrow backed up like a demon, ran hard, and made a more measured twenty-three. He'd only hit one ball in the air, which came down in a gap in the field. It felt like luck might be with them. Then the Sri Lankan spinners came on.

The ball was fizzing and dipping, the sound tying their guts in knots. He was only picking one ball in three, playing mainly off the back foot, and managing to keep them out. For three overs they were bogged down, besieged. Then Shep went on the attack, striding down the pitch and spanking the ball back over the bowler's head for SIX. That took the pressure off Harrow, and he managed to guide one between point and gully. They ran hard for the first. The fielder took his eye off the ball, and fumbled, allowing them to come back for two.

Shep had moved to sixty-four when he came down the pitch again – and missed. By the time he gathered himself, pivoted and reached for the white line with his bat, Hopman had taken the ball and removed the bails.

Hall got off the mark first ball, and the left-right combination made it harder for the Sri Lankan bowlers to settle into a rhythm. At last Harrow was starting to pick them, the bowler's stock ball anyway. He was turning them miles, you couldn't play for that. It was the one coming on straight Harrow had to watch out for. Second last ball of the over, he swept through mid-wicket for two. The full movement of his upper body got the blood flowing again and Harrow took over where Shep had left off. He came forward to a few, smothering the spin. Then he sent one into the crowd at long off, and another over cover, into the Lion Beer signage boards on the full. The bat was light in his hands, the ball finding the sweet spot every time.

After lunch, the Sri Lankans pulled their fielders back. Harrow and Hall started pushing singles and twos into the gaps, running hard. They'd just brought up a hundred when Hall hit one straight back at de Silva, who fumbled and fell but managed to tuck the ball into his belly.

Beade, the only Tasmanian in the squad, was bowled for a duck, bringing Peters to the crease. The big fella was one of their better players of spin, using his feet, and that big stride forward, to put the bowlers off their lengths.

When Harrow got into the eighties, he stopped looking at the scoreboard, stopped counting. He treated each ball he faced as a new day, blocking out the crowd, the chatter between the Sri Lankans. It helped not to understand them. Then they started muttering in English, something about Queenslanders not being the brightest. He managed to block that out, too, walking away between balls and humming to himself, to his bat – staying in the zone. He was pretty sure the tree near the fort was a fig, like the one back at his old Landsborough ground. So deep rooted it had survived the tsunami. There were birds, crow-sized, perched on top of the flagpoles, fluttering now, in the breeze.

The umpire called drinks, and Harrow groaned. It was bad timing, a break in concentration. He signalled for new gloves. The third change for the morning. He couldn't remember ever having sweated as much. He put the sports drink away in three long pulls and washed it down with water. Peters leaned on his bat, looking around the stands, while Harrow squeezed sweat out of his helmet lining.

'Beautiful ground, isn't it?'

'Reckon.'

The breeze was picking up, cooling his forehead. Gordo, their twelfth man for the match, handed over Harrow's new gloves and inners, took away the old. There was a line of them now, drying by the boundary.

'Just keep doing what you're doing,' Peters said.

Harrow nodded. The pitch would only get harder to bat on. They needed to put on a big score now, give the bowlers plenty to work with. But he wanted the hundred, too. It was starting to tire him, the nervous energy.

He waited for the right ball, the right moment, one that sat up a bit, and cut, watching the ball run away, over the rope for FOUR. He grinned and raised his bat, acknowledged the boys in the sheds, the crowd.

Peters enveloped him in a hug. 'Excellent work, Hars. Excellent.'

They were in sight of the break when one squared him up, hitting his pad, and then his glove, flying into the waiting hands of short leg. He waited for the umpire's decision, hoping against hope, but his finger went up. It had been a good ball, but he was filthy with himself walking off. It meant Mads had to come in just before tea.

Every single person in the crowd seemed to be applauding him, and he couldn't help smiling and raising his bat, their energy channelling through the willow somehow, into his body. His whole heart went out to Galle, to Sri Lanka. Cricket, too. What a game.

When he got back to the hotel, there was a message from Megan. She'd seen a snippet on the news, she said. It meant more than all the slaps on the back from the boys, the nod of approval from Freddie.

It was hard to put her out of his head but he had to, on the field anyway. His century wouldn't mean anything if they didn't win. He hung on to the feeling that thinking about her gave him, though, throwing himself around after the ball when they fielded the next day. The ground was so rough he had to wear long sleeves despite the humidity. Even then, he lost plenty of skin on his forearms.

The Sri Lankans were eating away at the total while the Australian bowlers wore themselves out. After lunch, Cowp and Sangha worked in tandem. Sangha was soaking up the pressure, bowling nice and tight. At home he didn't get a huge amount of turn, it was all variations in flight. But here, he was really troubling Sri Lanka's right-handed batters. As the other senior member of the squad, his role was to provide experience and leadership. But it was also a try-out, for their next tour of India, and Sangha knew it.

Harrow was hot under the helmet in at short leg, watching the bat, the batter's body language, to anticipate where the ball would go. If the batter swung hard, made contact, Harrow spun and crouched, turning his back to the ball, making himself small. A few had flown up, off the bat and one off the glove, but always landing just out of reach. He tried to stay relaxed, keep his hands soft, eyes sharp. He'd started carrying a little cloth, to wipe the sweat from his eyes between balls. They had the batter surrounded, with him in close, as well as a leg slip and, on the other side of the pitch, silly mid-off. One mistake, that's all they needed, and they were into the Sri Lankan tail.

Sangha gave one some nice flight and turn, it spun out of the rough, ran up Serendip's pad, onto his gloves and into the air. Harrow threw himself forward, watching it come down, in slow motion – into his outstretched palm. He softened his body, for the landing on the hard pitch, closed his fingertips around the leather, and held the ball aloft. OUT.

Mads lifted him up off the dirt, slapping his back, pulling him into the huddle. 'Some fucking catch, Hars,' he said. 'C'mon, boys. Let's keep the pressure on now.'

Sangha cleaned up the tail, taking a five-for. Everyone was happy for the old boy, as they called him, at the mature age of thirty-one. And then Harrow and Shep were running from the ground to pad up and do it all again.

The final morning started with scattered showers and the covers over the ground. Mist clung around the clocktower. The boys paced around the change rooms watching the rain. The forecast was for it to clear mid-morning but they were nervous all over again. His seventy-nine (close enough to another hundred to leave him gutted) had helped give them a lead of two hundred and seventy and a full day to bowl Sri Lanka out. But a draw would mean they couldn't win the series.

Freddie was relaxed, saying it just put more pressure on the opposition. So the boys tried to relax too, playing cards, drinking coffee, reading the papers. Harrow was already hungry, thinking about the curries that would be laid on at lunch. It had seemed a strange meal to have during a game at first, but now it seemed to fit with everything else, all the textures and flavours of international cricket.

He was trying to cheer up Sky, who wasn't having a great game, only bowling ten overs and yet to take a wicket. Cowp was feeling the pressure, too, always expected to clean up on day five. As Harrow knew himself, as soon as you were tense, the ball didn't come out the same. Then your head started up. It was a downward spiral, for sure.

As it turned out, when they got on the field, it was Peters' day. Touted as the next great Australian all-rounder, he was yet to post a big score, so his three wickets in two overs were a lifeline for him and the team. Bowled, caught and bowled, and leg-before. Quite the trifecta. The big fella couldn't stop smiling. Sri Lanka still needed a hundred and three to win, with only three wickets remaining.

Cowp did the rest, with the final wicket falling in the second last over. He pumped his fists in triumph. The sound of the stumps being broken was the perfect way to end the game.

They celebrated with a few Singha beers in the sheds, and the team song from Mads. Harrow sat back, head against wall, as all the stories started coming out from the old fellas of other tours, the highs and lows, the hijinks they got up to. Freddie told them that in his day, he and their strike bowler got lost in Colombo after a big night out and, with the cab drivers all gone to bed, ended up sleeping on a wharf somewhere, waking up with the gulls and fishermen. They turned up on the morning of the game just in time to get changed and take the field.

'Course, if any of you try that, you'll be sent home,' he said.

Harrow smiled and shook his head. They all knew they couldn't get away with that shit anymore. They were trying out to play for their country. The satisfaction of contributing to a win, a century to his name, and sitting around with the boys was more than enough.

postcards

Harrow headed out early to walk the cobblestone laneways and grassed fort ramparts one more time, looking down over the ground, trying to commit the win to memory. Women swam in the sea baths with their headscarves on, graceful as swans. Boys dived from Flag Rock in bright boardshorts, lithe and laughing. The water was a different blue than home, more greeny-white. From the limestone, Mads said. Straggly palm trees leaned over the white sand, while surfers made the most of a modest swell, their style more relaxed than on Sunshine Coast breaks. The rubbish washing up on the beach was a shock, though, a rainbow of plastic and paper. In front of the resort, staff swept it all away before dawn, but elsewhere, the real world crept in.

He offered to have a hit with one of the street cricket games and, after he smashed one down onto the beach, one boy asked him to sign their bat, just a fence paling held together by tape. The way they returned to their game as soon as he left was a reminder of what was important.

He peeled off his T-shirt, stepped out of his thongs and jogged down to the water's edge in his shorts. He waded into the waves and dived in, breaststroking underwater, light streaming down around him, until his breath was spent. The water was tepid but there was something thrilling about bobbing around in the ocean on the other side of the world. He turned and pushed off the bottom, and swam a few strokes of freestyle to catch the wave, aquaplaning with his right hand, all the way to shore. A little boy smiled as Harrow emerged, hitching up his shorts.

On the walk back to the resort, he let himself be talked into buying half-a-dozen postcards by the young woman. It was a photogenic kind of place. Back at the hotel, he picked out the best card, of the beach he'd just walked on, but at sunset, and scribbled a few words to Megan. It took ten minutes to decide how to sign off. In the end, he went with *Yours, Todd.* It had happened fast, but he *was* hers, or he would be if she'd have him.

He sent one to his parents, too, of the lighthouse near the fort amid palms, taken from above. He described the firm cheese, paneer, he'd tried in a butter masala, knowing Mum would be pleased that he was tasting the world as well as scoring runs.

The one of a local street cricket game was for Liv. He told her how he'd had a hit with the kids, and that he wished she could see it, instead of being holed up in that stuffy library.

The final postcard, a black and white picture of an historic game at the ground, took the longest to write, even though it contained the fewest words. He'd said to call him Allan but he always thought of him as Mr Reader. And how to thank someone he didn't really know for changing his life? In the end he kept it simple, hoping the gesture was what mattered.

The bus trip up to Kandy was long and quiet, the fast bowlers occupying the back seats as usual, stretching out their legs and talking shop. Peters was trying to bust in, arguing that his top speed of a hundred and thirty-three clicks qualified, but they were still knocking the big fella back. A few more runs, just one big score, and he could be sitting up front with the batters, but that didn't seem to carry the same attraction.

Harrow made sure he scored a window, to see as much as he could on the drive. It also made it harder for the boys to steal his bat if he fell asleep. Peters had already taken off with it while Harrow was in the bathroom and now all the bowlers were in on the game.

Shep sat next to him again. They chatted about the game at first, what had gone right, and what hadn't, and then they got onto family. Shep's father was pretty sick, he said. Undergoing treatment for leukemia. They didn't know what would happen. Harrow hadn't been sure what to say, but it seemed to help Shep to share the story, because he dozed off afterwards. Harrow felt a little nauseous, imagining Mum or Dad being sick while he was so far away. He put in his headphones, listening to the playlist he'd put together for the trip, as he stared out temples shouldering arms above the jungle. They were winding their way through high mountains, steep slopes sewn with tea plantations. It was all so lush and green, like when he first saw far north Queensland on those early family caravan holidays, before cricket took over their lives.

He'd probably be home before the postcards. He was already thinking about seeing Megan. Was the day he got back too soon for a date? He'd be jet-lagged, not at his best, and it would be a 'school night', as she called it. He didn't want to wait, after so much waiting, but he didn't want to mess it up, either. He'd never met anyone like her, never felt so comfortable from the get-go. But he'd never been so scared. Maybe he was kidding himself. She was older, more experienced, so smart and beautiful. What did he have to offer?

He felt calmer in Kandy, all temples and pale buildings reflected in the green lake. Maybe it was the still water, more muted colours, or perhaps he was finally adjusting to the pace of life in Sri Lanka.

The lake was man-made, Mads said. And there was a price to the stillness. At training, a series of short sprints across the field, followed by a couple of laps around the ground, the altitude and encroaching jungle had Harrow dragging his breaths. Just when he thought he had everything sorted, there were new challenges.

Freddie drove the team bus down to the crowded gold-roofed temple, supposedly housing Buddha's tooth. They didn't get to see the tooth itself, but the entrance was guarded by carved elephants and the chamber made of real ivory. There was a service going on and with the sun setting and the lamps being lit, it was a special place.

'Peaceful, isn't it?' Mads said.

'For sure.'

Mads hung back, sitting cross-legged. Harrow left him to it, wondering if he was praying and, if so, for what.

Sky was left out for the final game. When there was no sign of him at training, Harrow went looking. He found him out the back of the ground, bowling balls flat out at a rusted-out forty-four-gallon drum. The booming sound mirrored the look on the big man's face. He'd never seen him angry off the field before.

'Nets not big enough for you, Sky?'

'Needed a blowout. This is how I used to train back on the farm.'

'They're just giving Gordo a run, you know that.'

'I didn't get the wickets,' he said. 'You know that.'

Harrow dropped his kitbag and collected an armful of balls from around the drum. 'Tough conditions. There's no one harder to face, when you're sticking to line and length, banging the odd one in.'

'Should have done exactly that, instead of thinking I should be swinging it like Hilt.'

He threw a ball back to Sky and watched him run in. Already he had the easy rhythm that had gone missing in the second game. Going back to basics always worked.

The delivery was quick, a blurred circle of arms and legs. The ball speared into the base of the drum, bursting through a rusted patch and rolling around and around inside like a pinball machine.

Sky pulled up from his follow through, hands on thighs, laughing.

Harrow figured it was okay to laugh, too. 'Not a batter in the world could've kept that one out.'

Sky was super talented. But they were all only two poor performances away from losing sight of the dream. Somehow they had to keep their heads clear and stick to their own game, to be the best they could be.

coverage

Without television or radio coverage it's been hard work following Harrow's progress. A few seconds of footage on the news when he scored his century at Galle was something – to see his moment of triumph, and the bat in action. But not at all the same as seeing the whole journey: the conditions, the crowd, all the ebbs and flows of each session and the building of his innings. I've taken to wandering down to the corner shop before breakfast to buy the paper. It's a pleasant walk, down the lane, past the park and the school. A snapshot of the first stirrings of suburban life.

They only print the scorecards, which are twelve hours old by the time I read them, but if you know the game, they tell the story. Harrow is doing well. Consistent performances building to his hundred, three wickets and a handful of catches. A significant contribution. With just one match to go, there's a chance to really make an impression.

My own figures tell a different story. The manager down at the bank suggests I'll be hard-pressed to buy out Marlene. Before I even get to that stage, I have to do my quarterlies, and my tax for the last financial year. I don't need to sort through the mess of papers spread over the dining table to know it wasn't a great season.

The orders are starting to pick up again, thanks to Harrow. But I can only make so many bats on my own, and with the mass-produced bats so cheap, it's a challenge to stay competitive. I tried hiring a helper, but the work is part time and seasonal. The first guy, a hard worker and really good with his hands, moved on for something full time. And the next one, not half as skilled, eventually went the same way. I was so relieved when the last one quit – a smoker who talked too much – that I gave the idea away.

Dogs lead their walkers out of the mist, joggers disappear behind their garden gates, rose-cheeked. The few cars on the road have their fog lights on, eyes downcast, like a Clarice Beckett painting. Jim hands me *The Age* and takes my coins. I take the alternative route back, past the pink and purple house with its pink and purple fence and lavender-filled front garden beneath a weeping silver birch. For nearly a decade I've been trying to catch a glimpse of her clothes on the little line in the backyard, to confirm my suspicion that she only wears pink and purple, even underneath. But once again, the line is bare. Like every other Melburnian, I'm longing for colour, for spring to be properly sprung.

I make a cup of tea, put on the porridge and spread the paper out over the kitchen bench. Harrow has had his first failure in Kandy. Out for one in the first innings. The young quick, Hilton, took five wickets. He's putting himself in the frame for the Ashes this summer, too.

Once the porridge is bubbling, I turn off the heat, add milk, give it a stir with the old wooden spoon, wondering, not for the first time, why I don't make my own kitchen implements. Willow has been used for making tools since eight thousand years before Jesus supposedly walked the earth. The brown sugar melts as I carry the bowl back to the table. The workshop has emerged from the mist, the trees unveiled, wet and glistening.

When I was with the willowmen in West Moor, I saw willow coppiced to grow withies – or *withes* – the long flexible stems that can be bent, woven and shaped. In mid-November, once the leaves have fallen and the sap is sunk, the willowmen start cutting last year's growth, with their billhooks, to stimulate new shoots. The moorland was just about all withy beds in those days: Black Maul, Flanders red and Holton's black, plus all manner of hybrids, grown in rows, with a protective hedge of dogwood. Drainage ditches, or *rhynes*, kept the water level just high enough to moisten the willow roots, the banks were lined with meadowsweet, comfrey and reeds. It was a scene straight out of an eighteenth-century painting.

Like batmaking, it's labour-intensive. The willow osiers or rods are dried, left to season for a year, boiled to dissolve the tannins, and stripped of their bark. Then there's almost no limit on what they can be woven into: bicycle baskets, hot air balloon baskets, fishing creels, eel traps, craypots, hoddie pots – for catching sparrows – even coffins!

Everyone in those villages once worked the willow, in one way or another. I saw bundles of osier rods, bound with willow bark and knotted in the traditional rose pattern, still stacked criss-cross, floor to roof, in barns and sheds. But the industry was dying, even then.

Plastic pretty much killed it off. Then most of the withy beds were lost during the floods. And weaving fading away, like so many other traditions.

I brought back some willow gifts for Marlene. There was a bit of trouble getting them through customs, but it was worth it. A handwoven picnic basket. And, inside, nestled in a red and white checked tablecloth, a set of willow plates, cutlery and cups. Marlene exclaimed as she examined each piece, finally seeing the beauty of the timber.

We tried it out the next sunny day, entwined on a rug by the river, with champagne, pâté, cheese and a bread stick, a thermos of tea and a slice of Marlene's chocolate angel cake. We'd missed each other terribly and vowed never to be apart so long again. But the house was full of her paintings, leaning on walls and wardrobes, larger than ever before. It had been a productive time for us both.

The bats in progress are for a state player, a consistent performer, desperate for higher honours. I've been making his bats since he was playing for his private school Under-12s. He's filled out now, matured. I've tweaked this batch a little, given the bats a bigger sweet spot, and little more weight, to try to help him break through. At twenty-six, he's running out of time.

When I stop the lathe, I catch the end of the news. There's been a bombing at a hotel in Colombo. Six dead. The boys are safe, in Kandy, but it's the hotel they were going to be staying in before they flew out – a little close for comfort. The Tamil Tigers want a separate state, and though they're entitled to self-determination, religious freedom, they're killing innocent people, keeping cricket from everyday Sri Lankans, and Sri Lanka's cricketers from the world stage.

playing for the draw

Harrow recovered from the shock of losing his leg stump in the second over of the match at Asgiriya Stadium – a slower ball that moved off the seam – to anchor their second innings. On the ground where David Hookes had scored a Test century, he would've liked to throw his hands at everything, but once Mads was out, his role had been to steady the ship and build a big total. A nod from Freddie when he came off suggested it hadn't gone unappreciated.

Then the rain came down from the surrounding mountains, washing away any chance of a result. The boys were subdued on the bus back to the hotel. The end of any series brought a lot of relief, along with mixed feelings about their performance and, linked to that, a new anxiety about what lay ahead. A certain amount of sadness, too, at breaking up the gang. A-teams were always situational; the same group wouldn't come together again. The bombing had shaken everyone up, too. They would be bussed straight down to the airport in the morning, with a security contingent, flying out a day early.

Once home, there would only be a short break before it was back to pre-season training with their Shield sides. And, never far from anyone's mind, the announcement of the Ashes squad in just a few months' time, with England arriving in early November.

He couldn't wait to sleep in his own bed, have breakfast at the greasy café down the road. He couldn't wait to see Megan either, except that now it was close, a reality, he was starting to get nervous. Messaging into space was one thing, but whenever he started thinking about taking her out for a meal or kissing her, or what might happen afterwards, he felt himself seizing up.

He was already showered and packed, and carried his bags down to the hotel foyer to give himself time to buy Megan a gift at the markets. He found a carving Liv would like, of a local elephant. She'd loved them since she was a little kid. Mum said it was a metaphor for the way Liv went about things. But he didn't know Megan like that. Not yet. Luckily Mads came down the same crowded row and suggested a batik sarong. But there were so many colours and patterns to choose from, he was getting a headache.

'What colour are her eyes?' Mads said.

'Green.'

'There's a clue.'

He picked out a swirling abstract design that reminded him of swimming at Galle, the feeling of the water on his body.

'Good choice,' Mads said. 'Modern. Not too folksy.'

The lady wrapped it for him, including a card with information about where and how it was made. Her smile was so warm, he couldn't help smiling back. He would miss the Sri Lankan people, especially the kids. The way they played cricket, with next to no gear but all their hearts. Most people didn't have much, and he noticed now the signs of the civil war around the place. Freddie said the terrorist threats directed at the team were only what Sri Lankans had had to live with for a decade. But still, or maybe because of that, they seemed to know how to really appreciate the everyday – the ceremonies of food, family, cricket.

Mads had chosen an ornate timber jewellery box. 'Did the sarong last time,' he said.

'How long have you been married?'

'Five years,' he said. 'Best thing that ever happened to me.'

'Yeah?'

'Hands down.'

Judging by the stories, Mads had been a bit of a rogue before Jane. He was sent home from the academy, turning up to training after being out all night. Though the way he tells it, it was just because his room was messy. And there had been a few dressing room incidents: bat through a window, fist into a locker.

A short string of poor batting form, and losing the Ashes 4–0, saw him dropped from the Australian team. Harrow could see the hurt in him. Mads was still the best keeper in the country, a natural leader, and batted well with the lower order. His replacement was a dasher, opening the batting in the one-day format, but only competent with the gloves.

'C'mon. Time for a drink on the way back. I know a great little bar,' he said. 'We need to have us a celebratory Kandy Cocktail.'

He started to shake his head. They'd been warned not to stray too far on their own.

'I want to have a chat, Hars. Things are going to start moving for you now. You need to be ready.'

He followed Mads down an alley he would never have entered on his own, and then through a doorway he probably wouldn't have noticed. They emerged in a wood-lined structure, thick with smoke and incense. Mads led him to a wooden slab overlooking the lake and ordered. When their waitress brought the drink, it was in the tallest glass Harrow had ever seen, decorated with a tower of pineapple and melon segments.

'Cheers,' he said. 'Congratulations on your first tour. And, I'm betting, a start in the Australian squad this summer.'

'Don't get my hopes up,' he said. Still, he felt himself tearing up. At the thought of achieving what he'd strived for his whole life, but more so the acknowledgement from Mads, someone he'd come to respect so much.

'I'm right,' Mads said. 'You'll see.'

The cocktail tasted a bit like a Long Island iced tea, or the James Street Smash he'd had on big nights out with the Queensland team in the Valley. For ten bucks, he was set for the night. There'd been a few dates, too, mostly set-ups from the boys. Nice enough girls, and he usually had a good time, but he didn't really have time for a relationship. But maybe it was more that he hadn't met the right person. Until now.

The Kandy Smash was made with Ceylon Arrack, Mads said. It went down pretty well, warming his insides.

'They'll try to mess with your game, your technique,' Mads said. 'Everyone will suddenly have an opinion. Don't lose yourself, with all those voices in your ear. You're as natural a batter as I've seen with my own eyes.'

Harrow sipped his drink, nodded. Mads was speaking from his own experience. The hurt in him was close to the surface again.

'Find a way, a little mantra to centre yourself, play your own game, to bring you back to how you felt on this tour. And don't ever forget it.'

Dad had given similar advice, but coming from Mads, who knew what it was like at the top, and to drop back down, it meant more somehow. The moment he pictured was at Galle. Not reaching his century but walking from the field, holding up the bat, and feeling its energy, the energy of the crowd, coursing through him, as if he could conquer the world.

in rags

The Australia A team has made the news but not for their results. They're on their way home from Sri Lanka, flying out just ahead of another Colombo bombing. It must have been quite an education for the youngsters in the group. Their parents will be glad to have them home safe, I imagine.

Harrow's patient eighty in the last innings helped ensure the draw, leaving the series level. It was a good result overall, most of them touring the subcontinent for the first time. If Harrow starts the Shield season well, he'll be a shoo-in for the Ashes squad.

I apply oil to the bat in progress with a new cloth, one of my old work shirts with the buttons removed. For a time there, it was always Katie's clothes, recycled into rags as she grew out of them or tore holes in the knees. Marlene used them, too, when painting. One child wasn't enough to keep us both in rags.

'I'm a cricket widow, Al,' she liked to say, when I'd been out all weekend at a game or hadn't started dinner because I was too caught up listening to the radio commentary. It was pretty aggravating, especially after Nate died, because poor Jean really was a cricket widow. But she had a point, looking back. I thought she'd always be there, whereas the game is constantly changing, moments in history being laid down before my eyes. I didn't want to miss a thing. A relationship is just the same, of course. You have to be present, savour the moments, invest in the partnership, and celebrate the miracle of two people falling in love and enjoying each other's company, deciding to share a life.

Still, if I ever shack up with anyone again, she'll have to like the game, respect my love for it. There'd be no point otherwise.

It's not like it's something I can give up. Marriage is a team sport, and its disintegration a series of small decisions and relinquishments by both parties. Marlene's growing resentment of cricket meant I started shutting away a part of myself, keeping it separate.

We never even really believed in marriage. An institution that women would be better off without, Marlene liked to say. The whole performance of it was a waste of good money that could be put to better use. We agreed on that. And Marlene didn't have much to do with her family. An ongoing drama stemming from their refusal to support her art.

But when we got pregnant there was that pressure, to be respectable. For your child to be born in wedlock. So off we went, to the registry, in the second-hand outfits that we'd last worn to some opening or concert. Marlene's tiny Katie-bump was barely showing. Dad and Nate were there, and Marlene's mother drove up. But her father stayed put, out of pride. It didn't keep the smile from Marlene's face, but I saw a touch of sadness in her eyes, where there should only have been joy.

facing up

Megan didn't meet him at the airport. Arriving with the whole squad, the media there waiting to get their responses to the bombings, wouldn't exactly give them any privacy. They decided on dinner the next night instead. A proper first date, though it was almost as if they'd skipped that stage. But when the time came to get ready, he couldn't decide which shirt to wear, or shoes. Suddenly nothing was good enough. He needed to go shopping but there wasn't time. In the end he settled on the patterned shirt he'd bought in Kandy. At least there was a story behind it. It was a little summery, but he knew already he would sweat.

Megan had chosen Ecco, where he'd been once before, for Liv's sixteenth birthday, so he was less uncomfortable than he might've been. He'd expected Megan to stick to protein and salad, like his sister, but they started with champagne and oysters, then shared a bottle of red with their *bistecca con patatine fritte,* and a side of green beans. The food was good, the place bustly enough that he could relax. With Megan's beaming face finally on the other side of the table, he couldn't stop grinning. His steak was half cold by the time he finished it.

'Tell me about the bombings. That must've been scary.'

'The trip down to Colombo was pretty full-on. And armed guards escorting us through the airport. But we felt so welcome the rest of time.'

'What's Sri Lanka like?'

'Hot, humid, colourful. Kinda hectic but kinda country. It was all a bit much at first. But I really liked the markets and the food. Even the crazy roads in the end. Not that I had to drive on them. There's jungle and beaches and mountains and temples everywhere. But the people ...'

'It's somewhere I've always wanted to go.'

'Where have you travelled?'

She tucked her hair behind her ear, more red than blonde under lights. 'We lived in Malaysia for part of my childhood, so a lot of Asia – Borneo, Hong Kong, Thailand, Cambodia. And I worked in London, so the UK, holidays in France and Spain. A weekend in Portugal.'

'Favourite place?'

'Scotland. The Hebrides, maybe.'

'They're islands?'

'Yes, the Western Isles. Skye, Lewis, St Kilda. My mother's family is from there. Way back.'

'Cold?'

'It is cold. But it suits it. All misty and atmospheric. A different kind of wild. Tall cliffs, seabirds calling, ships coming and going in the fog.'

'I'd like to see that.'

She smiled. 'Maybe you will.'

He sipped his wine, hoping the blush he felt hadn't reached his cheeks.

'What about you?'

'I only really know cricket places: Cape Town in South Africa looks amazing. Saint Kitts in the West Indies.'

'I wouldn't mind going to either of those.'

He looked at her, to make sure she was serious, and she held his gaze. His stomach was in freefall, but he grinned all the same. 'Maybe you will.'

glasshouse

I'm cleaning the workshop properly, long overdue. I hear the postie stop and my guts twist. But when I duck out, she's delivered me a gift. A postcard from Sri Lanka! Harrow's description of how the bat plays is the best thank you I could ask for. And the picture, of players taking the field for the first Richmond–Mahinda Cricket Encounter in 1905, is a classic. The competition is still running today. I stick the card above my workbench and stare at it a moment, my world a little bigger and brighter.

He'll be starting training again soon, getting ready for another Shield season. I can't wait to see him back in action. Ashes fever is already here: the English squad has been announced, the commentators are weighing up their prospects and deliberating on our squad. All but one has tipped Harrow to debut.

There's a green thundercloud moving in, as if the Sri Lankan subtropics have come to the Melbourne suburbs. I'm stuck in traffic on the way back from the hardware warehouse, everyone trying to get home. The sky turns dark. It's already hailing when I exit the freeway. Only small at first, like frozen peas, pinging off the car and bouncing up from the street. People are running for cover, bringing in their signboards. The wind is picking up, too.

As I pull into the garage, it's getting larger, loud on the roof. I struggle to close the doors in the swirling wind. By the time I run inside, with just a newspaper over my head, they are golf ball-sized pieces of ice. My shirt and jeans cuffs are soaked. I stand on the deck for a moment, watching it all come down. The noise is incredible.

It doesn't last long, but the garden is smashed to pieces, leaves and flowers splattered over the lawn and paths. The power is out. It's only much later, in the quiet after dinner, that I think of the glasshouse.

In the morning, it's with some trepidation that I leave the house. My garden is a wilderness, the path barely visible for torn leaves. It's a miracle no lines are down. I step gingerly over fallen branches, wet foliage brushing my shoulders. The glasshouse is upright, but its roof and one wall are shot full of holes, like the windscreens and windows all across the city shown on last night's news – or war zones the world over.

The door is swinging off its hinges. I crunch through the shards and stand amid the mess to survey the damage. The seedlings are intact, just a few knocked over spilling soil. They've already shot. I pinch off the tiny leaves they've sent out, from the bottom half, so all their energy can go into the roots.

Unlike windscreens, windows break at sharp angles. I get to work cleaning up the mess: righting the willow sets, sheltering them as best I can in a corner, and fetching a pile of newspapers to wrap the broken pieces.

I stop wrapping. The words I've long dreaded are in print, magnified through glass. The article is from two weeks ago, hidden in the middle of the international section of *The Age*. There's been an outbreak of willow rust in Suffolk. Dendrologists have been flown in to assess the damage. I should call John May, see how the willowmen are doing – but it's still night time there.

I lift the glass and smooth out the paper. Willow rust has long been present in other *Salix* species but now, somehow, it's crossed over into white willow. Scientists say that with rising temperatures, increasing monocultures, it's expanded its range.

The fungus defoliates the trees. Yellow pustules appear on the underside of the leaves in spring and then rupture in summer, releasing their spores. They hibernate over winter in the fallen leaves, only to rise again the following spring. They need an accomplice – an alternate species like the larch – to spread their spores on the wind, so they can come back, for a second innings. It's the secondary infection that's killing white willows, not only taking all their leaves before they've pumped enough nutrients into the timber, but leaving them susceptible to further infestations, like scabs, cankers and blight.

Even if it doesn't kill the tree, the rust apparently stunts the willow's growth, leaving ugly lesions. When the affected trees are cut, their timber not only looks unsightly, but all the magic and lightness has vanished. I have to steady myself on the chair. It's a disaster for growers and makers, for cricket.

back in the nets

He removed his helmet and squeezed sweat from its lining, towelled his face and hair dry and headed back into the cage for another barrage from the quicks. It was another hot afternoon at the Gabba nets: sweaty gloves and pads. Their sessions were always in singlets and shorts, box strapped on the outside, like Superman. They couldn't play like that, not in public. It was still trousers all the way, though they had at least shifted into short sleeves by the time he started playing.

Training gave him a chance to get some sun on his legs, even up that cricketer's tan. Brisbane was so much hotter than the coast, too much bitumen and concrete, too far from the sea. Still, it was milder than Sri Lanka. If that tour had given him anything, it was an appreciation of home conditions. He still thought of Galle, sometimes, imagining playing there again, opening for Australia.

A climbing ball rapped him on the glove. He swore, shook his hand, gave the finger a squeeze. Last thing he needed now was an injury. In the form of his life, back-to-back centuries to open the season, he had to be there or thereabouts.

'You awake, Hars?' Klimt was halfway down the pitch after his follow through.

'That the best you've got? Reckon you've lost a yard since last season.'

It wasn't true. Klimt had dropped five kilos and picked up some pace. Enough to be considered a genuine quick. It had a lot to do with his new partner, Sean, who was super fit and lean, taking even more care with what food they bought and how they cooked it than Liv. Harrow knew first-hand how hard Klimt had worked; he'd moved into the spare room of Klimt's Woolloongabba apartment. Klimt's old flatmate (a club cricketer who was getting married) had moved out during the off-season and Harrow was sick of his share house, always full of students wanting to party until late.

Missing the final last season had knocked the Bulls boys around. They'd been unlucky, everyone said so. But it still hurt. Tank coming on board as the new coach brought new energy; they were desperate to turn it around. Harrow and Klimt were going to be a big part of that. Sky too. He was fit as and had been working on a slower ball that was hard to read.

Copes and Tank were old mates, understood each other. And Tank had been part of the Invincibulls Shield-winning team in 1994–95, scoring one hundred and fifty-one, so he knew how to win.

Life had changed so much, so quickly. He was finally feeling more settled in Brisbane, on a Queensland contract, and well and truly part of the squad. A few youngsters were coming up beneath him, which made him feel older, more experienced. He was going to meet Megan's parents, and they were already talking about getting a place together one day, somewhere with a view of the city or the river. Sometimes he wished he didn't have to spend so much time away from her. But that was the job. And it wasn't as if she was sitting around waiting for him. She had her own career, ambitions. That was something they had in common.

He pulled the next one around the corner, the ball jagging in the mesh. Maybe it was just him, or the afternoon heat, but the bat never did seem to respond as well during training as it did out there in the middle, with a crowd and real opposition.

Reid was smashing them on one side, Copes working on his defence in the other, which wasn't going that well. Sky had just knocked over his leg stump and was whooping it up. Poor old Frazer was kitted up waiting to bat. He was fully fit but with Copes dropping back to three, would start the season down the order, at number four or five. At thirty, his chance of national selection was probably gone. Harrow tried not to dwell on it, but he did feel bad for the bloke.

He shed his protective gear, piece by piece, and spread them out in the sun to dry. They lined up with their fielding coach for some catching drills, taking the same slips formation they did in the opening overs, before scattering for some high catches and boundary work. He didn't often field out there, but it was good practice, judging where the rope was behind you as you watched the ball drop out of the sky into your waiting hands.

As the batters packed up and drifted back to the sheds, Harrow stayed back to bowl some overs in the nets. It was just the bowlers left, getting in some hitting. Klimt thumped one back past Harrow's head.

'Am I meant to be cooking tonight?' Harrow said.

'Sean's coming over. Said he'll do that Thai beef salad.'

'Cool.' Lucky, because he hadn't even done any shopping, coming straight to training from Megan's. He liked his food but cooking was never going to be his back-up career. He bowled the next one a little slower, and Klimt was through the shot before the ball arrived, rapping him on the pads.

'OUT! That was plumb!' Harrow said.

the G

I carry the radio out to the greenhouse and plant each of the sets out into pots, burying them up to about halfway in a mix of soil, compost and manure. They're all bushy on top now, full of optimism. Willows are a great plant for beginners because you can't overwater them. Just keep the soil moist and the sun up to them, and they're happy.

'Queensland has won the toss and elected to bat,' the commentator says.

They're playing here, at the Melbourne Cricket Ground. The G, as we call it. Harrow will be batting. And soon. One more good score and Harrow is a lock for the Ashes squad.

I have plenty of work to do, paperwork pending, calls to return, but there's a fluttering in my belly that has nothing to do with financials. Something big is going to happen. I down tools, lock up, put on a clean long-sleeved shirt and hat, pack water and snacks, and take the train in to the city.

I emerge from the clocked mouth of Flinders Street Station, blinking into the glare, and cross the road. The walk down to the ground is one I've always enjoyed, the palm-lined path rolling over green grass, between tall trees. The sound of traffic falls away and the pedestrian bridge lifts me into the canopy of pepper trees and pines. And there's the stadium – the heart of the nation's sporting capital.

As I step into the shadows and pass through the gates, it isn't too much of a stretch to imagine entering a great stadium from the past. The Colosseum perhaps. It was the Greeks who invented sport as spectacle, with those first Olympic Games way back in

776 BC. Socrates, Plato, Herodotus – all the big brains – turned up in their day to watch the best athletes from every Greek city and colony. Common people weren't allowed in.

Once democracy came to Athens, theatre became the primary form of cultural expression. Every year, for four days, Athenians sat outside from sunrise to sunset watching the tragi-dramas of competing playwrights until a winner was decided. If you combine the athleticism of the Olympic games and days-of-drama as a competition, that's Test cricket. It's an expression of the best of us – and an outlet for the rest. Maybe that's where the saying 'cricket tragic' comes from. It's insulting, really, to suggest that a passion for the game is a negative.

More tourists are queuing for the museum than the stadium itself. For the footy, a one-day game, even a Test, if Australia was playing, the place would be abuzz. But the stands are almost empty, the ball making a hollow sound when it whacks into the advertising signage. I guess the players are used to it, but there's something missing from the equation without an audience. The boundary was Harrow's, a sweep shot played from one knee, with all the calm and precision in the world. I'd recognise that sound from back at Flinders Station. He's already away, fourteen from fourteen balls faced.

People are at work, I suppose; more might filter down in the afternoon. The Shield is a tough competition, stacked with current and former Test players, household names. England's equivalent, county cricket, doesn't even come close. It isn't as populated with current Test players either, though a few imported internationals lift each team. And yet every county game – and there are a lot of them – draws a crowd. The fans know their cricket, too, the history, and the implications of every player's performance.

The loss of interest in the long-form game reflects a changing society. People lack the patience and the time. Knowledge of the game and an appreciation of its nuance and subtleties are slipping away. I position myself on the boundary fence, next to the sightscreen, behind the wicket, so as to better see Harrow, and the shots I'm hoping he'll play.

And he doesn't disappoint. Once Harrow passes fifty, his shoulders relax and he treats me to an extra cover drive. Not many can play it as he does. That knee, that left elbow, the full face of the bat, the angle of the ball heading to the boundary, like destiny itself. There are plenty of players who'll guts it out, carry their teams over the line. But a batter like Harrow, you'd travel across town, across the country, across the world even, to see him play. He just has that natural grace and beauty. The bat helps, of course. But watching him wield it is like watching music being made.

When the players take drinks, I wander around to the bar for a beer. There's only one station open in a sea of stations on my side of the ground. The young woman fills a plastic cup with Victoria Bitter, long-time partner of the game.

I used to bring Katie along for a day out during the school holidays. She seemed to appreciate the occasion. Pies and soft drink and ice creams probably helped. But we saw the G evolve and Victorian players on the rise. Those playing out their sunset days, too. We were all down on the fence on the final day, when Victoria won the Shield. I knew they would, not just on statistics, probability, matching up the players from each team. Their season had built momentum in a particular way. It's hard to stop the team that gels and believes they will win.

It all came down to the final over. Nate got a wicket with the last ball of his career. Not that we knew that then. He was carried off on the player's backs, the start of a festival for the team, the city and the state. The best night of his life, Nate would say later. Marlene and I walked to the tram holding hands, Jean, Katie and the girls running circles around the palm trees, grinning. Everyone is happy when they're part of a winning side.

Harrow cuts again, the ball flying out of reach of the diving fielder, and rolling over the boundary rope for FOUR. It brings up his hundred, from eighty-seven balls. He raises the bat, nods to the dressing room, and takes his mark again. He's on a mission, you can see it. The Vics are doing their best to help. The bowlers have lost their lengths in the onslaught, serving the ball up too short and wide, right in Harrow's sweet spot. The young all-rounder, Peters, looks like he's warming up – a powerful-looking bloke, probably a bit heavy to be truly quick. Ideally, at this level, an all-rounder is good enough to be selected on the strength of either discipline. His stats don't suggest that on the face of it. Not yet anyway. Too often all-rounders are selected on promise, in the hope that they'll give a team more versatility. It was true of Nate, too. He grew into his bowling with the Vics, working with the coach and players at the higher level.

I think of Nate every time I come to the G. Well, he's on my mind every day, but it's here that I can no longer push the thoughts away. He was at his best out on that field, bustling in to bowl for his state, muscling a win for his mates. I miss the way he played, the way he was in the world. So much.

When anyone takes their own life, it's hard not to be angry. But your own brother … The guilt, the questions. *Could I have done more?* The answer is always yes. I was too wrapped up in myself at the time, trying to making the business work, ends meet.

He left behind two little girls, a beautiful wife. Their marriage hadn't been unhappy, not until the injuries, the axing. Quite the opposite. I've not seen many couples so in love. But that was Nate; he didn't do anything by halves. When he crashed, everyone crashed with him.

I used to drop in on Jean and the girls for a time, but it was always Marlene who organised it. The girls are grown up now of course, still in Melbourne, with all Nate's energy. It isn't hard to pick up a phone, I know. The truth is it's painful. But I owe it to Nate.

After lunch, Queensland are still only two down, and Harrow takes on Peters again, depositing the ball over long on for SIX, taking him to one hundred and fifty-four from a hundred and twenty balls. If all Shield games were played at this pace, the crowds might return. A few more have dribbled in, hoping for a big score, and perhaps knowing what it will mean for Harrow. He's a good-looking lad, strong cheek and jawline, and a big smile; he'll be popular with the fans, no doubt.

The Queensland captain, Copperfield – or Copes, as they call him – goes for a patient thirty, having fed Harrow most of the strike before spooning one back to the bowler. Scoring slows leading into tea. The whole crowd is willing Harrow to cut loose, reach the milestone of legends, so we can relax, but he's not going to risk throwing it away.

The players file off the field. I had intended to head home, beat the rush, but as if I can, with Harrow not out on a hundred and ninety! I fetch myself another beer. There are two stations open now, the suits filing in after work. There's a bit of a buzz around the ground after all. A camera crew has turned up and, with the binoculars, I spot two of the national selectors in suits and sunglasses up in the Members'. We're all waiting for Harrow to take his mark again.

I open a packet of spicy nut mix and stretch my legs. The light is softening, a few clouds drifting in from the sea, the shadows getting long. The gulls have settled on the ground, dressed in white, in imitation of the players. It's been too long since I spent the day at the cricket.

I've finished my beer and a whole packet of nuts before the players return. The Vics are focused on denying Harrow his double, but he scores a single off the final ball of the over to retain the strike.

Third ball of the following over, Harrow gets the loose one he was waiting for and guides it to the boundary for FOUR. It wasn't much more than a caress of the ball, but it flies away off the bat. Even better than I had hoped.

The bowler runs in hard, tries to punish Harrow with a bouncer, but he's waiting for it. He hooks, and the ball flies off the middle of the bat, clearing the deep square boundary ten rows back. SIX. I'm on my feet before the umpire can raise his arms. Harrow has a double century for his state. The crowd stands, applauding him. Harrow grins and raises the bat above his head with both hands, like a trophy.

The dropping sun catches the face for a moment, lighting the willow like the day I first pulled the cleft from the stack. Maybe there really is some magic there. It's showing no sign of wear and tear, but taking on a new life, singing its own song.

hurrying on

Play had run past five-thirty, thanks to injury time and Queensland's slow over rate. South Australia had them on the ropes. And then Tank called an impromptu team meeting. They'd dropped three catches and the bowlers were missing their marks, forgetting their plans. Sky had picked up a calf strain in his first spell. He was suffering but wouldn't give up.

Copes tore into them, while they all stared at their feet. 'We were sloppy today. We all need to step up tomorrow and help Sky out.'

Tank nodded. 'I want to see you bowling in partnerships. Talking to each other. We've got to get them out early if we're a chance. Make sure you all get your rest. I want a hundred and fifty per cent tomorrow.'

Harrow glanced up at the clock. He was already late for dinner with Megan's parents. There was no time to go home and get changed. Klimt grimaced from across the room. He'd messaged Sean, to see if he could drop off a clean shirt, but Sean was much taller. Harrow would have to go with the jeans stuffed in the bottom of his locker and the old shoes in the boot of his car.

He had the quickest shower in history, dressed and styled his hair. At least he had clean socks and jocks, and his hair looked pretty good. He ran to the car park bare-chested, kitbag over his shoulder. Sean was waiting, holding a brightly patterned shirt, still on its hanger.

'Emergency wardrobe.'

'You're a legend.'

'I know,' Sean said. 'You owe me.'

The players had started dribbling out of the rooms to their cars, and someone wolf-whistled.

Sean turned.

'Don't worry about them,' Harrow said. 'Idiots.' He slipped on the shirt and buttoned it. A little tight across the chest, and not really him, but it would have to do. 'Tuck it in or leave it out?'

'I think, for the parentals, you have to go the tuck,' Sean said. 'I brought a belt.'

He found a park not too far from the restaurant and sprinted to the entrance. It was fancy, as he'd expected. He paused at the door and took a deep breath, his stomach churning. At least they weren't sitting right in the window. He spotted Megan up the back on the raised platform.

A waiter stepped between him and the stairs. 'Can I help you, sir?'

'I'm joining the Quigley table.' He smiled and gestured towards them with an open palm.

'Of course. Go on up.'

He took the stairs two at a time, heart pounding. It wasn't the first impression he'd hoped to make. Megan's face fell, just for a second, when she saw him. And then she smiled, with relief that he'd made it, probably, and everything was all right. Her arms were bare and he could see the outline of her body beneath her dress, which was going to be distracting.

Megan's father stood, placed his left hand on his tie and reached out with his right to shake Harrow's hand.

'Mr Quigley, so pleased to meet you.'

'And you, Todd.'

'Mrs Quigley.'

Her handshake was firm and her eyes intense. 'Please, call me Helena.'

'I'm so sorry I'm late.' He smiled. It was all he could do.

Megan slipped her arm around him. 'We've just ordered some starters.'

Megan's father lifted a bottle from the ice bucket. 'Champagne?'

'Just half a glass. I don't usually drink during a game.'

He filled Harrow's glass to exactly halfway. 'So. Not a great day in the field.'

Harrow shook his head. Megan had warned him that her father was direct. 'Terrible. You follow the cricket?'

'I do. Played for Air Force, back in the day. Though we barrack for South Australia, I'm afraid.' He smiled. 'We've been following your progress of course. An impressive season.'

'Thank you.'

'Once you're in the Australian team, we'll be able to cheer for you without any conflict,' said Helena. Her smile was a lot like Megan's, warming the room.

'You'll have to talk to the selectors about that,' Harrow said.

'Oh, I think your bat is doing the talking,' Mr Quigley said.

When the waiter arrived with champagne, Megan leaned in to whisper in his ear. 'Is that Sean's shirt?'

Harrow grinned. 'Yep.'

The waiter cleared their dessert plates and brought Megan's father an espresso. Harrow was grateful for the smell wafting over, rousing him a little. He could easily have nodded off at the table. He'd been up since five, a full day in the field, and stressing all afternoon about dinner. He needn't have worried, Megan's parents were charming and warm under all that formality. Still, he would make sure he was better dressed next time. Everyone would be more comfortable, especially him. He knew Megan was out of his league, that he had yet to prove himself but he would. He smothered a yawn and excused himself to go to the bathroom.

On the way back, he stopped at the bar to pay. The tables were emptying out, a big group milling around saying their goodbyes.

'How was everything?' The young woman in charge of front of house wasn't much older than him but intimidating, with pale makeup and black hair slicked back.

'Very good. Thank you.' It had been, too. Not just the food but conversation had flowed and he felt included, part of the family. He kept his face still when he saw the total and calculated a decent tip. He could afford it now. And he wanted to make the gesture, show that he could play the game at their level.

Megan smiled when he returned to the table. As if a conversation had been had. A good one.

'Our waiter tells me you've beaten me to the bill. Very generous. Thank you,' Mr Quigley said.

'My pleasure,' Harrow said.

'Well, we'd better let you get some rest, though wearing you out would be in South Australia's interests.'

'They're doing fine without my help. A strong squad this year.'

They got up from the table and Megan slipped her arm through his. The warmth from her body was intense. There was relief there but something else, their relationship more solid than before. He felt a little taller, if that was possible. He shook Mr Quigley's hand, but Helena leaned in for a hug.

'When you play in Adelaide next time, we'd love to have you over for a meal,' she said.

'And we'll come to the game of course,' Mr Quigley said.

The waiter held the door and they walked out into the Brisbane evening, arm in arm. The lights of the city were bright, the Story Bridge lit up in pink and purple, reflected, upside down, in the river. Curlews called from the park across the road.

'Your parents are really nice.'

Megan leaned into him. 'I love you,' she said.

Ashes squad announcement

The week leading up to the announcement of the Ashes squad was longer than a wet summer holiday when he was a kid. In the end the call came a day earlier than he'd expected, which was just was well, because he couldn't have gone another night without sleep. Megan was fed up, too. She was such a light sleeper; even if he didn't move, she seemed to sense that he was awake. Perhaps she was anxious about his selection, too, though she didn't say so. Either way, she left for work with bags under her eyes, carrying a second cup of coffee in her little thermos.

He was averaging the highest in the Shield by a good margin. He hadn't had much opportunity with the ball, but there had been a few good catches and a run-out. He was feeling sharp. Ready. Still, when the phone rang, he dropped it on the floor of Megan's bathroom and had to call the chair of selectors back.

'Congratulations, Todd. We were pleased with how you did in Sri Lanka, and you've had an excellent Shield season. The double hundred, of course. And your century in Hobart in tough conditions was particularly impressive, I thought. At this stage, you're in the squad as the extra batter. But I'm sure an opportunity will come over the summer. We think you're a very exciting young cricketer with a big future for Australia.'

You never wished anyone an injury, let alone a fellow opener, so he had to put that out of his mind. It was another step up, and he'd be training with the Australian team, coaches. Legends! That's what he needed to focus on.

When he rang Megan, she choked back a scream. 'I'm so proud of you, babe,' she said. And then, 'Thank, fuck. Now we might get some sleep.'

Harrow smiled into the phone.

'Have you told your parents?'

'I'll call them next.'

Dad picked up on the first ring. 'I'm just going to put you on speaker. Your mother is here, too.'

'Were you waiting?'

'We just had a feeling it would be today,' Mum said.

'Well, you were right. I'm in the Ashes squad.'

'*Yes*!!' Dad said.

He heard Mum whoop and slap the kitchen bench.

'We're so very proud of you, son.' Dad's voice broke up. 'We'll come down for the First Test.'

'I probably won't even play, Dad.'

'We'd be happy to see you run drinks,' Mum said. 'We just want to be part of it. We ARE part of it.'

'Okay. I'll see about tickets.'

'For the first day? You know we like the anthems and everything.'

'Sure, Dad,' he said. 'Is Liv at school?'

'She's here. Studying for exams,' Mum said. 'I'll take the phone in.'

He could hear how annoyed she was, at being interrupted. But Mum insisted.

'What?' Liv said.

'I'm in, Liv.'

When she finally spoke, he couldn't tell if she was crying or laughing. 'That's brilliant, Toddy.'

He found a parking spot right out the front of Megan's apartment. It was on the river in the newly developed part of New Farm. Or *re*developed, one of the old woolstores made over. He followed a man in a suit in through the security doors and took the stairs. He sometimes imagined he could still smell the wool, amid the cooking smells and scented candles.

He knocked even though Megan had given him a key. The good food smells were coming from her kitchen. She answered the door still in her work clothes, a bright apron over the top.

'Hey, handsome.'

He kissed her in the doorway, one hand on her waist, the other hiding the bottle of champagne behind his back. It still made him a little light-headed, kissing her.

'I thought I'd cook something to celebrate.'

There were flowers on the table, candles lit, music playing. The breeze off the river shifted the blinds. Two champagne glasses were already set out. Megan took the bottle from his outstretched hand, her fingers brushing his.

'How do you feel? Has it sunk in?'

He plucked an orange from the fruit bowl and spun it from one hand to the other. 'I don't know. I mean I probably won't even play. Not the First Test anyway. But it's another step up. Recognition.'

'Well, here's to being recognised.'

He put the orange back in the bowl and took the glass. 'Cheers.' He tinked the glass carefully against hers, and held her gaze a moment, the way she liked.

'What should I say? Train well?'

'I've just been trying to see it as another opportunity.'

'Smart.' Megan opened the oven a crack and peered in, checked the clock above the fridge. 'So I was thinking I'd like to go to the Brisbane game. I can take the Thursday and Friday off work.'

'Really? I mightn't even get on the field.'

She sipped her champagne and smiled. Like it was the most natural thing in the world to be standing there with him in her kitchen talking about playing in the First Test with the last light in her hair.

'I have a feeling you will,' she said. 'But even if you don't, I'd like to be there. And it's obviously easiest for me to go in Brisbane.'

'True.' He swallowed a mouthful of the champagne and tried to focus on the bubbles over his tongue, the cold feel of it going down. 'My parents are coming. And my sister.'

Megan filled a saucepan with water, lit the gas, and set it down. 'Good. It's about time I met them, don't you think?'

'Okay.' He blinked. 'I mean, yes. Of course, I want them to meet you.'

'But it might be a bit much on top of everything else?'

He nodded. 'Maybe.' How was it that she knew exactly what he was thinking, even when he could not have put words to it himself?

'What if we met beforehand, somehow? Something more relaxed.'

'Drinks maybe?'

She put the beans in the steamer and the steamer in the saucepan, put the lid back on. 'People at work kept coming up to me all afternoon.'

'You've told them about me?'

'Of course. And Nina said to tell you congratulations. Now that you are actually *in* the Australian squad. You're on an *upward trajectory*, she says.'

Harrow smiled.

'She's coming back, actually – misses us too much.'

'Good.' He sipped at the champagne, and set the glass down, although he would have liked to scull it, and another, to steady himself. 'Mum and Dad said they're going to buy every paper, just to see the squad list in print.'

'That's cute.' She turned off the oven and pulled out a tray of potatoes and paper-wrapped parcels. 'It's barramundi. I'm trying something new.'

'My favourite fish.'

'Did you get a bunch of calls?'

'Yeah,' he said. 'A lot of the guys I used to play with back on the coast. They'll all want free tickets now. Mads, from the Sri Lanka tour. Sky, Klimt and all the boys gave me heaps at training of course.' Tank had grumbled about their lack of focus but was smiling when he said it. And, when everyone was drifting off, he took the time to shake Harrow's hand. 'Enjoy the time with the Australian set-up, Hars. Just be yourself.'

'It's nice though, right?' She arranged the parcels and potatoes on the plates, added the beans.

'For sure.' Harrow carefully refilled their glasses and carried them to the table.

'You sure you want to come to the game?'

She nods. 'I want to be there. And I'll have to get used to this wives and girlfriends business sooner or later, right?'

He unwrapped the parcel, releasing a rush of steam, and felt his cheeks go hot. Not for the first time, he worried that she was too good for him.

'Why is it WAGs, by the way,' she said. 'As opposed to wives and partners. What about Klimt and Sean?'

'Everyone's cool with that. But no one really talks about it.' He shrugged. 'And I guess WAPs doesn't sound so good.'

'True.' She sipped her champagne. 'Well, I'm glad Olivia is going; she can explain what's happening – on and off the field.'

rub of the green

They all trained as if they'd play, but one of the quicks would likely miss out, two unless they didn't play a spinner. One of the batters would miss out, too. It would be him, but Harrow managed to block that out. He had to be ready to seize whatever opportunity came his way. Even if it was fielding for ten minutes while one of the bowlers came off to retape an ankle, he would make a contribution.

In the meantime, he was batting in the nets with players like Gibson and Barker, or Dog, as they called him. He soon let you know if you messed up. Harrow made sure to arrive first and leave last, absorbing every action, word, and war story. Their batting coach spent some time with Harrow in the nets the second afternoon. He didn't try to change too much, just pointed out what he did well, showed him what was happening with his head when he first started, when he was nervous. The movement left him a little unbalanced, opening him up.

He even had a bowl in front of their bowling coach, reassured by the hard leather and proud stitching of a new ball in his hands, something he could grip. Their leg spinner, Jacks, spent an hour with him, seeing what he could do. He encouraged Harrow to take his time composing himself before each ball, which took some doing when he was so pumped up. Jacks talked, too, about focusing on how to get the batter *out* rather than where he wanted to land the ball. At first that felt like getting ahead of himself, but the guy was an absolute wizard, and Harrow saw the results immediately the next day at training, bowling Barker around his legs.

Starting at the Gabba, where the nets and training facilities were like old friends, the ball coming on to the bat just the way he liked it, helped him settle. The quicks were giving him a workover, especially the West Australian left-armer, Slim, who hit Harrow on the gloves, helmet, and box. That laid him out flat on his back, knees up, seeing bright white light until the pain began to subside, which had Slim, and all the boys, laughing their guts out.

Hilton was in the squad, too, a late inclusion after Russell pulled out with stress fractures in his back. When one of Hilt's bouncers hit Harrow on the biceps, he just shook his head and grinned. Who would've thought, back in Port Macquarie, that they'd both be in an Ashes squad? Those dreams seemed boyish now but somehow he and Hilt had made them a reality.

Drinks with Mum, Dad and Liv had been easier than he expected. Megan was charming, and his parents were just themselves, as ever. This time he'd invested in new pants, shoes, a nice shirt and tie. It had been worth it, too, for the smile on Megan's face when she saw him, to feel a match for her. She wore a new dress, as he knew she would, from the little store with the unpronounceable name she liked, in the city. Mum exclaimed over the *gorgeous* fabric. They talked cricket of course, but not just that. About her growing up in Malaysia, the orangutans in Borneo, and his parents' cheese business. They brought along a gourmet gift basket and invited her up to see the farm.

He needn't have worried about whether Megan and Liv would get along. They talked shop: *the law.* Liv had been accepted early at the University of Queensland, under some special scheme. She was already playing cricket for them, batting at five, and first change bowler. Megan asked Liv about the areas she was interested in specialising in, which was more than he'd ever managed to do. He'd never even heard of environmental law, though now that he thought about it, that was kind of what

Megan did. When Megan gave Liv some careful advice about being a female solicitor in a big firm, Harrow recognised the frown on Liv's face. It sounded a lot like cricket; being the best wouldn't necessarily be enough.

Dad had taken him aside afterwards. 'She's a great girl, son. Hang on to this one.' Megan would have something to say at being called a girl, but Dad meant well. And she was great – and even prepared to spend a day at the cricket. She didn't seem to care that he wasn't well-read and had only ever travelled with a cricket team and coach.

'You're smart,' she said. 'I just want to be with someone who makes me laugh. Besides, you're *kind*. It's not as common as it should be.'

After training he packed up his kitbag and wandered through the stands, to where he and Liv had sat as children. The Gabba was still his favourite ground, the way the field seemed to rise up before him as he walked down to the boundary fence. The hill was gone now, a bit of a shame, but it was still beautiful. Perfect sightlines, the scalloped awning, the multi-coloured seats around the ground. The new light towers, on an even larger scale, were like something from the future.

Commentators liked to say the Gabba lacked atmosphere, but that was just the usual bias from southerners. The Woolloongabba ground, in a previous iteration, was where the tied Test with Worrell's West Indies happened, way back in 1960. The First Test of the summer was nearly always played at the Gabba. And for good reason; it was Fortress Australia – the Gabbattoir. The bounce and pace of the pitch had upset plenty of touring teams, causing carnage and collapses. Especially the English. There would be early wickets, and then they had to tough it out in the blazing afternoon Queensland sun, the rowdy, beer-swilling, crowd giving them heaps from the boundary. It was how every home series began.

Game day dawned clear and bright. They were playing a warm-up game of soccer, out on the ground. A way of loosening up the mind, too. Harrow took shot at goal, missed, and dropped back. He was so distracted at the thought of Megan sitting up in the stands all day with Liv, Mum and Dad, plus Sky and all the Queensland boys set for a big day out, that he barely registered Macca going down while intercepting Gibbo's pass. The poor bloke had had that many hamstring problems you could write a book. He was built, so much power, but those big hammies, glutes and calves kept pulling away from the bone, as if they were too big for his body.

When he didn't get up, the physio jogged out and squatted beside him. It was only when Macca dropped his head in his hands, and Slim and the physio had to help him to his feet, that Harrow stopped.

This was how it happened. The rub of the green – that touch of the playing surface on bat, ball, player, team. Your luck could change in a moment. For Macca, finally getting back to full fitness, back in the team to open the First Ashes Test for his country, everyone saying it was his series to shine, and then *snap*, one lunge and it was gone. Instead, months of rehab, watching the summer play on without him from the couch. Cricket could be cruel.

But for Harrow, it was his big break. He had sixty minutes to regroup, prepare to bat, maybe even open the innings for his country in the First Test of an Ashes series, at the Gabba.

Somehow the staff found Megan, Liv, Mum and Dad and brought them down for the presentation. Damien Martyn happened to be in the Members' and had been roped into presenting Harrow with his baggy green. Only his favourite batter of all time! How good was that?

'There's a lot of value placed on this cap,' Martyn said. 'It doesn't make you any better than anyone else. But if you play with humility, with integrity, with complete commitment to this team … the people, our cricket family, will ride with you through the highs. And, when the lows come – and they will come – the cricket family will be there for you.'

Harrow didn't trust himself to speak, just shook Martyn's hand and nodded, took the brand-new green woollen cap, his very own number sewn beneath the Australian coat of arms, and fitted it on his head, grinning.

All the times he'd imagined the moment, and now it was actually happening. The current players – his new teammates – and coaching staff all shook his hand, slapped his back, put a hand on his shoulder. Megan was smiling, so still and perfect there in her flowery dress, taking everything in her stride.

Martyn was generous enough to pose for a family photo. Dad shook his hand, beaming, and Liv, all dressed up in a linen suit and her hair tied back, told him they'd been there for his innings in Brisbane. And then Martyn was gone, back to his own family, and a day out at the cricket.

Mum was crying and laughing and shaking her head. 'All those years spent sitting around at cricket grounds, just to see you in that hat!'

Dad held him in a long hug. 'Go well, son.'

Even Liv was wiping her eyes. But that didn't stop her punching him hard in the arm. 'Now, don't fuck it up.'

First Test

I turn up the radio. Harrow is playing the First Test! Sometimes the cricket gods have their own way of getting the right players on the field. McCann has been given more lives than a litter of pedigree cats. If it's not an injury, it's giving his wicket away at the worst possible moment. Jimmy Maxwell, the voice of cricket, lists Harrow's first-class statistics, comparing him to the greats: Bradman, Trumper, Ponting. The stage is set.

When I was a boy, I listened to the Ashes all night on the radio. That was the only way to follow it live. My mother never knew I went five days without sleep, five times during winter. I'd nod off through lunch and tea but wake up when play resumed, making sure I heard every ball bowled. These days, I watch it on the box but with the sound turned down. I prefer the ABC radio commentators. Their tone and style is more harmonious with the pace of the game. Though there's a slight time delay now, deliberate on the part of the television broadcasters, I think, which means if I've wandered away from the screen, I have time to get back to see the shot or fall of wicket after hearing Maxwell and company call it.

Nothing beats the anticipation leading up to the first morning of the first Test in an Ashes series. The build-up in the media, final composition of the teams, the pitch, weather conditions, quirks of the ground – a myriad of variables. The captains are walking out to the middle in their blazers, where the Channel Nine commentators are waiting, baking in suits and ties.

Barker, as home captain, tosses the coin high in the air. For a moment, the tiny metal disc is spinning. Time is suspended, and no one knows how the session, the day, the Test, the series, will turn out. Anything is possible.

'Heads,' calls Ashton.

The coin falls onto the pitch. The match referee bends to examine the upward face. 'Tails.'

'We're going to have a bat,' Barker says.

Yes!

I make a cup of tea and sit down to watch the Welcome to Country and the anthems. I want to see Harrow's face, his comrades' arms around him. Hopefully they'll show the footage of him receiving his baggy green at some stage. But the phone is ringing. It's the business line, too, so I make myself get up out of my chair to answer it, though nobody who knows anything about cricket would be calling *now*.

'Reader bats.' I stretch out the phone cord so that I can still see the players standing, arms around each other in a line. They're a fine-looking bunch, the right mix of experience and youth, their expressions a mix of pride and determination. Harrow is between Gibson and Davis, grinning, as if he can't believe he's out there. And he's padded up. He's going to open the batting.

'Dad, it's Kate.'

'Hey, love,' I say. 'Are you okay?'

I can hear voices, some sort of loudspeaker announcement. 'Listen. Could you pick me up from the station?'

'You're coming to Melbourne?'

'I'm here actually. At Flinders Street. I have … a few bags.' Her voice breaks up.

I blink. The players are running from the field to prepare for the start of play. 'On my way, love. I'll pull in near the National Gallery there.'

'Thanks, Dad.'

'I'll be about twenty minutes. Maybe grab a coffee?'

It will be the first time I've ever missed the start of play in the First Test. But it isn't every day your daughter calls for help. A quick look in her old room confirms that it could do with a clean. I open the windows, strip the bed, and put the sheets on to wash.

We can figure the rest out later. Hopefully Harrow is still in when I get back.

I find a place to pull over, ignoring car horns and the police car parked across the road. Katie has darkened her hair and cut it just below the ear. It suits her, though she looks small, standing there on the side of the road. I turn the radio down. Harrow has been beaten a few times and struck on the shoulder. He didn't even wince, Maxwell says. I squeeze out and flip the tray cover.

'Hey, Kiddo.'

'Dad,' she says. 'Thanks for this.'

'Not a problem.' I load her overseas suitcase, tote bag and an overfull backpack into the back. It isn't an overnight stay.

I focus on the traffic moving all around. Mid-morning isn't too bad, but it's not often I drive in the city these days.

'New ute?'

'I've had it a little while now.' Since her mother left and took the station wagon. I had to deliver the batch of bats due that day by taxi.

'Why didn't you answer your mobile?'

'It was on silent. Sorry.' The phone was a gift from Katie so I can't exactly say I don't like carrying it around.

She shakes her head and turns up the radio. I expect her to grimace, but she cocks her head to hear the score. 'We're batting?'

'Yep,' I say. 'The first few overs were really tight. Good line and length from the English bowlers.' But Harrow has battled through and is starting to score. He wasn't intimidated by the two veterans or the occasion. It might be one of those battles within the battle that sets the course of the series. That's what I love about Test cricket. Something that happens in the first hour of the First Test can have an impact on the last hour of the Fifth Test. Cracks appear, psychological pressure builds, and then one team takes the opportunity when it's presented.

'Sorry. I didn't realise until I saw it on the screen in the café.'

I shake my head. 'Happy to see you anytime.'

She watches the shops, suburbs and signs flashing by, face unreadable. As far as I know, it's been at least a year since she was in Melbourne. Not last Christmas but the one before. I hear that *crack*, unmistakeable even through the ute's speakers. Harrow has hit his first boundary, moving into the twenties.

'I've left David.'

I keep my eyes on the road. 'For good?'

She nods.

'You can stay as long as you need, love.'

'He doesn't know where I am. I'd like to keep it that way.'

The traffic is backed up ahead of us, my blood pressure rising. But I mustn't push. 'Got it.'

I take our exit and she lets out some air at all the development, the new freeway going in, dust and rubbish whipping around where once there was scrub and birdlife. It's good to see it through her eyes; I've grown numb, seeing so much change so fast. We cross the West Gate Bridge, that gave the city so much, but has taken its share, too. Thirty-five workers killed during its construction, most of them sitting eating their lunch beneath the span as it fell.

When we pull into the driveway, Katie's body softens. We unload her bags and carry them inside. I catch her looking over the garden from the deck, towards the workshop.

'I need to dry the sheets. I'll make the bed later,' I say.

'I can do it,' she says. She places her things inside the room, by her old trunk, and removes her shoes. She comes out to the lounge barefoot, somehow fragile in the house of her childhood.

'Cup of tea? A sandwich?'

'That would be great.' She turns on the TV and the radio and sits in the chair next to mine. 'So what's this English team like then?'

'On paper, pretty good. But a lot of them haven't played here before. And a couple of their greats, the bowlers, are on the wrong side of thirty-three. I guess we'll see.'

She nods, staring at the screen. I put the sheets in the dryer, boil the kettle, and make us a couple of toasted sandwiches. Ham, cheese and tomato with a few fresh spinach leaves. I have a hundred questions queuing, like what the hell David has done and why she didn't go to her mother's but it can wait.

From the sound of the applause, and Maxwell's superlatives, Harrow has scored another boundary. They've reached fifty with none down, which is a great start. Maxwell and O'Keeffe (or Skull, as they call him) are praising Harrow's temperament.

It's helping him to have O'Neil down the other end. He wouldn't raise an eyebrow in a cyclone, as O'Keeffe puts it. Of the current commentators, these two are my favourites. O'Keeffe provides the humour, Maxwell the experience and calm. He learned from McGilvray, the father of cricket radio in this country, who understood that cricket is an art. Like all the arts, it has a technical foundation. You don't need technical knowledge to enjoy it, but commentary and analysis not based in technical knowledge is just half-baked opinion – in my opinion.

'Hey, Dad.'

'Yeah, love?'

'This guy, Harrow, has one of your bats!'

I cut the sandwiches in half and set them on matching plates. 'I made it for him. How's he doing?'

'He's timing them well. If he makes a hundred, you might get a few orders.' She takes the plate and cup, and I head back into the kitchen for mine.

'Don't go jinxing him now. He's on debut.'

'Really? He looks like he belongs there.'

Katie and I don't dare move. Harrow is on ninety-two. He's been playing freely but hasn't scored for the last three overs. Barker is still out there with him. He's got a good head on his shoulders – and he's scored enough hundreds himself. Harrow couldn't have a better batting partner for the occasion. The cameras keep panning in on Harrow's family, chewing their nails. His partner – an attractive blonde with a lovely smile. And, Olivia, his sister, seated between their parents, an up-and-coming all-rounder, Maxwell says. No wonder she had looked familiar.

Harrow cracks one away through mid-wicket. It's uppish, but just wide of the fielder, and the ball runs over the rope for FOUR. Locke, one arm heavily tattooed, watches it go with his hands on his hips. He's making his way back from shoulder surgery and yet to look anything near as threatening as he was.

The next ball is full and straight, rapping Harrow on the front pad. He starts to run but is sent back by Barker. The English are still appealing.

'Oh god. I can't stand it,' Katie says.

'Missing leg stump,' I say.

The umpire shakes his head. Locke turns on his heel. The English captain polishes the ball furiously on the leg of his whites and throws it to Locke's bowling partner, Patten, who walks him back to the top of his mark, offering advice. Locke steams in again. It's short of a length. Harrow drops back in his crease and cuts. The fielder at point dives valiantly, but the ball is already past him, and runs away for FOUR.

'Oh yeah!' Katie slaps the arm of the chair.

Harrow leaps high into the air and pumps his gloved fist. Barker waits, smiling. They come together, mid-pitch, and embrace. Harrow removes his helmet, kisses the Australian crest. He points the bat at his family, thumps his chest. They're standing close together, arms raised, applauding. His partner wipes the corners of her eyes. Harrow taps the label of the bat, holds it high, and turns, acknowledging the crowd, right around the ground, charming even the Barmy Army with that boyish grin.

I'm finishing my second bat for the morning, going over it by hand with superfine paper, by the time Katie wanders down, spooning cereal from a bowl. 'Morning.'

'Morning.' She chews slowly and looks around, tilting her head at the radio. Grieg's 'The Bridal Procession' from *Peer Gynt*. Not at all appropriate but she won't recognise it. I'm pretty relieved she won't be marrying David, though it isn't the time to say so. More than anything, I'm glad to have her home.

'No cricket?'

'Hasn't started yet. They're an hour behind in Brisbane.' I'm still savouring Harrow's hundred. He was out four balls later, caught in the gully. All the adrenaline, no doubt, but he'd hardly made a false stroke until then. The team was buoyed by a new player making his debut, everyone sharp and happy. What a day. And four more to look forward to!

In the press conference afterwards, Harrow was bright-eyed and still grinning. 'I'm pinching myself, to be honest.' He thought to thank his family, coach and manager, and even mentioned me – or the bat – calling it his 'little bit of Reader magic'.

Katie sets herself on the quilter's stool to watch me work. Her face is softer than yesterday, but it's hard to tell what's going on underneath.

'Sleep okay?'

'Best for ages,' she says. 'Phone been ringing off the hook this morning?'

'A couple of orders.' One from the Victorian Under-19s coach. For the whole squad, which is promising.

'Cool. Who are these for?'

'A batch of second-grade bats. For the shop really, to keep a bit of stock on hand.'

'How's business going?'

I shrug. 'Never going to make me a millionaire.'

'But you love it, right?'

'I do.'

'Well, that's most important.' She wipes milk from her mouth with the back of her hand and places her empty cereal bowl on the bricks.

'Anything you need to do or organise today?' I say. 'Should we get some groceries? Things you like to eat?'

'I can go out for groceries.' She pulls a face I can't read. One of those mannerisms she picked up while I wasn't looking. Or after she left home, perhaps. 'Is it okay if I stay a while?'

'As long as you like.'

'The thing is,' she says, 'I've quit my job, too. It was a toxic workplace, and this guy, my boss, he made things hard for me. With everything going on at home, I just couldn't handle it.'

I stop sanding. It's the most she's shared in years.

'I won't get paid for a week or so. Then it will be, like, a payout, I guess. But not a huge amount.'

'There's no need to worry about money.' But my guts twist. There isn't exactly a lot of cash floating around at the moment

She watches a magpie on the lawn, white and black on green, like an umpire. 'Dave emptied our joint account. I have a few hundred bucks in my pocket. But I'm pretty well fucked, really.'

'Sounds like we'd better find you a solicitor.'

She nods. 'I just need a day or two to clear my head first.'

'Okay.'

'Besides, the cricket is on,' she says. 'Maybe we can have a few beers this afternoon?'

'Absolutely.'

Australia finished day one six down for two hundred and sixty-eight. They should be able to improve on that; Gibson is still out there, and our tailenders are always good for a few runs. Then I'm looking forward to seeing what the Australian bowlers can do with the new ball, how many English wickets they can snare by the close of play. Perhaps Harrow will take a catch or even have a bowl. Having Katie around has me feeling even more optimistic about our chances.

Second Test

He took a moment to take it all in before entering the ground. It didn't get much better than turning up to the white-domed Adelaide Oval on game day with the boys, sun shining, one up in the series and an Ashes century under his belt. England had capitulated in Brisbane, all out for eighty-seven and then, following on, for a hundred and forty. The game was over in three days. The South Australian crowd was pouring in to see more of the same.

The old scoreboard watched on from the treed hill area, full of families set for a day out. The outfield was mown in green cross-hatch, the pitch flat and dry. England had been forced to make two changes, while Australia's side remained the same. Even England winning the toss and choosing to bat couldn't put a dent in the day.

Dog asked Harrow to field at second slip, which felt like a promotion. He fielded there for Queensland, too, so it was a reflex for the body, watching the ball out of the bowler's hand, getting his stance right, his distance from Dog at first slip and French at third, Davis behind the stumps. They were always in his peripheral vision, such that he became accustomed to their movements, body language, as if they were extensions of him, or him of them. And it meant being right in the game, Dog throwing him the ball, keeping his hands warm, his body limber in the crouch down, hopping to his feet after the ball was bowled, clapping the bowler on, and examining every detail of the English openers: their techniques, mannerisms, flaws and flourishes.

Megan and her parents were up in the Members' Stand, watching. It was great to have them up there but also a pressure;

he couldn't help wanting to impress. He'd have to put that out of his head when he got to bat.

At drinks, England was none down for fifty-four and Harrow was fielding back out in the covers. Not the start they'd hoped for. There wasn't much for the bowlers in the pitch. Slim had had a leg-before shout turned down and a tough chance go down at gully. He was starting to drag his feet.

Dog pulled them into a huddle. 'We're still right in this. If everyone can just find an extra one per cent, we can break it open.'

Slim and Jacks got a good bowling partnership going, backed up by a couple of diving saves – one of them Harrow's, earning him a pat on the butt from the boys. After three back-to-back maidens, their energy was up. Ingram, the younger of the English openers, was still on nineteen, scratching at the crease, fiddling with his box and pads, starting to look anxious. The Adelaide crowd's attention hadn't wavered for a moment. They could sense the game shifting.

When Ingram slashed one through mid-wicket and called 'yes', Gibbo threw himself at the ball, seizing it mid-air, full-horizontal, and throwing in a single fluid movement. He hit the stumps, with Jones still grounding his bat at the other end. The roar of the crowd, the movement of them coming to their feet, gave Harrow goosebumps. The boys appealed as one animal, whooping and crowing. The umpires called for a replay. They had to watch it four times before it was given out and Jones trudged back to the dressing room, yet to make his mark on the series.

With a new batter for Slim to bowl at, Harrow was back at second slip. Slim found some extra zip for the English captain, Ashton, using the bouncer well to work him over. His wicket was the big prize. When a brute of a ball struck Ashton on the shoulder, Davis made sure to remind him of his poor record in Australia from behind the stumps, trying to get under his skin.

Meanwhile, Armstrong was bowling like a metronome at the other end, honing-in on off stump. He reminded him of Sky, so relentless. Three overs later, Ashton was still on nought, and Harrow could see the fear in his eyes.

When the opportunity came, Harrow had to leap, throwing up his right hand. And it stuck! The boys were to him before the umpire raised his finger, slapping his body, messing up his hair.

'Course, if you weren't so short, you wouldn't have to jump,' Slim said.

Harrow just grinned. How could he not. The English Captain out for one!

The second opportunity was low to his left. He went forward, both hands, and closed his fingers around the ball just above the turf. OUT. Slim ran down the pitch, arms outstretched like an aeroplane.

Coming into such a great and settled team, being made so welcome and, best of all, contributing, Harrow couldn't help but lift. Every cell of his being was absolutely alive, synched with the ball, the shifts and currents of the game, his teammates, the crowd. The team's confidence was up, they were riding the momentum, forcing their way back into the game. It was about belief, believing they could win.

Dog clapped his hands. 'C'mon, boys. Keep pushing. Foot on the throat, now.'

England were all out before lunch on day two and Harrow couldn't wait to get started. By the end of the second over, he'd raced to ten. The English bowlers looked as flat as the pitch and the sun was shining. It was time to cash in. O'Neil got his fifty and then gave it away, caught in the gully. Harrow batted on, slow and steady, with Dog and then Gibbo, determined to make it another big one.

He loved the Gabba but the Adelaide Oval was his favourite place to bat. The wicket always played so true. The crowd loved their cricket, too. He'd picked out Megan, from her green dress, by the end of the first over, sitting between her parents. Harrow acknowledged them when he finally reached fifty. He was so much more comfortable in his whites than in fancy restaurants. It was on the field that he could prove himself.

He set his sights on building a big partnership with Gibbo. He was great to bat with, turning over the strike, calling 'YES' or 'NO RUN' so loud and clear, and always cracking jokes between overs, usually at the expense of the English players. Some of his local Peramangk mob had turned up to watch the game. They were still giving him shit about not playing AFL, he said. Gibbo rolled up his shirt sleeves and put on a show, demonstrating why cricket was better. He hit a massive SIX into the second tier of the Bradman Stand and then executed a perfect cover drive, with an exaggerated high elbow. He was *on* and the crowd loved it. Harrow was happy to play second fiddle, giving Gibbo the bulk of the strike.

When Gibbo powered into the nineties, a group of men on the fence starting booing, yelling insults. Drunk, by the look of them. Gibbo glared but said nothing. But with his first Test hundred in sight, he was suddenly shaky, almost chopping on. Harrow was in the nineties, too, but tried to keep everything calm, standing with Gibbo during the break in play while police removed the men, who were not happy. It was a disruption for sure, stemming the flow of runs.

Two overs later, Gibbo was on ninety-six, and Harrow, down at the non-striker's end, was getting nervous for him, wanting him to just get it done.

And then, *crack*, Gibbo brought up his maiden Test century with another classic on-drive. Gibbo roared, really let it all out. He nearly crushed Harrow in a man hug, lifting him from the ground. The whole squad was out on the balcony, clapping and whistling.

Gibbo acknowledged his supporters with his bat, the Aboriginal flag draped over the fence at mid-on. He didn't carry on kissing the Australian badge, just raised his fist, and tapped the skin on his forearm. There were boos from the shaded area beneath the trees, but most of the crowd was with him. And why the hell not, he was winning the game for Australia. Harrow leaned on his bat, smiling. The atmosphere had turned electric, and he was out there, part of it.

Gibbo was pumped, smashing a FOUR and a SIX before holing out on a hundred and eighteen. That was how he played, what was good about him. Harrow brought up his century the following over, with a pull shot. He was hardly doing a thing; it was the bat, playing through him. He leapt and raised his face to the sky, before composing himself acknowledging his teammates, Megan, her parents, and the Adelaide crowd.

It wasn't premeditated, it just came, the three-swish flourish of his bat, held out in front of him, like a sword. The slight bow. And the crowd loved it. In a way, it meant more than the first century, proving it hadn't been a fluke. He was no flash in the pan. And this time, he wanted to cash in, push the scoring along, and make it a big one.

At close of play he was not out on a hundred and forty-two. Australia was four down for two hundred and nighty-eight. But a worrying band of high cloud had appeared on the horizon.

They lost a full day to rain. The bowlers sat in a circle, playing poker. Jacks was some sort of shark, winning round after round, but McAllister was the dark horse, often cleaning up right at the end. The stakes were low, Slim said, but Armstrong looked so glum every time he said, 'I've got nothing.' Sky would fit right in, when he got his chance.

O'Neil, French and Davis did cryptic crosswords, while Harrow worked his way through the weekend papers. There was a long article on one of Megan's 'matters before the court'. A shipping company notorious for oil spills had another ship run aground, on a coral reef. Not that he could say anything to the boys, but it did help him understand why she'd had to fly home after his innings. To brief the barrister, she'd said.

Meanwhile, Dog and Winslow, their head coach, were busy dealing with the media storm that had erupted over Gibbo's response to getting his century. Out on the field, it had just seemed right. But now it had been blown out of all proportion.

It's 'just not cricket' said one headline, while another called cricket the 'last great white male society'. Maybe they hadn't been to the subcontinent or seen his sister play. But when he read the piece, he knew Liv would agree with most of it.

'This wouldn't be half as big a thing if we could just get out on the field,' Gibbo said, head resting on his forearms, watching the rain.

'Shouldn't even be a thing,' said Harrow.

Gibbo smiled. 'Ah. But it is.'

Eventually Gibbo agreed to do an interview with Fox Sports. Dog said he didn't have to, and the boys offered to go with him, to stand united as a team, but Gibbo shook his head and walked downstairs alone. His line, about being proud to play for his country but not proud of what his country had done to his people, would be replayed the rest of the summer.

Third Test

'What can I do?'

Katie is up early, dressed in old jeans, boots and a long-sleeved shirt that has been worn for at least one painting job. After the draw in Adelaide, Australia is in a good position to pile on the pressure on the bouncy WACA pitch.

'You remember how to finish?'

'Like, the sanding, on the lathe?'

'I have a machine now.' I walk her over to it. 'There's the rest of this batch. You need to use three grades, starting from this one getting finer. It's easier if you do them all on one grade, then change the paper, and so on.'

'Okay.'

'It grabs a bit, so you need to hang on to the bat. And keep your hands well away from the paper.'

'Got it.'

I fetch a new face mask, goggles, an old pair of earmuffs and place them on the bench beside her. I don't wear any gear for sanding, so am not in a position to lecture. But she puts them all on and gets to work.

I watch her for a moment, her movements smooth and confident, working with the grain. Her help frees me up to get on top of the new orders and take my time picking out the right clefts for each bat. I find myself walking along the rows with a spring in my step, a little more willow and a little less batmaker. It's nice having company, even if the circumstances aren't great.

I trim and press three blades and cut in the splices. It's nearly lunchtime for us when the game starts in Perth, and by then I've glued in two handles and left them in the vices to set. For a real production line, I'd need more benches, more vices. And less cricket to watch. But I'm already producing half as much again.

I switch on the radio. England wins the toss and will bat first. Australia has brought in the young gun, Hilton, for McAllister, who has a stress fracture in his front foot. Fast bowling is rough on young men's bodies, their bones not fully hardened until their mid-twenties.

Katie carries one of the bats over to show me. 'Okay? I haven't taken too much off?'

I run my hands over it. 'Perfect.'

'What next?'

'The handles. But that's a bit tricky.'

'Show me.'

'Okay.'

We turn to the radio, drawn by Maxwell's rising voice. 'Hilton has got him playing and he's *nicked* it. Jones is OUT. First ball of the match! The ball moved away a fraction, just kissed the edge of the bat, the catch was chest high, and well taken by Harrow at second slip.'

'They've got this, Dad.'

'It's a good start. A very good start.'

I show her how to flatten out the handles on the machine and sand them down by hand. 'Just use your own grip as a measure,' I say. 'What feels natural. Most of these will go to under-sixteens, about your size.'

She pulls a face but nods.

We wait to hear the last ball of the over, sensing something. Ashton, coming in at number three, still hasn't scored. Hilton is steaming in, his Test career off to a dream start. 'BOWLED!' The sound, of the stumps being knocked out of the ground, is unmistakeable. 'The English captain is OUT for a *duck*. The stumps are scattered and the team is in total disarray.'

Katie pumps her fist. 'I don't remember cricket being this exciting,' she says.

Maxwell is still going, describing Ashton trudging from the field, head down. I can see it as if it's on screen.

'What next?'

'You could string the handles if you like? Finish them off?'

'You'd better show me,' she says.

I set up a bat up on the lathe and show her the process for starting and ending. 'The tuck is the trick.'

She did the next one herself.

'You're a natural.'

'Watched you enough when I was small.'

I nudge her boots with one of mine. 'Steel-caps?'

'Yep.'

'Much call for those in the office?'

She smiles. For the first time since she came to stay, I think. 'I did a woodworking course last summer. Steel-caps were compulsory.'

'That explains a few things,' I say. Her skills weren't all my doing after all. 'Where?'

She shrugs. 'Just at the arts centre.'

'Any good?'

'I loved it. We did some basic joinery and then woodturning. I wanted to do more, just … Things got a bit hectic at home.'

We grin at each other as the next wicket falls. Ingram out for ten. Three down for thirty-seven.

'I thought I might clean up the shopfront today,' Katie says.

'You don't have to do that.'

'May as well have everything looking schmick,' she says. 'We could make a new display?'

'Okay.' I watch her walk up the steps. There's still no sign of her calling the solicitor. Her laptop doesn't appear to have come out of its case, but she seems a little happier each day, and I'm reluctant to interrupt that process. She's eating, sleeping, smiling more often.

After bowling the English out for a hundred and thirty-four, the Australians will head back in this morning, none down for a hundred and fifty, and looking to build a good lead. Harrow survived an early leg before wicket shout but has been faultless since. He'll resume on seventy, hunting for another century.

I sense, rather than hear, something happening, and shut off the press. It isn't the cricket but raised voices from the shopfront. I'm through the doorway before I've registered moving. Light is streaming through the freshly cleaned windows, like a proper showroom. But it has let something else in. Katie is behind the counter, backed up against the display cabinets. It's Dave on the other side, looking way too angry for my liking.

'David,' I say in my deepest voice.

'Hi, Allan.'

'I was just asking Dave to leave,' Katie says.

'That sounds like a good idea.' I pick up the closest bat, hold it loosely by the handle, and take one step forward.

Katie puts her hand on the phone.

'I only want to talk,' Dave says.

Katie shakes her head. 'I'm not coming back, Dave.'

I take another step. A crow is cawing from the powerline out on the street, Dave's car, with its New South Wales plates, is badly parked underneath.

His face and neck turn red, but he leaves, banging the door. The bell is still clanging when the car starts and he roars off. I lock the door, lean the bat beside it, and go to Katie. She feels like a little girl in my arms, but I'm beginning to see that she is one strong young woman. 'Should I call the police?'

She shakes her head. 'He just … doesn't understand *no*.'

'You don't think he'll come back?'

'He's a coward at heart,' she says. 'You were great, Dad.'

I hold out my hand, trembling like an old man's.

'Have you done that before?' She gestures to the bat.

'Not in a long time.' Not since the days when I had to bail Nate out of a scrape or two. Literally in one case, when he was picked up for drink-driving after a Shield game. 'Should we have a break? Take the afternoon off?'

She takes a breath and releases it. 'Let's finish this,' she says.

Like her old man, she likes to keep busy when upset. 'Should I bring out some bats, put them in the window?'

'Sure. Do you have an old packing case or something?'

'I'll have a look.'

The cricket hasn't stopped for us. Harrow is out for eighty-three but Australia leads by over a hundred runs with only three down. I turn the radio off, so as to better hear any disturbance. I lock the gate and check the lane: just the bakery van and my neighbour backing out of his garage. The overgrown wisteria grabs at my hair, as if to encourage me to pause, smell its blossom.

I carry the bats through in three lots and stand an old soft drink crate on its end, like a wicket, and lean the bats against it.

Katie hops up in the window and makes a few adjustments. 'That's good. Do you have a box of balls? And what about that picture of Great-grandfather?' she says. 'There's a hook here.'

I hesitate; it's one of my most treasured possessions, though probably not worth anything to anyone else. He's sitting at his bench, in morning light, wearing glasses by then, but back straight, jaw firm, shaving down a bat, willow curls piling up around him.

When I return, she's filled out the window with pads and gloves, which I also sell, though not in any committed sort of way. She takes the picture from me. 'You're a lot alike,' she says. 'It must have been amazing, to see that workshop, learn from him.'

'One of the best times of my life, though I didn't recognise it the time.' With Mum sick, it had been mixed with sadness, of course, but the making of me all the same.

She glances at me but says nothing. The balls go in, amid the bats.

'I brought in a couple of clefts, too.'

'That's good. To remind people that these bats are made by hand. From real willow,' she says. 'And what about some shavings, like in the picture.'

We have an early dinner and set ourselves up to watch the final session. England are fighting, scratching their way to a hundred and ninety-nine. Their keeper, Millet, who plays for Worcestershire back home, is batting with the tail, desperate to put a lead on the board, something for their bowlers to work with. He runs the ball down to long on, to reach his fifty.

'Have you spoken to your mother?'

'I saw her before I left,' Katie says.

'How's she doing?'

'Okay. She's teaching at the college.'

'She liking it?'

'Creepy building, if you ask me, but she loves it. A good community.'

'A lot of history in that sandstone.' Callan Park, too. Not all of it good. The jacarandas in spring were more spectacular every year, softening the lingering pains from the folks who were housed in what was once a psychiatric hospital. 'All that green space, right in the city. The developers must have their eyes on it.'

'She's painting again, too. Preparing for a show next year.'

'At the SCA? That's a great gallery space – all those arches and high ceilings, like a church.'

'I think so. She's living in a shoebox, but that's Sydney for you.'

Of course – she wouldn't have room for Katie in her place. 'You didn't like it?'

'The city is fine, bright and sparkly. It was my *life* I didn't like. I needed to come back to Melbourne. Besides,' she says, nudging my boot with hers, 'I wanted to spend some time here, hanging out with you.'

Harrow chases a ball to the boundary, dives to cut it off, and leaps to his feet, throwing the ball back in right over the stumps.

'Have you told your mother about Dave?'

She nods.

'I was starting to worry, not hearing from you ...'

She watches the screen. Hilton manages to keep Millet from scoring from the last two balls of the over, meaning it's Patten, new to the crease, on strike next.

'You could have called.'

'I didn't want to intrude. And I thought, with being so close to your mother …'

'For *six* months!? You're meant to be my father!'

'Of course I'm your father!' My face feels hot. Surely it wasn't six months? I take a deep breath and let it out. 'Sorry, love. I've been conscious of you caught between your mother and me. But I shouldn't have left it so long.' I put my hand on her arm and leave it there.

accounts

I'm already on the back deck, finishing my tea when the sun comes up. After a convincing win in Perth, Australia is up two-nil in the series and Harrow has two hundreds and two fifties. The WACA pitch was more challenging, seeing him caught behind off a rising ball he couldn't control, but he took the shine off the ball, getting them off to a great start in both innings, and setting them up for the win. With England only able to draw the series from here, and a ten-day break until Boxing Day, we have some breathing room to attend to other business. My appointment with the solicitor is first thing. A strategy meeting, she called it. Katie has finally made an appointment, too, with someone in the same firm.

She brings out her cereal and sits beside me. 'Morning.'

'Morning, love.'

'Those your accounts on the dining room table?'

I nod. 'A bit of a mess.' Her mother used to do them. But Katie knows that.

'How would you feel about me sorting them?'

'You don't need to do that.'

'It's easy for me,' she says. 'Least I can do.'

'I'd be grateful. I'm behind with my BAS. And I need to lodge my return for the … process. Before we can get into negotiating. I've had trouble facing it.'

'It must be awful, Dad. I'm sorry.'

I watch her face. 'Is your mother okay with you being here?'

She crunches her cereal, swallows. 'A bit uncomfortable, I think. But that's her problem.'

'True.' How I ended up with such a wise child is a mystery. 'It's not my choice that we're not talking. Just saying …'

'I know. I think, in the beginning, she just wanted to make sure she didn't back out. And then she was angry. And now, with solicitors involved … Do you think you can buy her out?' Katie's expression is sympathetic and very much adult, carrying all the weight of the situation.

'I'll have to see what the solicitor says. And the bank, when I have all the figures together, I guess.'

'This is a nice piece,' Katie says. 'Piano solo?'

I nod. 'The composer, Mélanie Bonis, was a French woman. Very talented – studied with Debussy. But there weren't really women composers then. She used the name Mel Bonis and changed her style, made it sound more masculine, so no one would know she was a woman.'

'That's sad.'

'Her works were published – three hundred pieces, I think. A significant body of work. She was accepted in the end.'

Katie takes off her glasses, places them on the table and shuts her laptop. My tatty manila folder now contains neat bundles of receipts and statements. 'Are you sure you've got all your income in here? Is there anything you could add?'

'Not enough?'

She pulls a face. 'Maybe.'

'I didn't do much for a few months there.'

'It's understandable.'

I get up to put on a new record.

'Dad?'

'Yeah, love.' Something in her voice has me turning to look at her.

She sips her wine. 'I hate accounting.'

'I said you didn't have to bother yourself.'

'I *want* to help with your accounts. I mean – as a job.'

'Bit boring?'

'I don't know why I did it.'

'Because your parents were so artsy-fartsy I suppose.'

'Maybe.'

'If you could do anything, what would it be?'

'Don't laugh, okay.'

'Wouldn't dream of it.'

'I want to go to Art School. To do woodwork. I want to *make* things. *Beautiful* things, from timber.'

I can't help grinning. 'Then do it.'

'I figure I'll work part time to support myself, with the accounting. I can do that anywhere.'

'I'll help however I can.'

'Thanks, Dad.'

'What prompted all this?'

'Apart from hating going to work every day?' She stands, slides the chair in. 'Mum, I guess.'

'What do you mean?'

'She's so talented. It's what she's meant to do with her life. It's sad to see what happens when creativity is frustrated. She was raising me, then teaching.'

I lower the needle, watch the record turn, a piece Katie will recognise. 'It was harder to see that, somehow, when we were young. It was work and money, family and security that were important. That's what our parents drummed into us. And women were expected to carry more of the parenting.'

'I don't blame *you*, Dad. You gave up your music, too. But at least you're still doing something with your hands.' She holds up a bottle of red as a question. One of Frank's pinots from Mornington.

'Perfect.'

'This is that oboe piece from *The Mission*, right? I saw you play this, with the quintet.'

'That was a long time ago.'

'Are the others still playing?'

I nod.

She hands me a glass. 'You should take it up again.'

'I know,' I say.

'Here's to doing what you want, living your life.'

I'm poring over the weekend sport pages instead of making bats, analysing the cricket analysis. Cricket writers are a particular breed, some of them former players, but not all. Either way, the best commentators have that passion for the art of the game. It must be strange, gathering together in the media room over the course of the match, a series. They tour, like a team of their own, but are competing against each other for top stories, new angles, space on the page, and then they go out for drinks and dinner together at the end of the day.

At the moment they're all saying the same things: the English team is underdone and outplayed, Harrow is beautiful to watch, a nice young fellow, destined for big things, and McCann will finally be put out to pasture in state cricket.

Harrow and O'Neil are beginning to form an opening partnership. A bit like Hayden and Langer, without the size difference. Or Miller and Lindwall, perhaps, one of the greatest partnerships of all time, the bedrock for that team of Invincibles. Miller was the epitome of calm, famously responding to a question about how he handled pressure on the field so well, after he returned from the war, 'Pressure is a Messerschmitt up your arse.'

Miller was a music lover, too. One night, after a dogfight with multiple Messerschmitts, he made an unauthorised detour over Bonn in his Mosquito, to see Beethoven's birthplace. There's room for two passions in life and, occasionally, they cross over.

collector

The shop doorbell goes, and I tense, thinking it might be David again, until a tall shadow enters that can only belong to Frank.

He removes his hat. 'Looking pretty good in here, Allan.'

'Katie's been jazzing things up a bit.'

'Home for Christmas?'

'For a while actually.'

'Must be nice to have her around. Bright young woman that one.'

'She is.' Frank's in his city clothes, button up shirt and pressed pants. Only the R.M. Williams boots are common to both worlds, polished but well-used. 'On your way back to the farm?'

'Correct. I have looked into my last mouth for the year.' He puts a bottle and a parcel on the bench. 'Just wanted to wish you a Merry Christmas.'

'Thank you. Looks like a special drop.' It's a Hilltops shiraz with a decade on it.

'Not too heavy for turkey, either.'

I unwrap the parcel carefully, a book by the look and feel. It's a pristine copy of Cardus' *Days in the Sun*, dust jacket intact. His second book, and his best, in my opinion.

'Frank – this is a treasure.'

'It's a first edition.'

'Got something for you, too.' I reach under the bench and place the brown paper bag in front of him. He reaches inside and holds up the little tin. 'How …'

I smile. It's a 1932 edition Owzthat Cricket Game. Just two hexagonal metal dice. One for the outcome of the ball bowled, one for the score. Two people could play cricket at the bar, on a plane. Or a ship, I guess, in those days.

He turns the pieces over in his fingertips. 'This was the only year they used the patent number,' Frank says. 'To celebrate the patent award. After that it was just "made in Great Britain".'

I nod.

'You've done well. Very well.'

'Welcome.'

'I see Harrow is wielding one of your bats.'

'Doing okay, isn't he?'

'That big century in Adelaide was delicious! The cut shots, pull shots, cover drives, scoring all around the ground. He had the English in tatters. And the way he supported Gibson, sensing the moment, dropping back like that. Maturity beyond his years.'

'I agree.'

'And how's our willow coming along?'

'Want to have a look?'

He follows me out to the drying shed. 'Someone been throwing stones at your glasshouse?'

'That big hailstorm. Still haven't decided what to do with it.'

Frank has to duck to enter the shed door. I hand him two billets from the top of the pile. 'Feel how much lighter they are now?'

'Bit of difference between them, too.'

'That's right.'

'And when will you turn them into bats, do you think?'

One of the things I like about Frank is his predictability. It's comforting, like the parameters of the game. 'Thought I'd start with these two. In the New Year. Would you like the first one?'

'That would be marvellous. Just like Harrow's, please.'

I smile.

We head back into the garden, the sun bright after the gloom of the shed. Frank stops at the corner of the glasshouse. 'There's a skip full of old timber windows just been pulled out of a building site around the corner. Big reno going on.'

'Yeah?'

'They're only going to go to the tip. We could pick them up in my truck if you want.'

'You don't need to get going?'

'May as well wait for the traffic to thin out a bit now.'

'I'll get us some gloves.'

Katie sets the table, pausing in front of the picture of Nate getting his baggy green cap from Alan Davidson in Hobart. Bigger than his wedding day, he used to say, though not in front of Jean.

'I thought I'd visit Auntie Jean next week. Take over a Christmas hamper.'

'That's a nice idea.'

'How long since you've seen them?'

'Months now,' I say. It's over a year. Closer to two. Since before Marlene left.

'You've never told me about what happened to Uncle Nate,' she says.

'Didn't your mother explain?'

'She says it's your story to tell.'

That's a first. I serve up the chicken and pile potato, carrots, pumpkin and peas on our plates. Katie's appetite is back, helped by the physical work no doubt. 'You want to open a bottle of something?'

'Sure. From in here?'

'Yep. The dustier the better.' The first thing I did when Marlene moved out, once I picked myself up off the floor, was convert one half of the pantry to a wine cellar. Better for the wine, and saves me walking out to the shed of a night.

She opens a Yarra Valley pinot, one of only five hundred bottles. A gift from Frank when we first sealed his willow grove arrangement. I'm pleased with how the grove has turned out, but the friendship with Frank has turned out to be worth more.

'Where was I when it happened?'

'Staying at a friend's. We asked them to keep you a few extra days.'

'Mum said you found him?' She pours us each a glass and puts the bottle between us.

I focus on setting the plates down flat on the table, in the centre of the place mats.

'He was a bit of a mess when we spoke the night before. So I rang back the next day to check on him.'

'And he didn't answer?'

'He wasn't at work. So, I went over to his place. When I saw his car was missing, I just had a bad feeling.'

'How did you know where to look?'

I put down my knife and fork, trying not to clatter. 'A place we went often when we were young. A picnic ground in the Dandenongs. You only have to walk a few minutes and you're among mountain ash, giant tree ferns. He used to go there when he had troubles – on and off the field – to walk it out, I guess.' Though, that last time, he'd only made it far enough to hook a hose up to the exhaust.

'What was going on for him at the time?'

'He'd been dropped from the Australian team. His injuries weren't repairing. Or they did, but then he would injure himself again. The selectors could have handled it better. But he wasn't looking after himself too well. That didn't help.'

'Drinking?'

I nod. 'There was some question whether he would even retain his position in the state team. Maybe someone had given him the heads-up.'

'What did you do when you found the car?'

I empty my glass and reach for the bottle. How do you explain the worst night of your life to your child, something you hope they never have to experience? The panic, the things your body can do with adrenaline charging through it. Pulling the dead-weight of a grown man out of a car and trying to resuscitate him even though you know you're too late. The sounds that come out of your mouth, alone in the dark, as you begin to comprehend that the person who has been part of your life since you were born – part of you – is gone forever. And you let it happen.

'I drove back to the township at dawn. A young woman was just opening up the café. She called the police. I called Jean. Then your mother. My father was on shift – so she had to make that call when he came off.' Giving him the news no parent should ever have to receive.

The woman made me a cup of tea and sat me on a green couch. 'They will take at least twenty minutes,' she said. 'Please. Sit a moment, and then I'll drive you.' Just when you think the world is going to hell in a handbasket, a stranger shows you simple kindness. That's when I broke down. In cricket, you get to play again, adjust your shots. Even if you drop back down a grade, you're still playing. In real life you only get one innings. Another day, another moment, if something had been different, Nate might not have made that decision.

'If I'd been there, not hung up on him. I mean, he was being impossible but …'

'I think I remember seeing you upset when I came home.'

'Really? You would only have been five.'

'You were crying in the kitchen. Mum was holding you.'

For a minute I think I'm going to start up again. It's all still in there. Katie puts down her knife and fork and places her hand over mine.

'I'm sorry, Dad.'

concerto

Katie carries my tea and toast out to the deck, where we've been making a habit of having breakfast as the sun comes up, listening to the birds sing in the new day. My body is stiff and sore as I pull on my boots, telling me it's nearly the end of the year. We're working long hours to finish all the Christmas orders so we can have a bit of a shutdown until after the Fifth Test in Sydney.

The English will have to make changes. Too many of their batters are just not making an impact. But bringing new blokes in now is a risk, unsettling the team further. There's some doubt about Gibson's fitness apparently. Physical or mental, I'm not sure. But I'm worried about him. All the media attention must be taking its toll.

Cricket is a colonial game. It was just one of the comforts of home the English imposed on their subjects throughout the Commonwealth: India, Sri Lanka, Pakistan, Bangladesh, South Africa, Zimbabwe, the West Indies, New Zealand and Australia. The game has adapted to each environment, with the locals rising up to defeat their colonisers and, eventually, gaining their independence. With a few exceptions. Along with New Zealand, we still tip our baggy green for the Queen. Our cricket team does not yet reflect the broader community, or our much longer history.

Kate waves her arm in front of my face. 'Dad?!'

'I beg your pardon. Lost in thought.'

'Where'd all the windows come from?'

'Building site round the corner – courtesy of Frank.'

'Do you want to make a start on fixing it?'

'Big job, especially the roof. Took the quintet a full day to build it.' We played on the deck afterwards, admiring our handiwork. Mozart, of course.

'How long since you've seen those guys?'

I shrug. 'A while. Graeme and I were meeting for a drink regularly until your mother and I …'

'We could ask him over?'

'He's probably too busy.'

Katie lifts her eyebrows. 'Do you want me to call him?'

'I'll do it. I'm sure he'd be glad to see you.'

Graeme helps me carry the unused window out into the lane. He's still as fit as ever, it seems. My back is complaining, threatening to spasm, as we lean the frame against the fence, but between the three of us we've resurrected the glasshouse. We wave to Katie, as she pulls out of the garage, headed for the supermarket.

'What do you make of all this fuss about Gibson?' Graeme says.

'Seriously talented player. Bat, ball, fielding.'

'No doubt about that. But the political comments?'

'He was just expressing himself, on the field. Media's drummed up the rest.'

'Sport should just be sport, I say.'

'Politics has always been a part of cricket. What about Apartheid?'

'True. And that was a right mess.'

'Decolonisation is a slow process.' I shut the gate behind us and we stand for a moment, admiring our work. The glasshouse is a bit of a hotchpotch but a picture nonetheless, nestled among the foliage, and reflecting the late afternoon light, like the potting room of a botanical garden.

'Thanks so much for your help, Graeme. Appreciate it.'

'Pleasure,' he says. 'We could have a lovely little concert in here.'

I nod. The same thought had crossed my mind. Playing doesn't seem quite as confined to the past as it did when Marlene first left. 'What are you doing for Christmas?'

'A quiet one this year. Felix is hiking somewhere in Patagonia, Annie is still living in London. And Lois' mother is in a home now, so she'll go there for lunch, I think.'

'I'm sorry to hear that.' I say. 'Patagonia? On his own?' I was always fond of Felix. A lot of energy but gentle, somehow.

Graeme nods. 'He usually does something adventurous in the uni break but he couldn't be much further from home. Antarctica maybe.'

'We're going to the Boxing Day Test. Not sure which days yet, but would you like to come along?'

Graeme smiles. 'I'd love to.'

cricket family

Harrow knocked on O'Neil's hotel room door and let himself in. The smell of freshly ground coffee in the corridor was the signal. O'Neil carried coffee beans, grinder and a portable drip filter on tour. It was way better than the bitter brew (stew, O'Neil called it) on offer down at breakfast. They'd started their own openers' morning ritual: good coffee and a chat about the day ahead, making their plans against the opposition bowlers. O'Neil and his partner had just had a baby. 'Never been so sleep-deprived,' he said. The hotel room was a bit of peace and quiet for him.

O'Neil was already nursing his cup, hunched over the morning papers with his glasses on, reading all the expert opinions on his batting. Although they were coming off a win and could only win or draw the series, O'Neil was the only batter with a couple of single-digit scores and only one fifty, coming off the back of an ordinary Shield season. One of the commentators, who'd just released a book about Australia's best batting partnerships, had labelled O'Neil their weakest link in his weekly column in the national paper. They always had to find someone to pick on.

O'Neil gave no signal that he'd registered Harrow standing in the doorway.

'Don't listen to them,' Harrow said. 'We don't write books. We score hundreds.'

'All right when you're making them,' O'Neil said.

'You've made plenty before, and you'll do it again,' he said. He flicked on the kettle, threw the used filter paper in the bin, and set a fresh one in place. 'Those blokes all wish they were us.'

It took some getting used to, training with media, cameras, all around. He'd rather not have an audience for his glute stretches or the moment when he was clean bowled by a fourteen-year-old net bowler. But it was part of the modern game, Dog said, giving the public greater access to the players. It was hardest on him, as captain, locked into a press conference and string of interviews every day between training sessions. No wonder his batting suffered.

Gibbo, meanwhile, was in 'a cone of silence' he said, fed up with his words becoming headlines. He and the physio were working hard, trying to get his ankle right for game day.

The Gibbo storm, and not scoring a hundred in Perth, meant the press had lost interest in Harrow for the moment. He was glad to retreat to the gym, to work on his core strength, in the cool and relative peace. Peters was already there, piling weights onto the bench press. It hadn't been announced yet, but he was playing instead of French, who'd picked up a groin strain in Perth.

'You won't fit into your whites if you lift all that,' Harrow said.

'Train with me,' Peters said. 'Build up those baby guns.'

Harrow glanced at his biceps, flexed. 'I'm not big. I'm quick,' he said. But he stood behind the bar, to spot for Peters.

'Megan flying in today?'

Harrow nodded, taking the bar in his hands, and a little of the weight, as Peters dropped it back on the stand above his head. 'My parents, too. Liv's already landed.' They were all having Christmas with the team in Melbourne. The cricket family, as they called it, in their fancy hotel. The team wouldn't be able to drink, playing the next day, but it would be worth it, to bat in a Boxing Day Test. 'You?'

Peters' parents had died when he was young. Car accident, Mads had said.

'Just my brother, Cal. He lives down on the Peninsula. Not far to drive.'

'Does he play cricket?'

Peters forced another final lift, the veins in his neck bulging. Harrow took the weight of the bar on the way down, easing it back onto the rack.

'Nah. He's a winemaker.'

'Really? I look forward to meeting him,' Harrow said. Megan liked her wines, and might find him interesting to talk to. 'Will be nice to have a day off together.'

'Reckon.'

He was looking forward to all the food, Megan arriving, and seeing Liv and Mum and Dad, but it was hard to think of anything but game day. His first Boxing Day Test at the G, his whole family there, watching. He'd already shadow batted through an entire (century) innings overnight. The bat was ready; well and truly seasoned, and back in the city of its making.

But first, he had to find a Christmas present for Megan. He was going with jewellery. Liv had promised to take him shopping as soon as she got settled. Tiffany's, she reckoned.

'Classic. Like the movie,' she'd said. Whatever that meant.

The hotel foyer was strung with thick tinsel and giant gold stars. The Christmas tree was so big, it obscured the front counter, and it took him a moment to see Megan.

'Hey, beautiful,' he said. He kissed her, not exactly under the mistletoe, but it was exciting all the same. 'How was the flight?'

'Long,' she said. 'I just wanted to be here already.'

He took her bag. 'Is that it?'

'They're bringing up my suitcase.'

They walked to the lifts, hand in hand. Harrow pressed the button for the top floor, grinning. 'Flash, isn't it?'

'It's nice.'

She pulled him into a proper kiss as soon as the lift doors closed. They were travelling upwards at some speed, which didn't help him stay steady on his feet. The lift dinged, and the doors opened. He led the way to their room, at the end of a long hallway.

'I missed you,' she said.

'Missed you, too.'

He held open the door. Their room had a view over the city and the Yarra from the lounge and deck, their bedroom, too.

'Wine? Champagne?'

'Bubbles,' Megan said. 'Why not. Christmas Eve already! How fast has this year gone?'

'Tell me about it.' He opened a bottle from the fridge, exaggerating the pop of the cork, and filled a glass for Megan, half a glass for himself. 'Thanks for coming, I know it's probably not what you would've chosen for Christmas.'

'Happy to be where you are.'

She took the glass he offered and opened the door onto to the balcony. He followed her out and tipped his glass to hers. 'To our first Christmas together.'

'Cheers to that.' Her eyes were sparkling, the tension she often brought home from work leaving her face.

'What are your parents doing?'

'Lunch at my aunt's place, in Glenelg.'

'That's on the water?'

She nodded. 'Nice old house, with a big deck out the back.'

'That's where you had Christmas as a kid?'

'Sometimes. Or we'd go out, to a restaurant. The Grange, in the city, back in the day. That was a bit of an Adelaide thing. But in Malaysia, they didn't really celebrate Christmas. I missed all the traditions, as a kid,' she said. 'What about you?'

'Pretty simple. Cooked prawns and salads at home, a game of cricket.'

'Of course, cricket. You and Liv, you're peas in a pod.'

He nodded and sipped his champagne, thinking of how unlike Liv he'd felt while they were shopping. She somehow knew what Megan would like and where to find it. And she kept asking questions about Sky. So annoying. Liv's Christmas present had come early: she'd been pulled into the Queensland Fire one-day set-up, for the Women's National Cricket League, to be played in Canberra.

'Was it lonely, being an only child?'

'I didn't really know any different. But I guess I did become accustomed to being the sole object of my parents' attention. Though they were very social. In Malaysia, it was a bit lonely, the language, and I didn't necessarily click with the other Air Force brats.'

'Not spoiled?' he said, nudging her arm.

'In some ways. But I was expected to be a grown-up pretty early.'

'And to be perfect at everything.'

Megan smiled. 'Yes. That, too.'

'Lucky you are then.'

'Yeah, right.'

He gestured to the city laid out below them. 'What do you feel like doing tonight? Do you want to go out someplace?'

'You know, what I'd really like is to stay in, maybe get room service. A burger or something ordinary. And watch an old movie. I feel like I've hardly seen you for months.'

'Wait.' He ran inside to fetch the brown paper bag from the coffee table, and slipped out the DVD. 'What about *Breakfast at Tiffany's*?'

'Todd Harrow. I *love* that film'

turkey and trifle

The year I was working in Essex, I spent Christmas up in London, with Grandfather. Marlene flew in for a full traditional lunch at my great-aunt's, the table laden with dishes that actually made sense in the depths of winter, in a room full of distant relatives, most of whom we were meeting for the first time.

Marlene was jet-lagged and her dress a little crushed from her suitcase, but she charmed everyone with stories of growing up on the Gippsland Lakes and holidays at Wingan Inlet. The family's attempts to pronounce Croajingolong National Park had everyone in stitches. She'd painted a series of Gippsland landscapes, one for each family, as a present. Grandfather's face lit up as he unrolled the canvas: our local Footscray cricket ground, late afternoon – a surprise even to me.

'Why this is marvellous, Marlene. The light ...' Grandfather said. 'I can see why you love it down there.'

After pudding and port, my great-aunt produced a violin, and her son, Saul, a cello. 'We saw your oboe case in the hall,' she said.

We played Bach's *Christmas Oratorio* as a trio, everyone's chairs pushed back in a circle, as the snow started to fall. At first I thought Grandfather had fallen asleep, but that was how he listened to music, eyes closed.

When the time came to leave, he kissed Marlene on both cheeks, and closed his hands around mine, his skin paper-thin. 'I want you to know how proud I am,' he said. 'I can rest easy, knowing you're carrying the tradition forward.'

I saw then, how frail he'd become, and how precious the gift I'd been given. 'Thank you,' was all I managed.

'I'd better get the turkey on,' I say. 'Am I okay to step in here for a bit?'

'Plenty of room.' Katie's layering up her trifle, pouring what will be Calvados-infused jelly over the sponge cake she made herself, broken into squares in the base of the deep cutglass bowl that was my mother's. My father gave it to Marlene as part of our wedding present and now it's being used by his granddaughter. A shame they're not still with us, to see the young woman she's become. Marlene, too, for that matter.

'I'll be out of your way in ten,' Katie says.

'Plenty of room.' I set the oven temperature, unwrap the bird and give it a good rinse. Then I pack the apricot and chestnut stuffing in both cavities, stitch up the skin, baste it in olive oil, garlic, and lemon thyme, before sliding the dish into the oven. I wash my hands and wipe them on a fresh towel, and get to work cleaning up.

Katie layers slices of fresh peaches, blueberries, more sponge, and drizzles more Calvados over the top. I take my time selecting a record, Benjamin Britten's *A Ceremony of Carols*, and set the needle. It's festive, but more subtle than anything we'd hear down at the mall. I stand close to the speaker to savour the gold harp, all the singers cascading in, while Katie whisks a white mixture.

'What is that?'

'Mascarpone and yoghurt,' she says, adding a little rosewater. 'Whips up good but better for us than cream.'

I find a tablecloth and set the table inside the glasshouse, lay out cutlery and the champagne glasses. I cut a piece of Christmas bush, flowering just in time, as it always does, and lay it down the centre by way of decoration. We're lucky with the day, clear but not too warm. Sun glints on the panes, the greenery gathering around close again since the hailstorm. Honeyeaters are busy about the garden, adding to the festivities.

Katie stacks the dishwasher, and piles what won't fit into the sink. 'Smells so good. Your turkey is the best, Dad.'

'My mother's recipe. She taught me to cook. The only one interested, I guess. And, after she died, someone had to feed us. Dad and Nate were pretty useless in the kitchen. I still have all her cookbooks.' I open the freezer, pull out the bottle of Billecart I've been saving. 'Bubbles and blinis with presents?'

'Lovely,' she says. 'This feels nice, Dad.'

'It does.'

I spread crème fraiche, dill and salmon on the blinis, and arrange them on a plate. Katie carries out our presents, her face holding a hint of that old childhood excitement. I follow with the bottle and plate.

I fill our glasses and sit at the head of the table. 'Merry Christmas,' I say. And I do feel merry, the best I have in a long time.

'Merry Christmas, Dad.'

I hand Katie her parcel and sit back to watch her unwrap it. A leather carpenter's belt and tools, and a satchel of fine chisels. Not necessarily what I would have imagined giving my adult daughter back when she was born, but why not? We shouldn't start with any assumptions.

'Oh wow,' she says. 'They're beautiful!'

'All German-made. Should last forever.'

'And for you.' Katie hands me a square parcel that looks like it might be vinyl. I'm already grinning, eager to see what she has chosen.

It's a first pressing, Helen Jahren, with the Berlin Philharmonic, performing Mozart's 'Oboe Concerto in C major', composed for the great Giuseppe Ferlendis in 1777. When Mozart reworked it for flute, the original version was lost, until Bernhard Paumgartner recognised a handwritten set of parts in the Salzburg Mozarteum archives in 1920. It took Alfred Einstein, no less – aware of D major and C major copies of the concerto in the Gesellschaft der Musikfreunde library in Vienna – to put two and two together, concluding that that the concerto was originally intended for oboe. That's supported by Mozart's letters, and fine details in the music itself.

'What a treasure! Wherever did you find it?' I open the box and touch the covers and paper liners, inhaling that particular new record smell.

'Graeme put me onto a store in the city,' Katie says.

I nod, not trusting myself to speak, for the tears in my throat. I put the box down and reach to put my arms around my daughter.

Boxing Day Test

Katie and I join the line at the gates. Kids are buying stick-on tattoos and having their faces painted: green and gold, the Australian flag, and the occasional red and white Saint George's Cross. We file through the turnstiles, bag check, and make our way through the sea of people up the stairwell, and across to our seats. The Barmy Army are two bays over, their band already playing some new song about British pride on foreign soil. At least there's an acknowledgement that it's no longer theirs. It's not ours either, but that's a longer story.

The stands are overflowing, extraordinary for day five of a Test match – even for the home of sport. Graeme stands and waves, in his yellow terry towelling hat, and we shuffle along the row, past legs and knees, expectant faces. We were here for day one and now we're back, to see it through. Australia needs to bat out the day for a draw or score another three hundred and four to win the game, and the series. But it's Harrow, resuming on nineteen not out, and the possibility of him taking the team to a win that has brought so many people to the ground.

'Morning,' Graeme says. 'Great day for it.'

'Perfect,' I say as we shake hands.

We settle into our seats. I've brought snacks, a thermos of tea, and two pairs of binoculars. Katie has the water, sunscreen and somehow managed to purchase three ABC Radio earpieces on the way in while I was absorbing the atmosphere.

'Too early for a beer, Dad?'

'Never too early. But make mine a light?'

'Graeme?'

'Ditto.'

She nods and heads back down the row, holding her hair from her face. We're having a day out at the cricket while the workshop is closed. The solicitors' offices are closed, too. I'm hoping we can both forget about it all for a day. And so far, so good.

I check the clock again. The television commentators, sweating in their suits, are inspecting the cracks in the pitch, the bowlers' footmarks, predicting how tough it's going to be to bat against spin, the odds of win, loss or draw.

Katie returns with three brimming plastic cups in a cardboard tray, her bar experience showing – a steady hand and a shy smile as she steps over legs and squeezes past bags. She distributes the beers and pushes the tray under her feet for later. 'To a good day's play.'

Graeme tips his hat. 'Should be a treat.'

I sip my beer and take a few steadying breaths. Excitement has risen around the ground, anticipation as to how the day will unfold. To be a true cricket follower is a kind of faith, attending the grounds, sharing the pews with other devotees, learning the rules, the history, and the ideals – participating in the pursuit of perfection.

The secret is in the game's structure. There's the comfort of all the rules and restrictions but, within that, there's still room for endless variations. The ball is bowled, the batter plays it. Runs are scored, or they are not, the wicket is or isn't lost. There are fluctuations, rises and falls, an unending series of events, each pregnant with possibility, waiting to be realised. Those episodes, one after the other, make up the narrative of the game.

The resulting drama is not so much about the outcome, as the human factor, the individual gestures, the qualities of the best players shining through. As C.L.R. James – the finest of all cricket writers in my view – puts it, greatness in a batter is when they set in motion all the possibilities that are contained in the game. Watching Ponting's pull shot, on his way to another century, or him racing in on a ball and throwing one-handed from cover to effect a run-out. Even the purpose with which he walked, gestured and chewed gum, suggested something was about to happen.

And then there's the aesthetic appeal: the lines, curves and grace of human movement. That perfect cover drive, the articulation of limbs, the flex of forearm muscles, the flick of slender wrists. The perfection of form, shape and style in the player's execution of their skills, the infinite variety of movement from one stable base. Each motion can be observed and appreciated in detail, as part of something larger.

It's true of bowlers, too. The rhythm in their run-up, the fluidity of their stride, their wrist position and grip, propelling the ball with the power of their hips and glutes. The position of their fingers determining the potential for movement through the air, off the seam, off the pitch.

For the fielders, there are endless possibilities: running, diving, jumping, flying, turning, all their energy focused on stopping the ball, catching the ball, returning the ball, or knocking down the stumps. The expression of physical co-ordination, timing, the harmonious action between player and ball, player and team, all eleven players working together, truly is a concerto.

Cricket sceptics like to say that nothing happens in cricket – but that's just a lack of imagination. Something is always happening, and something is always *about* to happen. We just have to be watching.

At last the players have gathered on the edge of the ground. The two batters are standing by the rope, ready to run on. The opposition are in a tight huddle, their captain geeing them up, trying to force a win, change the fortunes of the tour. The clock ticks over. The players, in their whites, head out onto the field of green. The bowling side scatter in all directions, the batters head out to the middle together, then part to take up their respective ends. It's a team sport, but in the end, it's batter versus bowler.

Harrow's intentions are clear from the first ball, which he smacks to the mid-on boundary for FOUR. They're playing for a win, not a draw. O'Neil fully inhabits the anchor role, running hard, feeding Harrow the strike. The crowd applauds the first time Harrow steps into a square drive, and at every pure *crack* of the bat afterwards. It truly is a fine instrument, giving expression to the occasion, the summer holidays. By the end of the first hour, he's worked his way to forty-four.

The umpire calls drinks. The bottle-shaped cart comes out on the ground. Harrow removes his helmet and gloves, shakes out his hair. The audience stands around us, seats flipping up behind them.

Graeme gathers our empty cups. 'Another light?'

'Please.'

Katie hands him the tray from under her seat. Graeme makes his way out, squeezing past those staying in their seats, with a musician's poise.

I pull the Tupperware container from my bag, open Katie's rice crackers and sit them alongside the cheese and pickled onions.

'He's looking good, isn't he?' Katie says, smiling.

'Flawless,' I say.

The players are resuming their positions as Graeme makes his way back up the aisle towards us. The sun is shining, I'm at the cricket with my daughter and old playing buddy, Harrow is on his way to a half-century, and the game could still go any of three ways. The G is packed, rainbow beach balls are already bouncing around the ground on the upraised hands of the crowd. There's a sea of people dressed as Richie Benaud, with their beige suits and grey wigs and microphones, and a whole stand of Stormtroopers. The Barmy Army is belting out its songs. It's joyous, and not something you can experience through the screen.

Graeme sits down and hands over our drinks. Patten bowls the first ball of a new over and Harrow scampers through for a run to take the strike. The energy of the crowd lifts, conscious that he's two hits from a fifty, willing him to this first milestone. A buzz, a level of attention, connecting everyone present. Harrow senses it, squaring his shoulders. The English players call to each other cross the field. They need to get him out if they have any chance of a win.

It's a good ball, full and straight, giving Harrow no room to drive or pull. He plays it back down the pitch and takes his little walk out towards mid-wicket. I pass around the cheese and crackers, take some for myself. The next ball is only a fraction wide but Harrow cuts, guiding it to the point boundary for FOUR. The crowd clap it all the way. The Barmy Army counter, with drums and trumpets, trying to rev up their veteran bowler, Patten. It might well be his last tour, but the old dog still has all the tricks.

It's a slow ball bouncer. Harrow checks his shot, just lets it go through to the keeper and smiles. Next ball is on a length and he leans into another drive, pushing the ball back past the bowler. It's a beautiful shot. Ingram cuts it off but Harrow runs two, taking him to fifty. The Melbourne crowd stands to applaud him and Harrow raises his bat for a moment, but his face is serious, jaw set; he isn't done. He'll want to be there at the end, to hit the winning runs himself.

They go to lunch with Harrow ninety-eight not out. The English managed to keep him off strike, denying him the milestone. It leaves us hanging, anxious, but not half as anxious as Harrow will be. I let out the breath I've been holding and open our parcel of sandwiches and a packet of salt and vinegar chips. Katie is back with another round of beers, having set out the over before lunch to beat the crowd. She'd realised Harrow probably wasn't going to make the milestone, but I had to smile that she was still reluctant to leave her seat.

'Great session,' Graeme says, taking a sandwich.

'Outstanding.'

We look out onto the field, at all the girls and boys running around, playing miniature games of cricket. The joy on their faces just to be playing on the same ground as legends.

Graeme sips his beer and sets it down on the ground. 'We have a little concert coming up, Allan.'

'Oh, yes. Where?'

'At the Athenaeum,' he says. 'You should come along.'

'Great venue,' I say. Though my stomach feels a little sick. 'What's the date?'

'Twenty-third of March.'

'I'll check the diary.'

Katie turns and smiles, takes another sandwich.

'Just going to stretch my legs,' I say. 'I'll bring back the next round.'

I do need the walk, and the bathroom, but it's so long since I've been to a concert, the thought of it is discombobulating. Graeme might be working up to asking me about getting back into some sort of practice, and I'm not ready.

I do a slow lap of the outer and back, taking in the crowd in each of the tiers and bays, the children dragging their parents to the merchandise counter for a replica hat or T-shirt. The line for drinks is long but I'm happy to wait.

I arrive back in time for the start of play. No longer as sure or as deft as my daughter, I spill a little beer as I'm stepping over legs and bags and trying to get a look at Harrow walking out all at the same time. Katie and Graeme smile and take their drinks, and I get the feeling they've been talking about me while I'm gone.

The Australians are slow to get going again, as if they've had a heavy lunch. The English bowlers have had a conversation, too, tightening their lines and crowding Harrow, building the pressure. It's Patten and their balding spinner, Jenner, trying to break the game open. O'Neil goes in the first over after lunch, caught behind to a ball he shouldn't have played at. Barker strides to the crease to lead his team home. If they win, as looks likely, the Ashes are theirs. The urn will return. Barker plays all around a topspinner from Jenner but survives the over.

Harrow scores a single first ball of Patten's over but it's another two and a half overs before he scampers through for the run we're all waiting for. He leaps in the air and pumps his fist. Four tests, three centuries. Barker shakes his hand, half-embraces him. Harrow composes himself and removes his helmet, holds up the bat, turning in a slow circle to acknowledge the crowd, and points to his family in the stands. Then makes the sword-like flourish with the bat that's become his signature.

The television crew has found his parents, partner and Olivia, showing their nervous faces on the big screen as he approached his hundred. And now, the moment when he reaches the milestone, their relief and joy. Katie nudges my arm with her elbow. Harrow is looking up, into our stand, bat aloft, as if he knows I'm here.

Katie, Graeme and I are on the edges of our seats. The energy around the ground is electric. The Australians have upped the scoring rate. They're within a hundred of a win. But the momentum shifts when Barker, hitting across the line, is caught at deep mid-wicket. Then Gibson is run out, trying to turn a two into three. Harrow knuckles down, playing most of his shots along the ground and trying to settle Peters, on debut in a Boxing Day Test. Harrow and Peters have toured together, been in this situation before, and it shows in the innings they build. They're calling well, chatting between overs, bumping fists after every scoring shot. Peters is doing a good job, feeding Harrow the strike and running well. At tea, Harrow is on a hundred and forty and Australia only need sixty to win, with five wickets in hand.

I take another trip to the bathroom and, on my way back, purchase three ice creams from the young vendor in our bay. Sweet and cool is what we need now, as the stands heat up and the tension builds.

Second over of the final session, Harrow top-edges one down towards third man. Henley runs in, takes the catch easily, and throws the ball on the turf. It's relief from the English rather than a celebration. Harrow stands still a moment, as if he can't believe that a mistake has come. He walks off slowly, watching the replay on the big screen, but his job is done. He acknowledges the crowd, clapping his gloved hand against the bat face, and disappears down the race, into the change rooms.

'What a knock,' Graeme says.

I nod, looking at the shining faces around the stands. It's a gift to witness an innings built and delivered, coming so close to perfection.

Davis survives an appeal for leg before wicket. Jenner is on one knee, begging, as if the series depends on it. It probably does. And still the umpire shakes his head.

We watch the replay, hearts in mouths.

'It was missing leg,' Graeme says.

Katie is leaning forward, chewing her nails. I've somehow made a cricket lover out of my daughter after all.

Peters takes up where Harrow left off, finding the boundary twice and running two on a misfield. Jenner is getting a lot of turn out of the footmarks and Davis is OUT, sweeping, struck on the pad again. It's the left-handed fast bowler, Thomlinson, in next. He can hit a long ball, when he connects, but isn't that comfortable against spin.

Peters swings and misses. The ball catches his thigh guard, flies wide of the keeper and runs down to the boundary for four leg-byes.

Forty to win, four wickets in hand and I'm trying to manage my hopes.

Peters clubs one into the covers for two runs and drops the last ball of the over at his feet to steal a single and keep the strike.

The English captain brings back his young quick, Pilkington, spending a long time setting the field. He's fast, and lethal when on target, but the kid is under pressure, in his first Ashes series, his team desperate for a wicket. He's missing his lengths, giving the batsmen too much room. Against the lower order, the way they're playing, the bowler only has to bowl at the stumps, and eventually they'll miss and he'll hit – stumps or pads, either will do.

Peters takes full advantage, slashing a wide ball over the square leg boundary on the full. 'That's right in his hitting zone,' Maxwell says in my earpiece. 'They have the win in sight here.'

It means Thomlinson has to face spin. But he's focused, solid in defence. The first ball beats the outside edge of his bat but he's back in behind the next one, defending. Second last ball of the over, he takes one stride down the pitch and hits the ball straight back over the bowler's head. It flies high and long, into the stands. The crowd love it, those down on the boundary banging the signboards. What used to be Bay 13 starts chanting *'AUSSIE AUSSIE AUSSIE, OI OI OI'*, drowning out the Barmy Army. Thomlinson just grins. Peters comes down for a chat.

'Easy, Tiger,' Graeme says.

'That's exactly what he'll be saying.'

The crowd is chanting *SIX SIX SIX*, clapping the bowler in, whistles blowing. There's so much noise all around us, my skin is tingling. Thomlinson blocks, in an exaggerated movement. It's a great sign that he's enjoying the moment.

Peters faces Pilkington, using all his height and muscle to intimidate. Just twenty-five to win and he's in sight of a Test fifty on debut. He wants it. He clips a three, but only runs two to keep the strike. The next ball is wide, too wide, and Peters throws his bat at it. The balls flies over the keeper's head, one bounce and over the rope, beating the fielder at fine leg. It's ugly, especially after Harrow's innings, but it doesn't matter now.

Ashton comes down to talk to his bowler. The kid is nodding, but he's rattled, not hearing anything. The next ball is better, full and at the stumps. Peters digs it out, takes a stride, but Thomlinson calls, 'NO RUN.'

The batters meet in the middle before the last ball of the over, a strategy perhaps. Peters mis-hits the next one but Thomlinson is already halfway down the pitch, trying to give Peters the strike for the next over. Peters runs. The fielder at cover swoops and throws in one movement. Peters dives, slides his bat towards the white line as the ball breaks the stumps. The umpire signals OUT.

Katie puts her hands over her eyes. 'Oh god. I can't *stand* it.'

Peters picks himself up, his shirt and trousers streaked with brown, bellows a single swearword, and leaves the field on forty-nine.

Australia have sent young Hilton in ahead of Jackson. He swings and misses at two but survives. Next ball he stands tall and smacks it, into the sight screen on the full. The crowd roars.

Ashton's hands are on his head. Last ball of the over, the fielders come in close, trying to stop the single. Thomlinson guides it down to long off but finds the fielder. Hilton will be on strike next over.

The English captain brings back Patten. He looks cooked but he'll dig deep, find something. Hilton does well, playing with a straight bat, watching the ball. He manages to flick one off his hips, runs through for the single, and he's off strike. When Thomlinson slog-hooks one down to cow corner, the fielder slips, and his return throw is wide. They run four. We don't have to be on the field to hear what Patten says. Everyone can read his lips on the big screen.

The tail is wagging. Two wickets to lose, eight runs to win.

The next ball beats Thomlinson, has him in a tangle, and hits him low on the front pad. The bowler screams and turns to the umpire. The whole English team has their arms in the air.

Katie covers her face.

Graeme says, 'I heard two noises.'

The umpire shakes his head. The English are incredulous. But the replay shows bat onto pad.

'Good decision,' says Maxwell in my earpiece.

Hilton is on strike, facing Jenner. He swats at the ball, splicing it, but it lands safely between fielders. He and Thomlinson run two, laughing at their luck. They can afford to. Even if they lose here, there's another Test to take the series. Six runs to win.

Thomlinson removes his helmet to face the spinner, his shaggy hair dripping with sweat. He sees it early, takes a great stride down the pitch, and slogs. It's high, sailing over the long off fielder's head. We're up, arms in the air. The ball is taken one-handed by a woman in the crowd, without spilling a drop of her beer. SIX! Graeme's fists are clenched, I'm clapping and Katie is screaming like the little kid she used to be. Australia have WON. The fourth Test and the series. The Ashes are ours! We embrace, for a moment, and release.

The Australians come out to shake the hands of the English, two lines moving against one another, one all smiles, the other grim.

'Harrow set it all up,' Katie says, wiping away a tear.

under the Southern Cross

He stood between O'Neil and Gibson as the captains made their speeches. The crowd was dribbling out of the Sydney Cricket Ground, the Fifth Test all over on day four. Hardcore fans lingered, among the iron lace and green roofs, as the sun dropped low in the sky.

Dropped on ten, Harrow had gone on to score two hundred and one. Lucky he doubled up, because they only batted once. Dog declared on six hundred and then they bowled England out for one hundred and ninety-eight, enforced the follow on, and bowled them out again. Australia had won the Ashes 4–0. A whitewash!

He leapt up onto the makeshift stage to accept the awards for player of the match, and player of the series, the boys all clapping, whistling and yelling out. Taylor called it a 'Remarkable debut from a remarkable talent. And a big part of this Ashes win.' Harrow shook Taylor's hand and managed to say a few words, thanking the boys for making him feel so welcome, his family for making it all possible, and Reader for a magic bit of willow. The boys laughed at that but it was true. The fact that it was still going strong was evidence enough.

The personal accolades, the acknowledgement, was satisfying. But finally stepping up onto that podium with the boys, streamers and confetti raining down, champagne spraying everywhere, everybody jumping up and down, screaming, was the best moment of his life. Harrow posed for photo after photo with the boys, arms around each other, taking turns holding the urn, grinning like idiots. They'd won the Ashes!

Afterwards, all the old players came into the dressing room to congratulate them. Border, Steve Waugh, Taylor and Langer, all shaking his hand and sitting down for a chat. 'It was a great win,' Waugh said. Lang just smiled. 'Brilliant batting, mate. Just brilliant. I know how hard it is out there, on the frontline, facing that new ball.'

The boys sprawled over the floor and benches, still in their playing whites, arms around one another, spraying champagne over Winslow and the support staff. He had messages from Sky, Copes, and rest of the Bulls boys. All the songs had started up, of victory and mateship. They were sunburned and exhausted from two days in the field, a five-Test series – living the dream.

The WAGs came in, and the photographers with them. He posed with Megan and the little urn, and she didn't seem to mind the boys being rowdy. Liv, Mum and Dad came in, too. Everyone was part of the celebration.

Liv stood talking with the Cricket Australia CEO in the corner of the room. She'd been player of the tournament in the Women's National Cricket League, so that might've got his attention. Or she was giving him a piece of her mind about the lack of support for the women's game. Either way, he was nodding, and they shook hands at the end. She sensed the right moment to take Mum and Dad back to the hotel, and Megan left with them. She was having her own night out on the town with Nina, who was down visiting her parents.

'Enjoy yourself, *Hars*,' Megan said, smiling.

He kissed her, not caring that it was in front of the boys, and hugged her hard, to hide his tears. It meant everything having her there, not just to see the win but to be a part of it. A part of his life.

By the time the England players came into the rooms for a drink, everything was getting messy. Peters was drinking straight from a champagne bottle. There wasn't a dry spot on the floor. Most of the English boys turned out to be pretty good value off the field.

Harrow made time to speak with Patten, having heard he wouldn't be touring again. One of the greats of the game was almost done and it had been an honour playing against him. He said as much, with the help of a few beers. Patten just nodded, wished him well, all class despite their loss. There was a bigger picture, more than winning or personal milestones. It was the way you played the game, the respect of the other players.

It was Ingram he felt the most affinity with, as a fellow opener. He'd toughed it out to score a couple of good fifties. 'See you in England,' he said.

It was almost midnight when the boys staggered down onto the ground in their socks and jocks, carrying bottles and cans. The stands were empty, just the lights of the city and the stars above, the fading echoes of the game and the series that had come to a close.

They stood in a circle, arms around each other, and Gibbo led the team in a rendition of 'Under the Southern Cross'. Although it was Harrow's fourth time now, it still made the hair on his forearms stand up and brought all his emotions to the surface, threatening to overwhelm him. Pride, and love for his teammates, the game.

Afterwards, he and O'Neil sat on the pitch back-to-back, keeping each other upright, supporting each other as they had right through the series, and reliving the best moments. They were a team within the team, a partnership. Peters was clowning around as usual, throwing an empty bottle at Davis, like he was still keeping. Davis took it cleanly in his left hand, though his movement was hampered by the ice pack on his knee. Hilton was stretched out full-length, head on Slim's belly, beer bottle in his hand. Harrow smiled. He'd never seen either of them drunk before, always so careful with what they put in their bodies.

The stars themselves watched over them, the Southern Cross and the two pointers. The Opera House was lit up green and gold, someone said, the Ashes urn reflected in the harbour, like some sort of underwater treasure. The whole city was celebrating.

Playing cricket for his country was everything he could've imagined, everything he'd hoped. They'd trained hard, played hard, and they'd delivered. But now, it was all over. O'Neil fell quiet and Harrow shed a few tears in the dark. Remembering all those moments, on and off the field, which now bound them together forever. They were Australian Test cricketers. Ashes cricketers. And, for tonight at least, they were heroes.

AFTERNOON SESSION

We must dig in and get through to tea.
And we must play on.

~ MICHAEL CLARKE, Eulogy for Phillip Hughes

plantation

With the Ashes won, it's time to catch up with other things. Australia was ruthless in Sydney. Thomlinson and Hilton blasted the English out, Armstrong bowled better than his figures suggest, and Jackson played his role, taking apart their middle order. It was nice to see Harrow take his first Test wicket, too, a sharp caught and bowled. Harrow's innings was his finest yet. Not just the double century but how comfortable he looked with his game, being on the world stage.

'I need to take a drive out to the plantation today,' I say. 'Check on things out there. Would you like to come?'

Katie looks up from her laptop. 'Would we be back in time for class?'

'We can be.'

'I'll get changed.'

I pack morning tea, lunch, a thermos of coffee and a bottle of water in my old satchel. Then I give the ute a quick clean out and wipe the layer of willow dust that seems to settle over everything from the seats. It's going to be a beautiful day. I open the gates into the lane. They're just corrugated iron over timber but Marlene painted them to look like a brick wall obscured by lemon trees. Katie helped with that project, signing her name down the bottom next to Marlene's. It looks even better with a little wear, outlasting the marriage as it turns out.

Katie throws her bag in the cab and waits in the lane, ready to shut the gates. Under a cap, she looks younger again. Or perhaps it's her burdens lifting, a new life opening up. If Art School is anything like the Con, they'll be the best days of her life. It's a small class, she says, but she isn't the only woman doing woodwork.

It's so much easier getting out of the city than in. We take the freeway past the airport and the landscape expands around us.

'Geez – dry,' Katie says.

'It's been a hot summer.' Straw yellow is the dominant colour, scraggly iron barks persisting along the roadsides.

'How far is it again?'

'About forty minutes.'

'So you bought this block after Great-grandfather died, right?'

'I bought the land before that. But we paid off the mortgage with the money he left us.'

'Have you included all that, for the legals? As your contribution?'

I nod.

'And the plantation – it belongs to the business?'

'That's right.'

'Hey, look. Wedge-tail.'

'There's a pair, circling.'

She loves her raptors. Even as a little girl she always picked out every hawk hovering by the side of road.

'Did you ever take me out there?'

'When we did the plantings. You don't remember?'

She shakes her head. 'Maybe I will when I see it.'

I take the turn-off. 'And this … is the home of the Ashes.'

'Sunbury?!'

'There's a mansion, Rupertswood, where the ashes of a burnt bail were presented to the English cricket captain, Ivo Bligh – in a velvet pouch – to mark their victory in the 1882–83 Ashes series between Australia and England. It was kind of a joke: the ashes of Australian cricket. They did a re-enactment a few years ago, when the Commonwealth Games Queen's Baton Relay passed through.'

'I don't get it.'

'It was the series before, in England, when Australia *won* for the first time ever. The press reported it as the death of English cricket, a kind of mock obituary. "The body will be cremated and the ashes taken to Australia." And when Bligh led his team over here, he vowed to win back the Ashes.'

'I know *that* part.'

'What most people don't know is that the urn was presented here, some time after that second series. And there were four Tests played, actually. Australia won the final one in Sydney, but it wasn't counted.'

'Because we won?'

'That suggestion has been made.'

'Why out here though?'

'Rupertswood was one of the largest houses ever built in Victoria. It even had its own railway station – only closed down ten years ago. The English team were staying there, guests of the Clarkes, who owned the joint. Bligh ended up marrying their music teacher.'

'There's always a love story. Even in cricket.'

I point out my window. 'And Mount Macedon, of course. Some nice walks in there.'

'I thought it was just where serial killers dumped the bodies.'

I turn to look at her. 'Where did that come from?'

'The news!'

'Today's news?'

'There was something last week. But I remember another story, from when I was a kid.'

'It's a shame to make that association,' I say. 'I think of walking with my father. Camping out.'

'You did all that?'

'Only a couple of times, but I remember it. Me and him and Nate, learning how to put up a tent, light a fire, cook damper. The trees all lit up around us at night. I think it was the first time I saw a bower bird,' I say.

'He always said he'd take me, but we never got around to it.'

I glance over. 'He got pretty bogged down after Nate died,' I say. 'We should have taken you ourselves.'

'You were always working,' she says. 'We could still go?'

'We will,' I say. 'Oh – see that craggy looking rock there? That's Hanging Rock.'

'Like the book?'

'Yep.'

'See. It's *gothic*.'

I shake my head but can't help smiling.

'How did you know this would be a good place to grow willow?'

'It had already been done. An Italian family, the Tinettis, have been here since the 1850s. After the gold rush, they settled, started farming – and fell in love with cricket. They started growing willows, and their neighbours, the Crocketts, made bats.'

'Crockett cricket bats? You're making it up.'

'I'm not. It all comes back to another Ashes Test match.'

Katie groans.

'Back in 1902, Umpire Bob Crockett and English Test captain Archie Maclaren got talking during a break in play at the MCG. Maclaren couldn't believe that we didn't produce our own willow. A few months later – everything still travelled by ship in those days – Crockett received six willow cuttings from England. But only one had survived the boat journey. They'd packed them in steel tubes!'

'*One*?'

'One is all it takes. They rushed it to Shepherds Flat, where his brother nurtured it back to good health, planted it – and propagated five thousand willow trees. Crockett cricket bats was the first major supplier in Australia and sold bats all around the world.'

'Do we drive past it?'

I shake my head. 'Sad story. The English didn't want us having our own willow. When the owners sold, in the fifties, Slazenger bought them out. Their staff flew in to Melbourne, travelled to the plantation, and cut down every tree. Except for *one* … For decades, it was from that tree that all Australian white willows were cloned.'

'Did they use the timber at least?'

'I think the point was that *we* didn't,' I say. I stop in front of the gate, glad of the sunny morning, showing my own plantation, well established now, at its best. 'We're here.'

Katie leaps out to open the gate, removing the chain easily, and waits as I drive through. It's a miniature woodland, blue-green native grasses waving beneath the trunks. There'll be some farmers who'd like to take their sheep through right now, probably think I should let them. But they'd break up the surface and bring in the weeds.

Katie shuts the gate and walks to the ute, standing by my open window. 'It's beautiful. And big! How many trees?'

'About a thousand now.' I grab my satchel from behind the seat. 'Up for a little walk?'

We follow the track in silence. The breeze ruffles the leaves overhead, shadows play on the ground. We're surrounded by uniform trunks, textured and sure. Outside sounds drop away. We could be anywhere, any country, a made-up place. Any man walking through a forest with his daughter. Except for the cockatoos squawking in the distance. I put my arm around Katie's shoulder, and she doesn't shift it.

'I'm sorry you've had such a hard time, kiddo.'

'I'm glad to have figured some things out. Where I'm going.'

We reach the rise by the creek, the ground softer underfoot. I unroll the little picnic rug and unpack our morning tea. Green apples, cheddar cheese, the rice crackers Katie likes, and a cupcake each.

'Did you make these?'

'I did.' I pour us each a cup of black coffee, still steaming.

'I used to love these in my lunch box,' she says. 'I always thought Mum made them.'

'I mostly did the baking. She painted first thing. And then she was teaching nights.'

Katie looks over the willow grove. 'It's wonderful. And all the grasses.'

'That was your mother's idea, actually.' I'd forgotten that. 'We figured these trees would be a willow bank – a sustainable forest that keeps on giving. Not just bats: carbon sink, nature reserve, habitat.'

'Could you sell off some of the willow?'

'If I had to. There's a section ready to harvest, maybe two hundred.'

She twists a strand of her hair around her finger. I can almost hear her doing the figures. 'Would you let me do the paperwork for you?'

'It's not fair to get you involved.'

'They're just numbers, Dad. I can do the loan application and set out the details of the financial proposal – to give to your solicitor. I won't be directly involved.'

'I'll think about it.' I produce two sets of secateurs. 'C'mon. I'll show you how to debud.'

The sounds are different among the young trees. Something springy in their sap, a certain vitality rising from the soil.

'They're all so straight.'

'There's an art to that; nipping off every bud as soon as it forms for the first four years. You don't want any knots or kinks in the timber. You have to keep a close eye on these young ones during summer; they're inclined to shoot all over the place.'

I show Katie how I do it, take my time moving the blade. 'It's more of a shaving, really.'

An hour later we're only halfway through. Katie's overly careful but that's natural at first.

'Now I know why you were never home.'

I wince at that. I thought I was investing in our future but I didn't stop often enough to live in the present. 'Once the tree is more mature, you can drop back to pruning once or twice a year.'

I tie my pruning knife to the end of the pole, so I can reach up to amputate any higher buds or shoots. 'It's important to always work upwards, and with the grain,' I say.

She nods. And I watch her notice the changing light in the canopy, her face softening with the willow.

We walk back to the ute through the most mature trees, where it's quieter, wood absorbing sound, the sun no longer overhead. And in that quiet, I lean on one particular tree, a little bigger than the others, with more presence. I place both hands on her trunk and close my eyes. I sense Katie doing something similar beside me. I don't put it into words or thoughts exactly, that's not how trees work. But I ask permission, with my heart, my whole body. This tree can share information with every other tree. I don't know how, but I know it to be true.

Willows have long been harvested by humans; that's our relationship. We have an understanding; I take what I need, and only what I need, and replace what I take. But now I'm asking for a little more.

When I open my eyes, I'm dizzy. Katie slips her arm through mine, and we walk back between the trees.

'I keep remembering that last day at the cricket. And I can't help thinking that everything will be all right,' she says.

'I always feel better when the team is doing well.' And among my trees.

'It was nice to spend some time with Graeme, too.'

'He's a good guy,' I say. I've been wishing I hadn't avoided the opportunity to talk in our other shared language. Music. The truth is, I feel sad, not being part of that brotherhood anymore. Guilty, too.

'Do you think you'll go to the concert?'

'I think I will. Would you like to come along?'

She smiles. 'I would.'

numbers

I open all the windows and doors to cool down the house and take another beer from the fridge. The late afternoon light is streaming over the garden, the glasshouse backlit. The occasion calls for vinyl. I have plenty of CDs, and it is nice being able to have three of them playing consecutively, without having to remember to change them, but there's nothing like the ceremony of choosing a record and lowering the needle. And nothing like that old vinyl sound. I choose a German pressing of Delibes' *Lakmé*. It's an attempt to soothe myself, while I open the latest letter from the solicitor.

Every line is barbed, every numbered paragraph a gut punch. There's something about the combination of grief and finances that makes people a little crazy. Of course she deserves a share of what we built; I couldn't have done it without her. But it doesn't seem reasonable that she insists on selling when I'm offering her more to let me stay.

Rising house values have a lot to answer for. The place has appreciated. Once an outer suburb, it has become inner – and perhaps she thinks it's worth more than it is. The idea of all that cash gets people thinking they can recover their emotional losses with money somehow. But I guess it's easy for me to say; I'm the one with the asset, the home. The one who stayed put.

I force myself to read it through until the end, details swirling like poison: dollar values placed on holidays, artworks, raising Katie. I resist the urge to respond straight away, to let rip. The solicitor always trims my words back to the bare facts, anyway, which has taught me something.

I pause as 'Flower Duet' comes on. It has to be one of the most beautiful love songs ever written, and between two women – pretty remarkable for its time. It just goes to show that the feeling has always been the same, the world over. I close my eyes as the song reaches its crescendo, letting the notes wash over me.

This is how we make love now, Marlene and I, though our solicitors. Taking the same care and precision with our sentences and calculations, with these violent exchanges, as we once did with our words, hands, lips and hips, whole bodies. It's the same passion, inverted. We want our pain recognised. The thought that love is still there, underneath, comforts me somehow.

As the song fades, I find my face wet. I do love the house – but the workshop; it's not just real estate, it *means* something. Everything. The record has finished, the needle tick, tick, ticking, but I can't make myself get up.

I see the doorbell jag, the latest customers leaving, and Katie appears in the doorway, smiling.

'Another order?'

'Two women. They play for Victoria. They were telling me that the women's game is growing fast. Getting a lot of support from Cricket Australia and big sponsors. Like the Commonwealth Bank.'

'Is that right?'

'Is it really a thing? That women are given men's bats?'

'The big companies don't design bats specifically for women.'

'Well, there's a niche for you.'

'Maybe.' She has a good head for marketing. It sure didn't come from me. Grandfather must have made bats for plenty of women back in the day, but this is a new phenomenon. Or made new again.

'I have an idea.'

'Let's hear it.'

'What if I work here part time, while I'm studying? Like an apprenticeship. We could do it properly – I think maybe you could even get government support.'

'Would you want that? Assuming I get to stay.'

'Beats working with a bunch of boring accountants! I think we can make a go of this. Like all processes of globalisation, there are efficiencies, sure, but there's also a backlash, people who want bespoke. New gaps in the market open up. Like the women's game.'

Her face is alight: heart, mind, body fully engaged.

'True.'

'I could do your books, some marketing maybe. We could open the shopfront in certain hours. I can study out there if it's quiet. And I can help with the handles, the sanding. But … there's one condition.'

'Yes?'

'I'd like you to teach me the whole process. Start to finish.'

I place the draw knife down on the bench and focus on the shavings nestling together.

'But if you don't want that …'

I walk around the bench to hug her, fighting back tears. 'I'd like that very much.'

Katie is still at the dining table, surrounded by files and papers. It's the second full day she has spent there. I don't know how she can focus on numbers for that long but I'm thankful.

I start chopping onions, for the pasta sauce. We're going to watch the first day–night game against New Zealand, in Sydney. Harrow is to open, and Matterson is in for Davis, who has a knee injury. Hilton is playing, too, on the back of his Ashes performance.

'Beer?'

'Please.'

I find a clean glass and fill it.

She sips, and sips again. 'So, income wasn't great the last three years. Though it's picking up now.'

'That's with your help. Any more ideas?'

'What if I live here, officially. Pay you rent? And, what about running workshops, on the weekends. Teach other people batmaking,' she says. 'Someone rang up asking about it only the other day.'

'A few people have asked over the years.'

'You're a good teacher. You know *all* the game's history. *And* you're the descendent of a long line of batmakers. That's worth something. Authenticity.'

'I'd be happy to pass on the craft,' I say. 'But it still feels like it's going to be a stretch.'

She nods. 'Looking at the assets, this place will be worth a lot. That's good, but you'll have to pay Mum half, at least,' she says. 'Have you thought any more about selling off some willow?'

'I'm prepared to do it.'

'Any sense of what it's worth?'

I scribble a quick calculation on the pad she slides over: the rough price per tree to a batmaking company.

'What about these other smaller groves, like the one near Colac?'

'They're not on my land. We plant the willows, I help them get established, and I have first dibs on harvesting them, when the time comes.'

'Any formal arrangement?'

'Gentleman's agreement, I guess. Each case is a little different.'

'So we won't include that. Any shares, investments?'

'I've invested everything I have in willow.'

'What about super?'

'A bit from the factory days. And the years I was teaching. My old accountant set up a fund – a proportion of my income each year. And I did drop in a chunk of the money I inherited.'

'Teaching?'

'At the Con,' I say. 'Until you were born.'

'I didn't know about that,' she says. 'It's all in one fund?'

I nod, a little light-headed.

'Any idea what it's worth now?'

'A statement came the other day.' I shuffle through the most recent pile of letters and hand it over.

Her eyebrows shoot up. 'This is good. Mum won't have much – you could shift some of yours over to her as part of the property settlement.'

'You can do that?'

'If the court orders it.'

I feel tired and the night is only just getting started. 'I need to get this sauce on. The pre-match starts in a few minutes.'

'Okay. Let's leave it there,' she says. 'I think it's doable, Dad. Will I set us up with some snacks in front of the TV?'

'Thanks.' Sometimes I miss my own space, pottering around. But the company, the help, the chance to build something with my daughter, beats that, hands down. And, if Katie is right, and I can somehow keep the workshop and house, well, life is looking up.

The stadium is full, the game timed for the last week of the school holidays. And the commentators are talking up Australia's chances. 'Australia have won the toss and will bat. With New Zealand's firepower, Australia needs a big innings from Harrow, you'd think.'

'No pressure,' I say.

struck on the gloves

He would have to wait to bat. Dog had won the toss and sent New Zealand in on a green pitch. Slim, Hilt and Sky, replacing Armstrong for the one-dayers, were champing at the bit. Harrow watched from second slip as Slim stretched his great frame from the waist, swung his tattooed arms like the weapons they were, examined the ball, and stood at the top of his mark, glaring at the batter.

New Zealand's opener, Callan, was one of the most destructive batters in the game on his day. He'd scored a double century and two fifties in the one-day series against India, with a strike rate of over hundred. But if he failed, the team tended to fail. He was more than half their side. Last time the two met, Callan hit Slim out of the park, forcing Dog to take him off. It was a big call to match them up again. Dog said it was a gut thing. Slim had been bowling rockets in the nets and was totally psyched.

The crowd stilled. It was as if the stadium itself held its breath, attuned to the battle within the battle. Slim positioned his fingers on the white ball, gripping the seam, then covered the ball with his right hand. Inswinger or outswinger, that was the question. The question he wanted to remain a mystery. Callan scratched at the crease, settled. Slim rocked back, and started his run in.

His rhythm was good, making running in look effortless, just an easy jog, but when he leapt, landed, and slung that ball, it was *fast*, real fast. And it swung, late, beating Callan's bat and smashing into leg stump, sending it cartwheeling out of the ground. OUT.

The danger man was GONE!

The stadium erupted, every person stood, as one. Harrow couldn't hear for the roar. Slim came out of his follow through and ran past Callan, shaking his fists, face fierce. He was still running. Dog, Mads and Harrow had to chase him down. The boys came in from all around the ground to join the huddle, with Slim standing tall at the centre of it all, like the warrior he was.

It flashed up on the scoreboard that the ball had been bowled at one hundred and fifty-nine kilometres an hour.

'First fucking ball,' Mads said. 'Legend!'

They rolled New Zealand for a hundred and twenty-two but it was a tricky total and the pitch was still seaming. Harrow survived the first spell from New Zealand's strike bowler, Boyd, just four overs, the ball beating his bat more often than not. He'd worn plenty on his body, too. Ribs, forearm, chest, and biceps literally absorbing the pressure. It was only luck he didn't find the edge, with three slips and a gully waiting to pounce.

They steadied, moving past fifty and accelerating. Then they lost three quick wickets, bringing Mads to the crease. New Zealand kept Boyd on, trying to blast them out. It was their only chance at a win. Mads was pinned down for four balls before swatting one off his hip. Harrow had to scamper to make his ground, getting Mads off strike.

Boyd fired in yet another bouncer, which Harrow was expecting. With forty runs to win, he wasn't going to risk hooking or pulling. He watched the ball out of Boyd's hand, read the line and length, and jumped to get in behind it. But the ball reared up, hitting him on the right glove, jamming his fingers onto the bat handle. He knew straight away. The blinding white light that meant *broken*.

The crowd hushed, that collective intake of breath. He smiled back at the bowler, more of a grimace really, a show of white teeth. He wanted to get the spray onto it, freeze the pain. But then the bowler would know he'd won. It would mean a break in the game, a loss of momentum. The physio would want him to go off for scans. He still had a job to do.

He walked out towards mid-wicket, gave his hand a bit of a shake, and walked back. He should have just smashed the fucking ball. It probably would've flown over the keeper's head for FOUR. Now he'd be out for weeks. Just when he'd been daydreaming about batting in Adelaide again – that paradise. And practically his second home ground now, with Megan's parents and all their friends and family there.

Mads came down. 'Broken?'

'Think so.'

'Whatever you do, don't take your glove off. You'll never get it back on.'

Harrow nodded. 'Let's get this done.'

The pain he could manage, but he was struggling to grip the bat handle. The bowler started his run in, tail up, finding an extra yard of pace with an injured batter in his sights. Harrow watched his arm come over, started his movement back, and ran the ball down to third, relaxing his right hand at impact. It bobbled over the rope for FOUR, just beating the diving fielder. The crowd applauded, beating a rhythm on the boundary fence.

Mads took as much of the strike as he could, hitting big down the ground, while Harrow backed up and ran hard, frustrating the New Zealand bowlers and fielders. Harrow's FOUR off the last ball of the fortieth over, an almost one-handed lofted drive, got them over the line with ten overs to spare.

When he finally removed his glove, his index finger was red and swollen, streaked black, the last two joints sitting at a queer angle.

'Yep. That's busted,' Mads said.

They raised their bats as they walked, side by side, from the ground. But Harrow couldn't manage a smile. The physio was waiting at the gate, kitbag over his arm, car keys in his hand.

It was a lonely ride back to the ground in the car, his finger strapped, splinted and held against his chest with a sling. X-rays had confirmed two fractures.

There were three missed calls from Megan. Another one from Liv, and two from Mum. But he wasn't ready to talk. He kept his head down when they walked the gauntlet of interviews back to the dressing room. He couldn't keep the disappointment from his face, and he didn't want to see it on the back page of the papers.

The boys were good, patting him on the back, making jokes. He took the beer Slim offered him with his good hand, though he didn't feel like celebrating. He could see it in their faces. Who would replace him? What if their luck changed? Would he be back?

Afterwards, he sat down with the physio, Winslow and Dog for a debrief. He'd have to miss the remaining two matches, and the tour to the West Indies. He dropped his head, said nothing. His summer was over.

Mads helped him empty out his locker. 'Don't worry, Hars. Rest. Do all the rehab. You'll be back before you know it.'

willowmen

I'm on the couch, re-reading *The Summer Game*. Cardus is waxing lyrical, yet again, about the first time he saw Trumper bat. That was quite the love affair, between commentator and player. I'm a bit more sympathetic now, feeling so attached to Harrow. I could write a book about watching him bat, that's for sure. All the air drained right out of the one-day series with Harrow gone. For six weeks, he said, when I messaged. I'll have to wait until Pakistan turn up, in November, to see him bat again.

Katie and I did watch the last two matches, as we worked through our respective paperwork. New Zealand won the second, Australia the third, with Matterson opening. I'm happy for him to be doing well. He's probably my favourite after Harrow. And Walker and Hilton look to be the next generation of fast bowlers.

When the phone rings, I check the clock in the kitchen. It's after ten. No good news ever comes at that hour. For a moment, I'm stuck to the couch, remembering that long drive out to Dandenong in the dark. Katie had a night class, and then dinner with a friend. She should be on the tram by now. On her way home. But what if David turned up? Katie said she thought she'd seen his car, in the Art School car park the week after she started.

'Hello?'

There's a delay, and I'm about to slam down the phone, thinking it a junk call from India that has my heart thumping, when someone speaks.

'Allan? It's John May.' There are voices in the background – and blackbirds. It's morning there.

Relief floods my body. *Katie is fine.* 'John. How are you?'

'Pretty shite, actually, mate. You've heard about this rust in our willows?'

'Yes. I've been meaning to call.'

'It's here, too, now. In Essex. We spread it on our bloody boots and lorry tyres, apparently. We've had to burn hundreds of acres. We're all in lockdown, under quarantine. It's *big*. The Cabinet Office has called an emergency security meeting.'

'Will you be okay?'

'There's what we have in storage. We're focusing now on treating and protecting what's left. But we're knackered. It could be the end of us willowmen. It could be the end of *cricket*.'

'What can I do, John?'

'Well, there is something. A long shot but …'

flying willow

Cricket is a time machine, a way of travelling through history, seeing the world. I've been to all the great English grounds of course: Lord's, the Oval, Trent Bridge, Headingly, Old Trafford. And when I was still at the Con, I followed one Ashes tour around Australia during the summer break, watching every ball bowled in every day's play of every Test from the stands at the Gabba, the WACA, the Adelaide Oval, the SCG and, of course, the mighty MCG. But I've also been, vicariously, to Cape Town, Galle, Mumbai, Lahore, Kingston, and Christchurch. Great games in legendary venues, history laid down as I listened.

Nothing beats the ABC radio team for commentary and company, but I do enjoy the vision of each ground and their surrounds: winding streets and stone bridges, rivers running out into hills, mountains, forests, seas. Castles and forts looking on. It all sets the scene, the local context and conditions, building atmosphere before the lens zooms in on that calm green field, the pitch, stumps, line markings, sight screens, the umpires walking out and, eventually, the players – the two teams who will be taking to the stage. And I don't even need to leave the house.

It's willow trees travelling now, flying back to the old country. Operation Willow Tardis is underway. When the first batch – a prayer in more ways than one – went over for testing, it turns out that our willows are somehow immune to the rust. Their wild colonial upbringing, perhaps. My nurseryman, Roger, is on board, so to speak, bringing over all his stock and potting more. We're packing up sets and sending them to growers and nurseries around

Essex – trying to turn back time. We use breathable biodegradable tubes now, instead of steel, and the trip is somewhat quicker. Katie and I have two production lines going: bats in the morning, sets in the afternoon.

We even have biosecurity clearance now, as a 'known consignor', which is a fancy way of saying they trust us to pack our own seedlings straight onto the airline's pallets and net them together. We've grown so used to the sound of ripping tape that we no longer wince or try to talk over the top of it.

The courier turns up at four in the afternoon to take them to the airport, and off they go, flying in the hold of a Qantas 747. The packaging is a bit tricky but if we get that right, they're not held up in quarantine. The Brits have negotiated some sort of work-around at their end. Katie deals with all that, I just trim back the sets and wrap the base and soil. She calls it our cash crop industry.

Katie fastens the netting to the pallet. 'Are we keeping enough to replant at Shepherds Flat?'

'I've made sure we *set* enough aside,' I say.

Katie smiles but shakes her head. One too many dad jokes. 'They don't deserve our help, you know,' she says. 'They did this to themselves.'

It's a reversal, that's for sure. Roger reckons I'm mad not to let their industry collapse. 'This is our *opportunity*, Allan,' he said. 'For global domination.' But that wouldn't be in the spirit of the game. As it is, we're doing all right out of it. The British government is throwing money at the problem, paying us for our time as well as the plants, and compensation for the loss of our own stocks. I'm hopeful we can keep the business going, and that's enough for me.

Meanwhile the orders are rolling in, and this month's weekend workshop is fully booked. We had a fellow in yesterday putting in an extra bench and a row of vices. A couple of blokes who attended the early workshops have set themselves up as batmakers and are now ordering clefts from me. The willow keeps on giving.

We followed the team's progress in the West Indies but it was almost a relief when the series was over. It kept us up too late and felt hollow without Harrow. Australia won 2–1. Shepherd scored two centuries on flat wickets, as well as a sixty and an eighty, while O'Neil is back in form with a big hundred in the final innings. I'm not sure how Harrow is going to make his way back.

Harrow v O. Harrow

He played and missed, the ball clanging into the wire behind him. Liv had picked up speed since they last had a net at the suburban ground halfway between her place and his. Her run-up seemed a little smoother somehow. Or maybe it was her action. She'd start the season as part of the Queensland Fire four-day set-up, batting in the middle order, and bowling first change.

'You chucking 'em or what?'

That earned him a filthy look. He'd been telling her she bowled like a girl her whole life. 'Can't help it if you've forgotten how to watch the ball, Bro.'

The next one came in fast and low. He dug it out, but only just. Her arm came over so quick at the end, it was hard to pick out of the hand. 'Geez,' he said. 'I'm a bit taller than the girls you're used to bowling to.'

'Oh, please. We're the same height,' she said. 'And you boys would still be bowling underarm if it wasn't for us.'

'What're you talking about?'

'Women couldn't get the ball around their skirts.' She mimed the action, indicating the broadness of an outfit he couldn't imagine, particularly not on her. 'So they had to come up with an alternative.'

'No shit.'

'It was more round arm,' she said. 'Like this.' She demonstrated the action with a real delivery. Her left arm coming around like that was not unlike Slim slinging it at him in the nests.

'Whoa. You should send a few down like that.'

She grinned. 'Maybe.' She walked back, and jogged in easy,

focusing on her delivery stride and action. He jumped up on his toes and knocked it down.

'Better,' she said. 'Your head's still falling over. And what's that weird little shuffle you're doing?'

Batting coaching from his little sister. Cricket was such a stupid game.

Outswinger. He watched the ball right onto the bat, played it straight and nodded. 'Nice bit of hoop on that one.'

She smiled, bent down to pick up the ball and turned into her run-up, all in one movement. The next one was a bit quicker, tucking him up, but he got in behind it. He was starting to see them a bit earlier, find some rhythm.

The next couple were fast and straight. He defended, eyes right over the ball, and threw the ball back. 'They're coming out pretty good, Liv.'

'Or your batting sucks.'

He smiled. The next one was more of a fourth stump line, which he cut, the ball smashing into the netting with a clang. In his mind, it was flying over backward point.

'You want to have a hit?'

'Sure,' she said.

He peeled off his gloves, pads, unclipped his thigh guard, removed his box, and threw them all in his bag, lay the bat on top. Liv kitted herself up, all her gear well-used. When she leaned over to pick up his bat, he opened his mouth to protest but closed it again. She held it with the reverence he'd had, when it was first given.

'Can I have a go?'

'Sure.'

She strode into the back of the nets, swung the bat a few times, and played a nice cover drive. He didn't like to admit it, but they looked good together. Harrow took his time walking back to bowl. He stood a moment, planning his over, starting with his topspinner. She struck it cleanly, that same pure sound. He'd assumed the bat would be a bit more loyal, that it was chemistry only they had. Apparently not.

He worked through a few leg spinners, increasing in turn and flight and then the straight one. She read them all, meeting them on the front foot, and hitting the ball back to him.

She played the next over off the back foot, letting the ball come to her, soft hands, playing both sides of the wicket. He sensed she would come down the pitch, wanting to smash it, and bowled the next one flatter and faster. She swung and missed, the ball hitting middle stump. Harrow held up his fist.

Liv threw the ball back hard and wide, forcing him to lunge. He caught it just above the ground, wincing at the jarring of it. But he hadn't hesitated. That was good.

'How's it feeling? The finger?'

He stuck the heavily taped digit up in the air, a familiar gesture between them. He'd got through rehab okay, but was still doing the hand exercises.

'Working fine, then,' she said.

He nodded. Fine but not great. He still didn't feel like himself with bat in hand. It had taken longer than they'd said, multiple breaks where he'd a break before, back in the Under-15s, and longer still to feel confident.

'Just have to get back on the park, Toddy.'

It wasn't going to be that easy. O'Neil and Shepherd were a good right-hand, left-hand combination. All he could do was get himself right for the home summer and score a mountain of runs for Queensland.

The day was slipping behind the ground, the sky a soft pink, like one of those old paintings in the MCG museum.

'I have to get to work,' she said. 'Drop you home?'

'Still stacking shelves?'

'I don't mind it. It's the one place I don't have to think, you know?'

'Megan said you could work at her firm during the holidays. Earn more.'

'Maybe.' Liv handed back the bat. 'Plays *so* nice,' she said. 'I met him, you know. Mr Reader.'

'Really? What's he like?'

'Sweet. And younger than I expected. He fixed up my bat and picked up that I was going too hard at the ball.'

'I've been telling you that for years.' He held the Reader blade in his still-healing hand, watching her strip down, only one set of everything in her bag, one off-the-shelf bat. The idea seemed to come from outside, from left field, but once it settled, he knew it was right. 'Why don't you keep it?'

'What?'

'The bat. My manager says I have to use the ones from my sponsor anyway.'

'Oh – *my manager*,' she said, pursing her lips

'It's worth a hundred grand a year. I'd be crazy not to.'

'A hundred grand?' She whistled.

He shouldn't have said that. Liv didn't even get paid for playing.

'Just put their stickers over the top. Everyone else does.'

He shook his head. 'I don't think that's fair on Mr Reader,' he said. 'I'm serious.' He held the bat out in front of him and dipped his head, as if presenting it to her.

For a moment she didn't move, and then he felt a wrench, as the bat left his hands. It hurt, but she needed it more.

'Thanks, Toddy,' she said. 'I'll look after it.'

They walked back to the car, kitbags over their shoulders, Liv sneaking glances at the bat and smiling. 'How were Mum and Dad?'

'In their element,' he said. 'We must have moved a tonne of cheese.'

'Did you end up in the film shoot?'

'Yeah. Milking a cow.'

Liv laughed. 'By hand?'

'I know, right.' The dairy had been featured on *Good Weekender* and they had to do nine takes of him squirting milk into a bucket. And then nearly as many serving a customer at the shop, who was only one of the Flanagan boys grown up, over for a visit. It had been hard not to giggle.

'And how's the love nest?'

'Wait till you check out the view,' he said. Megan had found them a great apartment, the whole top floor of a new building in Hamilton. They could see up and down the river, the ferries passing, and the city lights at night. The deck alone was bigger than the flat he'd shared with Klimt. He and Megan had slept outside the first night, curled up on the daybed under the stars. At least he'd been around to help with the packing and moving, even if it was one-handed.

'Megan sent me a link to the listing. It's pretty glam, Toddy.'

He nodded. 'We'll have to have you guys over.'

Liv had been seeing Sky since the Bulls' end of season party. He'd seen them talking but hadn't thought much of it, what with the age difference. The height difference, too! But why not, he was a good guy. The best. From the country, like them. Maybe she'd been training with him. That would explain the extra pace.

They threw their bags in the back and Liv slammed the boot. He climbed into the passenger seat beside his little sister, somehow still amazed that she was grown up, driving her own car. Driving *him* around. Liv shut the door, put the keys in the ignition and just sat there without expression, looking through the windscreen at the green field, as a footy team arrived for midweek training, insect halos already forming around the lights.

Liv reached over to put her hand on his shoulder. 'I've been selected in the national one-day squad,' she said. 'For the Rose Bowl. It'll be announced tomorrow.'

He blinked.

'I wanted to tell you myself.'

'But that's fantastic.' He leaned over to hug her, though it was awkward with the high centre consol. Envy gnawed at his stomach but he'd had his chance. And hopefully it would come again. 'Congratulations.'

She looked away but he'd seen the tears. Still as proud as ever.

He felt a bit choked up himself. 'You deserve it,' he said.

'I can't believe it's actually happening.'

'We're hosting?'

'Yeah – in Melbourne.'

When she started the car, the radio came on. James Blunt, who he didn't mind, but it was too loud. And such a mournful song.

'You'll get back,' she said. 'You *will*. And soon we'll *both* be playing Test cricket for Australia. The first ever brother and sister!'

shouldering arms

I watch the willows coming down. Beautiful creatures crashing to earth, sending up a cloud of dust and wood particles that stick in my throat. A willow sacrifice, to keep my business and home. The buyer insisted on organising the harvest himself, as if I couldn't be trusted, but it's a good sawyer they've chosen. I had a word with him first, felt respect in the handshake, and in the way he admired the trees. He's taken willows down for this company before, he says. He'll supervise the loading of the logs onto the truck himself, to ensure they aren't roughly handled. 'I don't want any waste,' he says. But that's just his way of justifying care.

It's Wagner I'm hearing, 'Ride of the Valkyries', the full operatic version. When it's over, I walk among the fallen, touching each trunk. There's a hole in my willow forest, the remaining trees exposed to more sun, more wind. But we'll replant. They'll become cricket bats, which is what they were always going to be. I just won't be making them.

I should be thankful they're not all stricken with rust, being bulldozed. But with so many going all at once, I can't help feeling I've betrayed them.

There's an intensity about sitting down together to nut out an agreement, dividing up everything we built and worked for, that I hadn't anticipated. Just seeing Marlene again has me feeling a rush of love and regret. She's thinner than I remember, more fragile.

I'd forgotten how beautiful she is, something about her face I never tired of looking at.

I have to remind myself that we're saying goodbye. That this is it. Part of me wants to say I'm sorry, to go back and undo everything, fix all my mistakes. Part of me wants to stand up and shout *I don't want this!*

And part of me doesn't. I'm starting to build my own life. I've reconnected with my daughter – our daughter. There's a sense of things opening up, new things, which I wouldn't want to turn away from now.

The solicitor, immaculate in her dark suit and makeup, warned that I might feel confused, emotional. 'Just get through this process first. Any feelings can wait. Everything will be clearer once you reach a financial agreement. It's a good sign that she was prepared to come down for the meeting. A very good sign.'

I keep it together, through all the back and forth, with less and less air in the room. Marlene finally accepts my offer, after a bit of haggling. I give up most of my super but I won't budge on the painting. It was a gift, and the only work of hers she left behind, apart from what is on the workshop walls and the gates. The lawyer shakes her head, as if it's too trivial an item to waste her time on, but there's a shift at the corner of her mouth when Marlene agrees.

There's a weird closeness about the moment. We half-smile, across the room, but don't move towards each other. Real love doesn't die, the poets say, it just changes form. It isn't as if we can undo everything and wipe it from the earth: the music and paint, willow shavings, all that making love, raising a child, building a home, a life.

But this is an ending, not a beginning. I get to my feet and manage to walk out of the room with the solicitor. She stands just close enough to shepherd me into the lift, while Marlene heads for the back stairs. There's a wrongness to the away movement but I don't resist. Marlene looks back, for a moment. And then the lift doors are closing and we're plummeting downwards. We emerge into fresh air, bright sunshine and buildings, the world rent open. It's not death, not the afterlife, but it's close.

'That went pretty well, all things considered. We'll formalise this and then file the papers next week,' the solicitor says. 'You okay?'

I nod.

She touches my shoulder, her nails the colour of red wine. 'Is there someone you can be with this afternoon?'

'My daughter is waiting at home.' Katie offered to come but that didn't seem right.

'All the best, Allan,' she says. 'The rest of your life begins today.'

I find the ute in a sea of white utes, overflow from building sites nearby. Vehicles had a lot more character once, different shapes and styles. You could swap the badges on all of these, and no one would notice. I manage to fasten my seatbelt but can't get the key into the ignition. My hands are shaking, my arms ache, and the pain is moving across my chest. For a moment, I think it's a stroke. I can't take a breath.

I put my head down on the wheel. When the tears come, the pain eases, and I'm sobbing, just a white middle-aged divorced man inside his generic white vehicle in a multi-storey city car park in the middle of the day.

I'm still trying to do up my waistcoat when Katie emerges from the bathroom in a deep blue dress, contacts in instead of glasses.

'Wow. Glamorous.'

'Looking pretty sharp yourself,' she says. 'Want a hand?'

'Please. Everything's a little tight …'

'You okay?'

I nod. 'I'm looking forward to this.'

'Will we get a cab? In case we want to have a few champagnes?'

'Already ordered.'

Katie secures my last button and adjusts my tie as the cab's headlights sweep into the lane.

'Let's go,' I say.

I hold the door for my daughter and climb in after her. The driver turns. 'Going to Collins Street?'

'That's right. The Athenaeum.'

We sit in the back, all dolled up, smiling at the passing traffic, the reflections on the Yarra, our great city decorated by light. It's the arts capital of the nation as much as it is the sporting capital. The last time I went to a concert was far too long ago, and with Marlene. We're lucky. Our greying driver is playing classical music rather than the usual hip hop rubbish. J.S. Bach's *Cello Suite No. 2 in D minor* – always a treat. Those big chord shifts always seem to match my mood, whatever the landscape. It's a classic for a reason.

There's a queue of cabs and cars at the entrance, a red carpet rolled out. The statue of Athena looking down on it all.

'I'm so excited,' Katie says. Her whole face is lit up.

I pay the driver and Katie and I make our way inside. The building's ornate walls and ceilings are uplit, like a high church. Graeme said he'd get us good tickets, but I hadn't expected the front row. We make our way along the red velvet seats. The plush boxes above us are populated with Melbourne's musical royalty.

'Wow,' Katie says.

'I should show you the library one time,' I say. 'It's stunning.'

When I check the program, it's a Haydn special. The main act is the Australian Romantic and Classical Orchestra, performing Haydn's *Symphony No. 104 in D major*, a wonderful arrangement by the composer's friend, Johann Peter Salomon.

They lower the lights, and Katie nudges my arm. The men in black emerge, their instruments gleaming. They bow, to their audience. Graeme smiles as he takes his seat, so not too nervous. He's freshly shaven and much more trim than me in his suit. It's Mal on first violin, Ben on second, and Rick on the viola. His expression shows nothing, but from where we're sitting, we can see that the big man is sweating.

The lights go out, the doors are locked, the crowd hushes and stills. Then, that beautiful inhalation, the moment of silence before the music begins, loaded with anticipation. The first notes have my skin tingling, tears forming – a body memory. They begin with

No. 41 in D major, nicknamed 'The Frog', one of the Prussian set. It's a graceful piece but clever and light, showing Haydn's sense of humour.

They follow with one of our old favourites, 'The Lark' in D major. The best music really does sound like birds singing. The beauty of the string quartet is in its homogeneity, the intimacy of the interaction of all four voices. It's a musical conversation. There are the short periodic melodies, with the other three parts lightly accompanying the melody, and the adherence to the four-movement form. But within those structures, it's the theme and subtle variations, each instrument getting their chance to shine. They're extending the phrases, pushing the tempos. Mal's passion is expressed through his head and bow actions. For Ben, the only reveal is his foot gestures. For Graeme it's all joy, his whole body.

They close with the more dramatic *No. 49 in B minor*, 'Allegro spiritoso', dedicated to the Hungarian violinist Johann Tost, enough to stir the most stubborn heart. Katie puts her arm through mine, eyes shining. I'm only just holding back the tears myself.

There's another pause, following the final notes, before they stand, and step forward to bow to their audience. The circle is closed, the show over. The music has transported me, reminding me not just of the beauty of live performance, of my own time up there on the stage, but the beauty of life itself.

Graeme finds us afterwards, his tie loosened, with glasses of champagne.

'That was transcendent,' Katie says. 'And the best seats in the house. Thank you so much.'

A young man approaches, in black jeans, dinner jacket and an open mauve shirt, who was sitting a few seats along from us during the performance.

'You remember my son, Felix?' Graeme says.

'Of course,' I say. I should have recognised his hair, like a lion's, as if to make up for Graeme's shiny pate.

We shake hands, but his eyes are on Katie.

'I knew it was you,' he says.

Katie smiles. 'You're still in Melbourne?'

Felix nods. 'Last year of uni. You?'

'Just moved back,' she says. 'Art School.'

'Really? Painting?'

Katie shakes her head. 'Woodwork, would you believe.'

I turn back to Graeme. 'You were great. Faultless.'

'We worked pretty hard – and it came together on the night.'

Ben and Mal cross the room. We stand in a circle, like old times, and shake hands.

'So good to see you Allan,' Mal says.

Ben nods. 'Thanks for coming along.'

'Wouldn't have missed seeing you guys all suited up.'

'Still playing?' Ben says, taking a mouthful of red wine from a large glass.

I tilt my head. An apology of sorts.

They look serious for a moment. It's sympathy, I think.

'I'd better find Marg and Rick,' Graeme says. 'We're all going out for dinner. Why don't you and Kate join us?'

I sip my champagne and glance at Katie, who is laughing, head thrown back, at something Felix has said. 'That would be lovely.'

giving yourself room

I stand in the doorway of the room I've been avoiding. Marlene's studio has the best light, windows on three sides, and a view out over the garden to the fast-disappearing field between us and the cricket ground. It's been left bare since Marlene left, except for Katie's yoga mat and iPod on the floor. It took me a long time to recover from the shock of the empty rooms, blank walls, pale squares on the floorboards where pieces of furniture had stood, all the gaps and silences in the house.

I can still picture Marlene standing at the easel, hair tied back, one of my old shirts over her jeans, bare feet – even in winter. The colours on the canvas, the look on her face. This was her room of her own. It's not like I didn't appreciate her when she was here. She's *still* here, really. But I wish I'd understood that you can't take anything for granted, let alone another person, not even for a day. I get to work vacuuming the cobwebs from the corners, dust from the skirting boards. Then I throw open the windows and clean both sides of every pane of glass, and wipe the marks from the walls.

It's turned into a sunny day by the time I wander down to the back of the drying shed and flip through the framed artworks. There wasn't room for anyone else's pieces on the walls when Marlene was here, but there is now. I choose a landscape from out near Mount Macedon, which has a certain something: the light, a feeling for that country, carrying my childhood with it. The other painting was my mother's, though she bought it for me. An oboist, in middle age, wearing a green velvet coat, practising his instrument alone in a room on a walnut chair. As a young fellow,

I didn't really identify with him or see myself in middle age. I paid more attention to his finger positions, the instrument itself. But he's grown on me. His velvet jacket, too. Katie will know where I can get one of those.

I make a second trip for my old music stand and wipe it down with a soft cloth. I have to stretch to reach the oboe – my first love, you could say – in its case on top of Katie's wardrobe. When I release the clasps and lift it from the case, the smell, weight, feel – everything comes rushing back.

I warm the instrument first, against my body. It's been so long, it needs breaking in. Just ten minutes playing with a few hours' rest in between. Even after all this time without breath, it's a great beauty. The first oboe I ever bought new. As it turned out, only months before I stopped playing. Made of granadilla or *mpingo*, an African blackwood, the shining silver keys against that lustrous red-black timber was more than I could resist at the time.

I fit a fresh reed and carry in one of the dining chairs but in the end I stand, the way I first learned to play. Like cricket, playing the oboe depends on doing the basics well. I focus on my posture: straight back, shoulders above the hips, head above the shoulders. Air, the foundation for playing, needs space to occupy. I set my feet at shoulder width, a low centre of gravity, rooted in the ground.

Don't go to the oboe. I still carry the voice of my first music teacher with me, Mrs Troy, with her ever-upright stance and greying hair tied in a bun. I breathe again, still my head, and bring the oboe to me.

I take a proper three-stage breath, filling all parts of my lungs, imagining a continuous column of air from my abdomen to the reed. The push, inwards and upwards from my abdominals, returns almost without thought, a reflex.

Finding the right pressure with the reed is more difficult. I make a slow breath attack on A, gradually increasing the airflow until the reed begins to vibrate – that ethereal sound I've missed. Gradually, I increase the air until the reed speaks, and adjust until it's at mezzo piano. I repeat the process, increasing the air until the tone firms up to a solid, resonant mezzo forte. And just like that, my breath and the reed are matched. I'm playing against the resistance of the reed.

I play a few notes of the oboe solo from *The Mission* that Katie likes, just to hear the sound, to move my fingers. I repeat the exercises until my blowing feels stable and lower the oboe. The tone isn't there yet, but my air production is healthy. And it feels so good – I feel so good – I couldn't even explain now why I left it so long.

More importantly, the oboe is fine. Like a cricket bat, they're here for a beautiful time, not a long time. They're meant to be played. An oboe, like many musical instruments, reacts to changes in humidity. And, like a bat, they do age and wear. They can 'blow out', leaving you with unstable pitch and distorted tone. We're a ways off that, I think. But I may as well play it while I can.

By the time Katie comes home, I've cleaned the whole house and have dinner in the oven. I switch off the radio. Harrow failed twice in his first Shield game. Unlucky to be caught down the leg side in the second innings, but it's not the start he needs. And, as Peter Roebuck noted in commentary, he's not using the bat. Whether it has finally broken or the sponsors have spoken, I'm not sure. But I can't help but feel a little flat.

'Hey,' Katie says.

'How was class?'

'Good – theory today. But I do love it. The teacher's great. She's been to every gallery in the world I think.'

'That'd be nice.'

She heads for her room but stops in the studio doorway. 'Whoa.'

I make myself busy choosing a record, Gerald Finzi's *Interlude Op. 21 for Oboe and String Quartet*, a piece I played in one of my first public performances. It's the Cologne Chamber Soloists on this recording who, unlike me, don't lose their touch over time.

'You're playing again?'

'I blew out the cobwebs,' I say.

'I can move my yoga mat.'

'Plenty of room. Nice spot for it there.'

She comes back to the kitchen to hug me. 'I'm so glad, Dad.'

O. Harrow

I steal a few hours to get down to the ground. My happy place, as Katie is fond of saying. Footscray Oval is as pretty as ever. I'd often catch Marlene weighing up the composition, the angle of the light, when she used to come down, but she never did paint the scene again. As much as I wanted her to. I looked for the picture she gave Grandfather among the things that came over but someone else must have kept it. I'd like a photograph or a painting of how the ground looks in this moment, summer coming on again, before all the development creeping into the edges of the frame spoils things too much.

Australia is playing New Zealand, the first game of the Rose Bowl one-day series. When Olivia Harrow strides out to bat at the fall of the third wicket, I see the resemblance between her and Todd. A similar physique, the way she holds herself. On the field, they could be twins. *Wait.* I check with the binoculars to be sure – she's even carrying his bat! There must be a story there. A loan for the occasion, maybe. It has already scored a lot of runs, more than is natural, even for such a remarkable piece of willow.

She's a little lighter on her feet than Harrow if anything. She *dances* down the pitch. And when she hits the ball, it barely makes a sound, it's timed so well.

I watch, leaning on the boundary fence. She has all the shots, timing, judgement, quick wrists and hands, a gorgeous on-drive. But the thing that has me standing there transfixed, when I should be getting out of the sun and back to the workshop, is her attitude. She plays with such *joy*. There's no other word for it. She reminds me of Graeme playing the cello. Her grin when she scores a boundary or has a little luck, the smile and shake of her head to her batting partner when she misses an opportunity, her single fist pump back at the rest of the team when she reaches fifty – no dramatics. It's the way the game *should* be played. Now that I notice it, the whole team is smiling. Both teams. There's no sledging or smashing of bats on the way off. It's a tense international match played in the right spirit. And barely anyone here to see it.

Victoria was the first to set up a women's association. We had some of the best players, too. Victoria was at the forefront of the competition, but WWI put an end to that. When cricket resumed in the 1920s, it was all New South Wales. Their captain, Margaret Peden, led women into Test cricket, and an Ashes Test series at that, during the summer of 1934–35. The second Test, at the Sydney Cricket Ground, featured two sets of Australian sisters, including the Peden girls. Margaret Peden must have been quite a woman. When she married, her husband became Mr Peden – changed his name by deed poll!

O. Harrow is out in the eighties, trying to accelerate the scoring. It took a blinder of a catch on the boundary to stop her. The bat, I have to admit, appears to have found its way into the right hands. Cricket – it's always teaching me something. I think she's about to step out of her brother's shadow.

I bring my hands to the oboe, making sure not to squeeze too tight, though we have missed each other. This time I take more time finding my embouchure – or lip-shape – holding as little of the reed in my mouth as is possible. Too much and the pitch gets sharp, too little and it's flat. My tongue finds the tip of the reed, blowing firmly and tonguing hard until the pitch of the sound is C. I relax my jaw, the interior vowel shape of my mouth an open *awh*. It is not just about breath. Articulation comes from the tip of the tongue striking the tip of the reed. Technically, the tone starts when the tongue is released from the reed.

I do some warm-ups and scales, then a few etudes and exercises. My playing is flat and spread, that embarrassing mark of incompetence. And then I overcompensate, too sharp. The place to play from is 'barely not flat', which gives the greatest resonance and finest control. But I'm not finding it. I slow the metronome and start fresh, until my brain is ahead of my fingers again.

The oboe is one of the few instruments with a double reed. It creates the unique sound and tone that people love – but is also notoriously hard to play. It can take weeks to learn to make a sound and much longer to learn to control it. Hopefully not so long to *re*learn. I focus on the two places where there should be tension: my abdominals around my belt and the muscles at the corners of my mouth, and relax everything else. *The oboe is played with your whole body.*

Outside the window, pardalotes are flitting from branch to branch, the way I would like to be playing. I practise the first long statement of Strauss' *Oboe Concerto*, using the breathing spots to exhale, and circular breathing to inhale while playing the sixteenth, and am left with more energy than I thought to play the fortissimo at the end.

My phrasing and range are yet to return, all the things I once did without thinking. Each note should connect with the next, more like Harrow's fluid on-drive. I'm striving too hard for all the things that come only with daily practice. And maybe they will not return, not the way they were.

I focus instead on expressing myself. Like a batter exercising their full range of shots, fluid motion, their style, strengths and flourishes – weaknesses, too. To thwart that expression, to force a change, is often the death of a player.

Harrow has had another poor game, scoring just three and thirteen in Queensland's match against South Australia. Sometimes an injury can impact on a player's confidence. But I can't help thinking it's the bat. It seems he's switched to using a Kookaburra

Kahuna permanently. Ordinary, and way too heavy. His balance is off. He seems to be getting to the ball earlier and going at it too hard. He didn't bowl, and he's fielding in the covers, rather than in at slip or short leg, with his fingers heavily taped, so perhaps he's not a hundred per cent. I can only hope that he'll bounce back. The great players always do.

Katie and I are packaging up the last of the willow sets bound for Essex. They've been planting flat-out all across the county, John says. If there's a upside to the disaster, it's being in touch with him again. Even if it's just by phone. He says it feels good to get his hands dirty, having been confined to the office in recent years. He's divorced, too. Five years, now. His wife, Anna, was a lovely woman, and his partner in business as well as life.

'I'm rubbish without her,' he said. 'But let's face it. We're married to the game.'

He's offered to fly me over for the next Ashes, as a thank you. Business class, too. I said I'll think about it. Right now, I'm needed here.

the reed

It's tone that defines the oboe, and the reed that defines the tone. Making my own reeds is part of my music practice. It takes time, but done well, it's a player's secret weapon. I can craft a reed to match my instrument, my embouchure, my capacity. All that time making them for others taught me what I like and how to achieve that sound.

I sharpen my reed knife, as specific and critical as any of my batmaking tools, and sort the cane stalks, throwing out any that are less than straight, then split each tube into three equal parts.

At last, Harrow is finding form. A fifty in the game against Western Australia at the Gabba and now into the sixties against New South Wales at North Sydney Oval. A century would surely bring him back into the Australian set-up. Shepherd's figures look good, but his big scores have come on flat pitches, and too often he gets bogged down, unable to force the game. He also ran O'Neil out on ninety-eight, which must have tested the partnership.

Shepherd's feeling the pressure of selection now that he's home, failing to score a fifty in the first four Victorian games. Meanwhile, Needham, the towering youngster from South Australia everyone is talking about, has two centuries. The selectors will be hoping they have another Hayden on their hands.

When Harrow is struck on the hand for a second time, the radio commentators, both former fast bowlers, suggest it's a deliberate tactic to unsettle him. Play pauses while he removes his glove and examines his fingers but when they head into lunch, he's on eighty-nine and playing cut and pull shots, like his old self. I leave the canes to soak in warm water while I head inside for my own lunch, my appetite renewed.

I'm back before the resumption of play, trying not to hope too hard for a hundred. I cut the canes to length with the little guillotine, then flatten the surface of each cane with a straight blade so that it will fit in the gouger bed. And then the gouging itself, the elliptical blade leaving a tiny spine. I brush away the debris and measure the thickness of each cane, tossing out any that are too tough or too weak. Like willow, there's a lot of variation. The best cane comes away in smooth silky shavings, dropping among the larger willow curls on the floor.

Reid is not helping Harrow's cause, hogging the strike and slowing the scoring while he sits in the nervous nineties. New South Wales bring Hilton on to bowl, grown in stature since the West Indies tour, where he took his first ten-wicket haul. With the pitch flattening out, he'll need to find something special to displace Harrow.

The true test of a reed, like a bat, is by sound. I drop each cane on the tabletop. Those with a pitch close to C have the best vibration characteristics.

Harrow's bat is making better sounds now, if not exactly music. Consecutive boundaries take him to ninety-nine. I set down my tools and rest my head on my hands, eyes closed.

'Harrow is on the front foot and driving. A lofted shot. The fielder *hurls* himself at the ball and grasps it in his fingertips. Harrow is caught! OUT on ninety-nine. He can't believe it. He's still standing there, head thrown back, looking to the heavens.'

I fold the gouged cane over the template and trim off the excess. It's a narrow shape I'm after, for better tone and control. But too narrow and the pitch rises; the reed will never vibrate sufficiently.

That's the constant tension in reed making, playing too: weighing up vibrancy and stability. It's a fine balance.

I place a cane over the wooden cylinder I use as an easel. Marlene used to think that was hilarious, protesting that it was too small even to see. I scrape each end of the cane until it's thin and score the bark so that I can fold it over the knife edge. Then I trim the edges of the cane with a razor blade to fit over the tip. To join them, I coat a length of thread with beeswax and start the wind, tying it off with three knots.

Queensland is still batting, and I'm still listening. Still managing my disappointment, too. But I'm sure Harrow feels worse. It's funny how much impact that particular run has, the difference between a fifty and a century for the scorebooks. Perhaps I should shape him a new bat. I could make a few tweaks now, having seen him play so much more. But he chose to give it away, after all. I can't go forcing something on him.

'Copperfield has played a true captain's knock, here. Now he's really freeing his hands. With such a big lead, you'd think Queensland will declare before tea.'

I scrape back the bark from the reed, leaving rails up both sides and a heavy spine down the middle. Then I clip the reed and soak it for a few minutes to encourage a really good opening.

When I have a dozen, I set them aside to dry. Giving them time to adapt to their new surroundings now will produce reeds that last longer, with greater stability and consistency. I learned that the hard way, always trying to rush the process when I was a student. If they'd last half as long as the Harrow bat, I'd be happy.

I separate the back from the heart, and scrape away the excess cane. *Scrape them until they crow,* one maker says. The trick is to listen to the click the knife makes. As soon as it begins to quieten, I know I've done enough. And I set them to soak them again.

Once the canes have dried, I can make the final adjustments. It's a much finer process than batmaking, and I'm out of practice, but I'd forgotten how meditative it is.

Queensland declares, sending New South Wales in. Harrow didn't quite get the hundred, but he put his team in a winning position. Surely he's done enough for a Test recall for the upcoming home series against Pakistan, then the tour of South Africa. That *will* be a test. We've had the wood on them at home and away since they came in from the cold – a thirty-year break in playing, with South Africa's stance on apartheid dividing the cricket world – but they've rebuilt around the best fast bowler in the world, the best all-rounder, some fine batters and excellent fielders. It could be the making of Harrow.

the moving ball

He was relieved just to be back in the Australian squad, with the boys. His hand was still not perfect but, taped up, he could bat freely and field. It hurt whenever he was hit on the gloves, but he was training himself not to fear it, not to anticipate being hit. Of course, it would be better not to be hit at all. Their batting coach, Stevo, was spending a lot of time with him in the nets, trying to tighten his defence. It was doing his head in, to be honest, thinking about every movement.

Even though they were playing at the Gabba, Harrow was staying with the team at South Bank. He'd come straight from the airport, after their last Shield game, in Sydney. Megan said she could count the nights they'd spent in the same bed on one hand, and she wasn't joking.

He and O'Neil had picked up where they'd left off, heading out to training and gym sessions after their morning coffee, and hanging out in each other's rooms in between. He gathered Shep wasn't really into O'Neil's freshly brewed coffee, which Harrow had missed. Just the smell got him going. But it was taking time to resume their partnership.

The big news was that Mads was in for Davis on the back of his performance in the one-dayers, a record number of catches in the West Indies, and a match-saving hundred to top it off. He was an inspiration on how to make a comeback. Armstrong was fit but Sky had been added to the squad as an extra bowler. With Hilt now an automatic selection and Peters settling in as their all-rounder, it was almost like old times.

He was late to meet Megan and Nina, his hair still wet, thanks to Tank surprising him with a chat after training. It wasn't just his match schedule that meant he and Megan had hardly crossed paths for three weeks, it was her long hours. Some big case she and Nina had been working on. The girls were at a table outside, already sipping champagne, watching a Citycat churn up the river.

'Hey, handsome,' Megan said. She stood to kiss him. 'Missed you.'

'Missed you, too.' He put his hand in hers, watching her cross her legs when they sat down. Always so graceful.

'Has Megan told you?' Nina said. 'I've moved into the Penthouse. Since you're never home,' Nina said.

He glanced at Megan, to see if Nina was kidding, but she just shrugged.

He forced a smile. 'Plenty of room.' There was plenty of room and Nina was great fun, but they didn't get enough time alone together as it was.

'Bubbles?' Nina said, the bottle already in the air.

'Just half a glass,' he said.

Megan turned. 'You're playing tomorrow?'

'I'm in,' he said. 'Just found out. But it won't be announced until right before the match.'

'See! You're back,' Megan said. 'That's it. I'm taking tomorrow and Friday off. To go to the cricket.'

'Me, too.' Nina said, clinking her glass to theirs.

'Don't you have to work?' Harrow asked.

'We had a win today,' she said. 'That media matter I was telling you about. An out of court settlement – but good terms.'

'We were just bitching about one of the senior partners taking credit for all our hard work,' Nina said.

'Again? What are you going to do about him?'

Nina leaned forward to whisper. 'I thought a stiletto to the head?'

'Effective,' Harrow said.

'Or – do things differently when we have our own practice,' Megan said.

Nina drained her glass. 'If we ever get there.'

'You will,' Harrow said. 'You're the smartest, hardest-working people I know.' He wasn't just saying it. They were so dedicated, solving problems, finding a way to get the best outcome for clients. Without any fanfare either. And often without acknowledgement.

'Anyway,' Nina said. 'I have a *very* serious question to ask.'

Megan put her hand over her mouth, but her eyes were crinkled at the corners.

'Okay …' Harrow said.

'Is Peters single?'

He laughed. '*Peters*? I can find out.'

Padding up, he had butterflies all over again. Pakistan, the masters of swing, had won the toss and sent them in on a green pitch on an overcast morning. It had been one of those nights that never really cooled down.

Armstrong had pulled up sore after training the day before, so they were playing Sky instead. Harrow was nervous for him, all jittery during the anthems, and glad of Megan and Nina in the stands with Mum and Dad. Liv was playing in Melbourne but would be back for day three. 'To watch Sky, not you,' she'd said. She'd probably be batting, too, later in the day. Hopefully once Queensland had got off to a good start.

Seeing each other play had become a luxury. A few texts or a quick call at night was often the best they could do. Mum and Dad could watch him on screen, but seeing Liv play interstate wasn't always possible. They had to divide their efforts: Mum following one game and Dad the other. The Gabba was packed, and a big Pakistani contingent had turned up, waving their dark green flags.

He hadn't been able look at Peters during warm-up without thinking about Nina. It had never occurred to him before but there was something similar about them. A positive way of being in the world. All that joking around didn't fool anyone, though;

there was plenty going on under there. But Peters wasn't single; he'd found out that much. He was dating a netball player from Melbourne.

For now, he and O'Neil had to focus on getting the team off to a good start. Despite all the waiting, the focus on getting back, he didn't feel quite ready. He'd never played Test cricket without the Reader bat. What if all those runs hadn't been him at all? Other bats just didn't give him same invincible feeling.

Pakistan's strike bowler, Hakar, was a left-armer, *the* master of the craft. Harrow could only watch from the other end as the ball moved away in the air, towards four waiting slip fielders, trying to lead O'Neil into playing a shot. And then, the inswinger. The ball slipped through a narrow gap, between O'Neil's moving bat and his pads, cannoning into leg stump. He spun his head around to see the damage but there was no undoing it, he was on his way back to the sheds for a duck.

Harrow stared at the delivery replayed up on the big screen, over and over, guts churning, while Dog walked out, asked for middle stump, and scratched at the crease, trying to slow things down. Hakar was waiting at the top of his mark. The fielders were rubbing their hands together. It was only ever going to be an inswinging yorker, and Dog almost kept it out. But it struck him on the big toe, knocking him off his feet. It looked absolutely plumb. Hakar was dancing, arms in the air, before the umpire even raised his finger. Dog limped back to the pavilion for a golden duck. Two down for none. *Shit.*

He met Gibbo in the middle of the pitch. 'Let's just take it one ball at a time.'

'Got it.'

Gibbo defended his stumps as if his life depended on it, body in line, eyes on the ball. The only shot he offered he played straight, with soft hands, for no run. They'd survived the over.

At the change of ends, Harrow tried to clear his mind of what had gone before. He took his time, facing up, and watched the first three balls go past, moving away. The next one came in, forcing him to play. He flicked it off his pads and called Gibbo through for a single. Gibbo defended the final two balls, and it was Harrow to face Hakar with his tail up.

Inswinger. And another, forcing him to play. Then the outswinger. It went late, and the keeper had to dive for it. The next one was a tighter line, coming in. Harrow kept his hands soft, played straight. Still the ball found the edge, falling just short of third slip. Hakar's slinging action made it hard to read the line. Harrow wafted at the next one, wanting to feel bat on ball. *Idiot.* Hakar had him exactly where he wanted him, playing in the corridor of uncertainty.

They scrapped to twenty runs, and Harrow had almost seen out the final over of Hakar's spell, when he had no choice but to play at a ball that hooped in at his pads and then moved away. He felt the *snick* and turned to watch second slip scoop up a straightforward catch.

When he was showered and back in the dressing room, they watched the replay over and over. The deviation was at least six centimetres. 'Unplayable,' Winslow said. 'That ball would have got anybody out.'

But it had got him out. And Megan and Nina had been there to see it. He just didn't feel in charge out there the way he had before the injury.

Harrow watched, head in hands, as the wickets fell. Australia were all out for ninety-seven. Hilt took two quick wickets in his opening spell but then the sun came out for Pakistan's innings. Sky created a chance, but Dog dropped the catch, which was unheard of. He was usually Mr Golden Hands. Pakistan got away, building their lead to two hundred and twenty before the last wicket fell. Then, all too soon, Harrow had to pad up all over again.

He was OUT to an almost identical ball as in the first innings, for two miserable runs, and his dismissal sparked a mini-collapse. They fought back, thanks to a good partnership between Peters and Mads, but it wasn't enough. Pakistan scored the winning runs before lunch on day five. Hakar was player of the match, taking ten wickets.

The boys sat around in the change rooms afterwards, sharing a quiet beer, except the bowlers were all up one end, like on the tour bus. The batters knew all too well they hadn't given the bowlers enough runs to defend, without seeing their disappointed faces and their broad backs turned. Even Sky was avoiding him, walking away when Harrow stood next to him. The team was pulling apart.

In Sydney, they won the toss and batted first. Hakar came on second over. To bowl to Harrow. He'd started taking strike outside his crease to negate the swing, but for the first time, he was dreading batting. His hands were shaking as he retied his laces, his heart pounding as he and O'Neil walked out, without looking at each other, to face the King of Swing.

The ball was not swinging as much on a dry pitch and a clear day, but he was still a handful. Harrow played and missed at more balls than he could count but survived. They put on forty-five, with a little help from a wide, two no balls and four leg-byes, before he fended at one outside off stump and caught the finest of nicks, which was taken low by the keeper. Harrow examined the thick edge of the bat on his way off the ground, shaking his head.

This time the rest of the boys held their nerve, putting on a decent first-innings total around O'Neil's ninety-three.

Then it was Pakistan's turn to collapse. Hilt bowled both openers in his second over. Sky got his first Test wicket, and Jacks broke open their middle order. Dog had brought Hilt and Jacks back on to bowl, keeping it tight, trying to clean up the tail. With Shep released back to Shield cricket, they were without a twelfth man. So when Peters ran off the field to change his boots, a young grade cricketer, Salt, came on as replacement fielder.

Third ball of Jacks' next over, Aziz tried to sweep and caught the splice of the bat. Salt sprinted in from the boundary, eyes on the ball, launching himself into the air, flying forward, arms outstretched, to take the catch in both hands, well above the ground.

'You little *beauty*!' Mads was screaming.

The elation on Salt's face when he held up the ball gave them the shot of energy they needed. They ran to him, forming a scrum, messing up his hair. The cameras zoomed in. It was a classic catch for sure, a close-up already being replayed on the big screen. Salt would be a household name by morning. Hopefully he was ready for his picture all over the back pages.

Even Liv, when they caught up after the game, could only rave about the catch. At least she didn't mention his batting.

a game of fine margins

We're glued to the radio, when we should be gluing in handles. Harrow is facing Hakar, yet to score in the third over of the series decider at the G. There's no crowd noise, as if they sense a moment within the game.

'Harrow looks unsettled here. But if he gets a start, he'll punish them on this flat track you'd think,' Maxwell says.

'Getting a start seems to be his problem,' Roebuck says, always the wet blanket.

Pakistan is a mercurial team. Their First Test win was inspired, pure class from Hakar, one of the best bowlers in the world. Probably the best ever left-armer. Given their paucity of international experience and facilities, political turmoil and constant rotation of coaches and captains, it's a miracle they're fielding a side, let alone one that flogs the Australians. And then they completely gave it away in Sydney.

Hakar seems to have Harrow's number, getting him out cheaply in three of his four innings. That first dismissal was an absolute peach, planting a seed of doubt in Harrow's mind. Now he's wafting at balls he doesn't have to play. Of course, that club of a bat isn't helping. They say cricket is a game of inches but sometimes it's a matter of millimetres.

'Hakar is steaming in,' Maxwell says. 'Oh – he's *living* on that length. Harrow pushes forward. *Edged* and GONE. Caught at first slip. A brute of a ball. And he's OUT for a duck. His first in international cricket.'

Katie looks up from the bat she's sanding. 'What's happening to him?'

I shake my head. 'Got the yips.'

Katie has moved up to shaping bats on her own. She's still a little nervous around the pressing. The machine, the mystery, I'm not sure. But she can make a bat from scratch to finish. She has more to learn about balance, but it's a process. We had a laneway hit with her first one, to give her a feel for the weight and pick up. Just like old times, though my wobbly off-breaks are a little more wobbly. We had a beer on the back steps afterwards as the sun went down, just talking. I'm happy to see her laughing again.

During the days we're both in the workshop, we get quite a production line going, which flows right through the week. Together we seem to get more than twice as much done. Youthful energy, I suppose. And there's something about sharing the work, someone understanding what goes on in your day. Exchanging that knowing look across the workshop or passing over a finished bat and acknowledging the miracle of something special.

I'm even enjoying the teaching. It's only one weekend a month and the people seem to appreciate the willow. All but one have been men, from all over the country, but maybe that will change. There'll be a tribe of batmakers soon. People are already booking in for next year. It means working seven days during the season, but Katie and I are building a future.

Meanwhile, I'm making time for music. Just an hour of practice the afternoons Katie is at class. It's all coming back to me now. I'm wishing the same for Harrow. He made a decent start in the second innings, played a beautiful on-drive and a couple of nice cut shots, but was out, caught in the slips again, for thirty-nine. A big hundred from Barker and a seventy-eight from Peters meant three-sixty for Pakistan to get on the final day, which was too much pressure. They were dismissed for two hundred and twenty-three, with Walker taking four wickets. He looks very good indeed, easy action, consistent, and getting a steepling bounce from his height.

It was a dismal series for Harrow. A complete contrast to the Ashes. It's partly that the bowlers have figured him out, found a weakness, perhaps. But who knows how it would have panned out if he hadn't been injured. And if he hadn't given the away his bat! With Shepherd still pressing his claims in Shield cricket, and young Needham turning out another century, Harrow is by no means a lock for the South Africa tour.

I want to reach out to him, but what to say? In the end, I send him a text message telling him to hang in there and trust his skills.

Meanwhile, O. Harrow has scored her first one-day international century to secure the series against New Zealand. She also took ten wickets for the match, including a freakish caught and bowled. The bat had nothing to do with that. She's the all-rounder the men's team would love to have. And the new poster girl for Australian cricket as they head into the Women's One Day World Cup, which is to be televised. The Australians are favourites to take it out.

I hear Katie arrive home, and something heavy going down on the deck.

'You okay?'

'Get the door?'

'Sure.' I hold my arm out and press myself against the hallway wall. She staggers past, her satchel over one shoulder, tool pouch over the other, carrying something big in front of her. 'Heavy?'

'Just awkward,' she says. But she's puffing all the same.

I follow her inside and she sets it down in the studio and pulls away the soft cloth.

'That's beautiful. Stump stool?'

She grins. 'Exactly.'

It's the first piece she's brought home. The surface is glossy smooth and deep red, dipping into a tall, bottom-shaped seat. 'Red gum? Where did you get it?'

'A classmate and I went out to an old road-clearing site. Came back with a ute-load of these stumps. He's turning his into delicate dishes, but I wanted minimum interference. It's furniture but still half tree.' Her face is alight.

'It's wonderful. You can see all its growth rings there. How did you get that burnish?'

'Heat gun. And wire brush, on the drill.'

'Huh – like when cattle rub on a tree or a post.'

She lifts it to show me underneath. 'I turned out a heap of timber, so it isn't so heavy.'

'It's a lovely piece, Katie.'

'Hardwood is way more difficult to work than willow.'

'But this will last forever.'

'I hope I got the height right.'

'For me?'

She nods. 'For playing.'

I lower myself on it. A height between sitting and standing. 'Perfect.'

She grins. 'So, I have something for us.' She pulls a bottle of Bollinger from her satchel. 'I'll just pop it in the freezer for a bit.'

'We're celebrating your first piece?'

'And … I reached an agreement with Dave. He has to give me back a chunk of money. And not come near me for two years.'

A tension I hadn't been aware of in my body departs, as if all the close fielders have scattered for the boundary.

bad light

When Slogger's call came, Harrow was expecting the worst. But they were sticking with him; he was going to South Africa! Shep was in the squad, too, so no guarantees. But Slogger had suggested that the conditions over there would suit his style. Everyone said playing in South Africa was like playing at home, with dry bouncy pitches, the ball coming on. The two teams had similar styles of play as a result, and a particular rivalry. Klimt was going too, as cover for their quicks. A reward for a breakout season. He didn't really look that threatening, running in, but he kept getting wickets, and had a knack for breaking a big partnership.

He waited until Megan got home from work and he'd poured her a glass of wine before breaking the news.

'Are you pleased?'

'Relieved.'

'Me, too. You'll be out of my hair.' Megan smiled but he knew she wasn't fully joking. She was sick of him pacing around, shadow batting in the apartment, replaying all his dismissals against Hakar. And she was super busy, taking on someone else's clients, she said. One of the partners had left suddenly. A health scare.

'You don't want to come over?'

'I'm drowning at the moment. And I have a matter appearing before the court during that time. That shipping company I was telling you about. I need to be here.'

Okay,' he said. They hadn't really been able to plan anything, thinking he might not even go. And her schedules were changed around all the time, matters adjourned or dragging on longer than expected. But she used to say she wanted to come to South Africa with him.

'What about Cape Town? At the end. Just for a week,' he said. 'The other partners are all going.'

'Don't do that. I can't just drop my work for yours.'

Harrow stared out the window, the afternoon haze blurring the city. 'Fair enough,' he said. It wasn't like he wanted to make her go. But he was gutted, all the same. Not seeing her for a month, for a start.

'Sorry, babe,' she said. 'I'll be with you in spirit. And watching whenever you bat.'

They flew into Durban for the First Test. Kingsmead was below sea level, the Indian Ocean so close they could smell it. 'Watch out for the Green Mamba,' Mads said. That's what they called the pitch. When the tide came in, the ball apparently started swinging around corners.

South Africa won the toss and chose to bat. He'd have a chance to see how the pitch played at least. With Armstrong aggravating a side strain at training, Klimt would make his debut. But it was Slim to open the bowling from the Umgeni End.

The ground only had a few stands, it was all grass terraces, the crowd already baking in the sun. South Africa got off to a good start and were only one down at lunch. Slim and Hilt came back for their second spells with better lines and lengths. Klimt was immaculate. His first international wicket was thanks to a screamer from Mads, diving one-handed to remove South Africa's captain.

Maybe it was too much sun and beer but the crowd was hostile. They booed the bowlers running in, hooted at every little mistake in the field. Slim was copping it down on the boundary. The press had got hold of the story about his wife leaving him for the high-profile league player, Johnny-G. They had a young daughter, so it had all been a bit of a shock, and touch and go whether he would come away or stay home to deal with it.

A group in the crowd was really getting under his skin, holding up pictures of Johnny and making pretty filthy remarks about his ex. Dog moved him to mid-on but every time he chased the ball out towards the boundary, the crowd heaped on the shit. The South African batters had taken to saying, 'Uh oh. Here's Johnny,' every time Slim came on to bowl.

The upside was that Slim bowled mean. He hit the South African right-handed opener twice on the forearm and once on the shoulder. The next ball kept low and cannoned into his pads. Slim turned, absolutely upright, arm up, and raised one finger. When the umpire nodded, Dlamini had to go. Slim gave him a right send off, too. It was going to be one of those emotional matches.

Late in the day, thick cloud cover moved in. The lights came on and Klimt was starting to get some reverse swing. The batters were struggling to score. Their keeper muttered something in Afrikaans as Klimt fielded the ball.

'What was that?' Klimt said, hand to his ear.

'I told him you belonged back in state cricket, Fag.'

Dog, at first slip, held up his hand. 'Don't use it as an insult. There's nothing wrong with being gay.'

Klimt had the final word, knocking two of the keeper's stumps out of the ground with the final ball of his spell. He didn't say a thing, just took his hat and vest from the umpire and walked out to long on.

Dog brought back Slim, who only needed one more for a five-wicket haul. But the South Africans had complained about visibility. The umpires conferred, consulted their little meters, and called close of play for bad light.

'Fucking bullshit!'

Harrow and Peters had to drag Slim from the field.

They cleaned up South Africa's tail the next morning. Slim got his five-for with the final wicket, holding the ball up for the crowd – and the press room. His own kind of 'fuck you', for dragging his off-field dramas into the game. The boys gathered around him, trying to be his armour, his family. Harrow and O'Neil ran from the ground to get ready, psyched to build a big total.

O'Neil saw off the first over from their veteran quick, Coetzee, leaving Harrow to face their new young quick, Zungu, from the Old Fort Road End. No one had played against him and there was limited video footage so they weren't really sure what to expect. The first ball was short and wide, giving Harrow room to cut for FOUR. It was good to feel bat on ball, get the legs moving.

Their captain and keeper were muttering in Afrikaans, something about Harrow not being able to play the swinging ball. Not that Zungu was getting much swing. The captain brought mid-on up; a bouncer was on the way.

'He's no Hayden,' their keeper said. 'That's for sure.'

'And you're no Boucher,' Harrow said.

The slips fielders spat on their hands, rubbed them together, and dropped down into position, waiting.

Zungu sprinted in, gold chain flashing. The ball was just wide of off stump, right in his hitting zone. He dropped his knees and swung. 'Oh no.' He turned to watch the ball fly into the outstretched glove of the keeper.

Second time around, South Africa already had a lead of a hundred and fifty when Harrow missed a run-out chance. Not by much but there'd been more time to steady himself. Then Peters dropped an absolute sitter at gully. With his wingspan, he'd been taking blinders. But now this. Poor Sky, finally getting the breakthrough. Or so he'd thought. He covered his face with his hat to mask the swearing from the cameras but the stump mics picked it up, all the same, and the local TV station made a big deal of it.

Only Klimt managed to lift, taking two wickets in consecutive balls, putting him on a hat-trick for the first ball of his next over. It was a beauty, too, pitching in line, hitting Kruger low on the front pad. Everyone went up. Klimmy was in a crouch, arms spread wide, pleading.

'Not out,' the umpire said.

Replays showed it was going down leg, but the boys threw their heads back, as if Klimt had been robbed. The South African batters got on top and then got away, looking to build a big total.

When Peters took a low catch at gully and claimed it, Kruger walked. But replays made it look like it had hit the ground just in front of his fingers. The South African players had plenty to say and, when Mads and Peters fired up, the umpires had to step in. The crowd was booing and yelling obscenities, calling them cheats, throwing things onto the field.

Harrow let it get to him, fumbling a straightforward catch. All the energy drained out of them, like a deflating balloon. Even Dog was rattled, deciding not to review a caught behind despite Mads swearing there was a nick.

When South Africa finally declared, sending Australia in to bat late in the final session of day four, Australia needed four hundred and eleven to win. The crowd booed as he and O'Neil walked out, hurling rubbish and abuse. The South Africans were all over them, bowling good lines and lengths, sharp in the field. O'Neil went first, followed soon after by Dog. They sent in Slim as nightwatchman.

The clouds gathered around the ground and the lights came on, like a day–night game. The crowd clapping the South African bowlers in was all he could hear. And the sledging. 'Little man,' they called him. Nothing the umpires would stop but eating away at him all the same. Somehow, he hung on until the last over, only to be caught in the gully, slashing at the final ball of the day.

Slim tried to comfort him, as they walked from the field. Harrow left his helmet on, to hide the tears. A wide ball he hadn't even needed to play at. *Idiot.* Without the magic bat, he was no knight. He wasn't even a decent batter.

the bullring

He'd thought Durban was tough but it didn't compare to what was waiting for them at the Wanderers. They flew over a vast grassy plateau, into the seething city of Johannesburg. They weren't to leave the hotel alone, their manager said. The city had one of the worst crime rates in the world. It was the kind of a place where people were shot just going out to get their morning paper. The ground itself was ringed by trees, a nod to the distant Highveld. But the city had them surrounded, stretching on forever. Harrow could feel the history: the triumphs of the Rugby World Cup and the Africa Cup of Nations, the weight of apartheid itself. It was all so heavy. They were one down in the series and he was coming off back-to-back failures.

When he and O'Neil ran down the caged race and out on to the ground, Harrow understood why it was called The Bullring. People were throwing bottles, grabbing at their shirts, yelling obscenities. The outfield seemed to shimmer, the heaving stands to lean in. The crowd was too close, too loud. The embankment was a sea of colour, movement, and hostility. Their placards did not so much support the home team but attack the enemy: Australia.

O'Neil was close behind him, breathing hard. They slowed at the edge of the field to touch the Australian flags and pass between them. Harrow watched O'Neil take strike and guide the first ball down to fine leg. He ran through for the single and took strike, but everything had sped up, Coetzee running in before Harrow had steadied himself.

The ball reared off the pitch. Harrow played and missed, his bat clipping his pad. *Close.* Their keeper took the ball and appealed.

Second slip followed, then the bowler. Harrow shook his head to indicate that he hadn't hit it. But the umpire raised his finger, pointing the way to the dressing room.

Harrow tucked his bat under his arm and trudged back through the enclosed race, the mesh protecting him from all the projectiles the South Africans were hurling, but not their insults.

'Fuck!' He threw his bat through the door, into the dressing room, hitting Sky's locker door on the full.

Harrow made another round of coffees in the team kitchen. The dressing room was their inner sanctum. There were rules, traditions, where they sat during the game, and who with. Their routines before they went out to bat, and when they got out. If Dog was dismissed cheaply, he would take a long shower and sit out the back with a towel over his head, so filthy with himself he didn't want the others to see it. It wasn't a captain's place to show too much emotion. And Sky, if a decision went against him, or someone dropped a catch off his bowling, he would sit by himself, so quiet it was scary. They knew just to leave him alone. He would calm down, store it all away for his next bowling session, and be joking around again after the next meal.

When it rained, there was usually a poker game. The bowlers ran that, with Sky now known as the shark. They'd roped in Gibbo, too. Harrow had started doing the crosswords with Mads, Dog and O'Neil. Not the cryptics, just the regular ones. Sometimes he had to ask what a word meant, or where a place was. The boys gave him shit but he didn't care, it was satisfying to finish them. He was trying to make an effort, learn a few things. Megan never made him feel stupid, but he didn't want to embarrass her in front of friends and colleagues. They weren't all as easygoing as Nina.

While he'd put in the minimum effort with everything but cricket, Megan had put in the maximum, awarded dux of her year and some big state prize for English. And while he left school as soon as he could, she'd gone on to university, not once but twice, getting an MBA on top of her law degree.

He saw plenty of movies with the boys, and they were great nights. But he watched them differently on his own. Sometimes he'd watch a bunch from the same director, or actor, trying to get a sense of their style, what they were on about. He'd talk to Megan about it, later, which usually led to a really good conversation, especially if she'd seen it, too. It wasn't quite the same as their Tuesday movie nights, at the Palace back in New Farm, but it kept them connected.

During breaks in play, the fast bowlers would be on the bikes, keeping warm, or getting a work-over on the massage table. They were the team's racehorses, finely tuned machines, only ever a moment away from breaking down. Not that they were delicate. They played with pain every day: backs, shoulders, knees, hips, ankles, and their feet were gruesome. It took half an hour just to tape themselves up before play. Hilt cut the toe out of all his shoes in the end, just to ease the pressure on his front foot when he landed. They were warriors, no doubt about it.

When they were winning, the dressing room was the best place in the world. Travelling together as a group, they became a herd. And, sometimes, they were animals. But they had each other's backs. Winning made it easy. Team spirit, belief, came naturally. Success breeds success.

But sometimes the dressing room wasn't such a good place to be. There was a negative vibe on the South Africa tour that they were all feeding, and feeding from. The press was hounding them, trying to get pictures of Winslow, Dog and the players looking glum, writing about how shit they were, all the things they were doing wrong, all the mistakes they'd made. Why Harrow should be dropped.

In the team meeting on avoiding another collapse, Winslow, his shirt so crumpled he must have slept in it, insisted the whole squad put in writing what they could be doing better. Slim just sat there with his arms folded and Gibbo actually got up and walked out. Blokes were breaking off into huddles, bitching about the food, the bus, rooms, Winslow. They'd split into batters versus bowlers, coach, captain and staff versus players. Everyone was looking over his shoulder, expecting the axe.

Harrow kept to himself. He knew he'd let everybody down, that his position was the first one being discussed behind those closed doors. He'd tried calling Megan but she wasn't answering. Probably just busy but it didn't help, the places his head was going. He couldn't face talking to Mum or Dad; he'd let them down, too.

Liv called while she was eating breakfast. 'It looks tough,' she said. 'Just do what you do best, Toddy. Bat. Bat your way out of it. Lift the team, take them with you.'

'Thanks, Liv.'

between the ears

The oboe can be a treacherous instrument. You can do everything correctly and still get an unexpected bloop – those messy sounds between two intended notes. The trap is to play cautiously as a result, which leads to tense and unpleasant sound. To find the real resonance and beauty of the oboe, you must take risks. I practise my fingering sequences, minimising my movements, relaxing my fingers – and breathe.

I'm blaming the cricket. Another bad loss in Johannesburg and things are getting ugly between the teams. The commentators are calling for Harrow's head. It's not that he's lost his gift or technique. Cricket is a game mainly played between the ears. He knows too much. He knows disappointment now, the things that can go wrong, all the ways he can get out, the way the game can turn on him. He knows his faults; they've been pointed out to him by coaches, managers, opponents, the press. He's been watching his innings – his dismissals – replayed over and over on screen, analysed and dissected, until he's sick of himself.

He fears failure. I can see it in his body language, the way he holds himself, those micro-hesitations. And he knows what's at stake now: his income, livelihood, reputation and, most of all, his position in the Australian team. That most coveted, most valued but inevitably temporary thing – his dream. Instead of watching the next ball, the bowler's next move, he's anticipating his undoing, his decline. Instead of wanting to score runs, he's trying not to get out. I've seen it before, that self-doubt, in Nate and so many other players since.

It isn't just a cricket thing. I left music behind because I told myself I wasn't good enough. In reality, it was the *fear* that I wasn't good enough that got in the way. I lacked the maturity to check that feeling, hitching my goals to scholarships, grants, performances, prizes, standing and accolades, rather than the things I could actually control: my practice, my love for music itself. The pressure I put on myself paralysed me. I was too young for success.

When I said goodbye to Grandfather at Heathrow, we knew we wouldn't see each other again. He insisted on driving me, although it had been so long since his old Vauxhall had been out of the garage, we had to charge the battery. His driving was no longer up to the A-roads or contemporary parking procedures, but between us we managed.

We'd been up to Worcester on the train, the day before, to see the English String Orchestra perform *Serenade for Strings*, as part of the Elgar Festival. The closing piece, 'Sospiri', had me sobbing into my handkerchief, capturing better than I ever could have with words, what it is to say goodbye.

We spent a final reverent morning at Lord's, Grandfather's church. It was with fresh eyes that I examined the development of bats, from wooden club to willow blade. When cricket appeared in Suffolk in 1780, they were more like a hooked cudgel, and solid timber: ash, spliced with alder. Willow didn't even come into the story until the mid-1800s. Grandfather stood beside me, in front of the display case, our reflections more similar that I'd realised.

'The game's always evolving,' he said. Which was as close as I was going to get to his approval to go my own way.

He hugged me at the departure gate, which was the first and only time. My father was the same, never one for affection. My words got stuck in my throat, as usual, but sometimes things don't need to be said to be felt. I gripped his forearms, still strong and ropey, and took in every detail of his weathered face.

'Thank you.'

It was my cousin Saul who called to tell me Grandfather had died in his sleep – the best possible way to leave the field. We'd spoken on the phone at Christmas, and I'd been able to tell him about the batmaking, the growing plantation – and that we were expecting Katie.

the mountain

By the time they reached Cape Town, he felt like they'd been touring for months. Even the press back home had turned on them, labelling them bad sports and poor performers. There was ample footage (thanks to the South African broadcaster) of Peters claiming the grassed catch, Gibbo disputing an umpire's leg-before decision, Dog defending Klimt (without the context), Sky's string of expletives, and Harrow throwing his bat. They were examining his failures under the microscope. No one ever remembered the bad umpiring decisions, the unplayable deliveries. He wasn't scoring runs anymore and they wanted him gone.

Slim had it worse. Pictures of his wife's every movement at home, all the details of her affair. He'd already dropped five kilos, losing pace and struggling just to get through training. It was taking its toll on all of them.

He needed to speak to Megan but the time difference made it difficult. His parents were in the middle of the Easter rush, and Liv was busy with training, uni and work. When he texted her, 'Chin up, Toddy,' was all she had to say.

He took some time to walk around the ground, reminding himself that to finally be at Newlands was a fairytale come true. The great flat-topped bulk of Table Mountain rose behind the ground, the remnants of a vast pine forest creeping into the city's edges. The mountain's fissured faces and big shoulders, the scrubby trees sprouting from the most unlikely outcrops, reminded him of Mount Tibrogargan, back home.

Trees sprouted inside the ground, too, shading the umbrellaed hill areas, and dominating an entire section, like a stand. When he walked out into the middle, to visualise batting the following day, the scoreboard seemed to float in the forest. The ground staff had planted wildflowers right around the edges of the ground, as if to tame it, but the wild wasn't far away.

In his mind he started calling it magic mountain. It was everywhere he went, watching. He could see it from the hotel room window, the breakfast room, and the nets, where he was spending a lot of time with Stevo, trying to iron out the little forward and across movement, which had him playing inside the line of the ball. Mads watched from the neighbouring net, saying nothing. But when Stevo left, he leaned on the mesh between them

'Hars,' he said. 'Just let the ball come to *you*. Own that space out there.'

He and the boys took a tour up the mountain with the wives and girlfriends for sunset. Dog's partner, Sandy, was sweet, asking after Liv and Megan. After the guide's talk and a whole lot of photos, Harrow stood at the edge, looking over the city. The height and scale was almost too much, in a country he didn't know or understand. They were all licking their wounds from the Wanderers and Durban. Some of the others had a bit of extra baggage, with what had happened last time they played at Newlands (bowled out for fifty-six). But he hadn't been there for that. Neither had Peters, Hilt, Klimt or Sky. Mads said it was time they made their own history. He was the glue keeping them together.

He was trying not to feel disappointed that Megan hadn't come. He'd had half a plan of proposing on the mountain. It was probably just as well, given his performance. He didn't exactly feel like celebrating. And he was beginning to understand that marriage wasn't necessarily something Megan wanted, like touring full time with the rest of the WAGs. She had her own goals. He didn't want to get in the way of that. He liked that she was different to the others. But he missed her and needed her support.

Sky and Klimt broke away from the group to stand with him.

'Okay, buddy?' Klimt said.

'Yeah.'

Sky looked down at the ground, far below. 'How about we show some Queensland fight, turn all this around, eh?'

Harrow smiled. 'Deal.' There was one more chance to prove himself, to show what he was made of.

It was late on day two before he ran out onto Newlands to bat. He and O'Neil shook hands and headed to their respective ends. Harrow stared up at the mountain, trying to figure out if it was with him or against him. The South Africans had put a good total on the board; it was critical that he and O'Neil got the boys off to a good start.

Zungu was really getting it to zip. It wasn't until the last ball of the over that Harrow flicked one off his pads, called YES, and had to sprint to make it home after a quick pick up and throw from Dlamini. The South Africans were chirping, telling Harrow what a shit batter he was, that there were two better men just waiting to replace him. Blokes had a knack of saying what you were already worrying about yourself. Harrow just smiled, tapped the ground three times with the base of his bat. But the red of the umbrellas over the hill section, echoed in the advertising signage, had him thinking of war, the violence still so close to the surface.

O'Neil was in nice touch, picking off anything loose for a series of clinical boundaries, scoring ones and twos square of the wicket. Harrow focused on backing up well and running hard. Then he got one away off the front foot, through the covers, and a cut for FOUR right out of the middle.

'Looking good, Hars.'

'They're not getting me out today.'

O'Neil, then Harrow, raised their bats for half-centuries, seeing Australia through to lunch and frustrating the home crowd. Then the mist came down from the mountain, cascading over its hard edges, like a sea. It didn't have weather, they were moods. The sun disappeared, and the ball started swinging all over the place. Magic mountain was a black shadow, looming. The light towers leaned, seagulls circled in strange patterns. The brewery behind the trees, with its row of silver silos, let out a puff of steam.

O'Neil went first, chopping the ball onto his stumps. When Harrow faced up again, the ball had shrunk. Coetzee started his run-up from far away and rushed up on him, as if popping out of a tunnel. He didn't see the ball leave his hand, let alone the seam position. He barely saw it hit the pitch, which had shrunk to eleven yards instead of twenty-two. He only sighted the ball at the last moment: a red blur, whirring and spitting past him. It was too late to move his feet, he could only shift his weight back and waft his bat. The one sense that remained intact was his hearing, which had been dialled up. The noise from the crowd, the fielders talking, the scrape of the umpire's shoe.

Another bouncer forced him back in his crease. Harrow watched it whizz past. *Slap*, into the keeper's gloves.

'He's got no idea,' said their captain, from first slip.

Harrow grinned, walked out towards square leg, shook his head, jogged up and down to get the blood flowing. The crowd was muttering and booing, sensing a wicket.

He took his time walking back, taking strike. Owning the space. He stilled his head, his breathing. Dog made as if to come down the pitch, for a word. Harrow avoided eye contact, took his mark. *Watch the ball. Just this ball*

Coetzee was tearing in, arms pumping, face set in a grimace, the delivery stride and swinging arm just a blur of force and motion. Harrow saw it out of the hand, got in behind it, but the ball jagged up off the pitch, as if it had hit a crack. For a millisecond, he was uncertain whether to duck, sway, or hook. Then his body took over, swinging hard. But he was late on it, not yet through his shot when the ball struck. Everything was white: noise, light, pain.

The ground came up, fast. The bowler was leaning over him, speaking, but he couldn't make out the words.

Dog removed Harrow's helmet. Something wet was running down his face. He couldn't breathe through his nose.

'You're okay, Hars. You're going to be okay.'

bad blood

'Oh my god. How is that even possible?' Katie is off the lounge, hands out in front of her, as if to walk through the screen.

The slow-motion replay shows the ball smashing between the top bar of the grille and the visor of Harrow's helmet – into his face. He's down. On his knees first and then onto his back. When Barker, holding Harrow's head, gestures for the medical staff to come out, there's blood on his hands.

'Sometimes they bend the grille, so they can see better,' I say.

Every member of the crowd had been baying for blood, but now that it has been spilled, they're quiet, hands over mouths, watching on the big screen.

The players, both sides, are huddled around. The South African captain's hand is on his bowler's back. The Australian team doctor and the physio run onto the field, squatting either side of Harrow. The twelfth man brings out a towel, drinks and ice. The doctor is examining his face, skull and jaw, holding a towel to his nose.

Harrow raises his hand, a weak thumbs up.

I let out the breath I've been holding. 'He's conscious.'

The commentators, who have been quiet, start talking again. Harrow sits up. The doctor and physio help him to his feet, one either side, and assist him from the field. Blood is still streaming from his nose, staining his white shirtfront red. Walker carries Harrow's bat, helmet and gloves.

The crowd stands to clap him off. The game has changed. Just walking from the field is an heroic act.

Katie and I are up late again, watching. Harrow's injury galvanised the Australians. A hundred from Barker and contributions from all the players got them to within thirty of the South African total. But South Africa took their lead to three hundred and eighty and declared, sending the Australians back in. And they'd rate their chances. Harrow has a broken nose and concussion, leaving them a batter short. Barker opens with O'Neil and plays a captain's knock, raising his bat for his first century of the tour. But he's out shortly afterwards. Gibson scores another aggressive fifty but gives his wicket away, holing out in the deep. At tea, they're five down with a hundred and forty to get. Which, with Harrow injured, is effectively six down. South Africa know that if they can take one more, they're into the tailenders.

I get up to make toasted sandwiches and we open a second bottle of wine. Peters is playing positively, taking on the South African bowlers, and Matterson is backing up well, haring between the wickets. Every run counts. Then Peters doesn't quite get enough bat on a hook shot. The fielder runs around to take the catch. Peters walks off, looking despondent but he's done well.

Jackson is in next, the veteran spinner. He's had plenty of experience in tough situations. The batters have a chat out in the middle and Jackson deliberately takes his time getting settled, leaving Zungu standing hands on hips. He gets off strike with a single and then Matterson takes up where Peters left off, striking the ball straight down the ground for consecutive boundaries, and stealing a single off the final ball of the over to retain the strike.

'The South Africans were sloppy there,' Pollock says. 'They should have come in to stop the one, and made sure the new batter was on strike next over against the spinner.'

'Yes, poor match awareness,' Maxwell says.

When Jackson shovels one straight to extra cover, Australia still need eighty to win. Hilton comes out, swinging his long arms. If he connects with a few, it will push the scoring along. He nods to whatever Matterson has said, grins, and takes his mark.

The ball is short and Hilton whooshes, getting enough on it to see it run past the outstretched hand of slip, down to the boundary for FOUR.

'They might get there,' Katie says.

Matterson tries to steal another quick single but a pounce and throw at one stump from Dlamini, patrolling the covers, and Matterson is caught short of his ground. OUT. The South Africans are up and whooping again. That brings Klimt to the crease. I've seen him hang in there for Queensland, but they still need another forty-one with only Walker left to bat.

When the umpire calls drinks, I head to the kitchen to put on the kettle.

'Dad, look.'

I turn. The cameras are showing Harrow padded up. His face is bandaged, swollen – unrecognisable. 'Surely he won't actually bat. Barker wouldn't let him go out.'

Hilton is scoring along the ground, both sides of the wicket, frustrating South Africa. There's a bit of chirp between the players, too. Some bad blood on this tour. Australia is within twenty-five of the required total, when Hilton is struck on the pad, sweeping again, and the umpire raises his finger.

The cameras are already focused on the player walking out. It's Harrow.

'The noise is incredible,' Maxwell says. 'How the tide has turned. The crowd are behind Harrow here, acknowledging his courage. Surely it's dangerous, if he was to be hit again.'

'It's the batter's job to make sure he's not hit,' says Pollock.

Spoken like a true fast bowler. They bring back Coetzee, and the first ball is bouncer. Harrow sways out of the way and watches the ball go through to the keeper. The grin is gone but he nods and walks away, to centre himself, and back to face the next one. This time he uses the width and whips it away through mid-wicket for FOUR but can't get off strike last ball of the over, leaving Klimt to face their big quick.

Klimt mis-hits the second ball of the next over, spooning it straight to Zungu.

'Oh, goodness,' Pollock says. 'Zungu has dropped an absolute sitter.'

Meanwhile, they've run through for a single, giving Harrow the strike. 'These two are former housemates. They've batted together plenty of times for Queensland,' Maxwell says. 'Beware the injured batter, they say.'

I don't know how he's seeing the ball, with his face so swollen, but he threads the next one between short cover and extra cover for FOUR. The bowler is panicking now, hands on head, changing his field yet again.

The next one is short and wide. Harrow cuts. The fielder is running around, dives, arm outstretched, but can't cut it off. The crowd signal FOUR. The bowler shakes his head, as if the fielder has let him down, and walks back to his mark.

'The bowler is steaming in. Harrow drives, just missing the stumps at the other end, straight down the ground for another FOUR.' There's emotion in Maxwell's voice. 'This is an incredible display.'

'That was not a bad ball,' Pollock says.

Klimt defends the first three from Zungu. Then it's his turn, a beautifully timed cover drive. Fielders are running around the boundary from either side, but it beats them both to the rope.

'They're playing out of their skins here,' Maxwell says. 'Just four to win.'

Another dot ball and then Klimt hits a single towards mid-wicket but they don't take the run, putting Harrow on strike for the next over.

I make myself breathe. It's Coetzee to bowl. There are singles everywhere but Harrow won't want to put Klimt on strike this early in the over. The first three balls give Harrow no room to score two. Coetzee steams in again, Harrow defends.

'Another dot,' Maxwell says.

The fifth ball is only a fraction short. Harrow picks it early. It's a beautiful pull shot, bouncing over the rope. FOUR. And Australia WIN!

'They did it!' Katie says.

'That's my boy,' I say.

Klimt and Harrow are embracing in the middle of the pitch. The South Africans are coming up one by one, to pat Harrow on the back. The Australian squad are sprinting out onto the ground.

Katie and I high-five, as if we had something to do with it. And we did; we were watching. South Africa win the series 2–1, but the Australians dug in, and fought hard. That's what matters. And Harrow, what courage, determination. I wipe the tears from my face.

solo

'Off to school?' It feels like that, though Katie's not wearing a uniform but jeans, T-shirt and flannel shirt, with her steel cap boots. With the early morning sun in the windows behind her, she's a picture. Now that she's looking for her own place, I'm realising how much I'm going to miss her smiling face in the mornings.

She smiles. 'I have a present for you.'

I down tools and she hands me two parcels wrapped in brown paper with white string.

'It's not my birthday.'

'Just a little something to thank you for helping me get back on my feet.'

'You didn't need to do that.' I unwrap the brown paper and stare at the box. 'New headphones! They look flash.'

'They're bluetooth – so no cords. And noise-cancelling. You can listen to music or the cricket even when you're using the machines. And protect your ears.'

I unwrap the other parcel, already a bit choked up. It's a new radio. A really good one.

'It talks to the headphones,' she says. 'So whenever you put them on you can just keep listening. It will talk to your phone, too.'

'Thank you, love. That's very thoughtful.' I'm worried I'm going to cry, so I hug her. Her shoulders are much more solid than when she arrived.

'You have to charge the headphones. But they should run for thirty hours,' she says. 'You can use them on the train, too. Or a plane.'

'I can't wait to try them out,' I say.

She unpacks the radio and tunes it to ABC. 'Any news on Harrow?'

'Flying home. He'll miss the one-day series.'

'Just when he was getting it together again.'

'Katie.'

She turns.

'It's you who helped me,' I say.

'We helped each other,' she says. 'See you at dinner.'

At last the reed and the air are doing the work and I'm not getting in their way. Those rich overtones – the reason for playing – are starting to come in. The most beautiful sounds on an oboe are the ones with the greatest complexity. A truly beautiful tone expresses the entire spectrum of colour, ranging from a warm fuzziness at the bottom, to a brilliant, piercing quality at the top. That resonance is what I'm aiming for but it's elusive – and the most vulnerable part of the tone.

I've been working up to playing longer pieces, ensembles mostly. We all have our moments in the limelight, but the oboe is usually part of something larger, whether playing with the string quartet, a duo with piano, or a full symphony orchestra. It's a matter of understanding the whole, and my part in it. I was always a team player, but some occasions do call for a solo.

I decide on gnocchi for Katie's last night, a childhood favourite. Her little apartment is near the Art School, in the new Docklands area. There's even a glimpse of the Yarra from her bedroom. I will miss her but we'll still be working together two days a week. It's better for her to have her independence. Bad enough working for the old man, let alone living with him.

When I hear the back door, I lower the gnocchi into the boiling salty water and fire up the gas underneath my butter. Once it's sizzling, I drop in the sage leaves, one by one, picked fresh from the garden.

'I bought a pinot. Okay?'

'Perfect.' I serve up and sprinkle parmesan over the top. Katie steps around me to fetch the glasses.

We sit down for dinner. Not for the last time but the last time quite like this. I sip my wine and put the glass down, conscious that I need to maintain that line between physically relaxed and mentally sharp.

'This is so good, Dad.'

'I'm glad.'

'Is it okay if I borrow the ute in the morning, to take my stuff over?'

'I'll help you. Is there anything else you need to pick up?'

She shakes her head. 'They're delivering the fridge and washing machine.'

'Exciting,' I say.

'Hey, I've caught up with Felix a couple of times since the concert. He's going to pop over to the new place tomorrow evening. Would you like to join us? We could break open a bottle of champagne, get some takeaway? Christen the place.'

Her face gives nothing away. Maybe this is where I should ask a question. But that could go wrong. I'll know the answer when I see them together.

'That sounds lovely.'

I clear our plates and stack them on the sink. A movement draws my eye to the garden through the old panes. Something hops out of the light and behind the glasshouse, tall ears backlit for a moment. A hare! I'll take that as a good sign.

I wipe my hands on the towel and again on my shirt. I take a deep breath, fetch the oboe from the studio and stand in the doorway.

Katie looks up. 'You're going to play for me?'

'I am.'

'About time.'

landing

This time, when he touched down in Brisbane, Megan was waiting for him at the gate. Her smile was a little forced but she hugged him and that felt good. He was home.

'Oh my god. Your poor face,' she said. 'Does it hurt?'

'It's not too bad. A bit of a headache from the flight.'

She sat her handbag on top of his luggage and pushed the trolley towards the glass doors, where a handful of reporters were waiting. Someone must have tipped them off, let them know which flight he was on. He stopped in front of them and flashed a smile, blinking into the cameras.

'Facing South Africa's pace attack while suffering from concussion was a considerable personal risk. Were you asked to go out and bat, Todd? Did you feel you had to?'

He shook his head. 'I was advised not to by our medical staff. And Barker forbade it. He's still dirty at me, actually.' Harrow smiled. 'It was my decision. I wanted to try to save the game.'

'That was a pretty tough tour. Are you glad to be back on home soil?'

'I'm sorry to miss the one-day series, of course. But yes,' he said, putting his arm around Megan, 'glad to be back.'

'Enough,' Megan said. 'I need to get him home.'

They loaded the car and Harrow wheeled the trolley back to the lift entrance. Megan was already strapped in and had the car started by the time he settled into the passenger seat. She was quiet until they were out of the airport and on the bypass. The day was bright and clear. Looking back, it was as if South Africa had happened in some sort of haze.

'Was that true?'

'What?'

'That the medical staff advised you not to go out and bat? And John told you not to.'

He nodded.

'Do you have any idea how scared I was?'

'You were watching?'

'Of course …' She sniffed. 'All that blood. I mean, I guess I knew it was dangerous but–'

'They needed me, Megs.'

She shook her head, her jaw set like when she was angry. 'I need you,' she said.

He reached across to put his hand on her thigh. 'I hadn't posted a score all series. I had to.'

'Oh, babe,' she said. 'What does the doctor say about the concussion?'

'I'm supposed to have a proper assessment tomorrow.'

Megan kept her eyes on the snarl of merging traffic ahead. 'Where's the specialist?

'Spring Hill,' he said. 'At ten.'

She pulled a face. 'I can't be there. But ring me straight after. Okay?'

'I saved the Test, Megs. That's what's important.'

'No,' she said. '*You* are what's important.'

FINAL SESSION

Once upon a time it wasn't as likely for
a girl to pick up a bat as a boy ...

~ Belinda Clark

the basin

Katie has come over to watch Australia play New Zealand in the Women's World Cup final. O. Harrow is her new hero – second top scorer and leading wicket-taker for the series. We're getting a bird's eye view of Wellington on a stunning clear day, on the eve of another summer. Basin Reserve is a pretty ground, at the foot of Mount Victoria, with grassy viewing banks and picket fence, not far from the city. A big crowd has turned out for the occasion.

I've made us a curry for lunch, to eat in front of the screen. There's something comforting about a bowl of food that you only need a fork to eat. It also allows us to keep our eyes on the game.

The girls get off to a good start, and O. Harrow comes to the crease looking to build a big total. She's using the cut shot well and working the angles to manipulate the field. She and the bat are moving as one, like a master musician and their instrument.

'She's good, right?'

'Sure is.' Watching her still reminds me of her brother, yet to get a game in India on a tough tour. He's hardly played since being hit in the face in South Africa, just the one warm-up match. The sooner he gets out there in the middle, back on the horse, as they say, the better.

O. Harrow's quick-fire forty-seven takes the team past the two-hundred mark. She's run out in the end, taking on the fielders one too many times. From her smile as she walks off and her generous acknowledgement of the crowd, she's loving the big stage. The New Zealand girls have a strong batting line-up, but the total might be an ask with Australia's bowling attack.

I should be putting dinner on but we can't stop watching. The New Zealand openers are out of the blocks early, taking advantage of the powerplay.

O. Harrow is running in, looking fierce, and bowls a perfect bouncer, pushing Mears back in her crease. O. Harrow smiles, turns on her heel, and walks back to her mark.

The next one is on a good length but moves away. Mears plays and misses. The keeper is standing up to the stumps, despite O. Harrow's pace. Talk about gutsy.

'Was that a bit of swing there?' Katie says.

'Some kind of cutter, I think.'

The next ball is almost identical. Mears pushes at it. There's a noise and a deflection. The keeper takes the ball and raises her glove. The Australians are appealing.

'She looks guilty,' Katie says. 'Her head spun around.'

The umpire nods, points her finger. Mears has to go. O. Harrow does a little fist pump. The Australian girls are up and about now. O. Harrow has a conversation with her captain, and they make some adjustments to the field. Silly mid-on comes in, and another slip. The next ball is full and straight, thumping into the new batter's front pad. O. Harrow's arms are above her head, palms open, asking the umpire the question.

'Oh, that's plumb,' says O'Keeffe, in commentary. 'Taunton has been their rock this series, and she has to go.'

The umpire raises her finger. Taunton walks from the ground, helmet pushed back on her head, looking anguished.

'Harrow is on a hat-trick here,' says Clark.

The television camera pans to her parents in the stands, leaning against each other. O. Harrow is waiting at the top of her mark when the next batter takes strike. She runs in, ponytail swinging from side to side, a stripe of zinc across her nose. All the fielders are up: three slips and a gully. It's a yorker, spearing in at the batter's feet. She plays all around it, and the ball cannons into the base of the stumps. BOWLED.

There's no need to appeal. O. Harrow has her first international hat-trick. The girls run to her, screaming. It's a tangle of joy and emotion. For some reason it's Nate I'm reminded of, teammates hanging off him in that Shield final.

O'Keeffe is bubbling over. 'An incredible performance. I mean, a young player, under pressure. In her first World Cup.'

'We've just witnessed a star being born,' Clark says.

collapse

He and the boys were gathered around Sky's laptop. It was the joke of the tour that the tallest player had scored the smallest room in their Mumbai hotel, but it was the only one with wi-fi (that worked). New Zealand had scrapped and scraped to get within ten runs of a win, but they were nine down. The World Cup had all come down to the final over and it was Liv to bowl it. Harrow had already chewed his nails down to nothing and drained his second beer.

They rearranged themselves on the bed, leaning in to watch over Sky's shoulder. Liv was running in again, looking fierce. It was a good ball, and the New Zealand number eleven, Riley, got in behind it but couldn't score.

'She's getting a bit of reverse there?' Gibbo said.

Sky nodded, held up his finger for quiet.

Liv was running in again. Her rhythm was great, she wasn't seizing up at all. The ball was fuller and right on target, but Riley managed to scoop it past mid-off. It should've been three runs but an excellent gather and throw from Lane sent them scrambling back. Eight from four balls to win.

Liv bowled a wide yorker this time, right on the line. Riley had to reach for it, swinging hard and missing.

'Perfect,' Mads said.

Riley would be feeling the pressure, for sure. Liv sent down a slower ball, fifteen Ks off her usual pace. Riley was through the shot early, the ball hitting the handle of the bat, but flying just out of reach of the diving keeper, to the boundary.

Four from two.

Liv switched to around the wicket. She stood a moment, at the top of her mark, face serious, positioning her fingers on the seam, all intent. Harrow knew that look. Sky leaned forward, hands over his mouth.

Liv steamed in. It was fast and full. Riley played at it, but the ball was way too good. The bails were broken, middle stump jagged back. BOWLED!

Harrow jumped up onto the bed. The boys were yelling, slapping him and Sky on the back. He watched his sister, on screen, the girls mobbing her, jumping up and down. The World Cup! He'd known Liv was good but, somehow, he hadn't seen her potential to be *great*.

'That was brilliant,' Mads said.

If they'd been playing on the same continent, maybe the girls' win would have rubbed off on them. Instead, failure spread through the team like the stomach bug they'd all managed to pick up. Mads said that on his first trip to India, he had to leave the field while batting, his guts were that violent. He took off for a run and just kept going, across the field and up the stairs, into the dressing rooms. It wasn't easy to get all that gear off in a hurry either. Play just had to wait. 'It was that or shit my pants,' he said. 'And white isn't a forgiving colour.'

Harrow was grateful to have Mads on tour, earning his selection after a big one-day series against South Africa, despite Davis being fit again. Mads' century had seen Australia win 2–1, saving some face after the Test series. But after a few months off, they were all pretty rusty.

In Mumbai, they'd lost the First Test by an innings and a hundred and nineteen runs. In Chennai, they weren't much better, losing by two hundred and thirteen. O'Neil, Dog and Peters were on a string of single-digit scores, Hilt was struggling, Jacks wasn't at his best. Sangha's two five-wicket hauls were a positive; the subcontinent was his playground. Sky had learned from

Sri Lanka; he just stuck to his nagging line and length, using the bouncer well. This time, he was leading wicket-taker. He seemed to have grown, if that was possible, leading the attack and keeping everyone's spirits up with his clowning around.

The batters were the problem. *Collapse* was the word in every headline, like it was a national moral weakness. Sometimes conditions were just tough, the bowling too good. The more wickets that fell, the more the bowling side got cock-a-hoop. They were hurried in the dressing room, strapping on their pads without their usual rituals, not mentally prepared. Cricket was a team sport, but out there in the middle, they were on their own, trying to stop that ball from hitting stumps, pads, head, hands, arms, ribs, or finding the edge of their bat and the fielders' waiting hands. It was pressure, and it was hard to stop.

Once they'd collapsed more than once, they were like cattle in the yards, picking up fear from each other: the sight of the previous batter's stumps splayed over the pitch, the idea of what the ball was doing, what the pitch was doing. When two wickets fell together, they couldn't help thinking *don't get out* as they faced up, instead of figuring out where to score.

Harrow watched it all from the sidelines. His nose was long-healed, though forever crooked. A few months' downtime at home had been a good thing, spending time with Megan. Whether it was his confidence or some weird after-effect of the concussion, it had taken time to feel right in the nets again. He'd felt fine facing the new ball in the warm-up game against India A, but was out in the thirties. A soft dismissal, too. Shep, meanwhile, scored a hundred. So Shep was getting another chance.

Harrow ran the drinks, helped the players as best he could, on and off the field, tried to keep their spirits up. He trained hard, morning and afternoon, did extra work with the strength and conditioning coach, bowled to the batters in the nets, grateful to even be on tour. But the only way he knew how to win Test matches for Australia was out on that green field, scoring hundreds.

The press was already writing them off. South Africa had revealed 'a brittle batting order', they said. They'd turned on him, too. His game-saving effort in South Africa already forgotten. Unorthodox, they called him. Was he too small for an opener? Had being struck in the head affected his confidence? Could he play the bouncer? Did he have a proper defensive technique? How would he play in England? Would he even be in the Ashes squad, next year?

He was asking himself all the same questions. The specialist said he was vulnerable to concussions now; that there were implications if was hit again. He hadn't dared tell Megan. Only he and the medical staff knew. And Dog. But it would get out eventually. Meanwhile, it was playing on his mind, keeping him awake at night. And the longer it took to get back out there, the worse it got.

The boys all watched the rugby final against New Zealand from a nightclub. Mads had found the only place with a big screen and pay TV. 'It's a dump, but the drinks are cheap,' he said. It meant a late night but Australia's win gave them a boost. They had a joint video call with Liv and the Queensland girls afterwards, who were having a night out at Suncorp Stadium, which cheered them up, too. The cricket family was growing.

Afterwards, back in his hotel room, he was homesick for Brisbane, for Megan. They'd agreed she'd skip the India tour, but go to England next year, if he was selected, for the Ashes. The way things were panning out, it was just as well she hadn't come.

In Kolkata, he dragged his bags from the conveyor belt, piled them up onto his trolley and pushed it through the crowded gate into yet another arrivals area. He stood in line, waiting, headphones in, like most of the boys. Even his new playlist couldn't lift him. He'd started daydreaming about boarding a flight home, with just his wallet, phone and an overnight bag, walking straight out of Brisbane airport with no one noticing him.

The press was all over them in India, like some sort of feeding frenzy. Dog stopped for yet another interview, trying to put a positive spin on their losing streak. Poor bloke. They were easy pickings, in their team uniform and hauling so much kit. Cricket was big news in India. *The* news.

Airport to airport, waiting lounge to waiting lounge, hotel room to hotel room. Hotel room to the ground. Ground to the hotel room. Constantly in transit, turning in circles it felt like. The routine was the same, wherever they landed. Practise, play, recover. Or, worse, practise, practise, practise – and not play.

down the order

They hadn't won a Test at Eden Gardens since 1969. It was the oldest ground in India, the bench seating allowing an eighty thousand-plus crowd. The Indians called it the heaven of cricket but when Harrow walked out, with Australia four for eighty-nine, it felt a lot like being thrown to the lions. Though, being Bengal, it would probably be tigers.

The selectors had dropped Peters, batting Harrow at six. He hadn't come in that low since playing for Sunshine Coast. India had scored four hundred and sixty and, after another top-order collapse, the Australians only managed two hundred in reply. India put on one hundred and eighty and declared after lunch on day four, giving themselves a hundred and forty overs to bowl Australia out. No team had ever lasted that long there, batting last.

The light towers were like cranes on a building site, all scaffolding. Smog smudged the tangle of jungle beyond the gap in the stands, where parkland ran down to the great brown river beyond. The Hooghly, Mads had called it, when they visited the multi-domed temple on its banks. That was the new name for the Ganges (or its old name), but all he'd been able to think of was the number of googlies he'd be facing over the next five days. And then the crowd had spotted them, mobbing Mads for an autograph or photo. Police had to escort them into a waiting rickshaw.

If Sri Lanka had been a riot of noise, colour and smells, India was off the charts. The poverty was overwhelming: beggars in the street, people missing limbs and eyes, everyone desperate to sell them something, even the staff of the places where they ate. It was a country still hungry. But cricket – they lived for it. It was playing on every screen, a game in progress on every patch of dirt.

He scratched out his mark, tapped the bat on the crease three times. He was facing up to Sunhil from the High Court end. It was his batting on trial. The flags fluttered on top of the sightscreen, the crowd clapped Sunhil in, blowing their trumpets, willing him to fail. Harrow got off the mark second ball, just a deflection, but it eased the pressure. Dog was as reliable as ever down the other end. They had a job to do: steady the ship and then bat for as long as possible.

When the first bouncer came, it was a little off target, and Harrow was able to rock back, watch it fly past. He took his three-step walk, out towards mid-wicket. *Back yourself.* It was Galle he pictured, how he'd felt there. The next one was right at the badge on his helmet. Harrow got in line, eyes on the ball, and hooked.

It wasn't quite out of the middle but he connected, and the ball bounced once, into the boundary. Dog smiled, for the first time. 'Nice, Hars.'

Hars grinned. He was back.

He was still at the crease after tea the next day. Eight of the ten fielders were crowded in around him, just waiting for the ball to hit a glove or bat or pad and fly into the air. They were still trying to score, turn over the strike, not let the bowlers get on top of them. He was dead on his feet, from the heat, the sun, dehydration, the noise of the crowd, the concentration required to defend his wicket. They'd lost their nightwatchman early, coming in for Dog three overs before close of play the previous day, but Mads was still there at the other end, all steel, giving them nothing, not wasting one ounce of energy on chat. If they could stay upright, they could do it.

Peters ran out with drinks, between overs, and wet towels from the fridge to drape over their heads. 'Legends,' he said. 'Respect.'

Harrow drained a sports drink but threw it up by the side of the pitch.

'Small sips,' Mads said.

He tried again, with water. Tiny mouthfuls at a time.

The Indian players were waiting. He and Mads nodded at each other, and Harrow took strike.

The ball was turning big out of the rough. The fielders were chatting all around him, trying to get under his skin, but he'd already zoned out, no longer sure which language they were speaking. He watched the ball out of the bowler's hand, but played inside the line, the ball hitting his front pad and popping up enough for short leg to take it on the full. The Indian players were appealing. It had missed his bat by a mile so they were hoping for leg-before.

The umpire shook his head.

Harrow defended the next two. He couldn't even take his little walk between balls, they had him so hemmed in. To try to break the shackles, upset the bowlers' lengths, he walked down the crease to the next one and hit it on the up. The bowler ducked, to protect his head, and the ball beat the fielder in pursuit, running away to the boundary.

They were giving Mads the same treatment, whittling away, knowing it was only a matter of time before they forced an error. Harrow watched from the other end as an edge flew just out of reach of leg slip, and two appeals for leg-before were turned down. It was more stressful than facing up himself. Mads finally worked a single, and Harrow ran through. Only seven overs to go and three batters left in the sheds. They couldn't win, but they could still lose. And he and Mads weren't going to leave it to the bowlers to save the game yet again.

Harrow swept from one knee, sending the short leg scuttling out of the way, and ran though for a single to keep the strike for the next over.

The ball spun out of the rough, sending up a spray of dust. The Indian spinners were getting a lot of side-spin and drift, making every ball a lottery. Harrow used the crease, defending off the back foot, but missed. The ball hit his forearm, just above the glove and flew up. The fielder at silly point dived, taking the ball in one hand at the edge of the pitch. The Indians were appealing all around him. Harrow stood motionless amid the swirl of movement and noise, the fielder still lying at his feet. A few millimetres lower and it would have been all over.

'Not out,' the umpire said.

Harrow had stopped thinking in overs. The Indian players were appealing every ball, trying everything. It was so intense.

'Would you be anywhere else?' Mads said.

Harrow shook his head.

With one over left to bowl, the Indian captain pulled a stump from the ground and shook Harrow's hand. 'Well played,' he said.

He and Mads leaned on each other in an exhausted embrace. Harrow finished on eighty-one not out, and the match was drawn. For the first time, the crowd was silent. For a moment – and then they turned feral, throwing plastic bottles onto the ground, booing. Security staff had to use force to stop one stand emptying onto the ground.

The boys were running out, to celebrate, but Dog held out his arms and lowered his hands, to slow them. It was only a draw after all. And the crowd was volatile.

It wasn't his highest score or his most beautiful innings, and it hadn't been without chances, but he'd batted for seven hours and forty minutes, faced three hundred and sixty-three balls, complete with a Dean Jones-style hurl on the pitch and, at the end, he remained undefeated. Those two partnerships, with Mads and Dog, were etched in stone.

When Mads, red-faced and glassy-eyed, smiled at him from across the dressing room later that night, nursing a beer, and nodded, Harrow knew he'd played the sort of innings he'd always hoped he was capable of. If it was the last game he ever played, it wouldn't be so bad.

Megan would have gone to bed, knowing he'd have the press conference and then a celebration with the boys. He would have liked her to have been there to see his innings, but her not being on tour had probably freed him up, given him the opportunity to focus. It wasn't like he ever went along to work with her. She was on her own in that way, too, supported by Nina and her team.

When he got back to his hotel room, she'd left a message: *Tomorrow you'll be everyone's hero. But you've always been mine. M xx.*

Mr Reader had been in touch, too. *Incredible innings. One for the ages.* He never said much in his messages, but it mattered.

He took a bottle of water from the fridge and sat on the bed, bare feet on the worn carpet. He couldn't wait to get on the plane home. There were three missed calls from Liv. When he called her back, she answered straight away.

'Toddy. That was the best innings you've ever played.'

'I know,' he said. 'But they'll drop me. You'll see.'

I carry my empty glass out to the kitchen and stand at the window, the first glimmer of light gracing the Melbourne sky. They didn't win. But they played so very well. They dug in and showed character. And, in the end, it was a nail-biter. That's Test cricket right there; a drawn match can be so tense, so full of emotion, all outcomes still open, right down to the last overs. Harrow's eighty-one was not a hundred but it was heroic. Instead of trying to force a personal milestone, thinking of his own selection, he played for the team, taking all that responsibility on his shoulders. Hanging in there like that at the end, every fielder close in around him. What a show of mental toughness.

And the captain, the way he tempered their celebration, like a conductor, when the boys ran out onto the field. It was a great escape, but he remembers, no doubt, the Ashes series when the Australian team celebrated a draw, not with relief but jubilation. The moment the English saw that, they knew they had them. 'HOW LOW THE MIGHTY AUSTRALIANS HAVE SUNK' was the headline the next day. Revealing themselves in that moment had given the English the edge they needed to win the series.

And India, although they must have been disappointed to have let one get away, knowing they'll face the ire of their fans, were gracious in defeat, calling time on the game when it was clear they couldn't win, shaking Harrow's hand, touching his arm. I reach for a tissue and blow my nose. It's the gestures that get me, every time.

I like Australia to play well, and to win. But what I want most is a good game. Everyone expected them to fold, to lose quick wickets. To go too hard, yet again, and fail spectacularly. But they put their egos in a box and fought – and so the draw felt like a win. It was exactly what was needed after South Africa. They played hard but fair, without a single ugly moment.

I run the spokeshave over Frank's bat in soothing movements, channelling tall and thin. It's a good piece of willow, in the end. The best of the tree, I think, but we can do something with the rest. Sometimes when I really get into the zone, when that flow and rhythm is happening, it's as if I'm tapping into something larger. It brings me back to myself, a calmer centre, where nothing changes, where the timber is solid.

With Katie gone there seem to be a lot of hours in the day, and the evenings are a bit quiet. But now that I've re-established my daily practice, there's a spring in my step that flows into everything else. When I lock up the workshop of an afternoon, I can't wait to get inside, back to the oboe.

Every practice session is like starting from scratch, but I'm entering the flow more quickly and more often. It's a relief to be able express myself again, even if poorly. This evening, I'm ready for Albinoni's *Oboe Concerto in D minor, Opus 9, (No. 2)*. Albinoni was first Italian composer to write oboe concertos, an emerging instrument at the time. And it's almost perfect. With its energetic opening followed by a ravishing slow movement, the melody, it's full of joy and drama. A complete emotional journey.

The doorbell jags and a tall man in a hat is bending his neck to enter the workshop.

'Hello, Frank.'

'How good was our boy?'

We shake hands, smiling.

'If only they'd played him for the first two Tests!'

'That's exactly what Katie said.'

'You have to back a special player,' Frank says.

'Agreed,' I say. 'All that chopping and changing. And then pushing him down the order, like some newbie.'

'Madness.'

'I've got something for you,' I say. I pick up the bat, from where it has been leaning all week, against my work bench.

'Outstanding.' He plays a leg glance with a fair amount of elegance. 'It's beautiful, Allan. I can't wait to try it out.'

'Bowl a few to you in the yard if you like.' I choose a ball from the bucket at my feet.

He takes strike with his back to the house, and I roll my arm over.

Frank paddles the ball back. His long face splits into a grin. 'Oh, that's grand.'

I jog after the ball and retrieve it from against the glasshouse.

'You did a good job on that,' Frank says.

'Graeme and Katie helped me get it done.'

'Missing her?'

'I am.' I bowl another one, a bit fuller. Frank plays it on the back foot, flicks it off his hip into the garden. 'But she's still here a couple of days a week.'

He bends over to fish the ball out of the agapanthus, unfolds himself, and throws it back. 'It's a lovely bat, Allan. Thank you.'

'Sorry it took me so long.'

'I know you've been busy digging the Brits out of their hole,' he says. 'Cricket's unsung hero.'

'That's all done with now,' I say. 'Our part in it anyway. The willows are in and growing. I guess we'll see what the new season brings.'

'A good fellow I know writes for *The Age*. I was telling him about your willow rescue operation, and the workshop. He wants to do a piece about you, for the magazine. Up for it?'

'Sure.'

'Grand. I'll let him know,' Frank says. 'Is the rest of the tree this good?'

'Close.' I bowl a straight one but it turns off something in the lawn and ends up a bit of a mullygrubber.

Frank flicks it back to me with the toe of the bat. 'My granddaughter has started playing. I might get you to make a bat for her.'

'For Colac?'

Frank examines the face of the bat, the little red wine kiss where he struck the ball. 'Yes, we're launching a new local competition for women.'

'I'll have to come see her play. And we could bring another tree down.'

'Grand. Why don't we make a day of it?'

'I was thinking. Would you like to design your own label, a line of bats? Maybe we could even sponsor your granddaughter's team.'

dropped

He had a few weeks at home, catching up on sleep, remembering all their old routines. Megan had got used to him being away; they had to learn how to live together all over again. But feeling her skin on his, her voice vibrating through her chest, just seeing her bright spirit moving around the apartment, he felt whole again. It was a busy time for Megan, long hours, so he did what he could: took her car in for a service, did the grocery shopping, cooking (or at least preparing everything for her to cook her dishes) and working his way through the list of errands she left.

One Friday, he cleaned the whole apartment and washed all their bedding, thinking maybe they could have a weekend off together. The washer and dryer were still going when Megan got home.

'Hey, Handsome,' she said. 'You've been busy.'

'How'd it go?'

She pulled a face, twisting her mouth the way she did. 'Not great.'

He poured her a glass of wine. 'Tell me about it?'

She shook her head. 'That's just work. Let's sit out on the deck. There's something else.'

He shifted their chairs around, so that they were close together and facing the sunset. Another new skyscraper, apartments apparently, had worked its way into their eyeline. Its multi-coloured panels reminded him of India somehow.

'Dad's tests came back.'

He put his hand on her arm. 'And?'

'Colon cancer.'

'Oh, Megs,' he said. 'Do you want to go down there?'

'Not yet. They're operating tomorrow, and then there's a treatment process.'

'Your mum?'

'Stoic, as ever. I'll call her tomorrow, to see how it went.'

Before he knew it, he was back into training with the Bulls. All the years he'd dreamed of playing for Queensland, for Australia, he could never have imagined it, but cricket was starting to feel a bit relentless. Still, their first game was at home, against Victoria, and it was a chance to put some runs on the board, to get back into some sort of playing rhythm.

He scored a scratchy thirteen (run out) and a decent fifty before he was clean bowled by Peters. While fielding at second slip in the final innings, he put down a sitter. The ball just slipped through his fingers. Dropped. It was the loneliest word in cricket. He'd let Sky down, and the whole team. The Gabba seemed to triple in size, with him in its spot-lit centre. He wanted to dig a hole and bury himself.

Shep went on to score a big hundred, every single run a cut on Harrow's conscience, and Queensland never pegged them back. Their season had started with a big loss.

Liv's message was brutal. *Forgotten how to watch the ball, bro?*

Queensland Fire, meanwhile, were on fire, winning their first two games. Liv, batting at four, posted a big hundred against New South Wales, who had the strongest attack in the competition.

Peters had broken up with his girlfriend during the India tour. Harrow organised drinks after the game, him and Megan with Peters and Nina, at a new champagne bar in the Valley. Despite the obvious chemistry between the two of them, and Nina giving Harrow one of her big hugs to thank him, he still felt pretty flat.

'That went well,' Megan said, on their way home in the cab, the city lights reflected in the river. 'Glen's nice, quite the gentleman.'

He'd seen Peters be a lot less gentlemanly, but he was good guy, and they'd have some fun together, for sure. 'She likes him?'

'Oh, yes.'

Sky had forgiven him by their next training session. Though, facing him in the nets, maybe he was a little more fierce. They were both fired up, Klimt, too, wanting to turn things around for Queensland before they went back to the Test set-up.

Tank had tasked him with getting back to basics. Defence, defence, defence, unless it was in his zone, there to be hit. It was just a matter of watching the ball, protecting his wicket, waiting for the opportunities. Anything loose and he would hit it all right. *Back yourself.* By the end of the week, everything was flowing again. If kept his head right, all he had to do was face up and watch the ball, and then make the right decisions.

With Reid out for their first few games with a hamstring problem, Harrow had been promoted to vice-captain, which meant spending more time with Copes and Tank, strategising for their match against Western Australia in Perth. It was always one of the toughest games, the long flight, then the WACA conditions. The pitch would suit Sky; he was bowling out of his skin, settling into his body at last. Liv said it was all her influence, and Sky didn't disagree. Both their games had come on, leaps and bounds, since they'd been together. They were a good team.

This time, when Slogger's call came, it wasn't good news. He hadn't been included in the thirteen-man squad for Sri Lanka's tour. *Dropped.* There wasn't a hole deep enough.

'You're still in our thoughts. You really showed your maturity, determination in Kolkata. But we're worried about your technique, against the swinging ball, and the rising ball. We think you'd benefit from another big Shield season. I'm sure you'll get an opportunity over the summer.'

For Harrow, it may as well have been winter.

Megan arrived home early, saw him slumped in front of the television with a beer, an empty bottle on the kitchen bench. 'I'm sorry, babe.'

'Not even in the fucking *squad*.'

'I can't believe it. After your innings in India,' she said.

She stepped out of her heels, and came to him, eyes soft. When she hugged him, he lost it, sobbing like a baby into the shoulder of her new dress, wetting those tropical flowers like some sort of summer storm.

'Sorry,' he said.

'Didn't you tell me that every great player has been dropped at some stage? Like it was the making of them. You'll get back. You will. You can still play those hundred Tests.'

wired for sound

I'm loving my headphones, which allow me to use the machines and still listen to music. With the sound quality, and lack of other noise, I tend to lose myself. It's a whole new experience. Tognetti and the Australian Chamber Orchestra are taking me into the news, as the presenter puts it, with 'Jupiter', Mozart's final and longest symphony. Stunning. Every single note.

When they announce the Test squad, it's less harmonious. Harrow hasn't been included. I stop the lathe, lest I do myself – or the bat in progress – an injury. I did not see that coming. After an epic match-saving innings in difficult circumstances, coming in at number six, not having batted for months. Coming back from a head injury. What more do they want?

I've been looking forward to the First Test, the start of the summer, Sri Lanka touring, seeing Harrow bat again. For months! Now the landscape has flattened out completely. Sometimes it really is hard to understand what the selectors are thinking.

'Bah.' I down tools, remove my headphones and walk outside. Even the garden, the greenhouse gleaming, the smell of summer, another batch of sets coming on, can't soothe me. If Katie were here, I could vent at least. But she's not in until tomorrow.

I take my phone from my top pocket, thinking to call Graeme or Frank or Katie. But it's Harrow I should contact. Maybe not a call; he won't be feeling like talking. But a message, telling him I'm thinking of him. And that he'll be back. He's still so young.

I've been cleaning up the glasshouse: sweeping it out, rearranging the trestles and pots, blocking any gaps, polishing the windows. For my folly in the folly. I've started practising inside, for the acoustics, the novelty, I guess. And to work my way up to asking Graeme and the boys over for a session.

Framed by glass, warm inside on such a clear winter's day, it does feel like a performance. When I begin the fifth movement of Benjamin Britten's *Six Metamorphoses after Ovid*, it's my mother I think of. The piece was composed for Joy Boughton, who premiered the piece at the Aldeburgh festival in 1951. Joy was my mother's name. And she should've had more of it in her life. Meeting her granddaughter, seeing her grow up. Seeing her sons grow up for that matter.

The image that comes is of morning light streaming through the kitchen window, lighting her curls. Her smiling at me. It's the music working, of course. It would stir anyone. I let the tears run down my face, for all the years she lost, everything she missed out on.

retired hurt

When he walked out to bat against New South Wales, there were more things on his mind than surviving the first ten balls. Shep and O'Neil had put together two good partnerships in the First Test, setting Australia up for the win. He wanted Australia to do well, always. But he wanted to be in the team, too. To show them what he was made of. He'd even take number six. But Peters was back there, and having a bit of a runfest at the Sri Lankans' expense.

He and Megan were going down to Adelaide early, for Christmas. Her father's treatment had knocked him around, and it was still touch and go. Megan wasn't sleeping; he was worried about her. But he had to score hundreds, lots of them, if he was going to force someone out of the Australian side. Starting today.

Copes got the first ball away behind square. Harrow jogged through for the single and took strike. Hilt and Slim were out, training with the Australian squad, so it was only a second-string attack. He tapped his bat on the crease, and watched Raftopolous, the gym-built young gun from Western Sydney, run in. It was a short ball, rising steeply. Harrow swung hard but missed.

It struck him, behind his ear, at the base of his skull. Sound, light and pain were one thing, the white lines of the pitch rushed up at him.

'Hars?'

It was Copes' voice. But far away. Harrow rolled onto his back, staring up at the sky.

Copes put his hand on Harrow's shoulder. 'You with me?'

Harrow nodded. But when he tried to get onto all fours, he couldn't. His vision and hearing were off, his balance. The pain reverberated through his whole head somehow, brighter than white.

Copes was gesturing for the team doctor. And he could see the New South Wales players now, standing around him in a circle.

Copes helped him remove his helmet and gloves, checked the area where he'd been struck, face serious.

'I'm fine,' Harrow said.

By the time Doc got out onto the field, Harrow had used the bat to get onto his haunches. He took the water offered, answered the questions asked. But his head ached and his ears were ringing.

'I think you'd better come off, Hars,' Doc said. 'I need to do a proper assessment.'

'You can always come back, if we need you,' Copes said. 'We've got this.'

'How are you feeling?' Megan handed him a cup of coffee and emptied the grounds from the machine. The bang of the head on the knock box was too loud.

'A bit of a headache.'

'Groggy? You seem out of it.'

He nodded. A week on and he still didn't feel right. Queensland had lost, again, without him. And he was further away from playing for Australia than ever.

'So, the specialist said you're susceptible to concussions. But why didn't they pick that up last time. After South Africa?'

He sipped his coffee, hoping the caffeine would clear his thinking, show him a way out of the conversation. 'She did, actually. I mean, she suspected.'

'And you didn't tell me?'

'I didn't want to worry you.'

Megan waited while her cup filled with coffee, added the frothed milk, placed the jug on the bench, and turned to face him.

'Did you tell the Bulls? The Australian set-up?'

'The specialist report went to the medical team. Teams.'

She leaned against the bench, one arm crossed over the other while she cradled her cup. 'What exactly did the specialist say?'

'Like I said. If I get hit, I'm more inclined to get a concussion than most people.'

'What about long-term effects?'

'That would only be if I was hit a lot. Or got a really a bad knock.'

'Like just happened, you mean?'

'That was freaky. Like a blind spot,' he said. 'It wasn't that I was scared. I just misread the line of ball. I wasn't concentrating properly.'

Megan drank her coffee, watching him.

'What?'

'You kept this from me,' she said. 'And went back out there. And it sounds like you want to keep going out there. *You* mightn't be scared but–'

'Megs. This is what I do. Open the batting for my state, my country. You knew that when you met me.'

podshavers

I shouldn't read the papers. They only aggravate me. With Australia winning 3–0 against Sri Lanka, the commentators are crowing about our prowess, our prospects for the Ashes. And how Harrow, when he finally returned for the last two Shield games, hasn't looked the same since he was struck. That's as sick as I've felt, watching cricket, seeing the footage of him hitting the ground.

Only a handful of players have died on the field, but it can happen. A bowler hit in the head by a batter's return drive while completing his follow through. Or the umpire, standing still behind the stumps, when the ball is hit straight. Or a close fielder, struck over the heart. Everyone needs to keep their eye on the ball at all times.

The back of the neck is vulnerable, experts are saying, even with a helmet. It can't come down far enough, not without restricting the batter's movement. But it looked to be Harrow's thoughts that were restricting his movement, stuck on the crease and fidgety. Queensland didn't even make the Shield finals, Victoria either.

It wasn't much of a summer, cricket-wise. Though the women's final one-day match against South Africa was televised. O. Harrow, batting at five, scored seventy-seven, took three wickets, and a blinder of a catch at gully that turned the game, sparking a South African collapse.

She's retired the bat, I think. It must have failed, finally. And Queensland Fire are now sponsored by a woman maker, Sally Bradbury. She's good, I hear. Maybe it's just me but with Harrow and the bat gone, a little magic seems to have gone from the game.

Frank tells me that the word podshaving is one of a thousand words omitted from the latest *Oxford Dictionary* due to lack of use. As if I've been made redundant overnight. Katie was so offended, she had a definition printed and laminated – with a minor gender amendment – and stuck it in the window. So podshaving and podshavers won't be forgotten. Not in our neighbourhood at least.

podshaver (plural *podshavers*) Noun
A craftsperson skilled at carving cricket bats in a traditional manner.

We're getting more and more women customers, thanks to O. Harrow. And Katie, too. Her just being here, making bats. She also had a poster framed, of the women celebrating their World Cup win in a shower of champagne and pink streamers, and hung it in the shopfront – pure joy on every face. She's put a rainbow sticker next to the door, too, which is important, she says.

Harrow, meanwhile, will be in the Ashes touring squad, surely. They usually take at least fifteen players. Having performed so well against the English bowlers when they were here. They know how talented he is. He needs to be playing at the top level. And he needs to play in English conditions, to face the swinging Dukes ball. He learns by doing. A season in county cricket during the winter would have been ideal. There were offers from Surrey and Middlesex, apparently. But he stayed home for family reasons. His father-in-law is battling cancer. Or so I've read.

the outer

When the Ashes squad was announced via live press conference, Harrow was two kilometres out to sea, his stomach queasy. He kept his eye on the horizon, as Copes suggested, and his phone deep in his jeans pocket. He'd considered dropping it in the water, more than once, severing that nasty lifeline to the world he'd left. The cricket world that had left him behind.

Slogger had given him the heads-up, a few days earlier. With his head injuries, so little time on the park, there were just too many questions over his form, he said. He wasn't going to England. When he told Copes, he'd suggested the fishing trip, to avoid the media. Copes had announced his retirement, after Easter. The birth of their third child tipped him over, he said. And his knee reconstruction hadn't really come good. So they were in the same boat, so to speak, facing life without cricket.

Or not facing it, not yet. Motoring away from shore felt good. As did reeling in big fish, one after the other. He and Copes cleaned, cooked and ate them right there on the boat, washing them down with beers. But tomorrow they would have to head back. And then where could he go? Some country where there was no cricket, no news, no internet. A tropical island in the far north. But there was still Megan, and Liv, and Mum and Dad. All the boys he would miss hanging out with. Only other cricketers really understood, didn't need him to explain.

'The Bulls will need a new captain,' Copes said.

Harrow shook his head. He wanted to be over there, with the boys, playing Ashes cricket. He understood, in a way. He hadn't had much cricket, since the concussion, and only posted the one century for Queensland all season. But he'd helped win the Ashes last time. Player of the series! And this time, he didn't even get to go.

Liv reckoned it wasn't over. But O'Neil and Shep were settled now. And he was happy for Shep, whose father had died during the winter. Their family was doing it tough. But as a batter, Shep was 'a bit of sheep', as Mads put it. He was never going to change the course of a game.

The hardest thing, the thing that had him shedding tears, concealed by the sea spray at the back of the boat, was knowing that if one or two moments had gone differently, he'd be on that plane.

For the first time in his life, he hated cricket. He didn't watch it, read about it, or listen to it. He cancelled their Foxtel subscription. Just a glimpse of white on green made him feel like throwing up. Gutted was the best word for it, like those big fish on the deck of Copes' boat.

He'd fallen from the world stage. From the bright green field to darkness, oblivion. After all the noise of the crowd it was an unbearable silence. And where was his fucking cricket family now? A few messages asking after his well-being and his specialist appointments paid for. That was it.

Without training, there was no structure, no reason. He slept till midday and still he woke up tired. It was as if all those years of training, playing, driving, striving had worn him out.

Megan was tolerant at first, tip-toeing around him, trying to cheer him up. But working such long hours while he lay on the couch eventually wore thin.

'I'm going to be late home tonight. Do you think you could do some shopping, organise dinner?'

He sat up in bed, to watch her button her dress. 'We could just order in?'

'I need a break from that,' she said. 'Some fresh food. I've left a list on the bench.'

'Okay.' The idea of going to the supermarket, the shopping centre, outside, being seen in public (while the rest of the team took the field at Edgbaston) filled the room, crushing him on the bed.

She watched him in the ensuite mirror while she applied her makeup. 'What else are you going to do today?'

'Not much,' he said.

'C'mon, babe. What's happened to my man?'

'You *know* what's happened.'

'It's not the end of everything, Todd. You can keep playing. Pre-season starts soon. You should be in training. You'll get back if you want it enough. And you know, *I'm* still here. We still have a whole to life to live. Together.'

Harrow turned away. He didn't blame her for being fed up. He was fed up with himself.

When the tenants moved out of her old apartment, Harrow suggested he do the repainting. Megan was enthusiastic, saying it would save them a packet, and give them 'some space'.

She was in Adelaide, visiting her father in hospital after another procedure, the first time he spent the night on the old couch the tenants had left behind, just too tired to go home.

The physical work was mindless and satisfying, something tangible he could do and see. When he finished the painting, he told Megan he was staying on for another week. Sean, who was a bit of a gun renovator, had offered to help redo the bathroom tiling.

'That's good,' she said. 'I'm in Adelaide again until next Friday anyway. You'll be home before me.'

Sean was a hard taskmaster, working late into the night. When he turned up early with coffees, to do the final grouting, Harrow was still asleep.

'Rise and shine, Todders. Work to do.'

Harrow sipped his flat white. By the time he put on boots and gloves Sean had already mixed the grout, a perfect match with the 'Indian Ocean' tile.

'Plenty of people would still kill to be in your shoes, you know.'

'I know,' Harrow said. It was easy for Sean to say, Klimmy was having a good tour, a five-for and a hat-trick. He'd really mastered the Dukes ball and the English conditions, thanks to a season in county cricket.

After Sean left, Harrow scrubbed his hands clean and lay on the couch, the smell of fresh grout filling the apartment. He was hungry, but too tired to go out. Too tired to make decisions.

When Megan's call woke him, it was already dark.

'Where are you?'

'Still at the apartment,' he said.

'Um. You haven't been home since I left?'

'No.'

'Well, I wish you'd told me. I would've taken out the rubbish. There are maggots all over the kitchen floor.'

'Sorry.'

'The roof guy says he was here yesterday but there was no one to let him in.'

'I forgot.'

He heard her sigh. 'He says he messaged you.'

He wanted to ask how her father was. But it was too late. She was already annoyed.

'When are you coming home, Todd?'

'Do you even want me to?'

Megan sighed again. 'We can't go on like this.'

Betty

If it was a half-life without cricket, it was worse without Megan. The pain ran down the centre of his chest, like a crack on a day five WACA pitch. She'd made it clear there was a way forward, if he could get himself together. He needed to dig in and fight. But it was like he couldn't get his feet moving or judge the flight of the ball.

He was awake early, with the light. The whole day to get through. Someone buzzed from downstairs.

'Hello?'

'Hey, it's Liv.'

Not Megan. 'Yeah, come up.'

He gathered up dirty dishes, cups and glasses, kicked shut the bedroom door, opened the door of the apartment and waited.

'Hey, Bro.' She hugged him hard. 'Place is looking good.'

He nodded. 'Going for a run?'

'I thought you might come with me. Along the river.'

He groaned. 'Not feeling that flash today.'

'All the more reason.'

She pinched at his abs, and he twisted out of the way, already feeling the softness setting in.

'Maybe next time?'

'C'mon, Toddy. I need to train with someone who can actually push me,' she said. 'Buy you breakfast after?'

Liv hadn't ever been one to take no for an answer. 'All right, all right. Give me a sec to get changed.'

He pulled on a pair of shorts from the floor, an old team singlet, his last pair of clean socks from his bag, a cap, and sat on the step to put on his runners. Liv had stacked the dishwasher, set it to run, and was tying off a bag of rubbish to take down.

'You don't have to do that,' he said.

'I know.'

He took the apartment key from the hook and tucked it in his shorts pocket, held the door for Liv. She couldn't duck beneath his arm anymore, the way a little sister should, the way he still thought about her sometimes. She was an adult, strong, and more than his equal. The thought broke something open. He pulled his cap down over his eyes.

'What happened to your hand?'

'Renovating,' he said. There was a little truth to it. He'd punched a hole in the wall, late one night, and had to plaster it over, repaint. The wall looked fine, but his hand hadn't healed. He probably should have gone to casualty, had it scanned, but he hadn't been in any state to drive.

Liv draped her arm over his shoulder as they walked down the long empty hallway, the only people in Teneriffe up early on a Sunday morning.

They ran downstream first, to the end of the Riverwalk. There were plans for it to continue on all the way to Newstead and then on to Hamilton, but for now they had to retrace their steps, running past all of the apartments, past the fenced dog park, right around New Farm Park, before looping back to the café near the ferry terminal.

Liv didn't talk or ask any more questions. They just ran, on what he began to notice was a clear and beautiful morning, the sun sparkling on the river, more blue than brown. His legs and lungs burned but he didn't let on, wouldn't. He let Liv set the pace, sat on her shoulder and, once he'd settled his breathing, started to push. And she responded, keeping the same distance between them.

It had always been like this, since she was old enough to run in and bowl, throw cricket balls at him. Life had changed so fast, but some things, the things from their childhood, things between them, didn't change that much.

He pulled up, hands on his thighs, sucking air. Liv was still breathing evenly, but her cheeks were red, and the skin on her upper arms. They walked another lap, along the water, to warm down. Mangroves were growing back in clumps, and they passed a water bird too big for its legs.

'That's a night heron,' Liv said.

'But it's day.'

She snorted.

The day was well and truly underway, a ferry releasing weekenders into the park, the café setting up its tables, a dozen women doing tai chi, poses that reminded him of the heron, facing the river. The smell of coffee and bacon had him feeling hungry for the first time in weeks.

She chose a table by the edge, near the river. 'The works?'

'Green machine,' he said. 'It's really good. Poached eggs, avo, kale, pesto.'

'That does sound good. And a skinny flat white?'

He nodded.

She went inside to order, slipping between the tables and smiling at a young couple with a baby. A few people glanced at Harrow, as if recognising him, but no one even looked twice at Liv. He was torn between envy and indignation on her behalf. She'd basically won them the World Cup, and had been all over the media since.

Liv came back with a bottle of water, two glasses and a table number. 'That was a good run,' she said. 'Thanks.'

He helped her move the table into the sun.

'How long since you've trained?' she said.

'Few weeks.'

She nodded, smiled at the waitress when she delivered their coffees. Liv looked good – fit. And her hair was different somehow. 'How many weeks?'

'Three, maybe four.'

'I think that's called a month.'

He couldn't help but laugh. When their food arrived, he cut into his eggs, spilling their yellow insides over the brown toast and green kale. He stuffed a forkful in his mouth and chewed.

It was good to be outside, eating good food with his sister. The future no longer seemed as unfathomable as it had when he finally crashed the night before.

'So, Bro. We need to talk.' She had her serious face on, not the pretend-to-be serious face.

He chewed as slowly as he could, eyes on his plate.

'First, what's happening with Megan?'

'She's sick of me, that's what happened.'

'Do you blame her? Moping around.' She reached around to pinch his side. 'Getting fat.'

'Piss off.' He twisted out of her reach. 'And I didn't tell her about the concussion, after South Africa.'

'What are you going to do about it?'

'Do?'

'Well, I don't care so much about you, but Mum, Dad and I aren't ready to let go of Megan. She's ace.'

'She might have different ideas.'

'*She* wants to work things out.'

'You think so?'

'I know so.'

So they'd talked. That was important. 'Okay.'

'Just go back to the Penthouse. Give yourself a chance.'

'With Megan?'

'With everything,' she said. 'You could still be playing.'

'What do you know about it!' He slammed his hand down on the timber table, making the couple on the table next to them turn. 'They dropped me. The game's moved on. I've moved on.'

Liv raised one eyebrow but kept her body very still. 'You should've gone to England. You should have been playing from the start in India, and against Sri Lanka. It isn't fair. And we'd probably be winning with you at the top. But you could still captain the Bulls, score a tonne of runs. Force your way back.'

So she knew about that. He scraped his plate clean and put the fork down. 'I'm going to say I'm not interested.'

'*Oh* – too good for them now?'

'I just need a break, Livs.'

'We get a break when we retire. And that's too soon. The game is our *life*, Toddy. You need it; it needs you.'

He sighed, shook his head.

Liv grinned, still the same dimples she'd had as a little kid. 'You know I'm right.'

'Shut up,' he said. 'My hand is fucked. Everyone knows about the concussions.'

'Just make sure you don't get hit.'

He shook his head. 'Have you ever faced the new ball against those guys?'

'Only Sky, in the nets.'

'Anyway. What's happened with Loz?' He'd heard the national batting coach had taken compassionate leave.

'Leukemia. He's having treatment but …'

'That's terrible.'

'That's the other thing I wanted to talk to you about. What about filling in, as batting coach?'

'Won't they just replace him?'

'It's a bit tricky with him being sick,' she said. 'Why don't you come down to training with me tomorrow? Just to help out?'

'I don't know.'

'Please. When have I ever asked you for anything?'

It was as if she'd punched him in the solar plexus, like she used to when they passed each other in the hallway at home. Only he hadn't tensed his abs in time.

They walked back along the river. The day was heating up, the boardwalk filling with people. More prams, strollers and toddlers than he remembered when Megan lived there. The breeze off the water was just enough to shift the leaves of the frangipanis.

He glanced across at Liv. The image that kept recurring was of her final wicket, to win the World Cup. And the girls' faces, when they stood on that podium, spraying champagne in a sea of streamers. Their joy. The sense that he'd witnessed one of those great moments in sporting history.

They waited to cross the road, watching a steady procession of prestige cars with dark tinted windows, cruising for a park. The area was changing, and not in ways he particularly liked.

Liv stopped beside her white Hyundai hatch, looking at him over the top of her sunglasses. 'So I'll see you in the morning, right?'

'I'll be there.'

He turned up to Allan Border Field early, watching the girls warming up in the practice nets, going through their paces. His stomach had been churning in the car park but soon settled among the familiar sights and sounds: leather on willow, the ball clanging into the nets, the occasional shout, laughter and chatter among players. He knew a few of the girls from the Queensland set-up. Chooky was national keeper, too, and a bit of a dasher with the bat. He watched her making the most of a high back lift to play some expansive strokes. Her defence could probably do with some work; she'd lost her stumps twice to their off-spinner, Maz.

Harrow leaned on the mesh. 'Hey, Chooky.'

'Hars! What am I doing wrong here?'

'What's your scoring shot?'

'Sweep, I guess.'

'You could try coming down to her, upset her lengths? She'll hate that.'

'True,' she said.

Their left-arm strike bowler, Lane, was bowling to Robinson, their veteran opener, and not cutting her any slack, either, firing one after another at her ribs. They were a couple, Liv said, which must be interesting for team dynamics.

When it was Liv's turn in the nets, she smashed one back at Lane, forcing her to jump to avoid being hit. Harrow smiled, shook his head. She hadn't had that kind of power as kid. The bat gleamed in the sun, an extension of Liv's arms and hands, part of her, as it had been part of him. It wasn't quite jealousy, but something twisted inside.

'*Nice*, Betty!' Chooky said.

'The bat's still going, Liv?'

'I only use it for special occasions now,' she said. 'Just wanted to feel a bit of the magic today. For your visit.'

He watched everyone bat and bowl, helped out with their fielding drills, and even bowled a few of his leg spinners to Chooky in the nets, encouraging her to use all of the crease. 'If you're going to come forward, come all the way forward. Or go all the way back. Don't get stuck on the crease.'

What stood out was how tight they were as a group, smiling and laughing, even when they messed up. Not that they weren't serious. He wouldn't want to stand in the way of any of them. They were world champions for a reason. But still, there was room for improvement here and there, especially with the young players coming through. The girls just didn't get as many games at the top level, to develop that match fitness.

Before he knew it, he was helping pack up. The day had flown by.

Liv walked him back to his car.

'So, what do you think?'

'They're a great group. Tight. Strong skills.' Stronger than he'd expected, he had to admit. 'Just not sure I've got much to offer. And I couldn't do this and captain the Bulls.'

'I'm pretty sure we could sort that out.'

He looked away, back towards the ground. 'Why do they call you Betty?'

'Like Betty Wilson.'

Harrow shrugged.

Liv rolled her eyes. 'She was the female Bradman. Except Bradman never took a Test hat-trick. Scored a century in the same match. First player *ever* to do that.'

'How long ago?'

'1958.'

'You'll do better,' he said.

change of pace

He stacked the fridge shelves with packets of brie, cheddar, mozzarella, parmesan, and the new halloumi. Dad had barbequed some the night before, and it was pretty good, all squeaky on his teeth. It had been Liv's idea to spend some time back home, helping out, where everything was so simple, to clear his head. Mum and Dad hadn't said a word about cricket since he arrived, which felt pretty weird, given it had been *the* conversation for their entire lives. He'd timed the visit between the Fourth and Fifth Test, so it wouldn't be on. But there would normally be plenty to analyse with their top-order batting collapses, and England dominating the Australian bowlers.

'You right to look after the customers this morning?' Dad said.

Harrow nodded.

'You're sure? You feel okay?'

'I'm fine, Dad.'

He rubbed at his forehead, more lined than Harrow remembered, and his hair receding. 'Thanks. Gives me a chance to run some errands.'

'No worries.'

'I'll be back by lunch. Your mother wants to show you how to make cheese this afternoon.'

'Don't rush,' Harrow said. He was keen to learn, he just wasn't sure he was ready to hear what Mum would say about the state of his relationship. 'Do you want me to try fixing that sliding door?'

Dad smiled. 'That'd be great.'

He tightened the screws on the door's tracks, brushed them clean, and found a can of WD-40 out the back to try to get the door moving properly again. Not perfect, but better. He cleaned the glass, with paper towel and Windex, looking out over the green grass to the mist-streaked range, and flipped the sign to *OPEN*.

The till was a bit challenging, and the whole EFTPOS thing, but the rest was really just talking to people. They were usually on holidays so in a pretty good mood, curious to hear all about the farm. Only one person had recognised him, so far, and she'd only talked up his batting, which wasn't so hard to take.

It was a lot like batting, having to kit up before heading into the dairy: steel-caps, gloves, gown, hairnet. Mum took him through the whole process, from separating the curds from the whey to checking the progress of the great rounds of brie and parmesan on the drying racks. She had him make a batch of ricotta on his own, which tasted pretty good, if he did say so himself. They had afternoon tea out the back, looking over the old cricket ground, with ricotta instead of cream on their scones and jam. Sixer lay at their feet, gazing at Harrow. He was grey about the muzzle now, but his eyes still imploring for a ball to be thrown or a bat to appear.

'It's been lovely having you home,' Mum said.

'Why didn't you teach us about the cheese as kids?'

'Cricket,' Mum said.

He smiled. 'Well, glad to help out now.'

Mum set her mug down on the table. 'I appreciate the extra pair of hands, that's for sure. But what I most want,' she said, 'is for you to go back to Brisbane.'

He turned, mouth full. 'What?'

'You need to go home, sort things out with Megan. A woman like that doesn't come along every day. Or two people who get along so well.'

'It wasn't so good at the end, Mum,' he said. 'I really let her down.'

'So, the relationship is real now. Cricket, too.'

They watched Dad making his way across the muddy paddock in his gumboots, dragging a coil of fencing wire.

'What's that supposed to mean?'

'You have to work at things, and keep working at them, in this life. It's not a fairytale.'

When he turned up at the apartment with his bags, he wasn't surprised to find Nina still staying in the spare room, or to get a punch in the arm.

'Nice to see you, too,' he said. The apartment seemed bigger, somehow. And he'd missed the river, so wide and strong. After all the rain it was brown, a half-submerged log and a plastic drum floating out to sea.

Megan smiled, from the other side of the kitchen bench. 'Welcome home.'

They'd spoken a few times, while he was up the coast. It had begun to feel like the old days, staying on the phone till midnight, because they didn't want to go. 'Just come back,' she'd said. 'We'll work it out.'

'I'll cook dinner,' Nina said. 'And tomorrow, I'll get out of your hair. Give you two a chance to talk.'

Nina's apartment was finally finished, across the river. They'd be able to signal from each other's balconies, she reckoned.

true note

I lean on the workbench, looking out at the garden, tossing a new cricket ball from one hand to the other, yet to get started for the day. Another Ashes series over, another loss to England. I watched or heard nearly every ball bowled. The upside of living alone again. There's a satisfaction in that, being part of a big series. Though I'm tired, and did feel cross, the entire time, that Harrow wasn't there. The Australians just don't have the same power at the top without him, that capacity to dominate.

The stand-out player of the series was Walker. He's really matured, adjusting to bowling different lengths on the English pitches, and just plugging away to get his wickets. Barker was good, too, averaging over fifty, though some of his captaincy decisions were a bit conservative, in my opinion.

Watching it all unfold on the box, I did feel regretful, in the end, that I didn't take up John May's offer, and go over, watch it live. I could have seen all those willow sets settling in, too. Next time, maybe. If I was ever to take a world tour, it would be of all the great cricket grounds. Lord's, of course, the Oval and Old Trafford. If I planned it right, I could do an Ashes tour and then just continue on, following the game to Cape Town, Kingston, Bridgetown, Galle, Mumbai, maybe even Dharamshala – the highest ground in the world, with the Himalayas as backdrop. Now *that* would be a heavenly game.

There are cricket grounds in places you wouldn't expect, cold-climate cities like New York and Calgary. There's even one in Berlin, built as part of the 1936 Olympic Games extravaganza. With a seventy-seven-foot-high bell tower looming over the ground, like Hitler's shadow, the Berlin Cricket Club would be more aware than most of the nation's sporting history. It must be a strange mix with the spirit of cricket, however that translates *auf Deutsch*.

It's not the only fascist cricket ground in the shadow of an Olympic stadium. Mussolini built the Stadio dei Marmi – Stadium of the Marbles – in Rome during the 1920s as part of the Foro Italico, a faux-classical sporting complex. With its grand Carrara marble statues, from a distance it looks like just another ancient monument. But when you get closer, the figures are all holding sporting equipment. A blocky wicketkeeper in shorts, wielding an enormous bat, is one of the few graced with any clothing. A fig leaf, after all, doesn't offer much protection against a cricket ball.

Playing cricket surrounded by statues, the terracotta running track and grand marble steps up to ancient olive trees, must feel like being part of the early Olympics.

I always dreamed of playing with the Berlin Philharmonic or the Sinfonica. Watching cricket where no one at home knew it was even played. Berlin and Rome were the two cities Marlene and I were equally keen on. We were halfway through our respective grant applications when we found out about Katie. She was unplanned, which is another way of saying that all the plans we did have went out the window.

We thought we'd travel the world with our music and our art. And, in a way, we did. Every time I played a piece of music or put on a record, every time Marlene entered the studio, whenever we went to a concert or a gallery. It was a rich life. But I'm not sure either of us ever completely let go of those dreams. I wouldn't trade Katie for any of it – for anything – but, looking back, maybe Marlene and I blamed each other, deep down, for our disappointment.

I've fallen in love with the oboe again, building up my practice to three hours a day. Any more and I find my embouchure collapses. Other things, too, are falling into place, but it's through music that it's becoming real, my body and mind working together. My heart space is expanding.

My confidence, too. Enough to tackle Handel's *Oboe Concerto No. 3 in G minor,* an old favourite. I still have to remind myself, every time, to play with an open heart. Without frustration at what I have lost, without expectation.

Until, at last, with the morning light dancing on the glass all around me, in the green of the garden, I forget myself. And it happens. The music is playing me. More and more true notes, that purity of sound I remember. Until I'm not sure if the light is coming from the music or the music from the light. I'm vibrating, fully alive, every cell connected to every other cell of this life, this universe.

I may never have learned Italian or lived overseas, but I have a universal language. I can read all those little marks on the page, set down centuries ago by composers from all over the world, and translate them into music. Their work, their inner and outer landscapes, live on, through the oboe, connecting us all. It's only through music that humanity and nature work as one. We can all transcend our own lives, given the opportunity, if we're open enough.

on the back foot

The first time Harrow turned up to training he was nervous all over again. The Bulls got around him, made him feel welcome, and it was good to be back at the Gabba, but it was a downwards and backwards movement. Having been part of the national set-up, an elite squad, and everything that went with it, anything else was less. He missed the boys, the coaching staff, the entourage, the crowd. The buzz of it all. A lot of it was ego shit. Embarrassment at being dropped. He sensed sympathy from the Queensland boys, but also a little satisfaction that he'd been brought back down to their level.

But when Tank announced him as captain, Harrow did feel proud. Klimt gave him a nod and a grin. Sky already knew, of course, but didn't let on.

They had some new young guys, exciting talent. They were like puppies, brimming with enthusiasm and no idea of any of the realities. When he chatted with them in the nets, some of their enthusiasm even rubbed off. He put them through their paces with some throwdowns, and gave them the heads-up on the bowlers they'd be facing against the old enemy, New South Wales. He answered their questions about the national team, playing with greats like Dog and Gibbo. It was his job to inspire, bring out the best in them, not bring them down. And it would really be something, something worthwhile, if he could lead them to a Shield win.

He was striking the ball well in the nets, but had yet to translate that feeling to the field of play. Tank asked him to bowl some overs before the next game. They'd lost their other part-timer to a shoulder injury, throwing himself too wholeheartedly at the ball on the boundary and colliding with the advertising signage.

'I'm pretty rusty.'

'Well get unrusted, we need you.' Tank walked away to take another phone call, rubbing his already balding head. Being needed was nice, after so long being superfluous. He put some effort into rolling his arm over, practising some of his variations on the new pups. It was good to feel the seam against his fingers, something tangible. But his fingers weren't what they'd been. It was harder to grip and spin the ball. He focused on flight and bounce, trying to work in a few variations in speed.

Arhus, one of the newbie bowlers from Gold Coast, tried to smash him, and succeeded, more than once, but then lost his off stump to one that didn't turn. That was the game in a nutshell, right there.

'Don't try to play for the spin,' Harrow said. 'It's the ones coming straight on you have to worry about.'

His first few innings were a bit scratchy, a twenty-three and a forty-two. The bowlers were targeting his head and he was yet to find his hook and pull shot, overthinking everything. His hand was giving him trouble, too, jarring every time he connected with the ball. He'd been taking painkillers to get through, which Megan had her views about. She'd made him an appointment with the specialist, to 'deal with it properly'. He knew she was right, but he wasn't sure he was ready to hear what they said. In the meantime, he changed his grip, keeping his right hand tucked behind and a little loose on the handle of the bat.

In their game against South Australia at the Adelaide Oval, he felt a little of the magic returning. After surviving an early dropped catch, he figured the rub of the green was with him and started freeing his arms. Megan's parents were up in the Members', backing the home team, no doubt, but hopefully behind him, too. Her father had come through the latest treatment okay, and they were just keeping their fingers crossed.

Once he reached his century, he stepped into a nicely timed off-drive without thinking about it and felt almost back to his old self.

South Australia looked like stealing the match though, with young Needham playing his shots, and passing the one-fifty mark. It didn't feel right to bring himself on to bowl as captain, but he did; they were desperate. And it worked. His wrong 'un, when he could pull it off, still had the surprise factor. Needham hit the ball straight back at him and Harrow snatched the catch. His bellow of triumph had more than a little to do with thwarting a rival.

The quicks cleaned up South Australia's tail, bringing home another Bulls win. They were gathering momentum and, this time, he was determined to see them all the way home.

With another hundred at the WACA, he thought he might've done enough to get a call up for the home series against South Africa. Shep had been solid again, but O'Neil had barely reached double figures.

When the call came, the news wasn't good. They were giving the young gun, Needham, a shot. He was still in their thoughts, still had a big future for Australia. *Blah blah blah.*

Mads said the word was the selectors thought he was vulnerable to the bouncer, and that the South Africans had his measure. 'Just keep scoring runs,' Mads said. 'Knock the bloody door down. You're too good not to be playing for Australia.'

After missing out, the pressure was somehow off. He was free to enjoy cricket again. The Bulls were a good bunch of lads who were really giving their all. On the back of Harrow's batting, Queensland had a dream end-of-season run, helped by Tasmania's unprecedented collapse at home, and Sky's freaky ten-wicket haul to wrangle a last-over win against Western Australia. In the semi against New South Wales, Harrow scored a quick-fire hundred before one of Hilt's bouncers struck him on the glove and then another on the helmet, forcing him to retire hurt. But it was enough.

Klimt saw them over the line, with Sky hitting the winning runs. They were not only through to the final, but would play in front of a home crowd, a once-in-a-lifetime opportunity.

specialist

Harrow paid at reception and walked out into the bright Brisbane day. It took a few minutes to remember where he'd parked. He opened the windows and sat for a moment behind the wheel without putting the keys in the ignition. The specialist said he would need surgery, pins and some sort of plate. He'd rebroken his finger, punching the wall, and it hadn't knitted properly. The new (Hilt) fracture in his neighbouring thumb was compounding things. Even if the surgery was successful, he probably wouldn't ever be pain-free. And any time he was hit again increased the risks.

He could get through the Shield final, with painkillers and careful strapping, but he'd have to have the surgery straight afterwards. Even if it went well, his movement would always be impaired, and arthritis likely from middle age.

As the specialist put it, 'Hands aren't just for batting, they're for life.' The images came thick and fast: holding Megan, helping his parents out in the dairy, throwing a ball, maybe to a daughter or a nephew, buttoning a shirt, even just washing his hair.

And then there was the concussions. The knock he'd copped on the helmet hadn't been too bad, but it was a few days until he felt a hundred per cent. Megan was right onto it, insisting on getting a second opinion. 'I've already paid for the appointment,' she said. 'And this time I'm coming with you.'

The woman explained about repeated trauma to the head, even if the knocks were only small. She showed brightly coloured images of footballer's brains on the screen, listing the impacts later in life, like loss of memory and 'cognitive ability', mood swings.

He sat there next to Megan, watching her fingernails tapping the arm of her chair. He was barely smart enough for her as it was without brain damage.

If he knew for sure he'd open the batting for Australia again, it would be one thing but … The selectors didn't believe in him anymore. The press was just waiting for him to fail. All the effort it took to keep going, all the work to get back, now felt like an even bigger mountain than it had.

He had a couple of black-hole days. Not sitting around, like before, but empty. He walked, listened to music and watched old movies. Megan gave him plenty of space, cooked his favourite meals, and ordered take-out from the new Japanese place he liked. Mum and Dad, Liv, Sky, Peters had all called but he didn't have the heart to call them back.

That Friday night, after dinner, he talked it through with Megan out on the deck, until the stars faded and the ferries were warming up. 'I just don't know if I can keep putting myself through it,' he said. 'And I'm putting you through it, too.'

'You need to be sure it's what you want.'

So he made another appointment. With the sports psychologist Mads had recommended. She asked, in the middle of a barrage of questions he had to answer without hesitating, if he wanted to keep playing.

'Yes, but …' he said.

She leaned forward. 'But what?'

He shook his head.

Afterwards, he took a long walk along the river, listening to one of his old Powderfinger albums. They were the voice of Brisbane, the Gabba, his youth. A lot of memories from when cricket had been everything, when batting was simple.

The psych's 'take-home question' had been 'Who would you be if you didn't play cricket?' He'd walked out thinking it was a stupid fucking question. But the truth was, he just didn't have an answer.

interstate

Katie and I are cleaning up after the weekend workshop with the radio on. The news is the usual wrap-up of disasters and doom but I stop sweeping to hear the sports round-up. The squad for South Africa's tour should be announced any day now. With the mountain of runs he's scored and his winning streak as Queensland captain, displaying his leadership ability, Harrow has to be in. Shepherd's shortcomings at Test level were really shown up during the Ashes loss. O'Neil is out of form. Young Needham's double century will have impressed, but it was on a flat wicket against a second-string New South Wales attack when they'd already won the game. It's *when* a player scores their centuries that matters. But the selectors may well want to pin their hopes on a new young thing with no scars or baggage.

'In breaking news, Todd Harrow has announced that he will retire from all forms of cricket. New Cricket Australia CEO, Belinda Clark, made a statement shortly afterwards: "Todd Harrow is one of the most gifted batters to ever play for Australia. We thank him for his contribution, all the fans and young players he has brought to cricket. And we hope that he will continue to be involved in our great game."'

Katie looks up, on the other side of the bench. 'No way,' she says.

I lean on the broom to keep myself upright. 'There must be something we don't know.'

It isn't even mid-morning and all the life has been sucked out of the day. You can't make someone play, keep putting themselves on the line, but … Harrow is to me what Trumper was to poor old

Cardus. Except Trumper played out a good career. Harrow is yet to even show us his best. I'm not ready for him to give it all away. I'm not ready.

When I watch the evening news, it's the lead story on every channel. At the press conference, Harrow struggles to hold back tears as he reads a written statement, lights flashing, cameras, microphones and phones pushing into the frame. 'Cricket has been my life. I've loved every minute. But I'll struggle to play on at my best with my injuries. And I'm told that if I'm hit in the head again, it could be life-threatening.

'I'd like to thank Cricket Queensland and Cricket Australia for the opportunities I've been given, and their support in making this difficult decision. My family and my partner, Megan, for helping me to realise my dream of playing for Australia. To my teammates ...' He swallows, his hands are shaking, holding the single page. 'My teammates at the Bulls, and all the Australian boys. It's been an absolute honour to walk out onto a cricket field with all of you, you've been mentors and mates. I'll treasure the memories.' He takes a deep breath. 'I look forward to leading the Bulls in the Shield final this year. After the game, I'll be retiring from all forms of cricket. To the fans, the public, the followers of our great game, here and around the world. Thank you for all your support. I'm sorry if I've let you down.'

He folds the piece of paper in half. The journalists start firing off questions. Harrow looks at the publicist sitting next to him, even younger than him.

'Todd won't be taking any questions at this time. Thank you for your understanding.' She stands, puts her hand on his shoulder, and escorts him from the room.

I stare at the television, through the barrage of stories about war, destruction and corruption, at home and abroad. And I can't make myself care about any of it. One more game. That's all there is.

I fire up the computer, remember my password on the third try, and log on. Tickets to the Shield final aren't a problem, but the airfares, at short notice, are going to set me back. I find an early morning Jetstar flight that isn't too bad, telling myself there's no price on history, on the closing of a career. And it's Victoria they'll be playing; I'm supporting my state, too.

Queensland have a great chance at home, with Harrow strengthening the batting, and Klimt and Walker released from the Australian squad to lead the bowling attack. The Queensland bowlers know exactly how to extract the best from the bouncy pitch and a boisterous home crowd. The Victorian boys don't tend to do that well at the Gabba. They'll be relying on Shepherd to set them up, Peters to play a role with bat and ball, and maybe some magic from the new fellow, Salt.

But I'm only doing it for Harrow. The last time I caught a plane was to my Uncle Rory's funeral, in Hobart. He was my favourite as a young fellow, a lot easier to get along with than my father. Or so he seemed, from a distance.

He just dropped dead on the spot. Blood clot they reckoned. I can't remember much of the trip. Or even booking the flight. Maybe Marlene did all that. Two flights, four cab rides, and an outdoor funeral on a miserable day that only Burnie could put on. I barely remember it. My last international flight had immediately preceded a funeral, too, of course. It's not a great association.

But Harrow isn't dying, just retiring. And I want to be there for the occasion. The sports pages are full of analysis: his stats, injuries, best performances. Concussion experts are taking the opportunity to speak of the dangers of repeated head injuries. What a tough decision to have to make, so young.

sleepless

Megan dropped her satchel on the bench and slipped out of her shoes. 'Hey, handsome. You cleaned.'

'And I made a curry,' he said. He poured her a glass of white wine and slid it across the bench.

'Thank you,' she said. 'Something happen?'

'They've formally offered me the job as batting coach for the women's team.'

Megan smiled.

It still did it for him, that smile. Reminded him how lucky he was.

'You going to accept?'

'I wanted to talk to you about it,' he said. 'There'd be a bit of travel.'

'Their schedule isn't as full-on as the men's though, right?'

'No, but it's building.'

'I just want you to be happy. And I really want to make partner sometime this decade.'

He nodded, sipped his mineral water. 'You will,' he said. 'And I want to support that. I'd be around a bit more. The coaching won't be forever – three years. But the girls are really good, Megs. They bat right down to number ten, they can nearly all bowl. It's practically a team of all-rounders. They could be best in the world in all formats. They *are*. And Liv ...' He swallowed. 'Well, she's basically their best player.'

Megan nodded. 'You'd be okay with that?'

'I'm around the game, involved. But not so personal,' he said. 'Not quite, anyway.'

'Let's make it work then,' Megan said. 'I think you still have a lot to contribute.'

'That's exactly what Liv said. Did you two talk?'

Megan smiled. 'Maybe.'

'What else did she say?'

'That you owe her, with all the balls she bowled at you.'

'Made her the player she is.'

Megan laughed. 'You must be feeling better.'

He woke in the middle of the night, heart pounding. Eventually he got up and made a cup of herbal tea, one of Megan's concoctions. She had a lot of trouble winding down, and it seemed to work for her. It tasted like grass but he'd give it a chance to work.

She came out and sat with him on the couch in the dark, looking out at the moon, which had risen over the wide, winding river, like a god. A god he'd been asking for help.

'Can't sleep?'

He shook his head.

'Me either,' she said. 'What are you worrying about?'

'Letting the boys down. Not winning.' He leaned his forehead against Megan's. 'Whether I've made the right decision.'

She stroked his cheek, her fingers lingering on his scarred nose. 'What's most important to you, about this game?'

'Contributing. Being fearless.'

She nodded. 'Well, I've seen you do that, time and time again. And you have nothing to lose now, really. You can leave everything out there,' she said. 'Why don't we put off all our fears until after the game. I'll do it, too.'

'You're worried?'

'*Yes*,' she said. 'When I saw you go down again like that …' She wiped her eyes with her fingertips.

'Last game, Megs,' he said. 'And I won't get hit.'

'You'd better not.'

flying batmaker

And I thought flying seedlings was complicated. Since I last flew, there's a whole lot more rigmarole just to fly interstate. Since the September 11 attacks, apparently. Me and a whole lot of other blokes have to back up and remove our belts and boots. It's disconcerting, giving up my phone and wallet, my jeans threatening to fall from my hips at any moment. When I sit down to put myself back together, on the other side of the conveyor belt and an explosives test, I find that I'm wearing mismatching socks.

I have a beer in the departures lounge, to settle the nerves. And then line up to board. The in-flight experience is no longer communal. Everyone has their own little screen, their own headphones, and no one listens to the stewards' announcements or safety demonstrations – they're far too smart and sophisticated for that. Except me. Falling out of the sky seems a possibility, and I'm not ready to die, just yet. I have a game to get to.

Harrow's announcement has taken the whole cricket world by surprise. Shock, bewilderment, even outrage. Suddenly everyone is nostalgic, replaying his greatest shots, his greatest innings, mourning the loss like a death. What could have been. I can't help wishing they'd shown more appreciation while he was playing. And that the selectors had backed him. Maybe the confidence would have made a difference. He wouldn't have had to be always fighting his way back, doubting himself.

I've chosen an aisle seat in case I need the bathroom. My neighbour is just as ill-fitted to his confinement. We bump arms, shoulders and thighs as we struggle to strap ourselves in. We're already on the runway by the time I put on my headphones, plug them into the socket, and find the classical music channel. I close my eyes for take-off and grip the handrails.

They've chosen the perfect soundtrack for my flight. The Berlin Philharmonic's performance of Respighi's *The Pines of Rome* transports me more gently than any aircraft could. He was all about creating an impression of nature through tone. The oboe solo is the highlight, making me yearn for the Villa Borghese.

Somehow I've ended up in the midst of a Victorian contingent, a bunch of bankers and investment brokers in matching Hawaiian shirts and Mexican hats who are getting in ahead of the south of the border remarks from the majority Queensland crowd by being loud and obnoxious. One of them has brought his young daughter along, wearing a Victorian cap, who seems unperturbed by all the noise and obscenity, intent on the action out on the field.

The Gabba is almost full. Cricket fans are pouring in to witness the final appearance of one of the finest batters ever to play the game. The press and photographers are all here to capture his last moments, those final images. Hopefully they're triumphant.

The big day has dawned fine and clear after an overnight storm. Scott wins the toss. Victoria will bat first. As the sun heats up and the moisture rises from the pitch, it will be steamy for the Queenslanders out in the field. But it might be a blessing, something in the pitch for bowlers in the first session. I'm looking forward to seeing what Walker can do. He has a big heart, that fellow.

After so much anticipation, the game is about to begin. The only threat to the big event is the rain forecast for days three and four.

Walker looks nervous at the top of his mark, fussing with his shoelaces and socks. There's more at stake for the Queensland boys than the Sheffield Shield. But when he runs in, his body takes over. The ball is full and fast, swinging late. It beats Shepherd, cannoning into the base of the stumps. OUT!

Walker is bellowing, swamped by Harrow and his teammates. Shepherd is trudging from the ground with a golden duck to his name. It's a dream start for Queensland.

It's an hour into play on day two before I get to see Harrow bat. Victoria rallied, after losing their top three before lunch on day one, to put two hundred and eighty-nine on the board. It feels like not quite enough but we won't know what's par on this pitch until we see the other side bat.

I'm applauding the moment Harrow connects. I don't care what my Mexican-hatted mates think. It's a glorious straight drive, running away to the boundary. The focus on the team has freed him up. He plays beautiful shot after beautiful shot, all style.

As he approaches fifty, I need the bathroom, and my legs are sticking to the yellow plastic chair, but I can't move, lest I change his luck. And I don't want to miss a moment.

Harrow brings up his half-century with a simple glide to fine leg. The stadium of Queenslanders stand to applaud the milestone and the new scoreboard's summary of Harrow's achievements at state and national level. I'm the solitary man on his feet in the sea of Victorians.

'Siddown, mate. I want to see that fucker get hit in the head again.'

'I beg your pardon?'

'You heard.'

'Yes, and it was offensive. Inappropriate for a young person's ears.'

'Whatever.'

I sit down. The bowler certainly was aiming for Harrow's head. Three bouncers in the over so far. The crowd has stilled, understanding the implications. But Harrow hooks the next one, sending it sailing into the second tier of the stands. He's grinning, the way he used to.

It's a very good start. There's a message from Katie on my phone. *Felix and I are watching. Everything crossed.*

carrying your bat

The rain had held off and Queensland needed three hundred and fifty-seven on the final day. It was a big ask. They only had to draw the game to win the Shield but the boys had a talk, and they were all agreed: they wanted to have a shot at the win. Harrow's plan was to try to build a total in the first session and see where they were after lunch, take it from there. His seventy in the first innings had left him hungry. If this was to be his final innings, he would make it count.

He and Reid started well, no risks, no chances, rotating the strike, pushing the singles and the twos. Then Reid started striking the ball hard, taking advantage of the short boundary. He was looking like he would never get out and then, just on drinks, lofted one straight to deep cover.

Harrow and Frazer steadied, putting on a hundred-run partnership. They shook hands on that, slowing things down, staying calm. 'Nice to be out here with you, Hars.'

'Ditto.' Harrow took a moment to savour the atmosphere, check the field placings. They were tracking well, but he tried to clear outcomes from his mind. He glanced up at where he knew Megan, Liv, Sean, Nina and his parents were sitting. What would he be without that support? Where would any of the players be? Nina was in a bind, wearing a Bulls cap in support of her home state but waving a Victoria flag for Peters. The thought made him smile despite all the pressure out in the middle. Life was funny, sometimes, the way things worked out.

When Frazer tried to steal a single to bring up his fifty, Salt was waiting. He'd switched states for a three-season contract, all on the back of his reputation as a gun fielder. He swooped, picked up and threw, one stump to aim at – and hit. Frazer grounded his bat with outstretched arm as he ran but it was close. Harrow turned to look at the umpire. OUT. Frazer had to go.

From there, Queensland wobbled, losing three quick wickets. Tank was rubbing his head, in the dugout, but Harrow leaned on his bat, watching the crowd, a strange sense of calm coming over him.

Klimt gave Harrow a look of steel when he arrived at the crease. 'If this is going to be the last time I bat with you, let's make it fucking count.'

They knew they could; they'd done it before, and on bigger stages. They settled into a rhythm, taking no risks, but rotating the strike, pushing the scoring along. Klimt hooked or pulled anything loose, while Harrow used his cut shot and drive to thread the ball through the fielders to the boundary. It was trust, the glue between them, and it was absolute. If Queensland were going to win the game, it was up to them. And there was something else, something beautiful: the joy of being out there, playing for their state, for each other, every moment all the sharper because it was almost gone.

He was still batting at tea, on a hundred and sixteen. Klimt holed out to deep backward square, but his sixty had given them a sniff. They needed a hundred and twenty in the final session with only three wickets in hand. A long shot, for sure. But while he was still at the crease, Harrow believed they could do it. It was just one of those feelings; that it was their day.

Harrow farmed the strike, but it was too soon to get silly about it. Franco had started out as an all-rounder, batting four for his club side. Harrow had to trust him to hold up an end and score when he could.

He nudged one off his pads, round the corner to fine leg to bring up his hundred and fifty. He raised his bat, for the crowd, the boys back in the dressing room – for his parents, Liv, and Megan. They'd reduced the runs required to seventy-four, and neither of them had played a false stroke. He could sense it in Franco, too. The purposeful note in his running, watching the ball, backing up. They were *on*. Every moment, every decision, every movement counted.

The Victorians, on the other hand, were getting frustrated. With their big second-innings total, they had probably started to think about holding up the Shield, celebrating a long hard summer with a win. That was a killer, for the bowling side, to get ahead of yourself, and take your foot off the pedal without even realising it. Peters bowled a no ball, his third for the day, which Franco hit for SIX. It was just an edge, but he was wielding one of the new Big Kahunas, basically just for boundary hitting, and it went all the way. Franco didn't move, he was grinning before the ball even cleared the fence. Seven runs off one ball was a bonus and brought them within thirty runs of winning.

Peters glared at Franco, the umpire, and scratched at his footmarks, as if they were the problem. Harrow walked away, gazing into the stands, where he'd once sat as a boy. There was a new generation of kids out there, girls and boys, families of all shapes, sizes and shades. People who had come to support their team, see them play. It was humbling, somehow.

Peters came running in again, a face on him like fury itself. The ball came straight for Franco's head. He played off the back foot, setting himself to hook. Harrow knew from the sound it was SIX all the way. They watched it sail over the cover fielder's head into the grasping hands of the crowd.

But there was another sound. Somehow, Franco had trod on his wicket. The Victorians were appealing. Franco looked back at the bails on the ground. The roar that came out of his mouth as he walked off was primal. He'd wanted to be a hero, and it was over.

But he'd brought them close. Sky strode out, all legs and arms. They'd been here before, too, and delivered. The big man was emotional, breathing too hard. 'Let's get this done,' he said.

'Plenty of time,' Harrow said.

Sky swung big, connected, depositing one into the crowd down at long off, which had everyone on their feet. SIX. It was probably the best shot he'd played in his life. And now the adrenaline was really pumping. Harrow tried to make him laugh, slow things down. But Sky wasn't listening. He tried the same shot next ball but didn't get quite get hold of it. They set off for a run, just hoping.

Harrow watched the two fielders running around on the boundary rope. Salt dived, arm outstretched, and flicked the ball back into the field of play while still mid-air. Shepherd pivoted, threw himself full-length, and took the ball cleanly in both hands. OUT.

They'd crossed before the ball was taken, putting Harrow back on strike. He couldn't look at Sky as he walked off, head back. The anguish he knew he would see on his face would do him in.

Arhus didn't have many shots, but he could defend, and when he did connect with one, it went a long way. He liked to remind everyone of Gillespie, the Australian fast bowler who scored a double century. Gillespie batted at nine, and came in as nightwatchman in that match, so technically, at number three. But Harrow knew Arhus would never give up, and that was gold.

He waited for him in the middle of the pitch. 'Right, youngster,' Harrow said. 'Play straight. Be ready to back up, every ball. But be careful, they'll try to run you out. Keep that bat grounded behind the line.'

'Got it.'

'One more wicket, boys,' was the constant refrain from Mads, behind the stumps. 'Let's spoil this little retirement party.'

Second last ball of the over, Victoria brought all their men in to stop the single. Harrow dropped the ball at his feet, yelled 'YES!' and ran. Arhus was already haring past him. Harrow heard the stumps go down. But when he turned, Arhus was home and Mads, one glove off, was cursing.

Arhus took his mark, faced up, cool as a cucumber, and blocked an absolute thunderbolt with a stride forward and an upright bat. The home crowd applauded the effort. Arhus grinned, loving every minute.

Harrow focused on scoring a boundary early in the over, a single towards the end. Arhus had only scored three runs but the kid was a fortress of calm. The Victorian bowlers were getting frustrated, anxious. A wide and four-leg byes put Queensland within ten runs of a win going into the final over.

Harrow assessed the field. He could go for the boundary over mid-wicket, but there was risk. Finding a two somewhere was the safer bet. The ball, when it came, was a wide yorker. Too wide, on the other side of the white line. He let it go through to the keeper and waited for the umpire's call. One less run to get. But the call did not come.

Arhus shook his head. 'What?! Were your eyes open?'

Harrow held up a glove. *Easy now.*

He pulled the next one behind square, didn't quite time it – and called two. When he turned to come back, Arhus was shouting 'NO!'. And just as well, because it was Salt firing the ball back in, straight over the stumps. Eight runs, four balls, one wicket, and Arhus was on strike. Harrow didn't give any advice, or instruction. The kid would do what he could. A draw would be enough. That's what he told himself.

When Arhus punched the next one past gully, they ran two, they had to. Harrow dived for the line and lay there, his mouth full of dirt, while the Victorians appealed all around him. He looked up at the umpire, who was shaking his head. Not out.

Six runs to get, three balls to get them in, and Harrow was helpless at the other end. Arhus settled himself, took a stride down the pitch and drove the ball back past the bowler like a pro. *Yes.* The diving fielder brushed the ball with his reaching fingertips but could only watch it run away for FOUR.

Two runs, one wicket, two balls.

The next delivery was straight and *quick*, cramping Arhus in his shot. He connected, the edge flew high in the air. Harrow ran. They'd turn for two no matter what. He saw Peters sprinting in, heard the crowd groaning. Peters dived, arms outstretched, and, for a moment, had the ball in his hands. But when his elbows, his great body, hit the turf, the ball bobbled out, onto the grass.

Harrow grounded his bat as the crowd erupted. A roar so great that it shifted the sails on the stadium. Arhus turned and lifted his arms in the air, like the champion he was. They ran to each other and embraced, mid-pitch.

'Well done, youngster. Well done.'

The boy was sobbing, all the relief, adrenaline pouring out of him. They weren't the first tears to be shed on a cricket pitch and they wouldn't be the last.

'We *had* to win, Hars. For you.'

stumps

The rest of the Queensland team are storming onto the ground, hugging and jumping in a delirious huddle, lifting Harrow and Arhus into the air. The final, and the Sheffield Shield, go to Queensland. If I was at home, in the privacy of my lounge room, I would weep with relief. What a game. I wanted, *needed*, Harrow to go out a winner at least.

The Mexican hats have been silenced, boozy disappointment pouring from their pores. The youngster is inconsolable, beating her father's chest with tiny fists, as he lifts her, Victorian flag trailing, from the litter-strewn ground. 'No, Daddy. *No.*'

That's the two faces of sport right there: winning and losing, careers beginning and ending, players made and unmade, heartbreak or elation.

The Victorian players are picking themselves up, their support staff dribbling out onto the ground to congratulate the victorious team. Matterson is the first to shake Harrow's hand and embrace him.

Peters is still lying on the grass. Harrow and Arhus go to him and kneel, their hands on his back, trying to console him. And in that moment, I *love* those men. Seeing that gesture, unscripted, unnecessary, completes the day.

Katie's message is a line of happy faces, Graeme's a line of expletives. I have to laugh.

I wipe my face on my sleeve and gather my things together to begin the slow shuffle out with the crowd. The aisles are littered with empty plastic cups, rolling in the breeze that has picked up, as if from nowhere, cooling things down at last.

Harrow is doing a lap of honour, held high on the shoulders of Klimt and Walker, waving to the fans. He's smiling, but who knows what's going on underneath. I break away from the throng, and take the steps down to the boundary fence, to lean on the white pickets, just to be a little closer.

Harrow taps Klimt's shoulder. They lower him to the ground and he jogs towards me.

'Mr Reader?'

'Allan.'

'I saw the big article about you. Thought you might be here.'

'Wouldn't have missed it.'

'Should never have let go of your bat.'

'Well, a bit of willow like that tends to have a say in things.'

'You might be right.' He glances back to Klimt and Walker, still waiting. 'I'd better go. Good to finally meet you, Allan.'

'I've loved watching you play, son.'

We shake hands and he turns to rejoin his teammates, to continue his final circuit.

I choke back an unmanly sob. Todd Harrow will finish on a hundred and thirty-nine not out, one of nineteen first-class hundreds, at an average of sixty-nine. And his Test figures are up there with the greats.

If he'd been told at the start of the career that's what he would achieve, I'm sure he would have taken it, no question. But he's way too young to retire, even in cricket. And, as he would know better than anyone, as the analysts and experts are already saying, his Test career could have been so much better, so much longer. He should have played a hundred Tests for Australia.

CLOSE OF PLAY

Reading poetry and watching cricket were the sum of my world, and the two are not so far apart as many aesthetes might believe.

~ Philip Lindsay

growing the game

I sit down with my dinner in front of the first ever T20 game between Australia and India, at the MCG, more out of curiosity than anything else. The crowd is huge, with such a large ex-pat Indian population. And the game certainly moves quickly. India are all out for seventy-four, and Australia make the runs in eleven overs, to win by nine wickets. A bit of an anticlimax, really.

What *is* interesting is the number of wickets taken by part-time spin bowlers. Perhaps the short-form game isn't going to be the fast-bowling festival everyone expected. Taking the pace off the ball means the batsmen have to generate it themselves, forcing more errors.

So, it's still cricket. But all the fireworks, dancers and mascots bouncing around cheapen the occasion, in my opinion. Cricket was developed by artisans, demonstrating not just players' skills but craftsmanship: the making of bats, balls and wickets. When the Factories Act of 1847 gave workers Saturday afternoons off, there was more time for weekend cricket, clubs and associations. There was plenty of food and drink – and bookies on hand to take bets. It was the money at stake that saw noblemen and the rising middle-class take an interest in the game – and then take it over. Now it's the administrators, the boards and corporations making the decisions. And those decisions are all about money.

Graeme rings after the game to see what I make of it.

'Shame it wasn't a bit closer,' I say. 'Thought the Indians were masters of this format.'

'I know. When you think how many Test matches come down to the final ball,' he says. 'I would've liked to have seen Harrow out there.'

'Yes.' My voice catches in my throat.

'I hear you're back playing?'

'And enjoying it, too.'

'Why don't you practise with us again? We still meet every Sunday. And we'll be performing this winter, at the Con. It's a charity event for the orange-bellied parrot,' he says. 'We really need the oboe for this one.'

'I'm in,' I say. 'I thought we might have a session in the glasshouse.'

'I'll tell the guys.'

I light the fire and leave the door of the stove ajar until it's away. I pour myself a glass of red, a gift from one of my workshop participants. The record I chose is a special one. Rubinstein's performance of *Piano Concerto in A minor, Opus 16*, Grieg's only completed concerto. Written when he was just twenty-five, it was a raging success. Everyone expected Grieg to produce another, but it never came. It takes a few minutes to find Jean's number, and I'm a little nervous. But I'm determined not to back out. Katie wants to have a dinner, introduce Felix to her aunt. And I said I'd organise it. Just when I think she's not going to answer, I hear her voice.

'Hello.'

'Jean, it's Allan. How are you?'

Frank, Katie and I spend the morning digging holes, which is no one's idea of fun, but it's a nice day, and good to be out in it. Frank is the tallest, with the oldest spine, so we give him the job of working the crow bar, loosening the soil. Katie and I take turns with the digging, piling up soil beside the holes, which we've spaced a stride apart.

Two hours in, we're desperate for a break. Frank brought the tea, in a big silver thermos, and mandarins. We hand around chicken, mayonnaise and lettuce sandwiches, and cupcakes, eating like labourers for the day. We stretch out our backs afterwards, on the hard ground in weak sun, watching high cloud building. A kookaburra is working over the earth we've dug, for grubs. Scrub wrens and fairy wrens keep to the undergrowth, busy being birds.

Frank pushes back his hat. 'You watch the Test?'

'I did,' I say. 'Pretty good effort from our bowlers.'

'Hilton was brilliant. And that Klimt, he's really come on.'

'Can hit a long ball, too. Always good for some runs down the order.'

We turn to look at Katie, peeling the paper from another cupcake. 'I only really follow the women's game now.'

Frank nods. 'Does Felix like cricket?'

She smiles. 'He does. Though perhaps not as much as you two.'

We get back to work digging holes, taking turns on the shovel. The sets don't look much, not yet. Even when they reach twelve feet, they're still just a stick, an unbranched straight stem. In the big plantations in England, they used to plant three times as many as they felled, investing in the future. Now they're all starting from scratch. It looks like the rust has been contained, for now. But it will always be lurking there, in the soil. There's such a delicate balance in everything we do: playing the game, making music, living on this earth.

When we wash up for lunch, Katie's knees are muddy and Frank's hat is askew. I can't see myself but my body is telling me I'm working hard.

After quiche and salad, more tea, leftover cupcakes, and a green apple to finish, we lay around on the picnic rugs, resting.

'That's a hell of a lot of holes,' Frank says. His boots are crossed on top of his bag, hands behind his head.

Katie rubs her face, leaving a smear of dirt across her cheek. 'Well, we've got a hell of a lot of willows.'

I watch the clouds passing overhead, one of them the shape of a batter's helmeted head and shoulders. 'All right,' I say. 'Final session.'

We plant to a depth of thirty inches, leaving nine or ten feet above the ground. For the next few years, we'll have to be careful to trim off any lateral shoots, but the process has begun. I picture the trees maturing, flowering for the first time. Female catkins are green – the males are yellow – appearing in late spring and releasing white fluffy seeds in early summer. They bring the bees of course, and butterflies and moths come for the leaves. It's not just a plantation; it's a forest.

I pat down the soil around my last sapling and water it in, the late afternoon sun in my eyes. When I stand and stretch out my back, Katie is packing up, Frank is leaning on his shovel, and the new grove is bathed in golden light. It's Beethoven's 'The Awakening of Joyful Feelings upon Arrival in the Country', from *Pastoral*, that I can hear, his hymn to nature. We're a long way from Heiligenstadt, but that symphony always was an expression of feelings rather than a portrait of place. Beethoven knew how to leave room for the listener.

We're not just planting seedlings, we're growing the game. The face of cricket may be changing, but its spirit lives on, in the willow. And in the hearts of the next generation of girls and boys, the women and men who will play in their backyards, for their club, their state, and maybe even their country.

ladies and lords

He was back in the rhythm and routine of flights, customs forms, hotel rooms, bus rides and training sessions, but without his kitbags or the pressure of performance. Not that coaching was without pressure. In some ways, it was harder watching from the sidelines. As Liv liked to point out, his hairline was already receding.

'So much for retirement,' Megan said, while he was packing. But he knew she didn't really mind. She and Nina were finally going out on their own, a practice run 'by women, for women,' she said. They'd found the right premises, in the Valley, but wanted to renovate first. She was flying in as soon as it was done.

The coaching role was challenge and reward, keeping him fit. He trained with the girls, and still got the occasional batting practice in, facing their bowlers in the nets. Lane was tough but his sister was definitely the worst. She swore she wasn't *trying* to hit his hand. It had healed as well as could be expected. The ache in his joints wasn't too bad, so far, just a reminder that he'd once opened the batting for his country.

He still hit the gym, between training sessions. Not every day, as he used to, but four times a week. He wasn't going to be one of those blokes who turned to fat once they stopped playing. And he definitely didn't want to be a fat coach. It was hard enough getting the girls to take him seriously. He was older than most of them, and no longer playing, which was still beyond their capacity to imagine.

England had a good record at the ground but the Australians, with their all-round game, were a threat. He'd suggested an adjustment to the batting order, putting Liv in at three. A gamble, but she was in the form of her life. He couldn't wait to see how they lifted for the big occasion.

The girls had drawn the one-day series, so a lot rested on the First Test at New Road, worth double points. It wasn't exactly Lord's (where they would all like to have been) but it had its own history of women's Ashes matches. Back in the day it had been a three-Test series. But the new combined format meant they didn't get to play as many Tests. Liv was good at all three forms, but the baggy green was as much her dream as any player's. It was true of all the girls. But they weren't just playing for themselves. Cricket Australia needed to bring people to the women's game and get more girls playing the sport.

Worcester had really welcomed them, organising special tours and holding events in their honour. The flags of both teams had been flying all the way along high street for weeks. It was a pretty setting, beside the Severn and surrounded by trees and parkland. The English girls said they'd seen Elton John play there. And, the previous summer, the river had risen and the ground flooded, cancelling all games. The ground staff said they did most of their work that season from a rowboat.

Everyone would be flying in for the first ever T20 between the sides, and the big double-header wedding afterwards: Liv and Sky (who was over playing a season with Yorkshire) and Lane and Robinson. He wasn't sure who would toss the bouquet there. Lane had the height but Robs the better throwing arm. She had dual citizenship, so could get married in the UK. It still wasn't legal at home, and everyone was showing their support.

The cathedral bells ringing out over the ground were a constant reminder of the upcoming nuptials. 'It's not too late to change your minds, girls,' Chooky said, just about every practice session.

He and Megan were taking off afterwards, for their first real holiday, up in Scotland. The highlands and islands, Megan said; she'd already organised everything. It seemed like decades ago that they'd discussed faraway places over dinner, barely knowing each other. And now they were going. Not a honeymoon, exactly, but it felt a little like it. He wanted to see wild country like in the films *Rob Roy* and *Braveheart*. And puffins, those cartoon-like birds on the cliffs. There was just something about them that made him feel happy.

Australia won the toss and chose to bat. They lost Robs cheaply, out leg before wicket to an absolute seed, but Chooky and Harrow rallied. Given a chance to play against the new ball, coming onto the bat with pace, Harrow played her shots, all around the ground. An hour into the second session, with no more wickets down, England had almost given up trying to get her out, focusing instead on drying up the scoring.

'I don't understand this strategy,' Holding said, in the commentary box. 'The only way to ensure a batter doesn't score any runs is to make sure they are back in the pavilion.' Todd smiled; Holding would know, with all the wickets he took for the West Indies back in the day.

It was a nervous few overs, with Harrow in the nineties, Mum and Dad's faces up on the big screen, Todd's, too. Just one of the many stories of the game. Harrow was using the old Reader bat for the occasion, a deep divot worn in its face now, from her finding the middle over and over, again, scoring so many runs. It was yellowed, a few fine cracks in the face, but still beautiful. Some kind of magic at work that it didn't really age. In the soft English sun, the bat was golden, containing all the hope and possibilities of the game.

And then, that particular *crack*: a classic on-drive, high elbow, lovely follow through. The ball ran away, over the clipped green grass, making its way to the boundary, bobbling over the white rope, its trajectory sure and inevitable, the fielder's wholehearted pursuit futile.

Harrow grinned, with the satisfaction of having timed it perfectly, all her skills coming together in that moment, white willow striking red leather, the sound of cricket, of summer, echoing over the ground. The crowd stood to applaud what Vaughan called, 'the shot of the day from Harrow, to bring up her first Ashes Test century'.

Todd leapt to his feet, with every member of the team and support staff, out on the balcony for this moment, whooping and clapping. Chooky was down the pitch and hugging Harrow before she could even remove her helmet. Todd raised his arms, fists clenched, mirroring Mum and Dad in the stands.

Todd found himself sniffing back tears. It wasn't just the hundred or that she'd put the team in a winning position, how hard she'd worked, or even what it meant for the game, the team. It was the joy on her face.

Harrow calmed herself, acknowledged her teammates, support staff, parents, the crowd (bat in one hand, helmet in the other, as you do). When she looked up at that blue sky, it wasn't because she believed in god, or thought herself a hero. She was thankful, for the rare English sun shining down on her, for the moment, the miracle that she was out there at all, doing what she loved – playing in an Ashes Test for Australia.

Harrow took a deep breath, put on her helmet and gloves, and took guard, once again, tapping her bat on the crease. Todd sat down, still smiling, still shaking his head. In some other moment, this ball or the next, another innings, another game, she would be undone, through a lapse of concentration, the skills of her opponent, or just bad luck. And, one day, it would all be over; she would play her last innings. It was that knowledge, ever present, that made the good times, moments like this, so very sweet.

That was the game. That was cricket.

acknowledgements

Thank you to Lachlan Fisher for his generosity, in time and stories, to teach me about batmaking, growing willow and the Victorian landscape. And for making me a beautiful harrow bat.

Leta Keens for her piece on Lachlan Fisher and traditional batmaking in *Shoes for the Moscow Circus: Scenes from a Hidden World,* which provided the initial idea (and my mother, Barbara, for giving me the book in 2011).

Simon Castles for throwing up the challenge with his 2015 article: 'Just Not Cricket: Where are the Great Australian Cricket Novels?'

Phillip Hughes, who should have played a hundred Tests, for the motivation to write this story. I loved watching you bat.

Billy Barge (Vandal bats) for a batmaking refresher and a Southern Highlands perspective.

Andrew, for giving me the link between batmaking and music. I'm glad you're playing again.

Frank, for all the treasures of cricket literature which kept me 'researching' for an extra couple of years.

Peter, for sourcing a beautiful antique spokeshave (at a bargain price) and a kangaroo bone.

Malcolm Knox for reading the novel so closely and generously in draft form, and for such warm support for the project. Stephen Vagg, for a detailed expert read. Ted Hill for the final cricket nuffie read, Test cricket conversation, and for being my man on the ground in Pakistan.

The brilliant team at Hachette for their belief in this book and for bringing *Willowman* into the world in such beautiful form, especially Rebecca Saunders, who pushed me to deliver the book I had always wanted to write, and: Emma Rafferty, Emma Harvey, Chris Sims, Lee Moir, Kate Taperell, Madison Garratt and Emma Dorph.

Jo Butler and Alice Grundy for editorial support, Libby Turner for proofreading – thank you for being (or becoming) literate in cricket, as well as story and sentence.

Debra Billson for the perfect and most beautiful cover.

Lisa, for walking this trail, and wider landscapes, with me.

I could not have written this book without the financial support of an Australia Council for the Arts Projects grant and a Queensland Writers Fellowship (State Library of Queensland and Arts Queensland in partnership with the Queensland Writers Centre).

I owe so much to the hundreds of books and articles I read whilst researching *Willowman*, too many to list. In particular, Allan Reader's ruminations on W.G. Grace and cricket as dramatic spectacle lean heavily on C.L.R. James' *Beyond the Boundary.* On batmaking and its history, I could not have written the book without Hugh Barty-King's *Quilt Winders and Pod Shavers.* On the oboe, I'm indebted to *Oboe: Art and Method* by Martin Schuring.

Damien Martyn's cap presentation speech owes a great deal to Adam Gilchrist's cap presentation speech to Alex Carey on 28 December 2021.

Key books:

Shoes for the Moscow Circus: Scenes from a Hidden World by Leta Keens
Quilt Winders and Pod Shavers by Hugh Barty-King
Beyond a Boundary by C.L.R. James
Wildwood: A Journey Through Trees by Roger Deakin
The Art of Cricket by Sir Donald Bradman
Remarkable Cricket Grounds by Brian Levison
Phillip Hughes: The Official Biography by Malcolm Knox and Peter Lalor
Captain's File from Peden to Haynes: Australia's Women Test Cricket Captains by Rob Harvey

Stroke of Genius by Gideon Haigh
The Meaning of Cricket by Jon Hotten
In the Firing Line by Ed Cowan
Crossing the Line by Gideon Haigh
On Warne by Gideon Haigh
A Beautiful Game by Mark Nicholas
Fair Game by Alex Blackwell
The Keepers: The Players at the Heart of Australian Cricket by Malcolm Knox
First Tests by Steve Cannane
Steve Smith's Men by Geoff Lemon
By His Own Hand: A Study of Cricket Suicides by David Frith
Ashes to Ashes by Peter Roebuck
Chasing Shadows: the life and death of Peter Roebuck by Tim Lane and Elliot Cartledge
Ponting: at the close of play by Ricky Ponting
No Spin: the autobiography of Shane Warne, with Mark Nicholas
The Commonwealth of Cricket by Ramachandra Guha
Netherland by Joseph O'Neill
Chinaman by Shehan Karunatilaka
Selection Day by Aravind Adiga
The Art of Fielding by Chad Harbach
The Natural by Bernard Malamud
Shoeless Joe by W.P. Kinsella
Oboe: Art and Method by Martin Schuring
Whole Notes by Ed Ayres

THE LAST WOMAN IN THE WORLD

A remarkable literary novel from the multi-award-nominated Australian writer

After the fires. After the virus. *They* came.

It's night, and the walls of Rachel's home creak as they settle into the cover of darkness. Fear has led her to a reclusive life on the land, her only occasional contact with her sister.

A hammering on the door. There stands a mother, Hannah, with a sick baby. They are running for their lives from a mysterious death sweeping the Australian countryside.

Now Rachel must face her worst fears: should she take up the fight to help these strangers survive in a society she has rejected for so long?

The Last Woman in the World looks at how we treat our world and each other – and what it is that might ultimately redeem us.

> 'Creepy and chilling, this becomes a hell-for-leather survival race through burning countryside' ***The Observer***

> 'Enthralling … a powerful allegory … every passage swells with the momentum of an action-flick. Each page is shaped with an impressive, world-building cinematic scope' ***Sydney Morning Herald***

UNDERSTORY

A memoir about staying in one place, told through trees

'The understorey is where I live, alongside these plants and creatures. I tend the forest, stand at the foot of trees and look up, gather what has fallen.'

This is the story of a tree-change, of escaping suburban Brisbane for a cottage on ten acres in search of a quiet life. Of establishing a writers retreat shortly before the Global Financial Crisis hit, and of losing just about everything when it did.

It is also the story of what the author found there: the beauty of nature and her own path as a writer. *Understory* is a memoir about staying in one place, told through trees, by the award-winning author of *Mr Wigg, Nest* and *Where the Trees Were.*

'A controlled and literate work that earns its emotional peaks'
Saturday Paper

'A delight' ***The Australian***

'Something powerful ... takes hold of the reader and transports [you] to the forest floor in a kind of awe' ***Sydney Morning Herald***

Inga Simpson began her career as a professional writer for government before gaining a PhD in creative writing. In 2011, she took part in the Queensland Writers Centre Manuscript Development Program and, as a result, Hachette Australia published her first novel, *Mr Wigg*, in 2013. *Nest*, Inga's second novel, was published in 2014 and was longlisted for the Miles Franklin Literary Award and the Stella Prize and shortlisted for the ALS Gold Medal. Inga's third novel, the acclaimed *Where the Trees Were*, was published in 2016.

Inga was awarded the final Eric Rolls Prize for her nature writing and has obtained a second PhD, exploring the history of Australian nature writers. Inga's account of her love of Australian nature and life with trees, *Understory*, was published in 2017. Her first book for children, *The Book of Australian Trees*, illustrated by Alicia Rogerson, was published in 2021. *The Last Woman in the World*, her critically acclaimed environmental thriller, was published in 2021 and shortlisted for the 2022 Fiction Indie Book Award. Her bestselling and critically acclaimed 2022 novel *Willowman* was shortlisted for the BookPeople Adult Fiction Book of the Year 2023. Inga lives on the NSW south coast among trees.